image comics presents

THE WALKING DEAD™

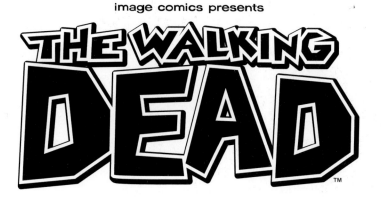

ROBERT KIRKMAN
CREATOR, WRITER

CHARLIE ADLARD
PENCILER

STEFANO GAUDIANO
INKER

CLIFF RATHBURN
GRAY TONES

RUS WOOTON
LETTERER

CHARLIE ADLARD
&
DAVE STEWART
COVER

SEAN MACKIEWICZ
EDITOR

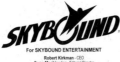

For SKYBOUND ENTERTAINMENT

Robert Kirkman - CEO
Sean Mackiewicz - Editorial Director
Shawn Kirkham - Director of Business Development
Brian Huntington - Online Editorial Director
June Alian - Publicity Director
Rachel Skidmore - Director of Media Development
Helen Leigh - Assistant Editor
Dan Petersen - Operations Manager
Sarah Effinger - Office Manager
Nick Palmer - Operations Coordinator
Lizzy Iverson - Administrative Assistant
Stephan Murillo - Administrative Assistant

International inquiries: foreign@skybound.com
Licensing inquiries: contact@skybound.com

WWW.SKYBOUND.COM

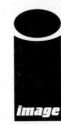

IMAGE COMICS, INC.
Robert Kirkman – Chief Operating Officer
Erik Larsen – Chief Financial Officer
Todd McFarlane – President
Marc Silvestri – Chief Executive Officer
Jim Valentino – Vice-President

Eric Stephenson – Publisher
Ron Richards – Director of Business Development
Jennifer de Guzman – Director of Trade Book Sales
Kat Salazar – Director of PR & Marketing
Corey Murphy – Director of Retail Sales
Jeremy Sullivan – Director of Digital Sales
Emilio Bautista – Sales Assistant
Branwyn Bigglestone – Senior Accounts Manager
Emily Miller – Accounts Manager
Jessica Ambriz – Administrative Assistant
Tyler Shainline – Events Coordinator
David Brothers – Content Manager
Jonathan Chan – Production Manager
Drew Gill – Art Director
Meredith Wallace – Print Manager
Monica Garcia – Senior Production Artist
Addison Duke – Production Artist
Tricia Ramos – Production Assistant
IMAGECOMICS.COM

THE WALKING DEAD, VOL. 22: A NEW BEGINNING. First Printing. ISBN: 978-1-63215-041-7. Published by Image Comics, Inc. Office of publication: 2001 Center Street, 6th Floor, Berkeley, California 94704. For information regarding the CPSIA on this printed material call: 203-595-3636 and provide reference # RICH – 583745. PRINTED IN THE USA

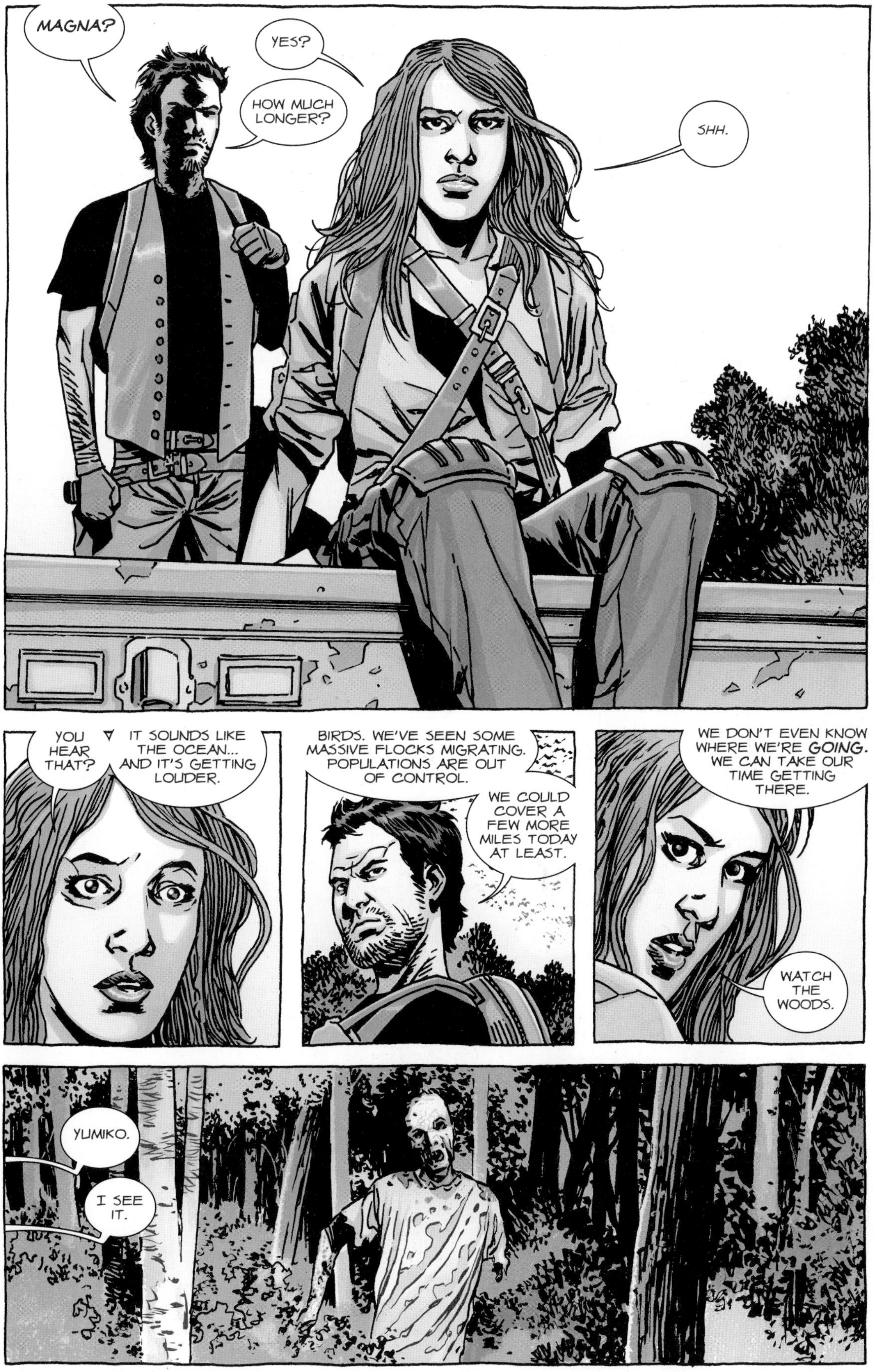
MAGNA?
YES?
HOW MUCH LONGER?
SHH.
YOU HEAR THAT?
IT SOUNDS LIKE THE OCEAN... AND IT'S GETTING LOUDER.
BIRDS. WE'VE SEEN SOME MASSIVE FLOCKS MIGRATING. POPULATIONS ARE OUT OF CONTROL.
WE COULD COVER A FEW MORE MILES TODAY AT LEAST.
WE DON'T EVEN KNOW WHERE WE'RE GOING. WE CAN TAKE OUR TIME GETTING THERE.
WATCH THE WOODS.
YUMIKO.
I SEE IT.

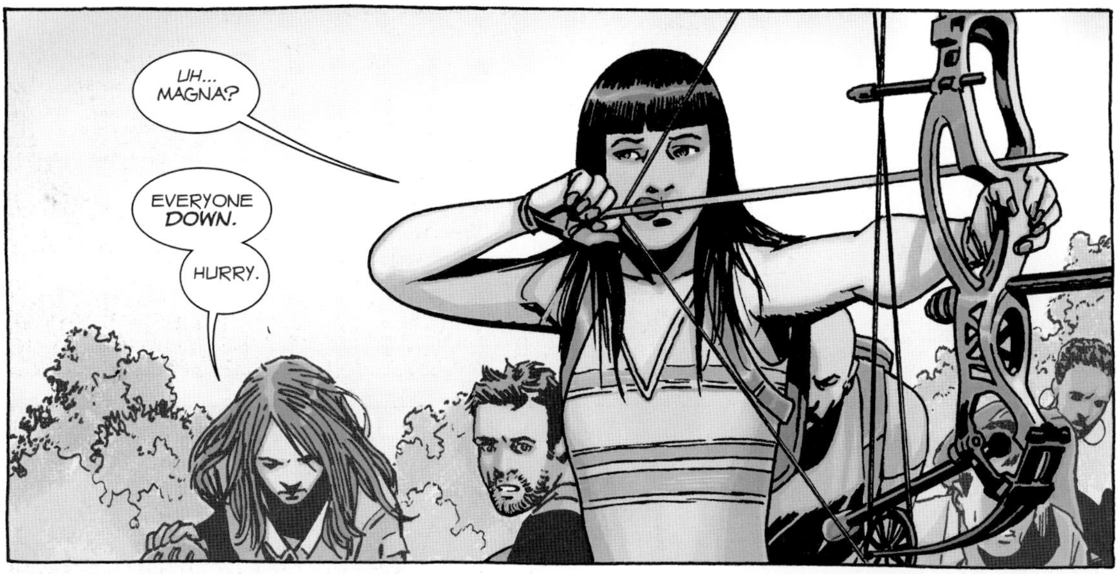
UH... MAGNA?
EVERYONE DOWN.
HURRY.

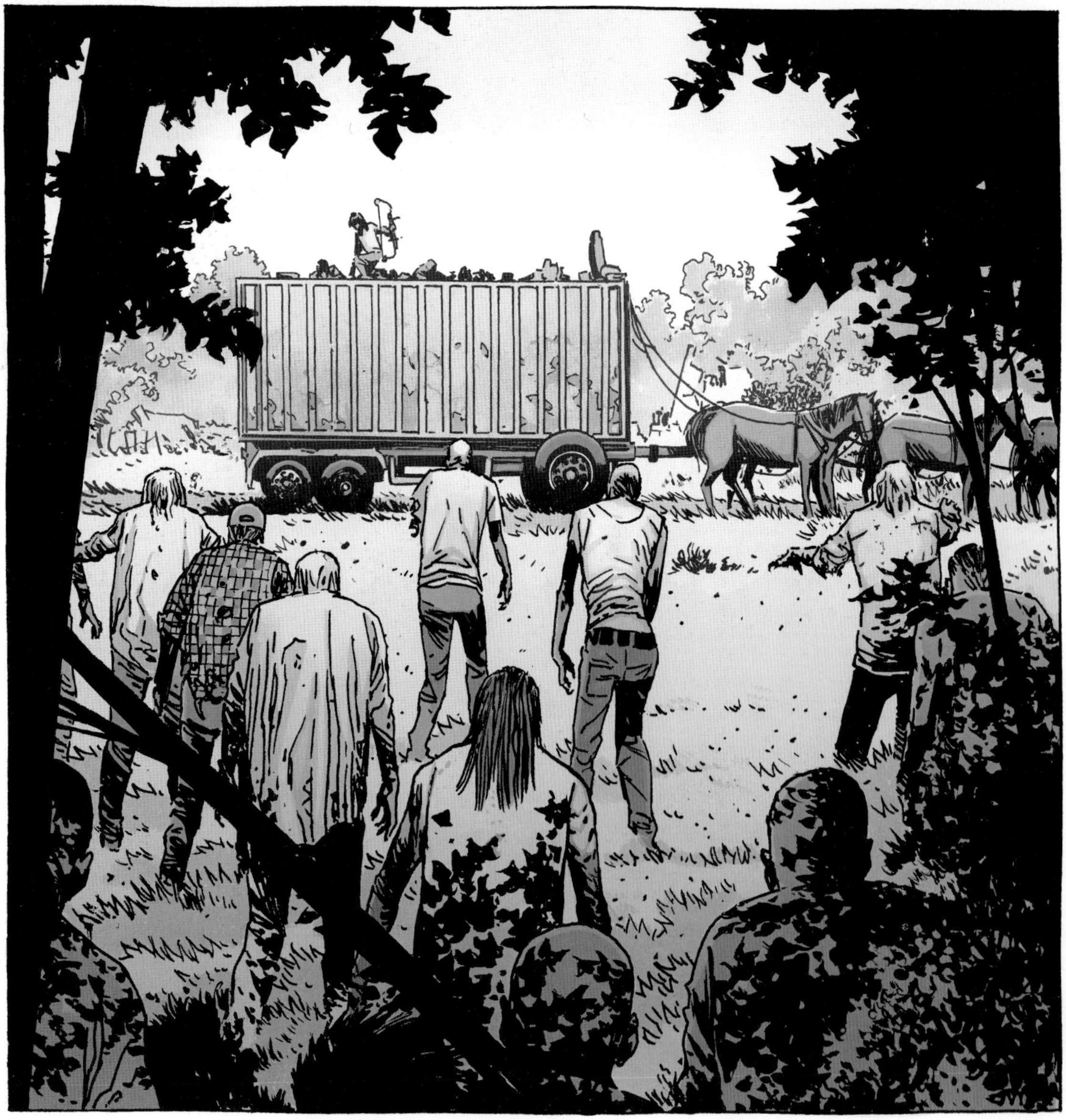

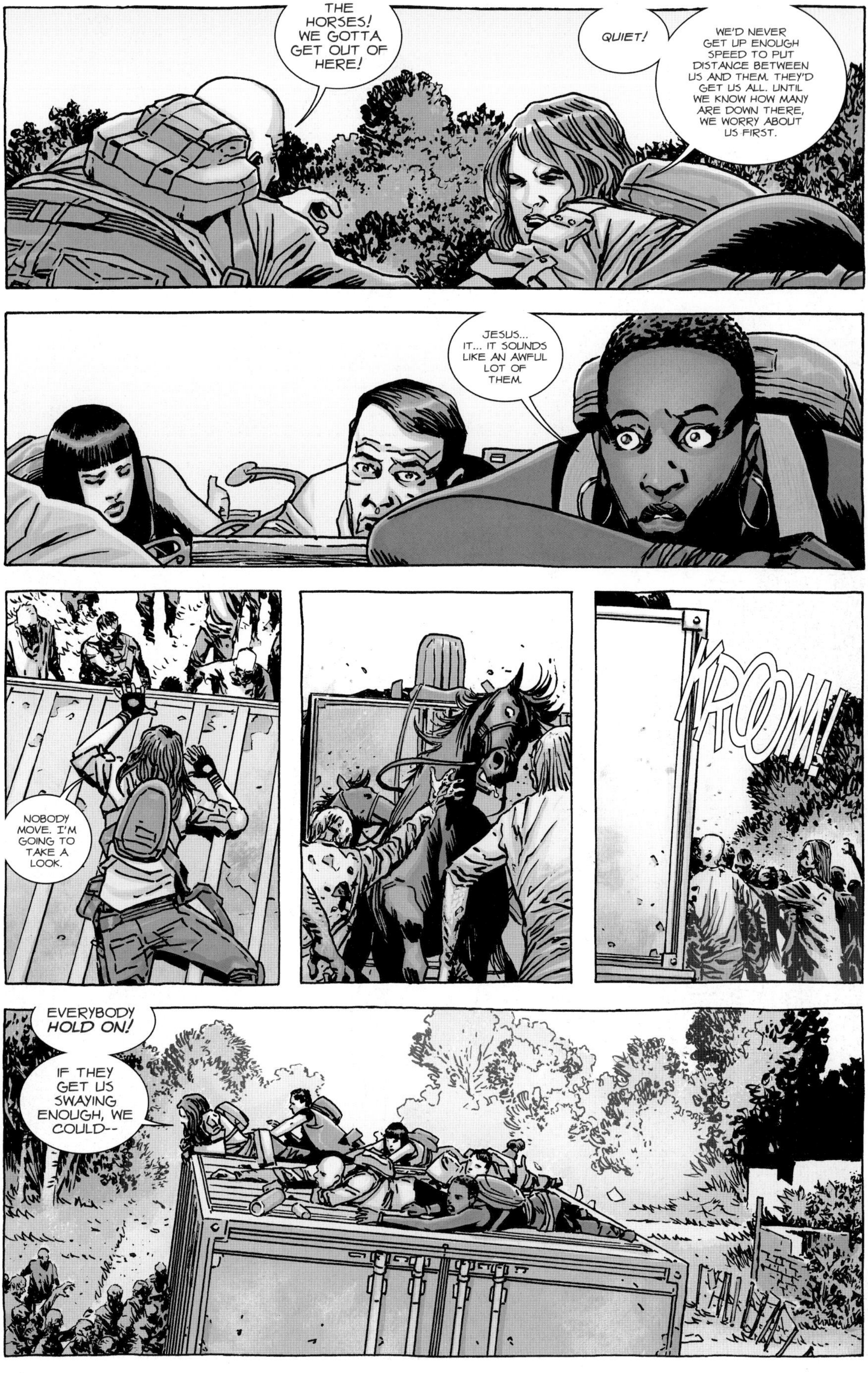
THE HORSES! WE GOTTA GET OUT OF HERE!
QUIET!
WE'D NEVER GET UP ENOUGH SPEED TO PUT DISTANCE BETWEEN US AND THEM. THEY'D GET US ALL. UNTIL WE KNOW HOW MANY ARE DOWN THERE, WE WORRY ABOUT US FIRST.
JESUS... IT... IT SOUNDS LIKE AN AWFUL LOT OF THEM.
NOBODY MOVE. I'M GOING TO TAKE A LOOK.
KROOM!
EVERYBODY HOLD ON!
IF THEY GET US SWAYING ENOUGH, WE COULD--

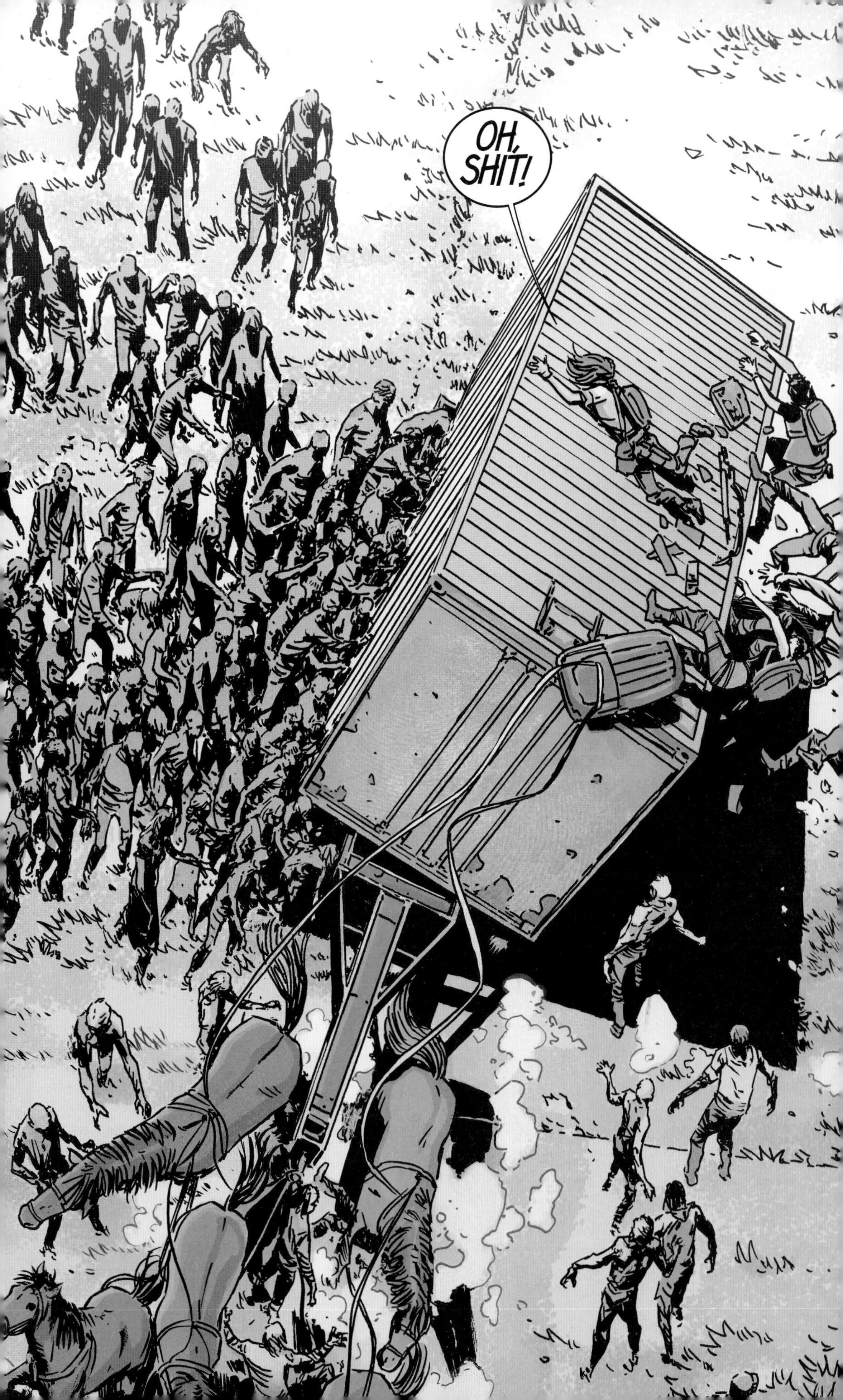
OH, SHIT!

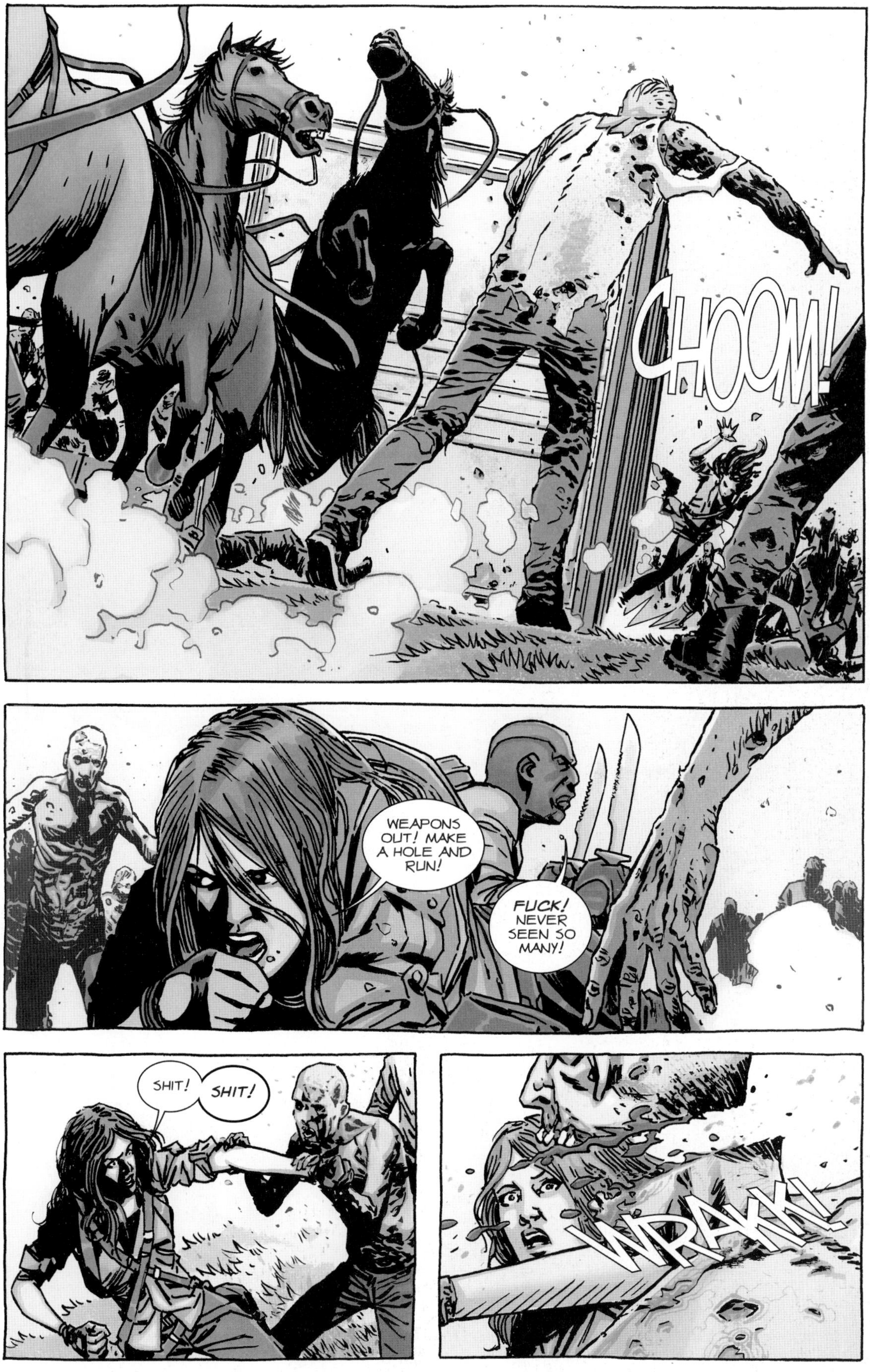
CHOOM!
WEAPONS OUT! MAKE A HOLE AND RUN!
FUCK! NEVER SEEN SO MANY!
SHIT!
SHIT!
WRAKK!

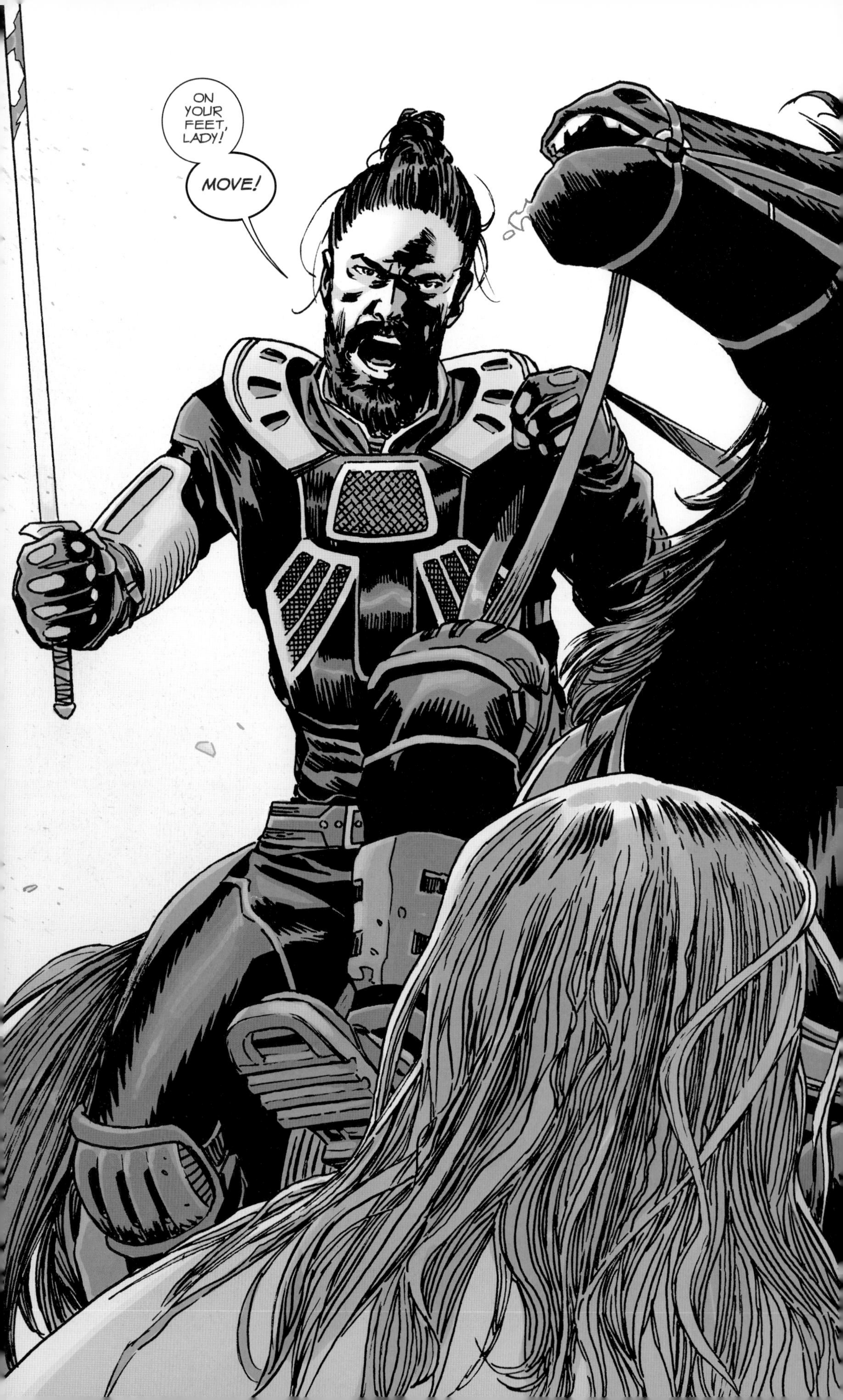
ON YOUR FEET, LADY!
MOVE!

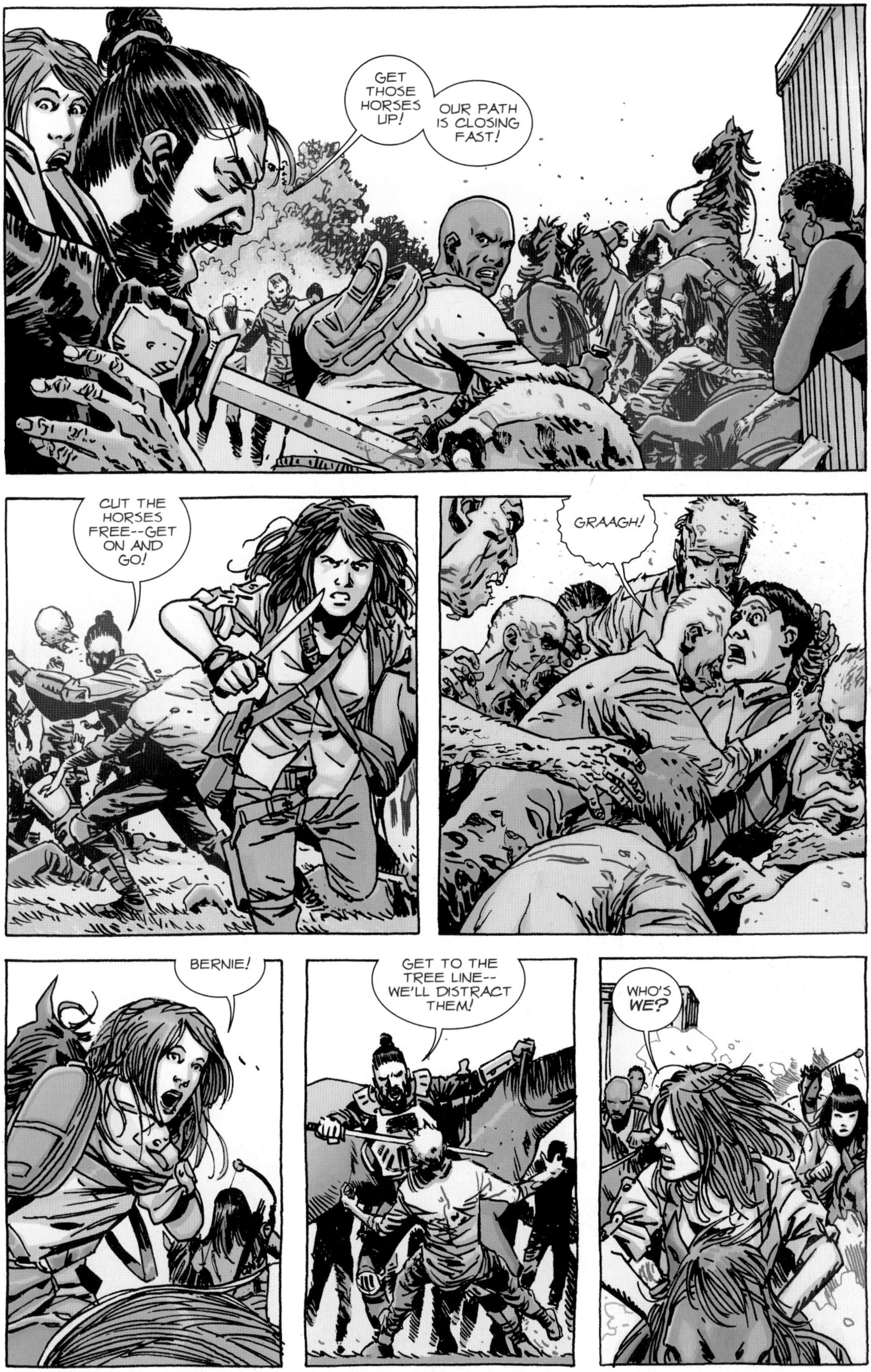
GET THOSE HORSES UP!
OUR PATH IS CLOSING FAST!
CUT THE HORSES FREE--GET ON AND GO!
GRAAGH!
BERNIE!
GET TO THE TREE LINE-- WE'LL DISTRACT THEM!
WHO'S **WE?**

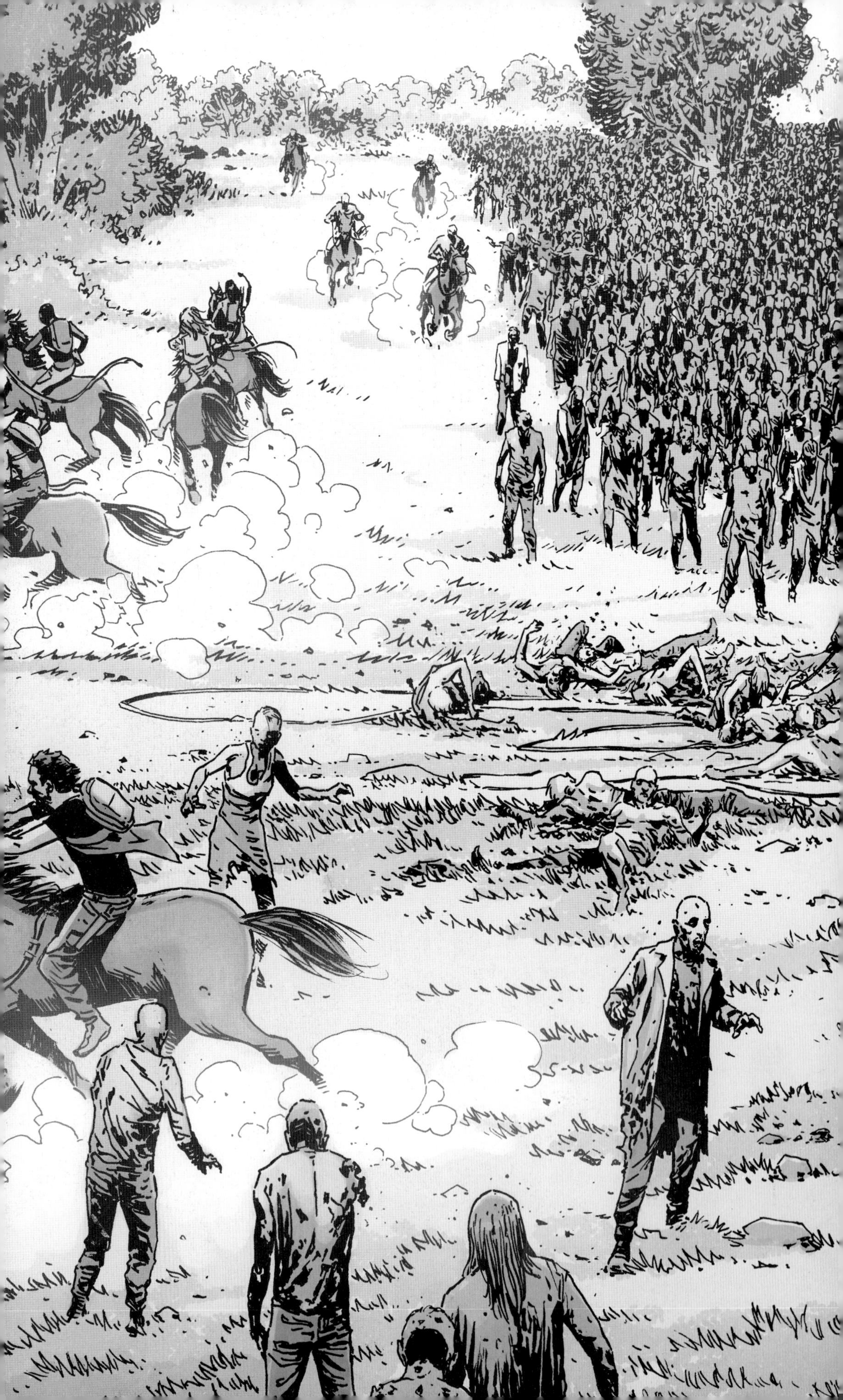

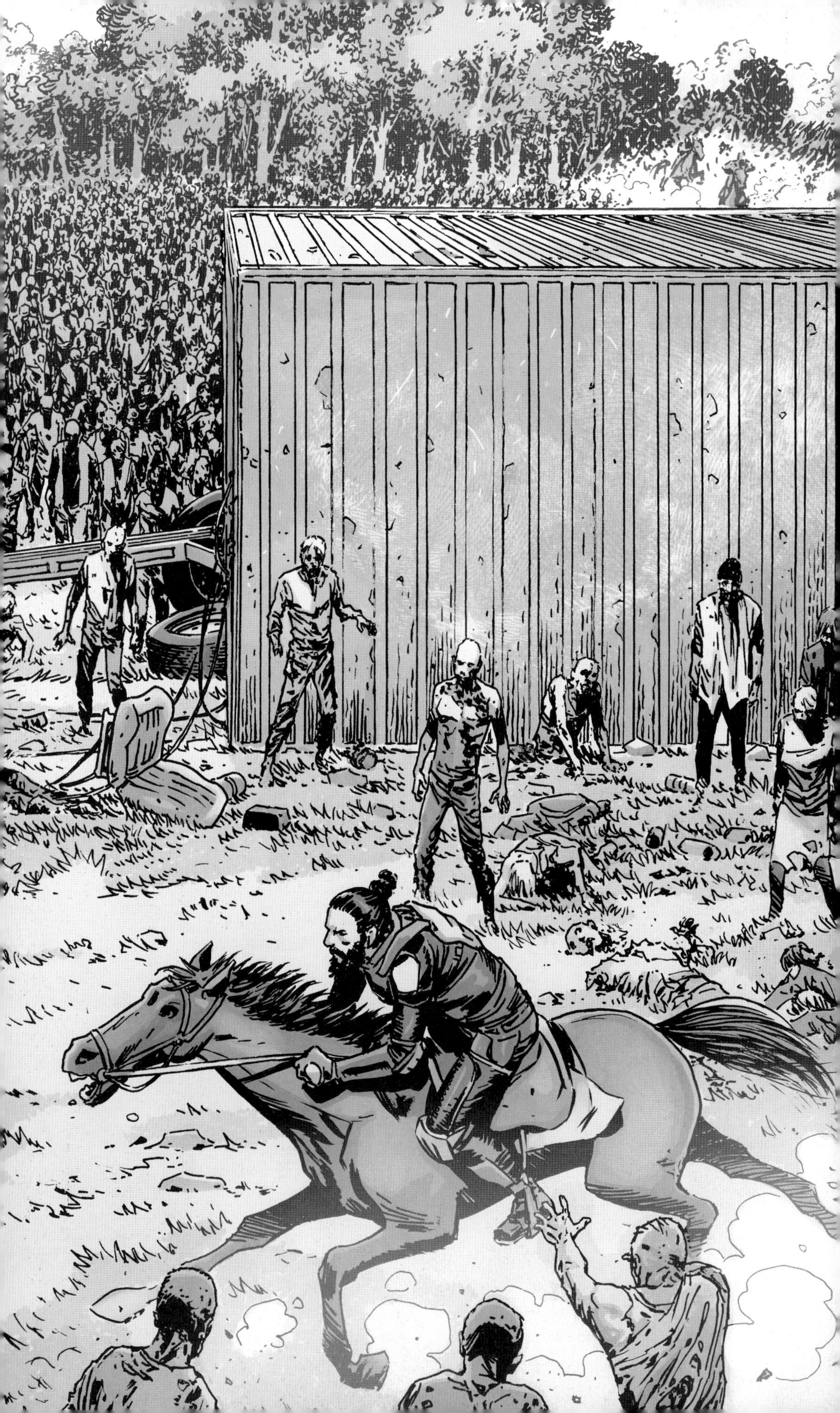

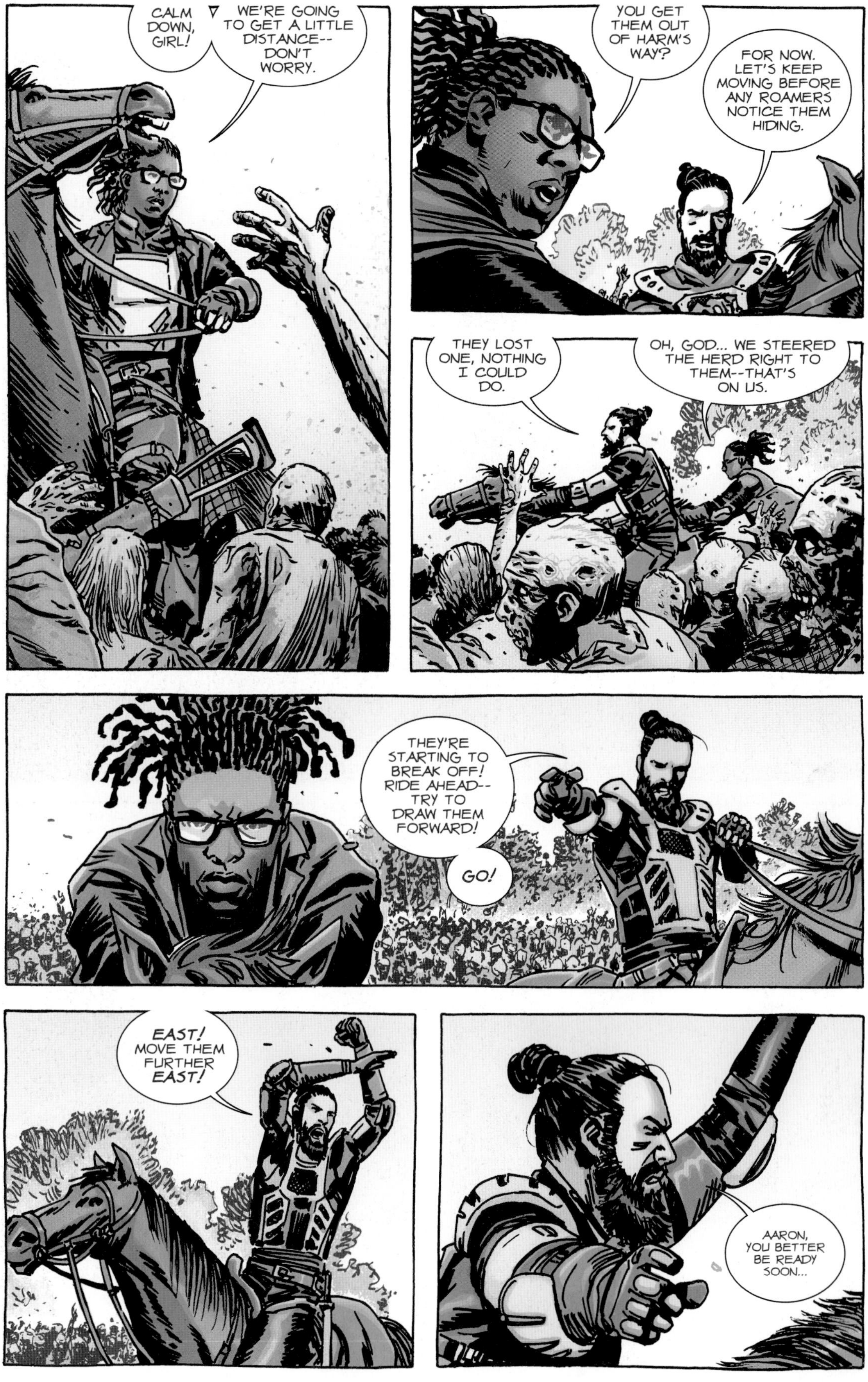
CALM DOWN, GIRL!
WE'RE GOING TO GET A LITTLE DISTANCE-- DON'T WORRY.
YOU GET THEM OUT OF HARM'S WAY?
FOR NOW. LET'S KEEP MOVING BEFORE ANY ROAMERS NOTICE THEM HIDING.
THEY LOST ONE, NOTHING I COULD DO.
OH, GOD... WE STEERED THE HERD RIGHT TO THEM--THAT'S ON US.
THEY'RE STARTING TO BREAK OFF! RIDE AHEAD-- TRY TO DRAW THEM FORWARD!
GO!
EAST! MOVE THEM FURTHER EAST!
AARON, YOU BETTER BE READY SOON...

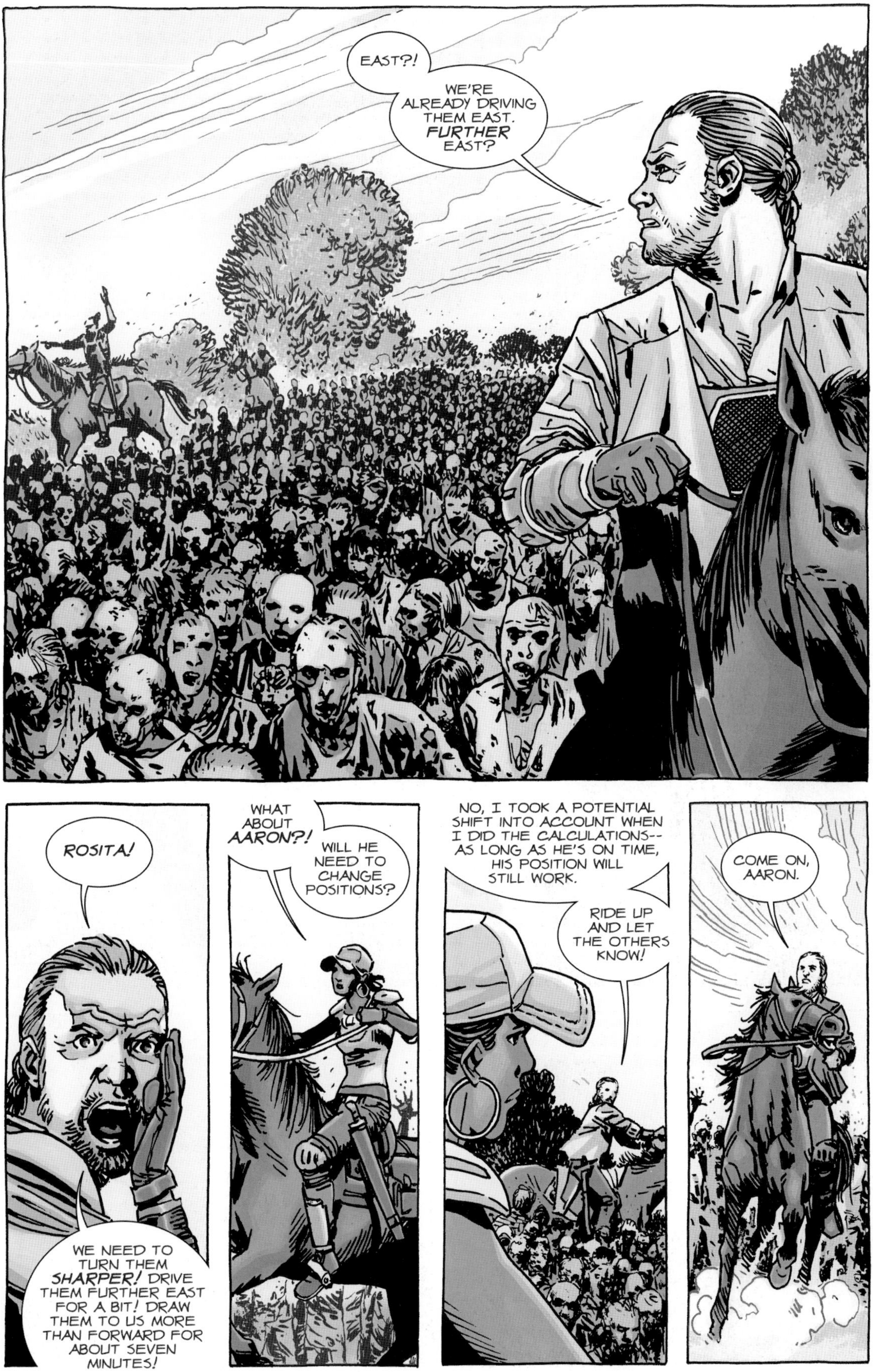
EAST?!
WE'RE ALREADY DRIVING THEM EAST. FURTHER EAST?
ROSITA!
WE NEED TO TURN THEM SHARPER! DRIVE THEM FURTHER EAST FOR A BIT! DRAW THEM TO US MORE THAN FORWARD FOR ABOUT SEVEN MINUTES!
WHAT ABOUT AARON?!
WILL HE NEED TO CHANGE POSITIONS?
NO, I TOOK A POTENTIAL SHIFT INTO ACCOUNT WHEN I DID THE CALCULATIONS-- AS LONG AS HE'S ON TIME, HIS POSITION WILL STILL WORK.
RIDE UP AND LET THE OTHERS KNOW!
COME ON, AARON.

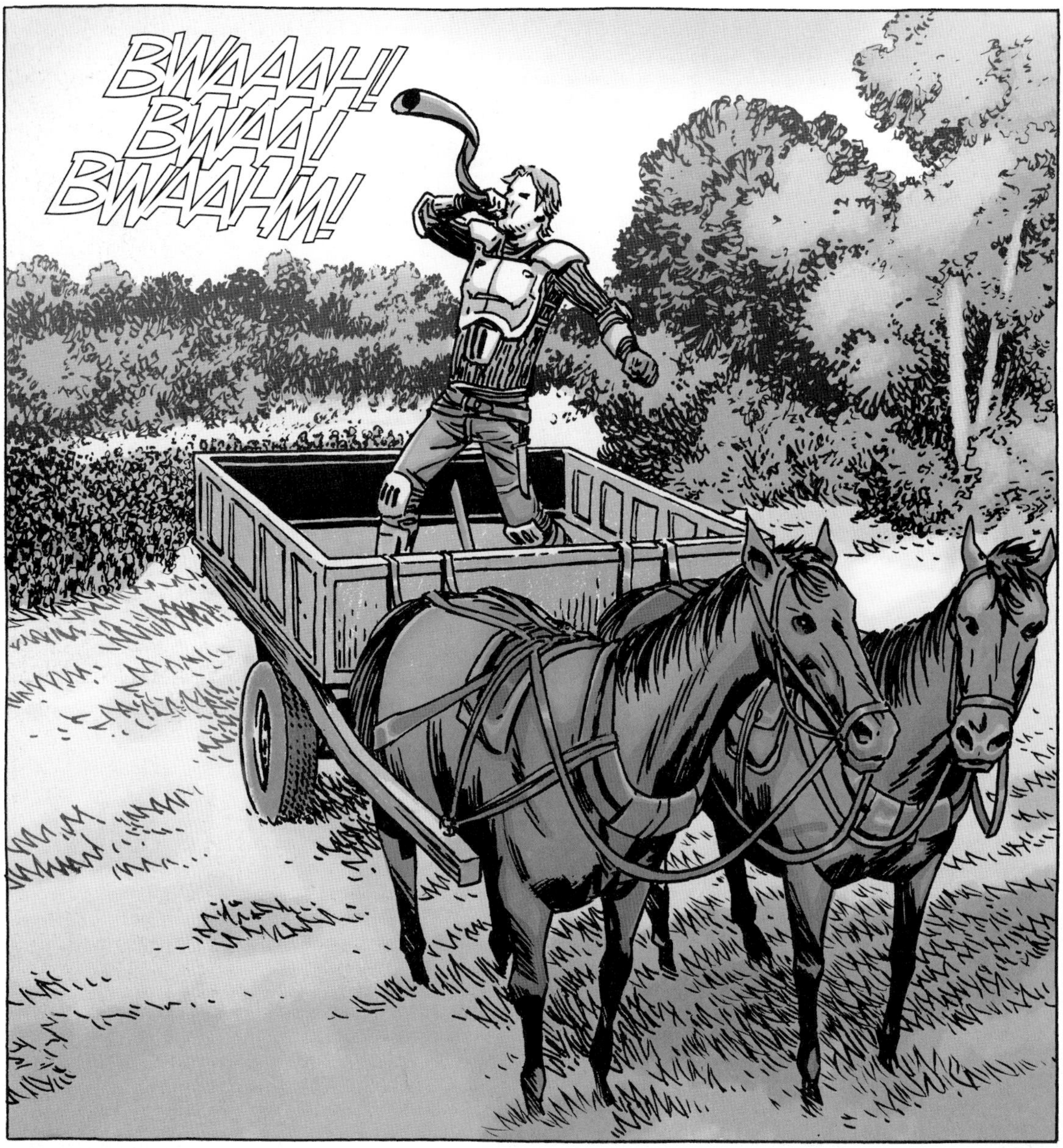
BWAAAH! BWAA! BWAAHM!

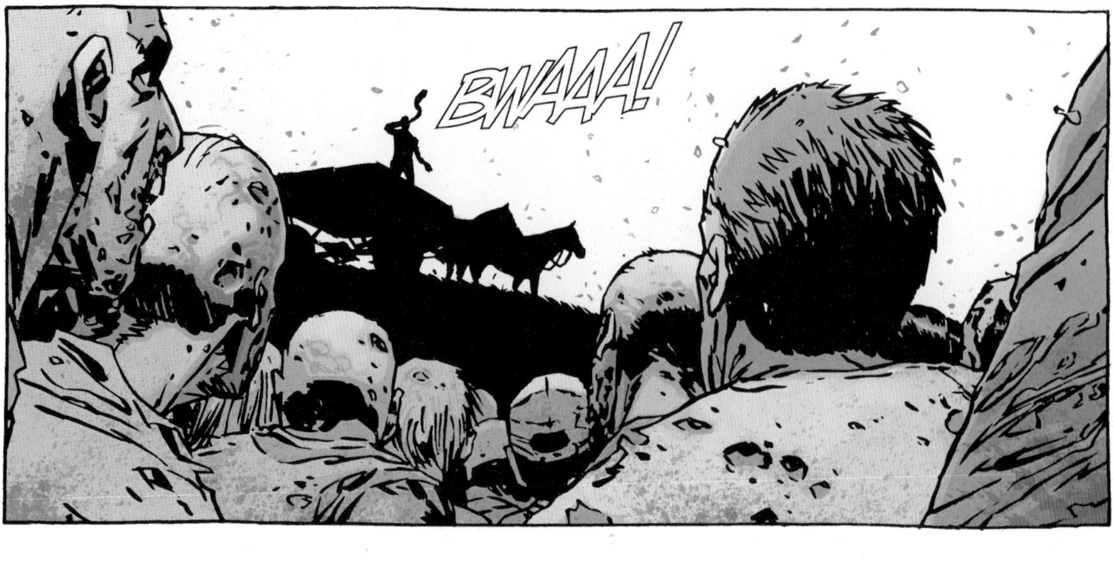
BWAAA!

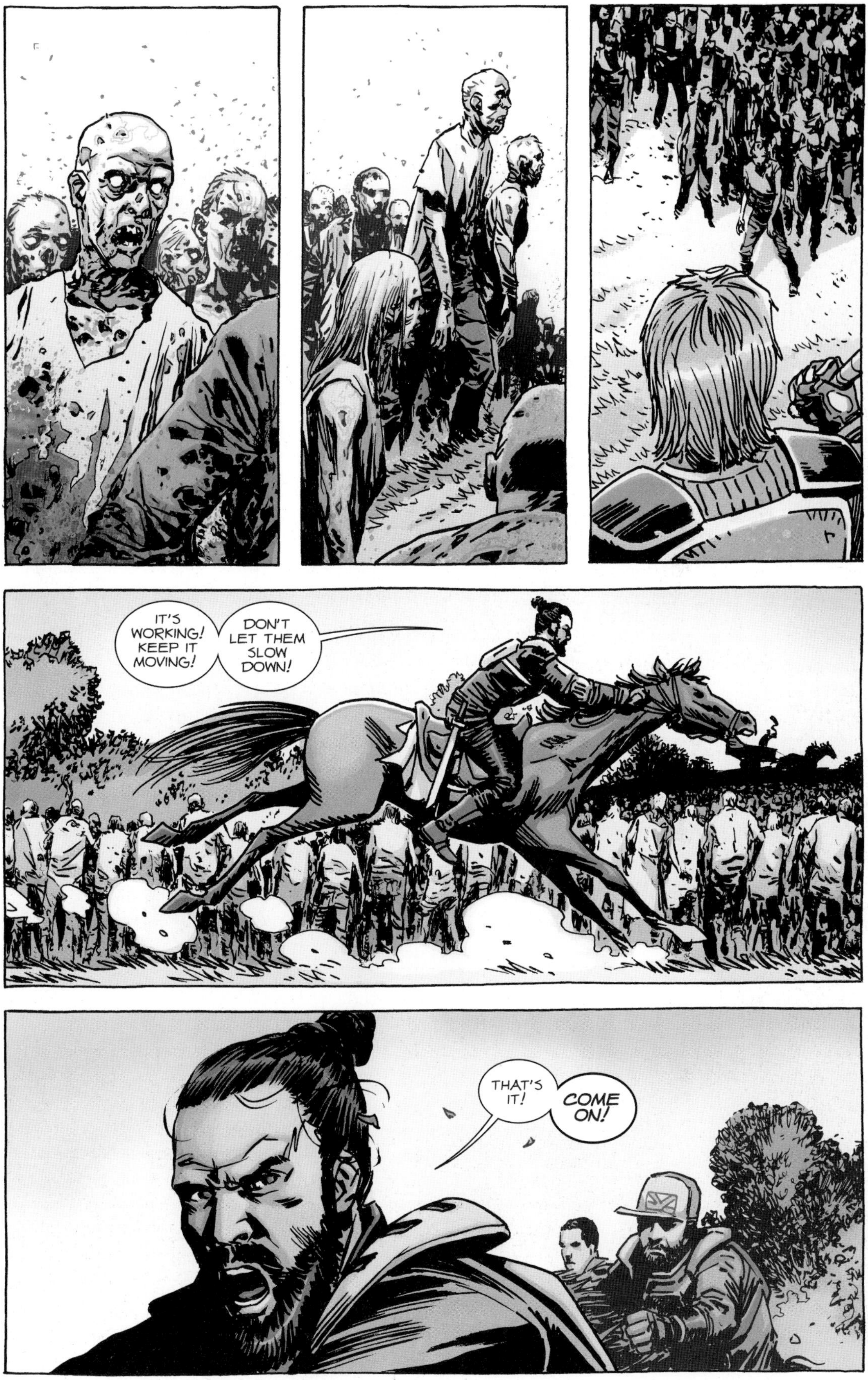
IT'S WORKING! KEEP IT MOVING!
DON'T LET THEM SLOW DOWN!
THAT'S IT!
COME ON!

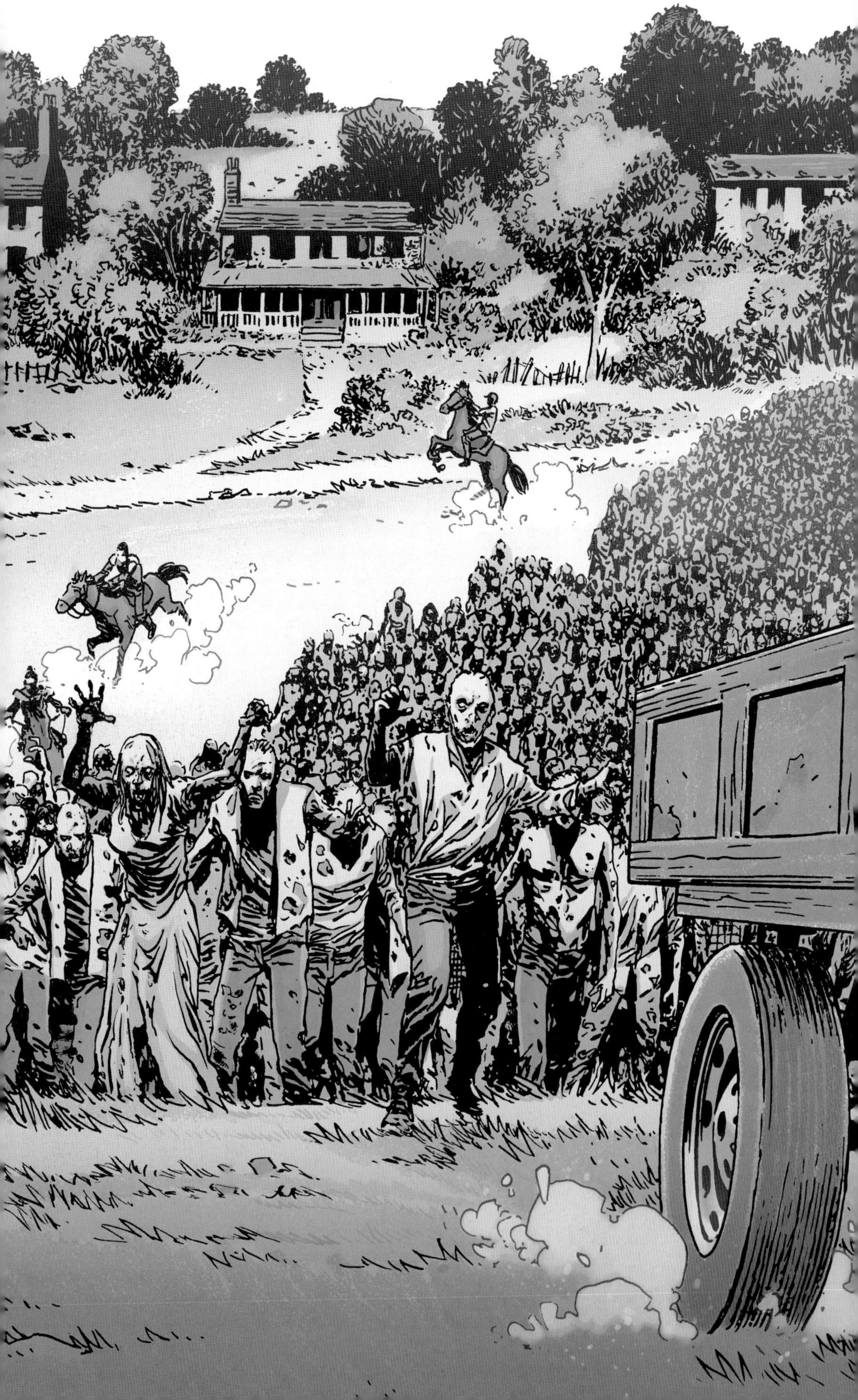

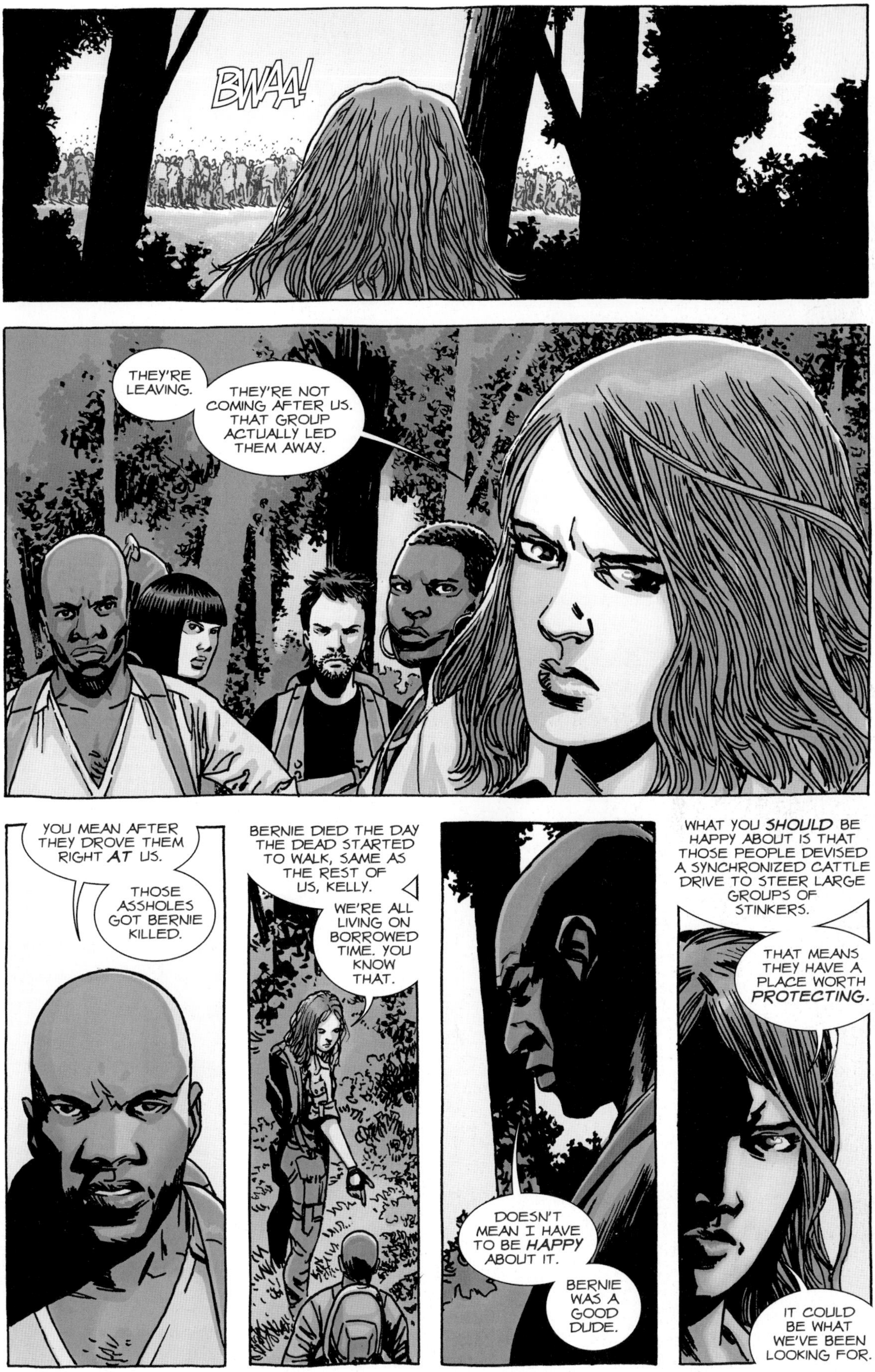
BWAA!
THEY'RE LEAVING.
THEY'RE NOT COMING AFTER US. THAT GROUP ACTUALLY LED THEM AWAY.
YOU MEAN AFTER THEY DROVE THEM RIGHT AT US.
THOSE ASSHOLES GOT BERNIE KILLED.
BERNIE DIED THE DAY THE DEAD STARTED TO WALK, SAME AS THE REST OF US, KELLY.
WE'RE ALL LIVING ON BORROWED TIME. YOU KNOW THAT.
DOESN'T MEAN I HAVE TO BE HAPPY ABOUT IT.
BERNIE WAS A GOOD DUDE.
WHAT YOU SHOULD BE HAPPY ABOUT IS THAT THOSE PEOPLE DEVISED A SYNCHRONIZED CATTLE DRIVE TO STEER LARGE GROUPS OF STINKERS.
THAT MEANS THEY HAVE A PLACE WORTH PROTECTING.
IT COULD BE WHAT WE'VE BEEN LOOKING FOR.

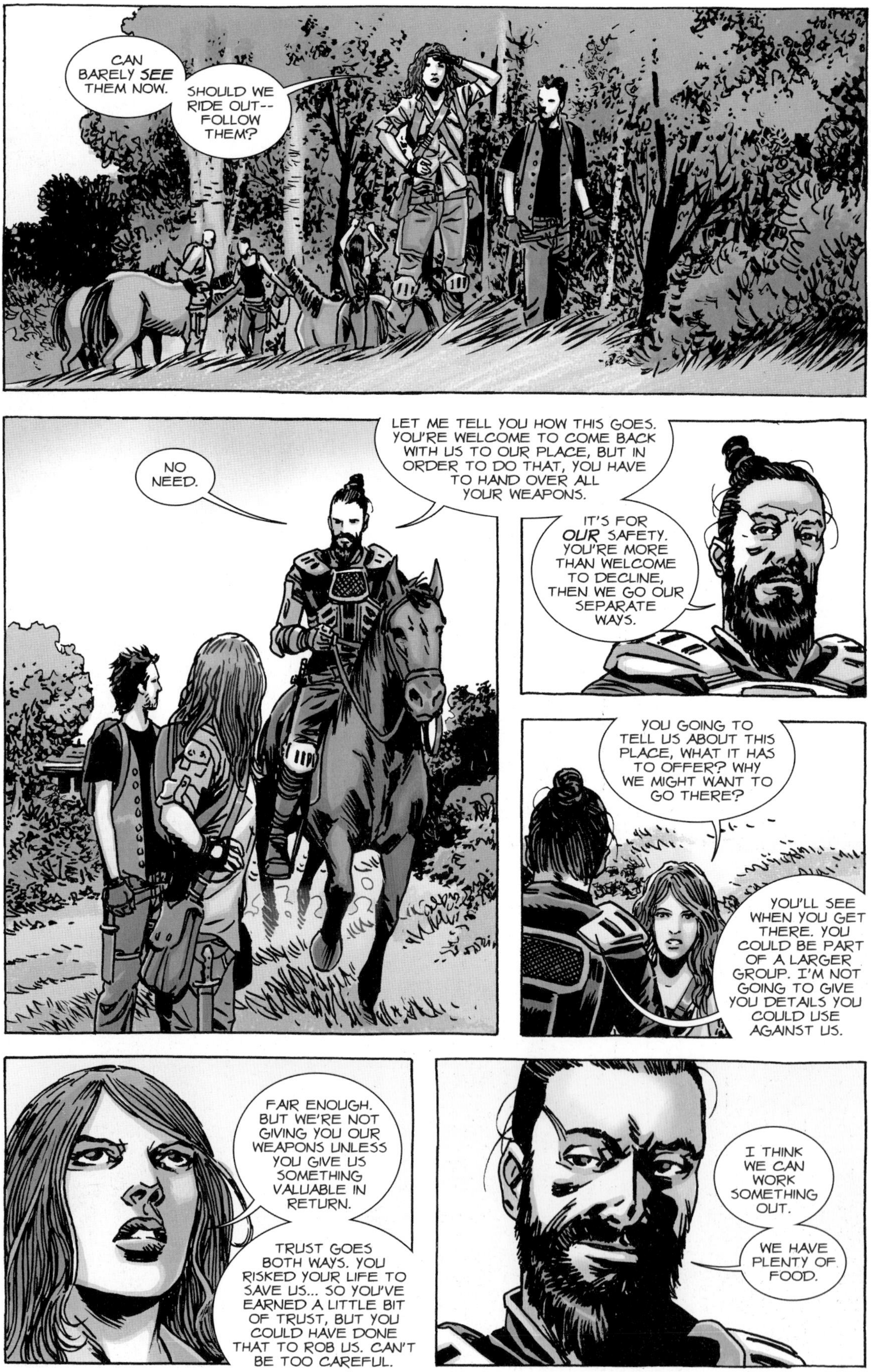
CAN BARELY SEE THEM NOW.
SHOULD WE RIDE OUT-- FOLLOW THEM?
NO NEED.
LET ME TELL YOU HOW THIS GOES. YOU'RE WELCOME TO COME BACK WITH US TO OUR PLACE, BUT IN ORDER TO DO THAT, YOU HAVE TO HAND OVER ALL YOUR WEAPONS.
IT'S FOR OUR SAFETY. YOU'RE MORE THAN WELCOME TO DECLINE, THEN WE GO OUR SEPARATE WAYS.
YOU GOING TO TELL US ABOUT THIS PLACE, WHAT IT HAS TO OFFER? WHY WE MIGHT WANT TO GO THERE?
YOU'LL SEE WHEN YOU GET THERE. YOU COULD BE PART OF A LARGER GROUP. I'M NOT GOING TO GIVE YOU DETAILS YOU COULD USE AGAINST US.
FAIR ENOUGH. BUT WE'RE NOT GIVING YOU OUR WEAPONS UNLESS YOU GIVE US SOMETHING VALUABLE IN RETURN.
TRUST GOES BOTH WAYS. YOU RISKED YOUR LIFE TO SAVE US... SO YOU'VE EARNED A LITTLE BIT OF TRUST, BUT YOU COULD HAVE DONE THAT TO ROB US. CAN'T BE TOO CAREFUL.
I THINK WE CAN WORK SOMETHING OUT.
WE HAVE PLENTY OF FOOD.

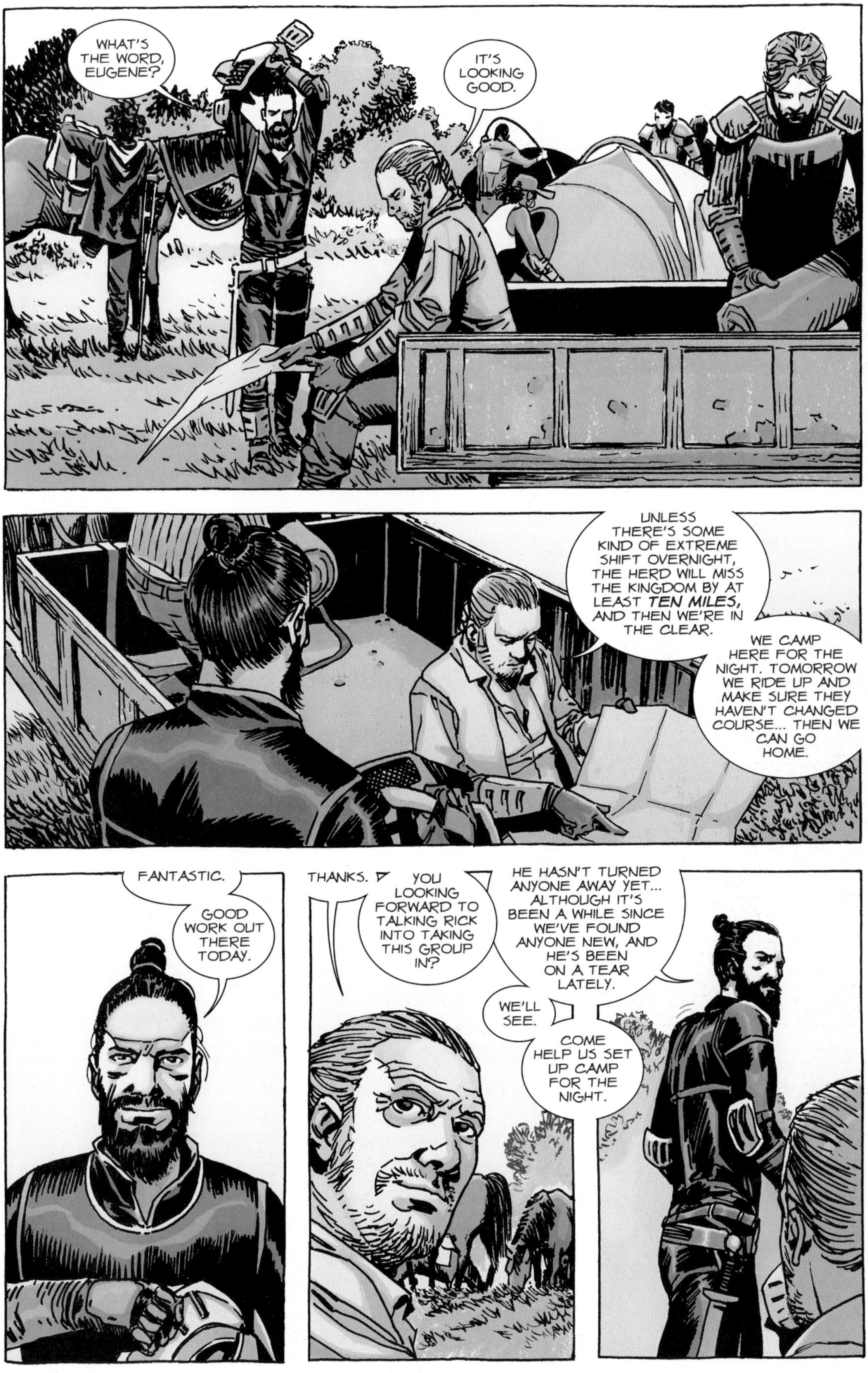
WHAT'S THE WORD, EUGENE?
IT'S LOOKING GOOD.
UNLESS THERE'S SOME KIND OF EXTREME SHIFT OVERNIGHT, THE HERD WILL MISS THE KINGDOM BY AT LEAST *TEN MILES,* AND THEN WE'RE IN THE CLEAR.
WE CAMP HERE FOR THE NIGHT. TOMORROW WE RIDE UP AND MAKE SURE THEY HAVEN'T CHANGED COURSE... THEN WE CAN GO HOME.
FANTASTIC.
GOOD WORK OUT THERE TODAY.
THANKS.
YOU LOOKING FORWARD TO TALKING RICK INTO TAKING THIS GROUP IN?
HE HASN'T TURNED ANYONE AWAY YET... ALTHOUGH IT'S BEEN A WHILE SINCE WE'VE FOUND ANYONE NEW, AND HE'S BEEN ON A TEAR LATELY.
WE'LL SEE.
COME HELP US SET UP CAMP FOR THE NIGHT.

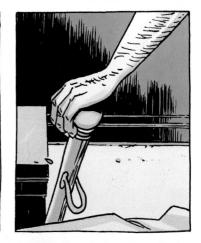

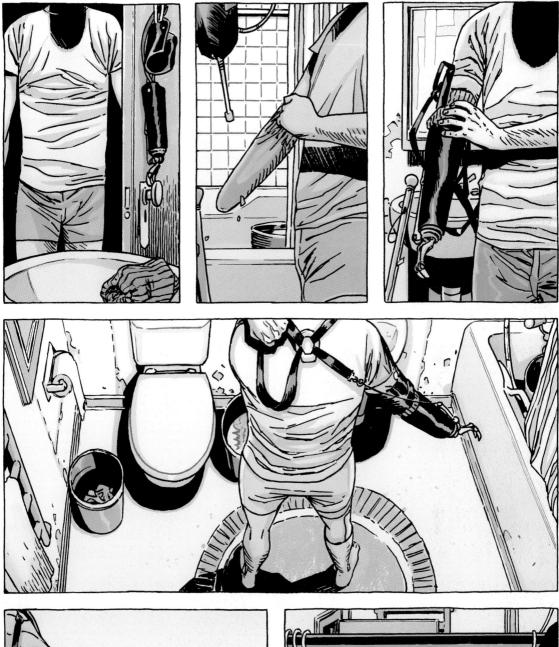

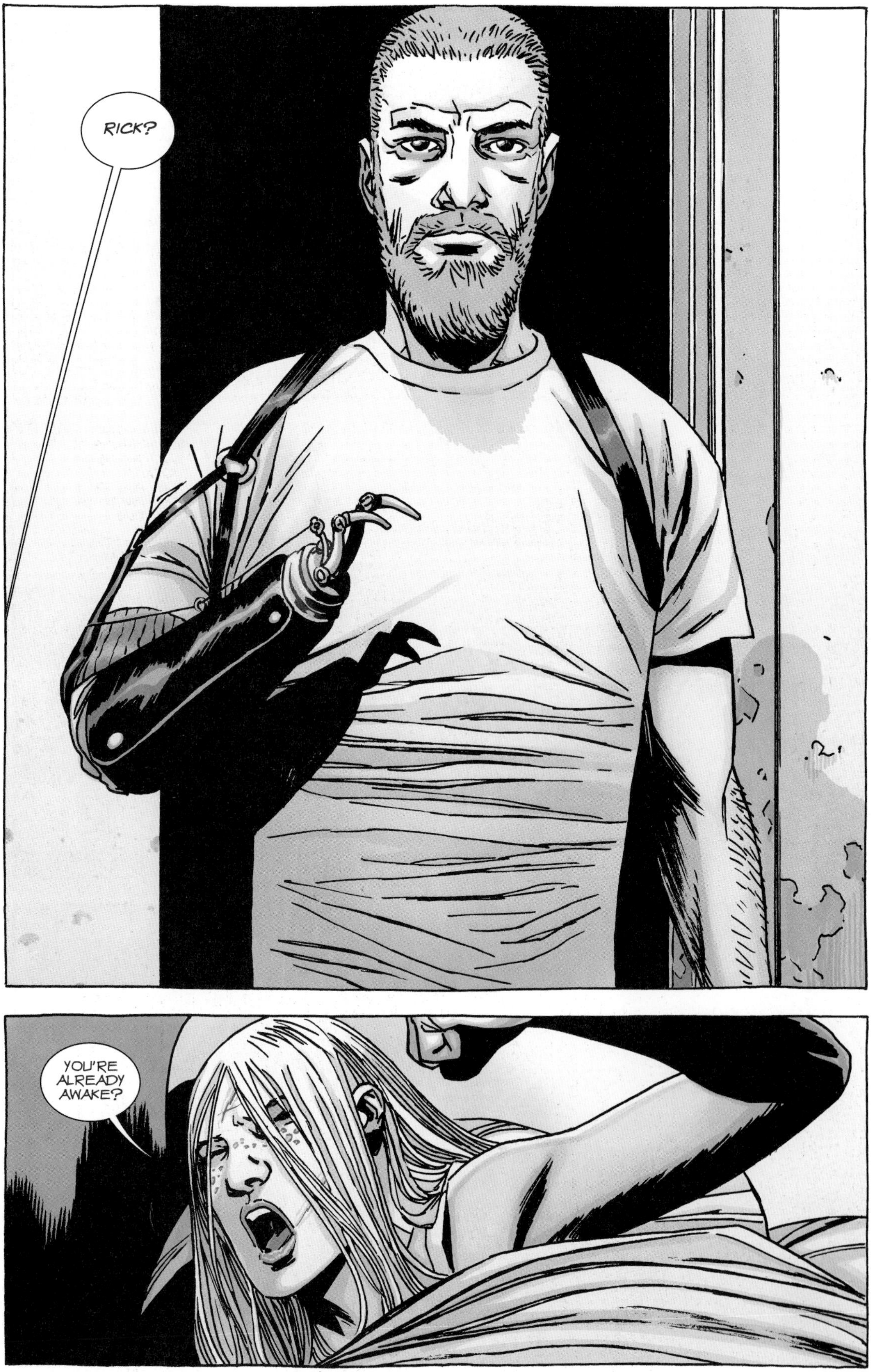
RICK?
YOU'RE ALREADY AWAKE?

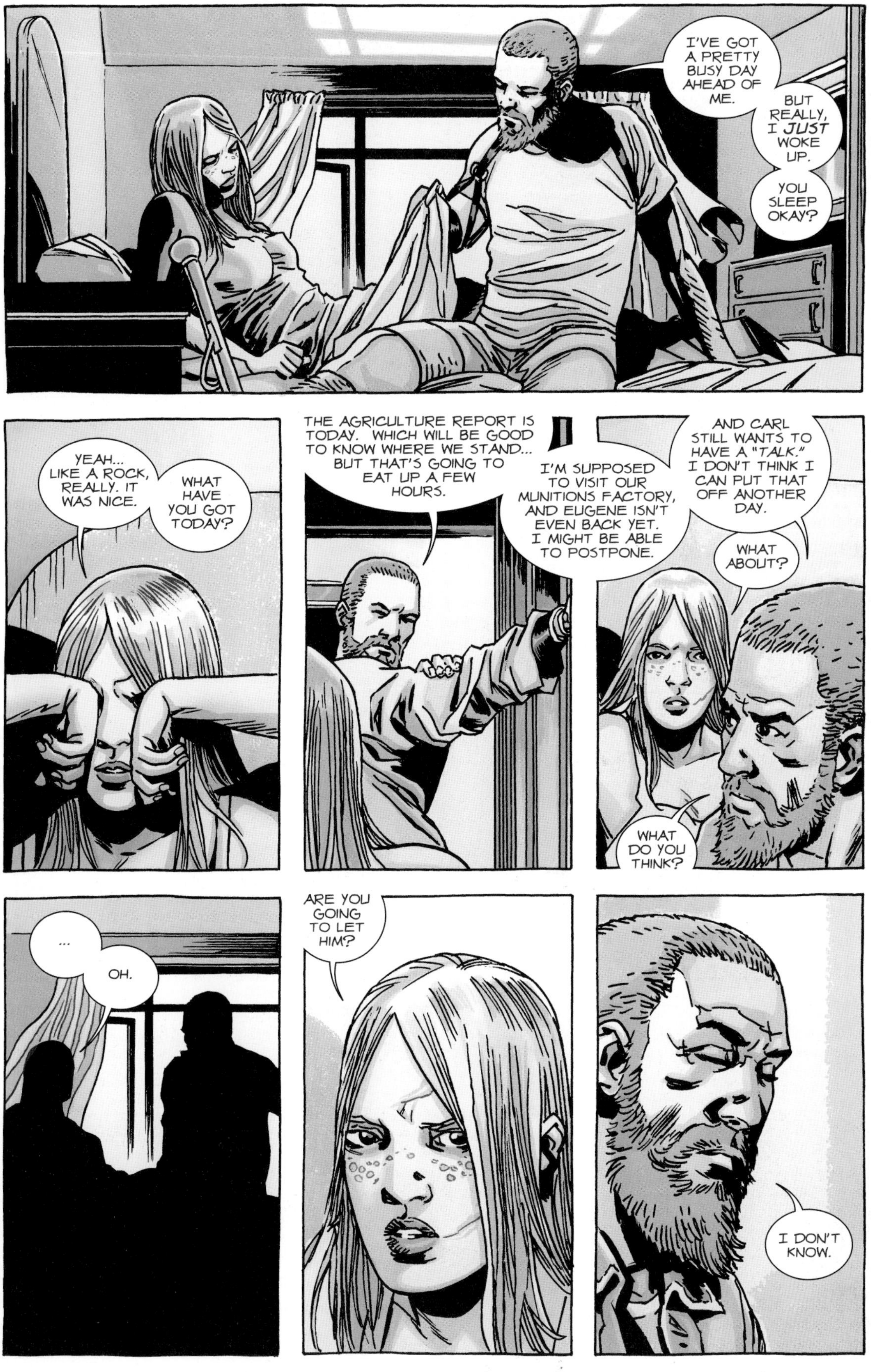

I'VE GOT A PRETTY BUSY DAY AHEAD OF ME.
BUT REALLY, I *JUST* WOKE UP.
YOU SLEEP OKAY?
YEAH... LIKE A ROCK, REALLY. IT WAS NICE.
WHAT HAVE YOU GOT TODAY?
THE AGRICULTURE REPORT IS TODAY. WHICH WILL BE GOOD TO KNOW WHERE WE STAND... BUT THAT'S GOING TO EAT UP A FEW HOURS.
I'M SUPPOSED TO VISIT OUR MUNITIONS FACTORY, AND EUGENE ISN'T EVEN BACK YET. I MIGHT BE ABLE TO POSTPONE.
AND CARL STILL WANTS TO HAVE A "*TALK.*" I DON'T THINK I CAN PUT THAT OFF ANOTHER DAY.
WHAT ABOUT?
WHAT DO YOU THINK?
...
OH.
ARE YOU GOING TO LET HIM?
I DON'T KNOW.

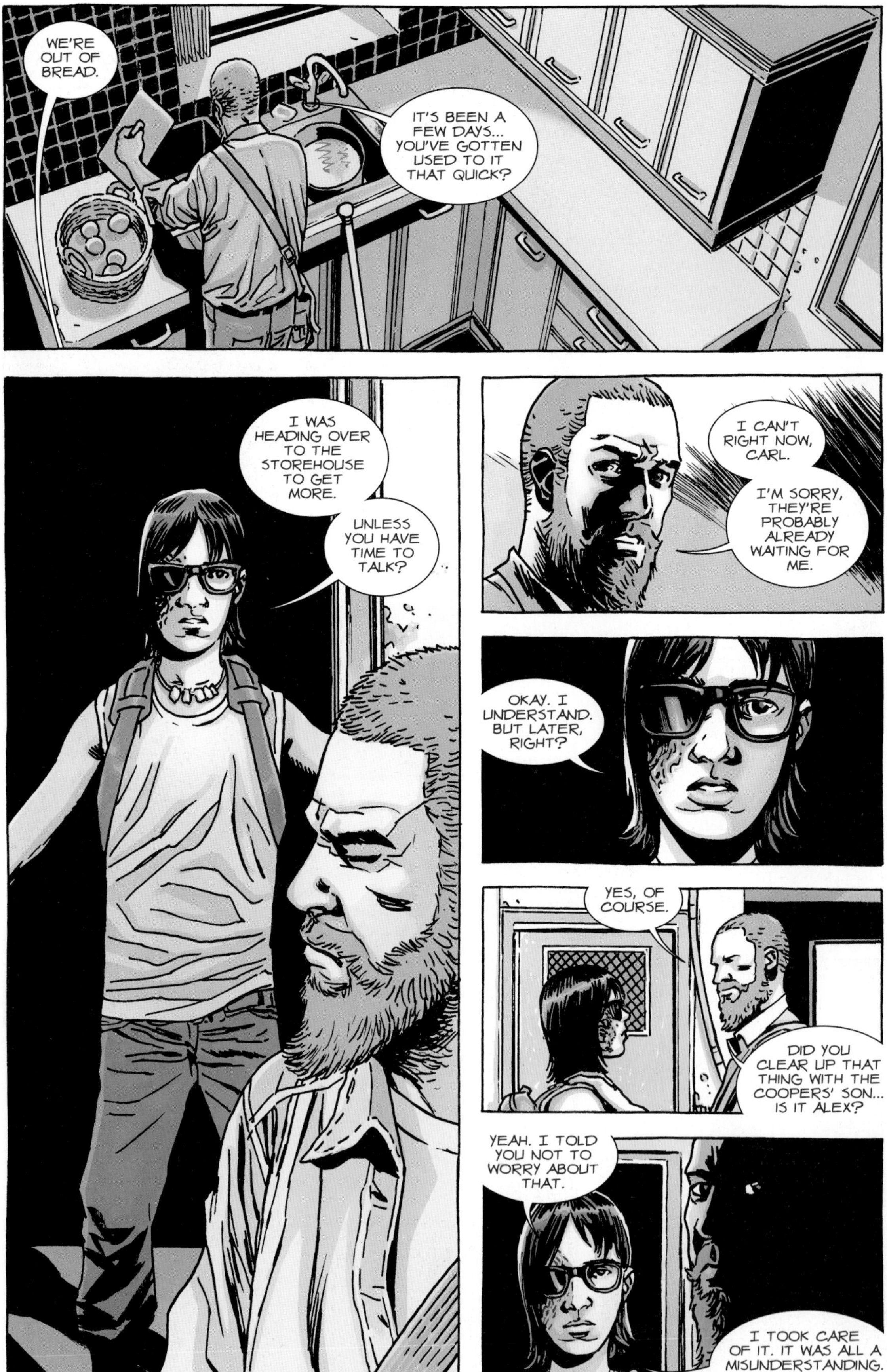
WE'RE OUT OF BREAD.
IT'S BEEN A FEW DAYS... YOU'VE GOTTEN USED TO IT THAT QUICK?
I WAS HEADING OVER TO THE STOREHOUSE TO GET MORE.
UNLESS YOU HAVE TIME TO TALK?
I CAN'T RIGHT NOW, CARL.
I'M SORRY, THEY'RE PROBABLY ALREADY WAITING FOR ME.
OKAY. I UNDERSTAND. BUT LATER, RIGHT?
YES, OF COURSE.
DID YOU CLEAR UP THAT THING WITH THE COOPERS' SON... IS IT ALEX?
YEAH. I TOLD YOU NOT TO WORRY ABOUT THAT.
I TOOK CARE OF IT. IT WAS ALL A MISUNDERSTANDING. WE'RE COOL, NOW.

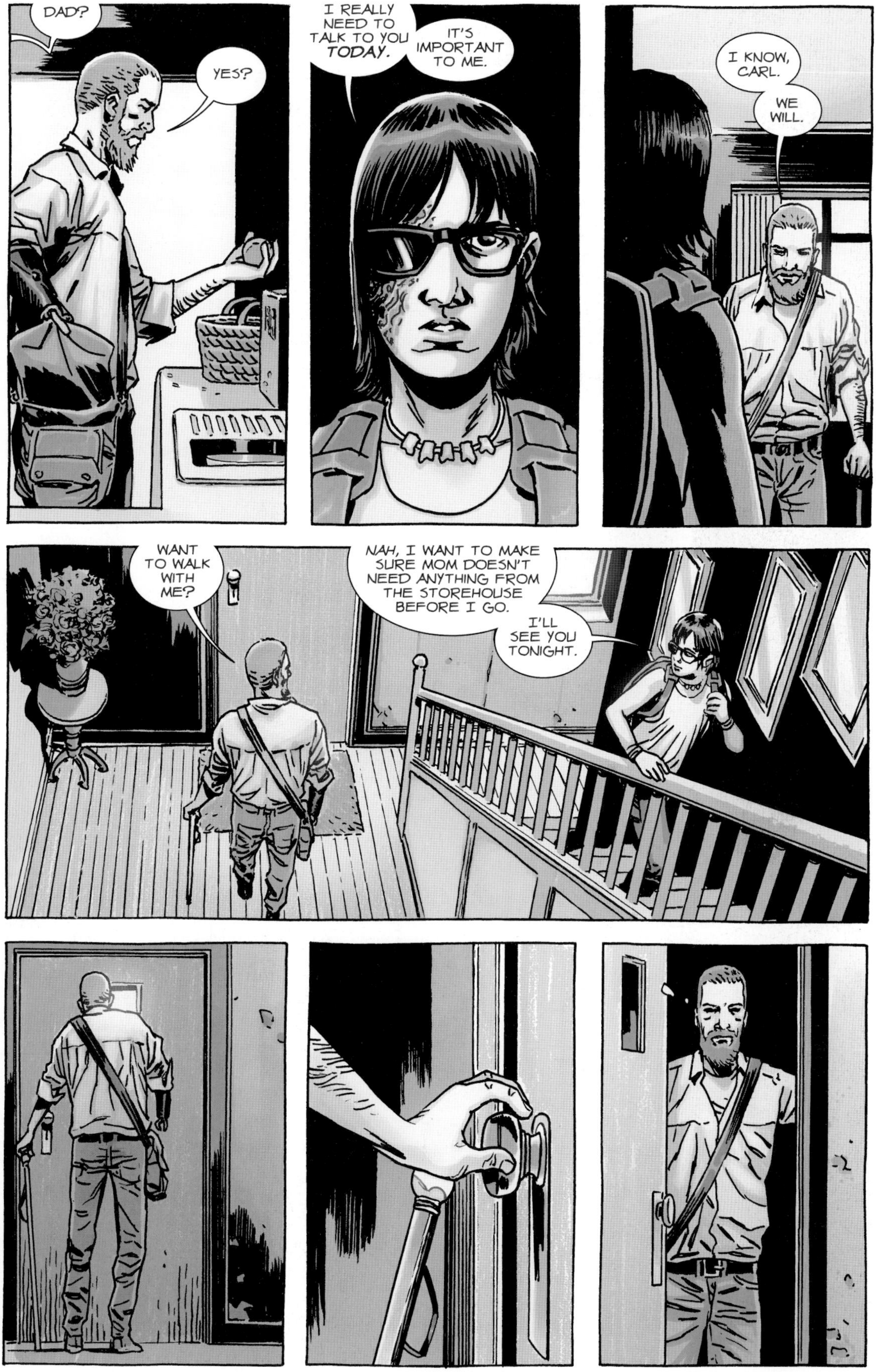
DAD?
YES?
I REALLY NEED TO TALK TO YOU *TODAY*.
IT'S IMPORTANT TO ME.
I KNOW, CARL.
WE WILL.
WANT TO WALK WITH ME?
NAH, I WANT TO MAKE SURE MOM DOESN'T NEED ANYTHING FROM THE STOREHOUSE BEFORE I GO.
I'LL SEE YOU TONIGHT.

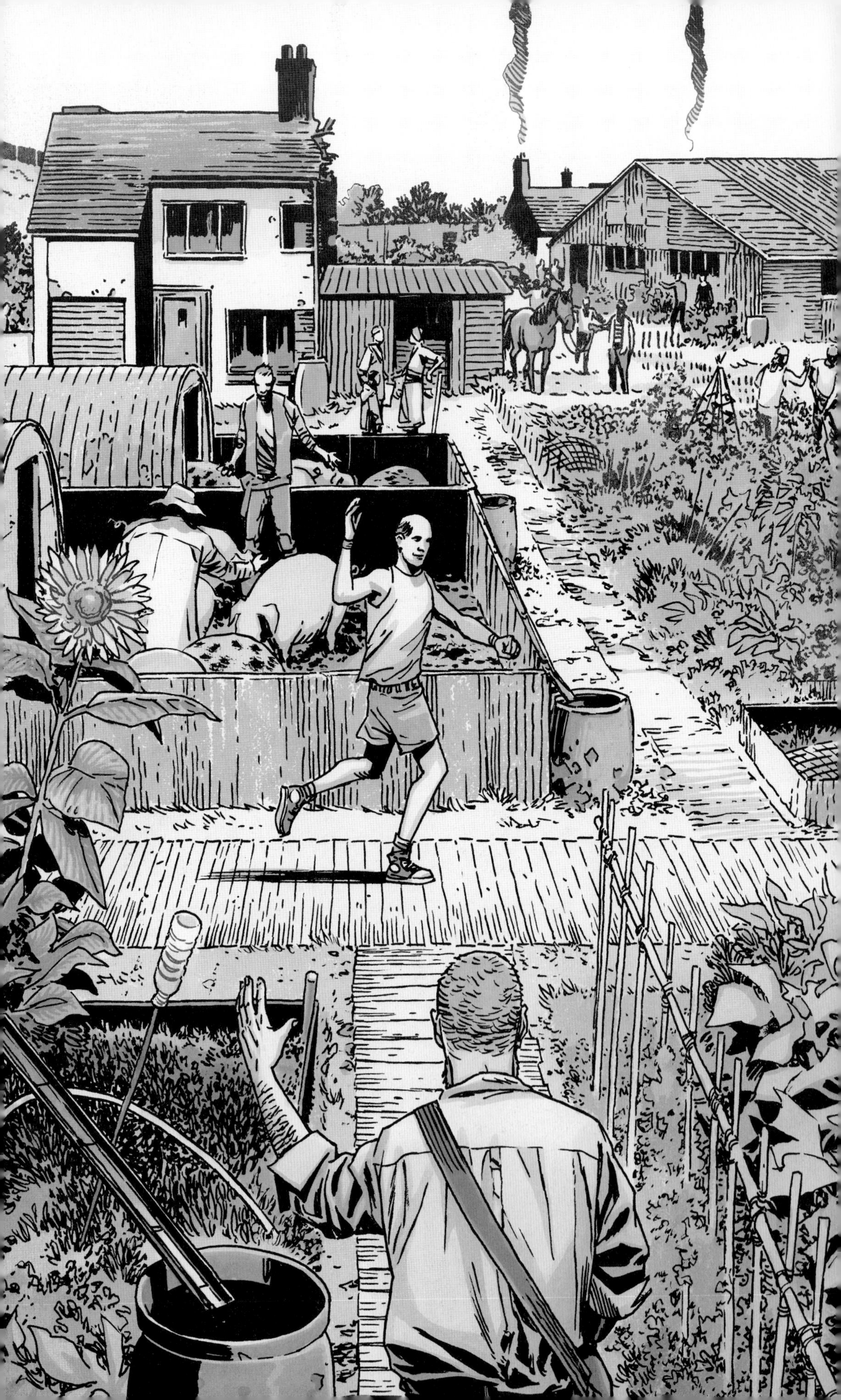

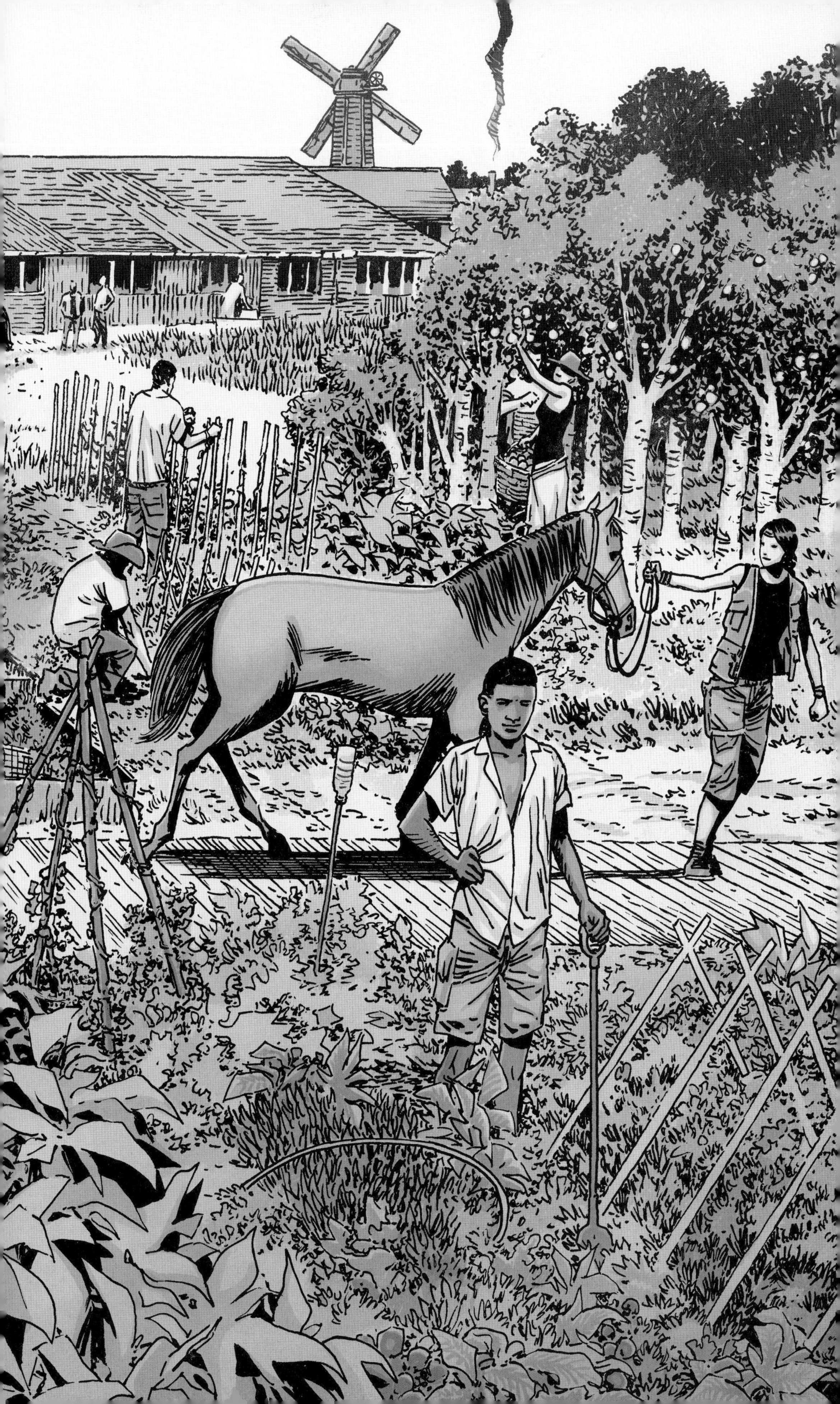

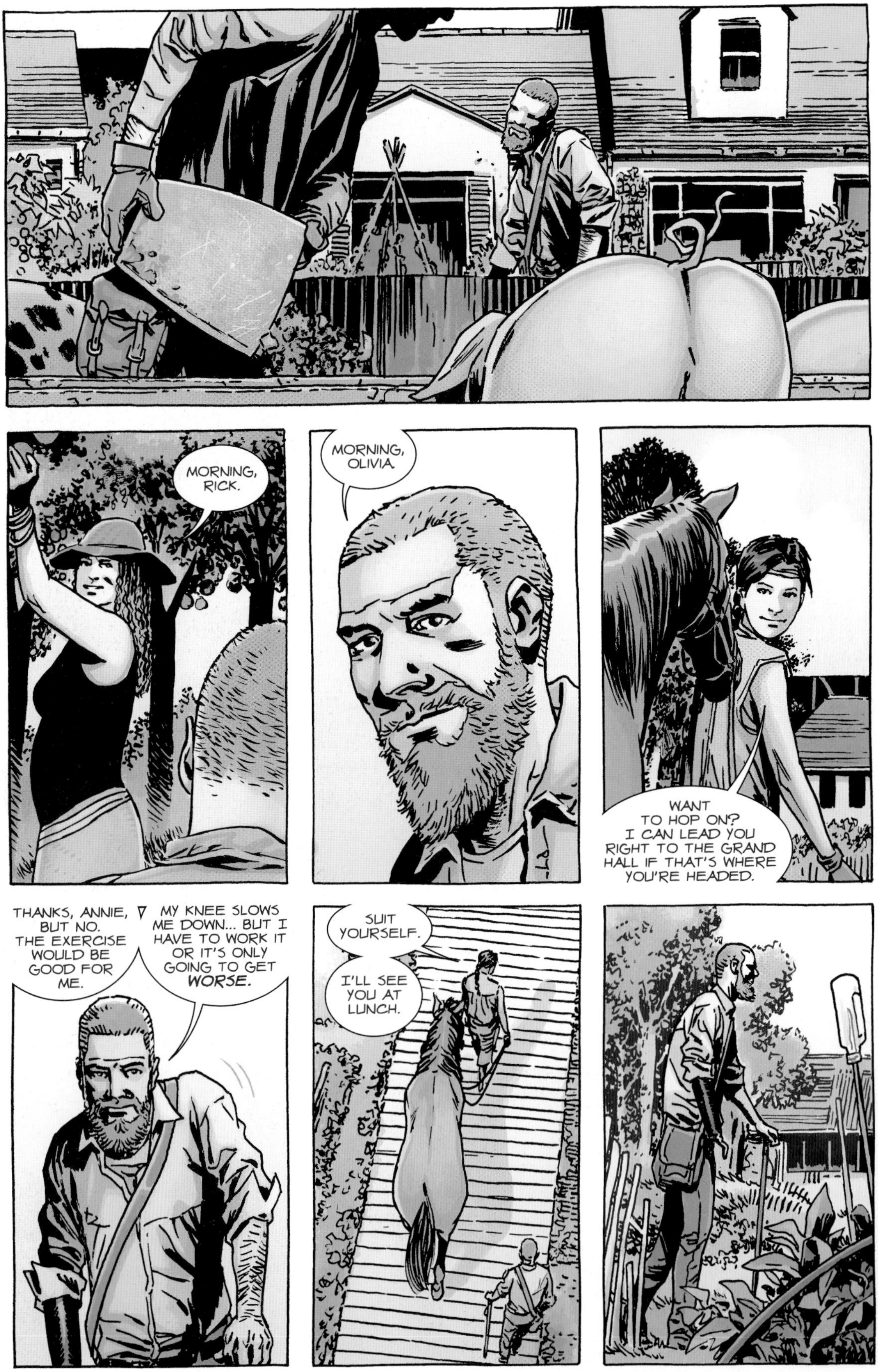
MORNING, RICK.
MORNING, OLIVIA.
WANT TO HOP ON? I CAN LEAD YOU RIGHT TO THE GRAND HALL IF THAT'S WHERE YOU'RE HEADED.
THANKS, ANNIE, BUT NO. THE EXERCISE WOULD BE GOOD FOR ME.
MY KNEE SLOWS ME DOWN... BUT I HAVE TO WORK IT OR IT'S ONLY GOING TO GET *WORSE.*
SUIT YOURSELF.
I'LL SEE YOU AT LUNCH.

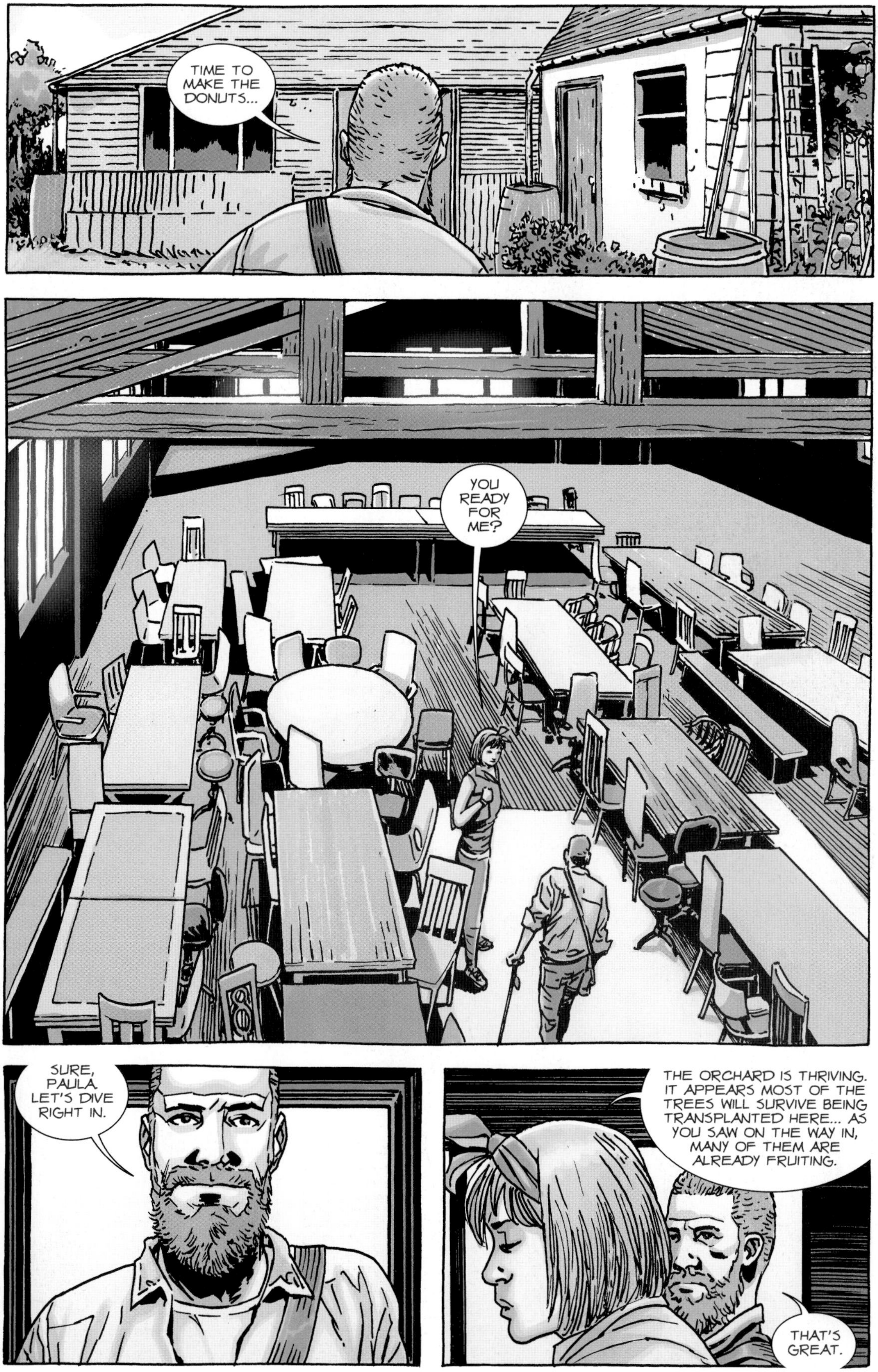
TIME TO MAKE THE DONUTS...
YOU READY FOR ME?
SURE, PAULA. LET'S DIVE RIGHT IN.
THE ORCHARD IS THRIVING. IT APPEARS MOST OF THE TREES WILL SURVIVE BEING TRANSPLANTED HERE... AS YOU SAW ON THE WAY IN, MANY OF THEM ARE ALREADY FRUITING.
THAT'S GREAT.

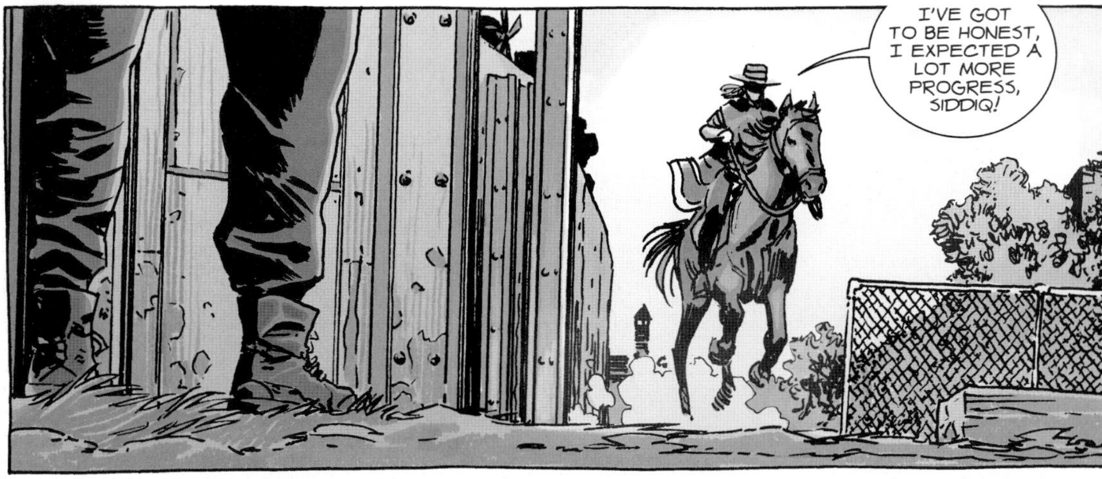
I'VE GOT TO BE HONEST, I EXPECTED A LOT MORE PROGRESS, SIDDIQ!

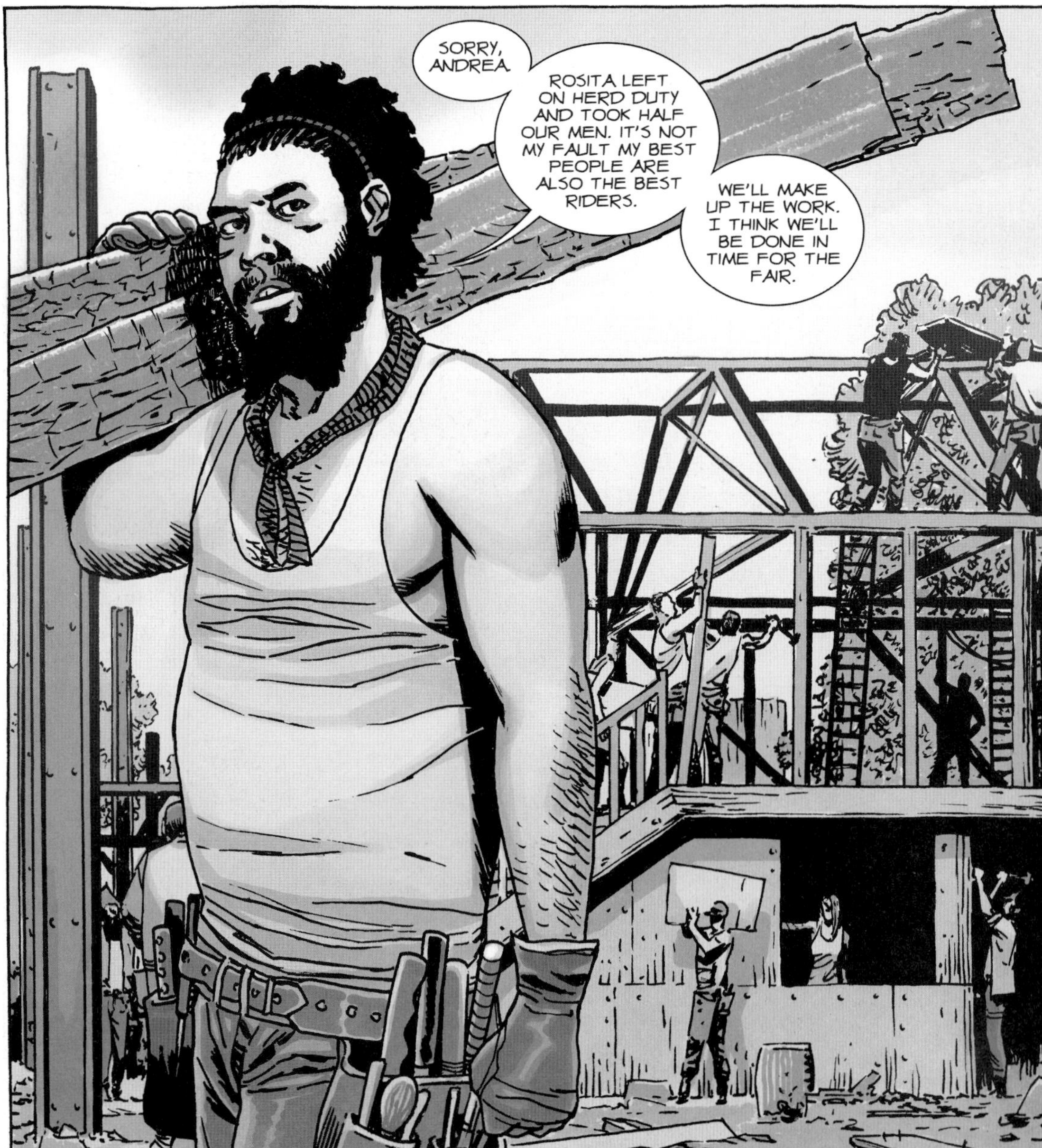
SORRY, ANDREA.
ROSITA LEFT ON HERD DUTY AND TOOK HALF OUR MEN. IT'S NOT MY FAULT MY BEST PEOPLE ARE ALSO THE BEST RIDERS.
WE'LL MAKE UP THE WORK. I THINK WE'LL BE DONE IN TIME FOR THE FAIR.

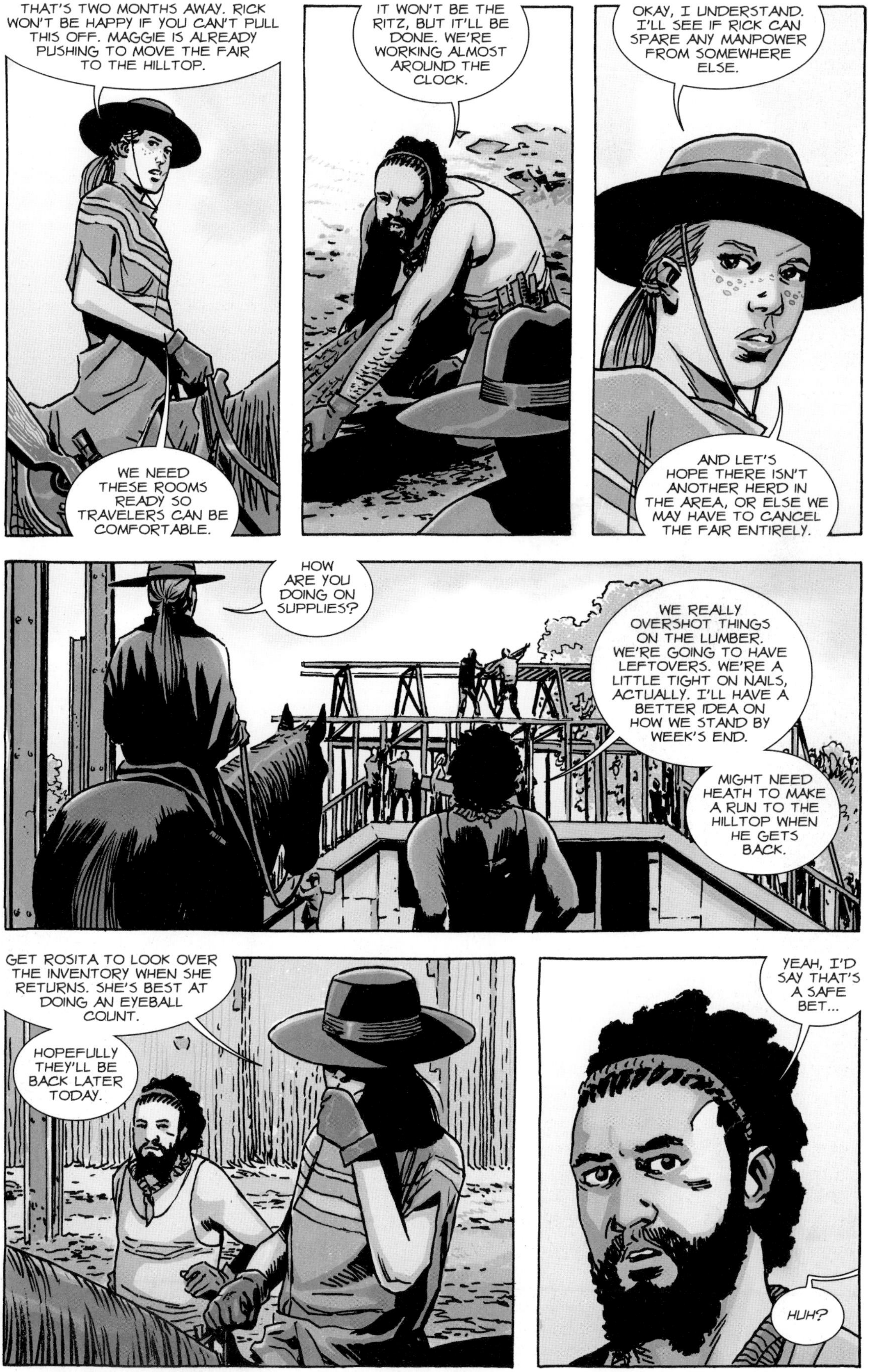
THAT'S TWO MONTHS AWAY. RICK WON'T BE HAPPY IF YOU CAN'T PULL THIS OFF. MAGGIE IS ALREADY PUSHING TO MOVE THE FAIR TO THE HILLTOP.
WE NEED THESE ROOMS READY SO TRAVELERS CAN BE COMFORTABLE.
IT WON'T BE THE RITZ, BUT IT'LL BE DONE. WE'RE WORKING ALMOST AROUND THE CLOCK.
OKAY, I UNDERSTAND. I'LL SEE IF RICK CAN SPARE ANY MANPOWER FROM SOMEWHERE ELSE.
AND LET'S HOPE THERE ISN'T ANOTHER HERD IN THE AREA, OR ELSE WE MAY HAVE TO CANCEL THE FAIR ENTIRELY.
HOW ARE YOU DOING ON SUPPLIES?
WE REALLY OVERSHOT THINGS ON THE LUMBER. WE'RE GOING TO HAVE LEFTOVERS. WE'RE A LITTLE TIGHT ON NAILS, ACTUALLY. I'LL HAVE A BETTER IDEA ON HOW WE STAND BY WEEK'S END.
MIGHT NEED HEATH TO MAKE A RUN TO THE HILLTOP WHEN HE GETS BACK.
GET ROSITA TO LOOK OVER THE INVENTORY WHEN SHE RETURNS. SHE'S BEST AT DOING AN EYEBALL COUNT.
HOPEFULLY THEY'LL BE BACK LATER TODAY.
YEAH, I'D SAY THAT'S A SAFE BET...
HUH?

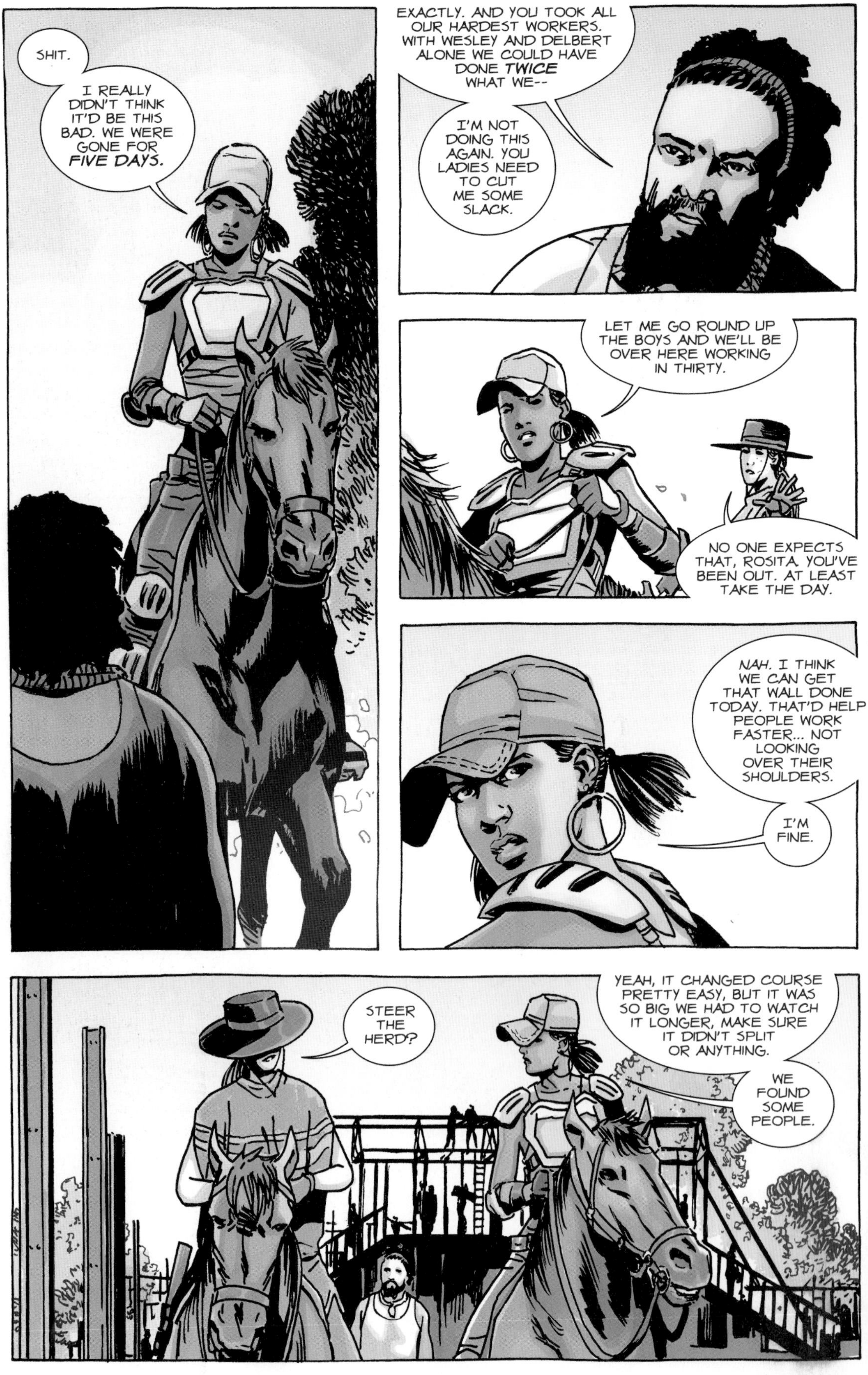
SHIT.
I REALLY DIDN'T THINK IT'D BE THIS BAD. WE WERE GONE FOR *FIVE DAYS.*
EXACTLY. AND YOU TOOK ALL OUR HARDEST WORKERS. WITH WESLEY AND DELBERT ALONE WE COULD HAVE DONE *TWICE* WHAT WE--
I'M NOT DOING THIS AGAIN. YOU LADIES NEED TO CUT ME SOME SLACK.
LET ME GO ROUND UP THE BOYS AND WE'LL BE OVER HERE WORKING IN THIRTY.
NO ONE EXPECTS THAT, ROSITA. YOU'VE BEEN OUT. AT LEAST TAKE THE DAY.
NAH. I THINK WE CAN GET THAT WALL DONE TODAY. THAT'D HELP PEOPLE WORK FASTER... NOT LOOKING OVER THEIR SHOULDERS.
I'M FINE.
STEER THE HERD?
YEAH, IT CHANGED COURSE PRETTY EASY, BUT IT WAS SO BIG WE HAD TO WATCH IT LONGER, MAKE SURE IT DIDN'T SPLIT OR ANYTHING.
WE FOUND SOME PEOPLE.

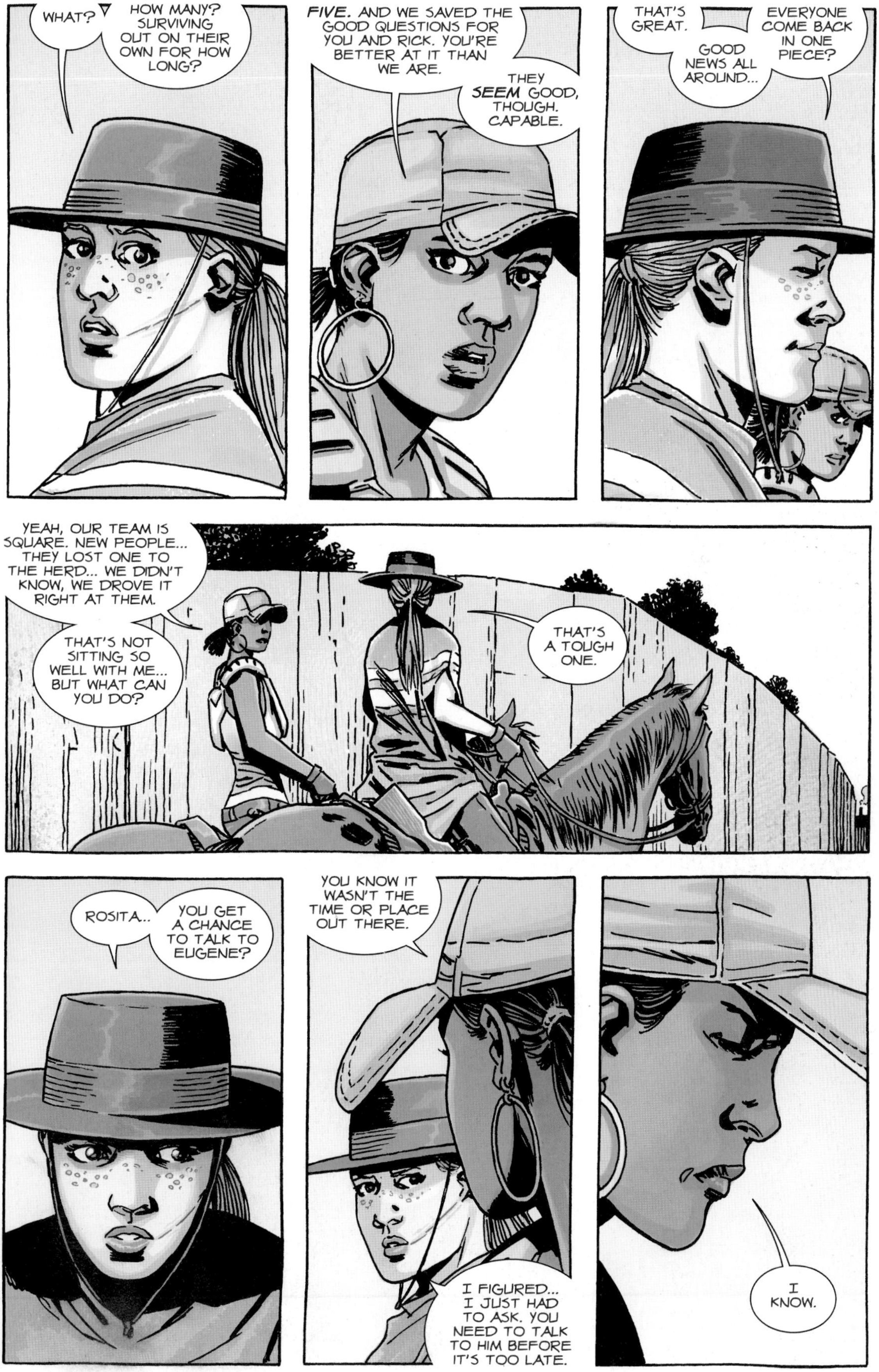
WHAT?
HOW MANY? SURVIVING OUT ON THEIR OWN FOR HOW LONG?
FIVE. AND WE SAVED THE GOOD QUESTIONS FOR YOU AND RICK. YOU'RE BETTER AT IT THAN WE ARE.
THEY SEEM GOOD, THOUGH. CAPABLE.
THAT'S GREAT.
GOOD NEWS ALL AROUND...
EVERYONE COME BACK IN ONE PIECE?
YEAH, OUR TEAM IS SQUARE. NEW PEOPLE... THEY LOST ONE TO THE HERD... WE DIDN'T KNOW, WE DROVE IT RIGHT AT THEM.
THAT'S NOT SITTING SO WELL WITH ME... BUT WHAT CAN YOU DO?
THAT'S A TOUGH ONE.
ROSITA...
YOU GET A CHANCE TO TALK TO EUGENE?
YOU KNOW IT WASN'T THE TIME OR PLACE OUT THERE.
I FIGURED... I JUST HAD TO ASK. YOU NEED TO TALK TO HIM BEFORE IT'S TOO LATE.
I KNOW.

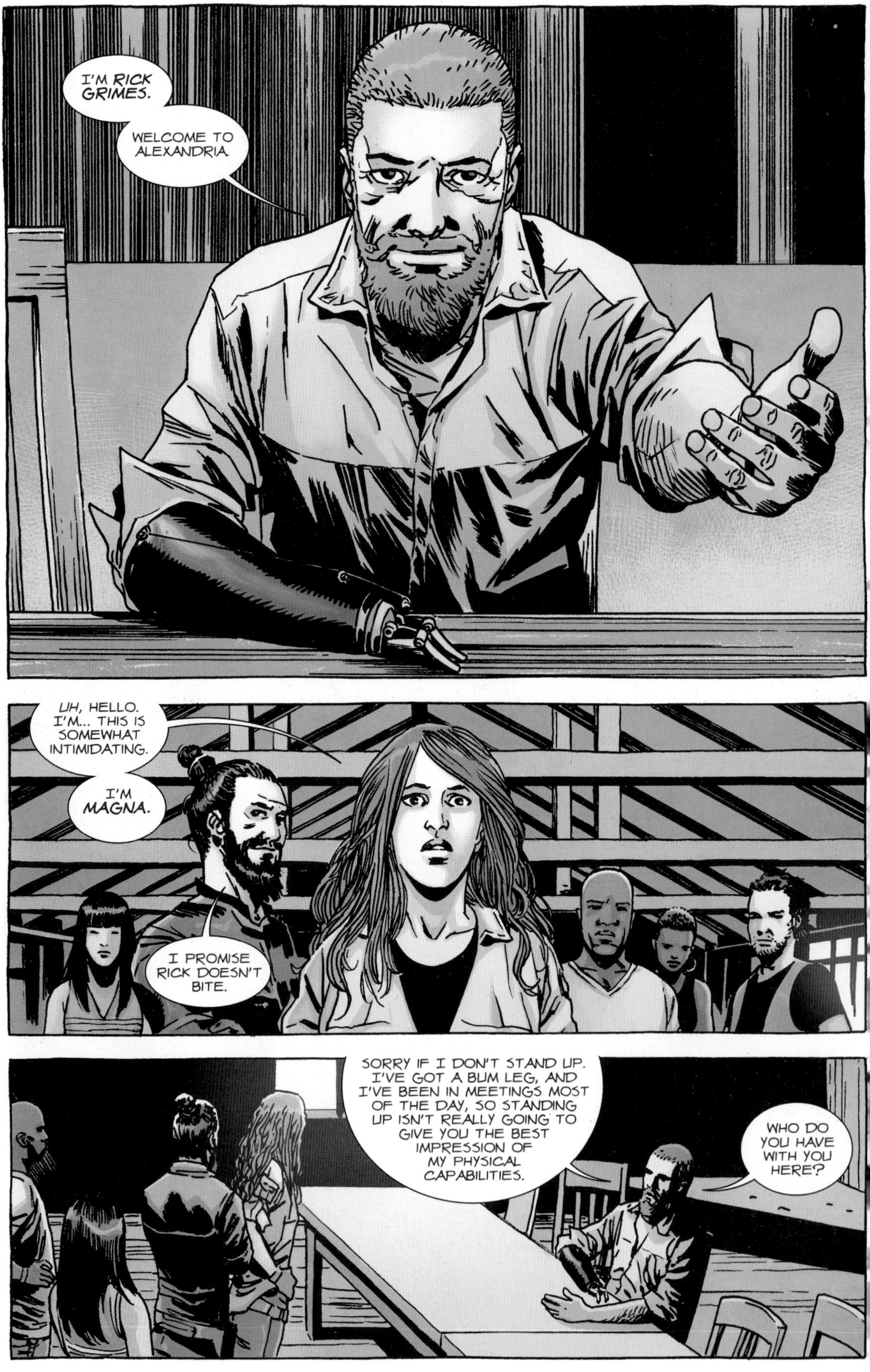
I'M RICK GRIMES.
WELCOME TO ALEXANDRIA
UH, HELLO. I'M... THIS IS SOMEWHAT INTIMIDATING.
I'M MAGNA.
I PROMISE RICK DOESN'T BITE.
SORRY IF I DON'T STAND UP. I'VE GOT A BUM LEG, AND I'VE BEEN IN MEETINGS MOST OF THE DAY, SO STANDING UP ISN'T REALLY GOING TO GIVE YOU THE BEST IMPRESSION OF MY PHYSICAL CAPABILITIES.
WHO DO YOU HAVE WITH YOU HERE?

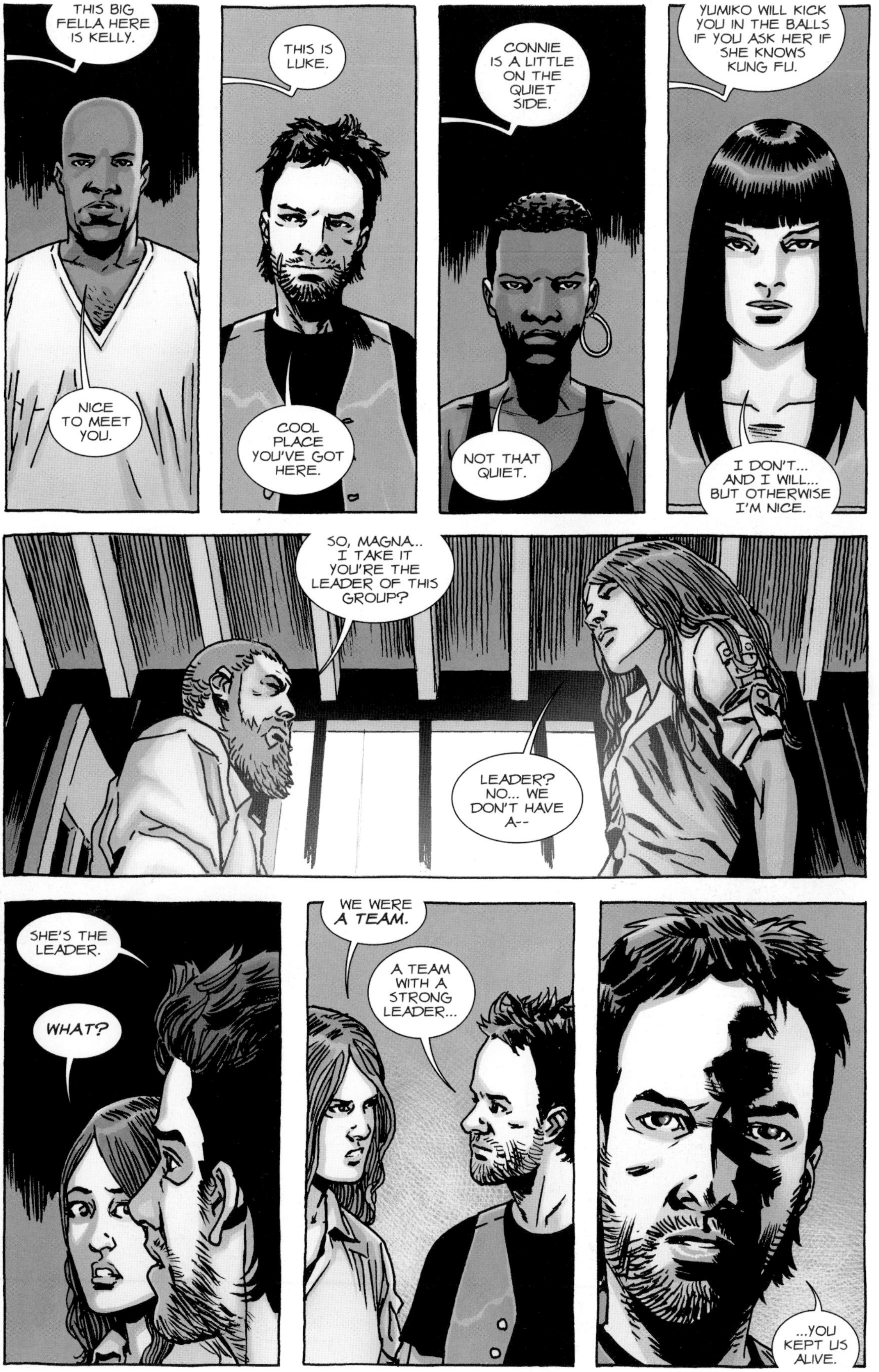
THIS BIG FELLA HERE IS KELLY.
NICE TO MEET YOU.
THIS IS LUKE.
COOL PLACE YOU'VE GOT HERE.
CONNIE IS A LITTLE ON THE QUIET SIDE.
NOT THAT QUIET.
YUMIKO WILL KICK YOU IN THE BALLS IF YOU ASK HER IF SHE KNOWS KUNG FU.
I DON'T... AND I WILL... BUT OTHERWISE I'M NICE.
SO, MAGNA.. I TAKE IT YOU'RE THE LEADER OF THIS GROUP?
LEADER? NO... WE DON'T HAVE A--
SHE'S THE LEADER.
WHAT?
WE WERE *A TEAM.*
A TEAM WITH A STRONG LEADER...
...YOU KEPT US ALIVE.

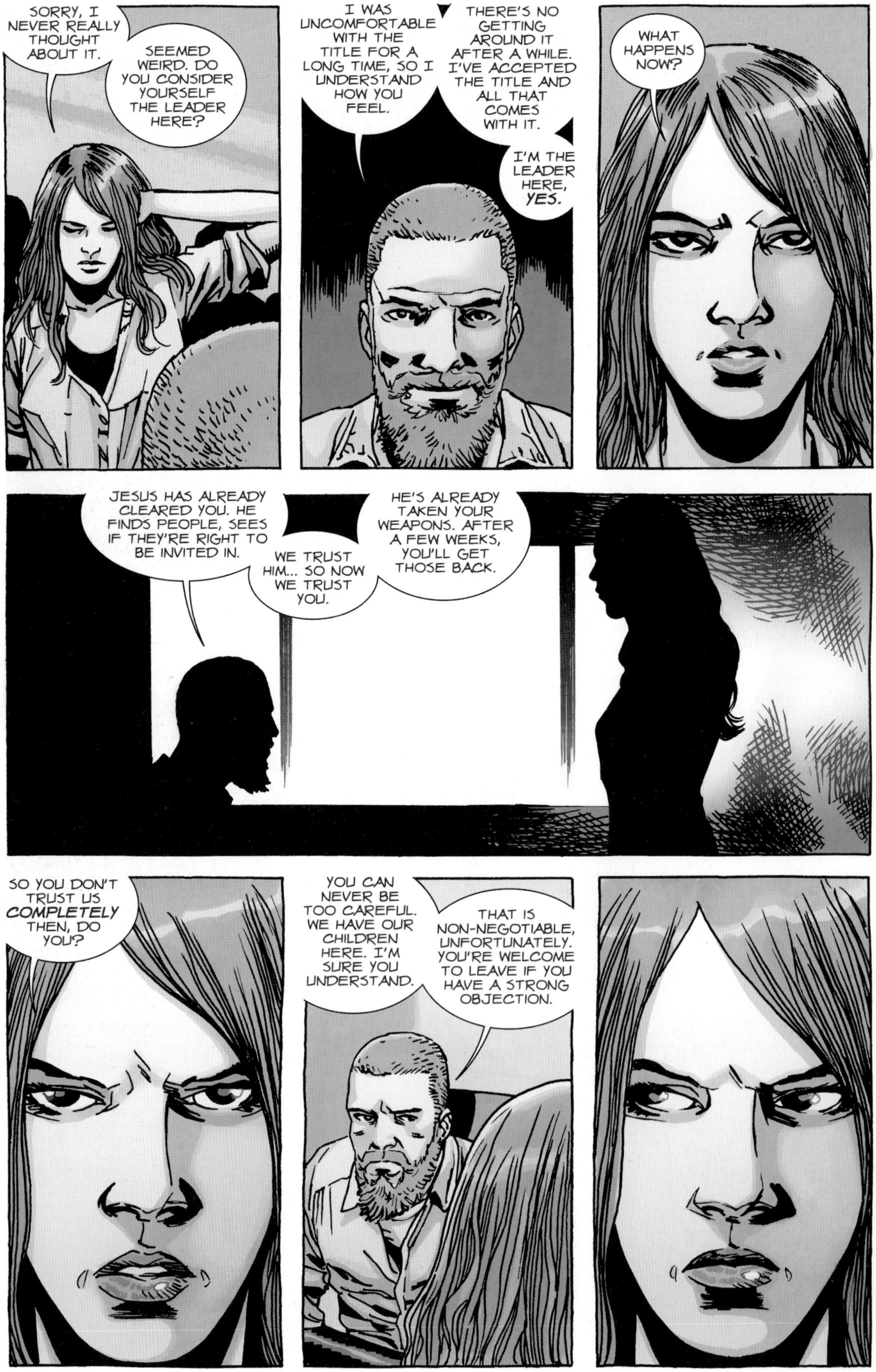
SORRY, I NEVER REALLY THOUGHT ABOUT IT.
SEEMED WEIRD. DO YOU CONSIDER YOURSELF THE LEADER HERE?
I WAS UNCOMFORTABLE WITH THE TITLE FOR A LONG TIME, SO I UNDERSTAND HOW YOU FEEL.
THERE'S NO GETTING AROUND IT AFTER A WHILE. I'VE ACCEPTED THE TITLE AND ALL THAT COMES WITH IT.
I'M THE LEADER HERE, YES.
WHAT HAPPENS NOW?
JESUS HAS ALREADY CLEARED YOU. HE FINDS PEOPLE, SEES IF THEY'RE RIGHT TO BE INVITED IN.
WE TRUST HIM... SO NOW WE TRUST YOU.
HE'S ALREADY TAKEN YOUR WEAPONS. AFTER A FEW WEEKS, YOU'LL GET THOSE BACK.
SO YOU DON'T TRUST US COMPLETELY THEN, DO YOU?
YOU CAN NEVER BE TOO CAREFUL. WE HAVE OUR CHILDREN HERE. I'M SURE YOU UNDERSTAND.
THAT IS NON-NEGOTIABLE, UNFORTUNATELY. YOU'RE WELCOME TO LEAVE IF YOU HAVE A STRONG OBJECTION.

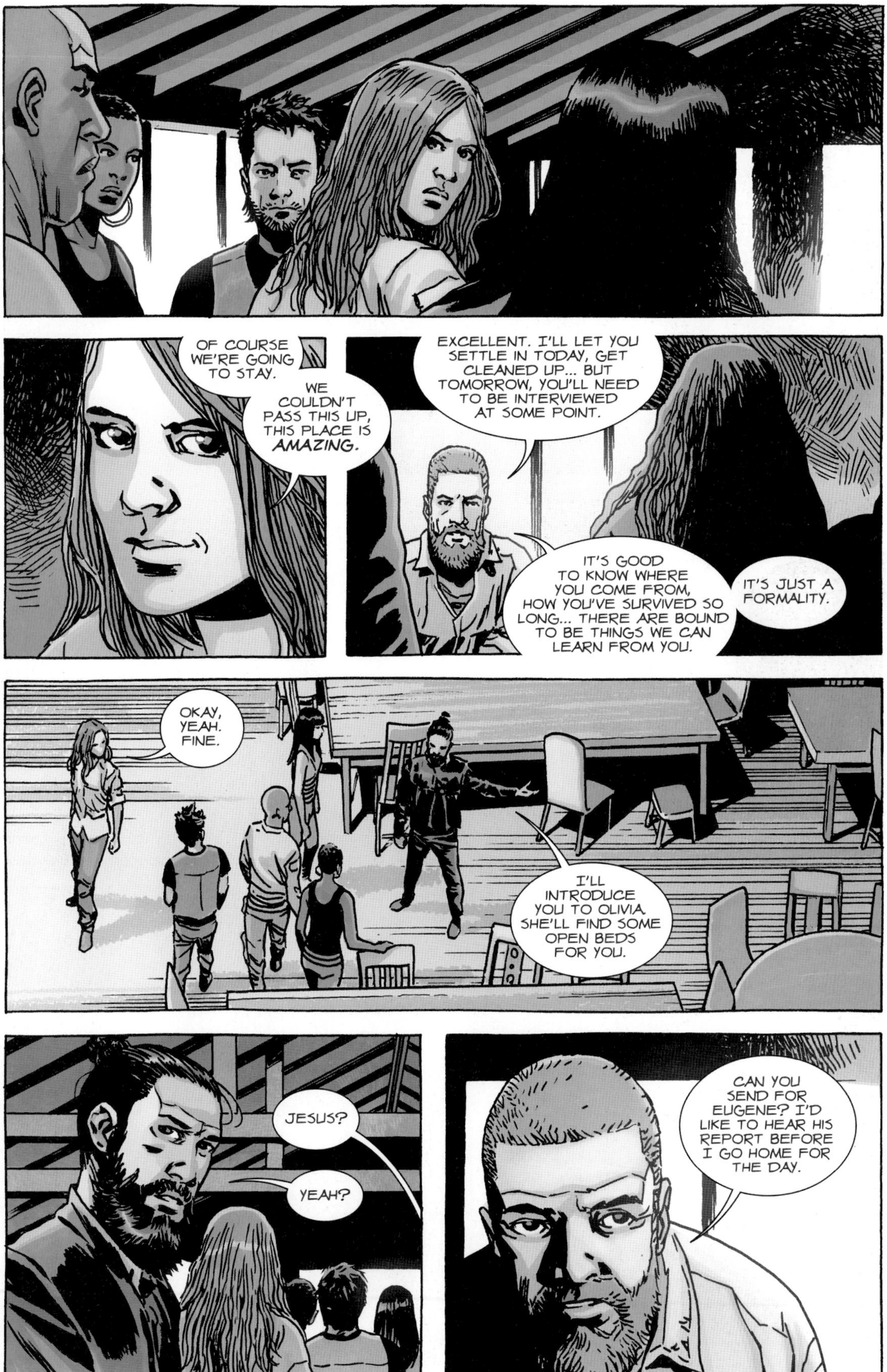
OF COURSE WE'RE GOING TO STAY.
WE COULDN'T PASS THIS UP, THIS PLACE IS AMAZING.
EXCELLENT. I'LL LET YOU SETTLE IN TODAY, GET CLEANED UP... BUT TOMORROW, YOU'LL NEED TO BE INTERVIEWED AT SOME POINT.
IT'S GOOD TO KNOW WHERE YOU COME FROM, HOW YOU'VE SURVIVED SO LONG... THERE ARE BOUND TO BE THINGS WE CAN LEARN FROM YOU.
IT'S JUST A FORMALITY.
OKAY, YEAH. FINE.
I'LL INTRODUCE YOU TO OLIVIA. SHE'LL FIND SOME OPEN BEDS FOR YOU.
JESUS?
YEAH?
CAN YOU SEND FOR EUGENE? I'D LIKE TO HEAR HIS REPORT BEFORE I GO HOME FOR THE DAY.

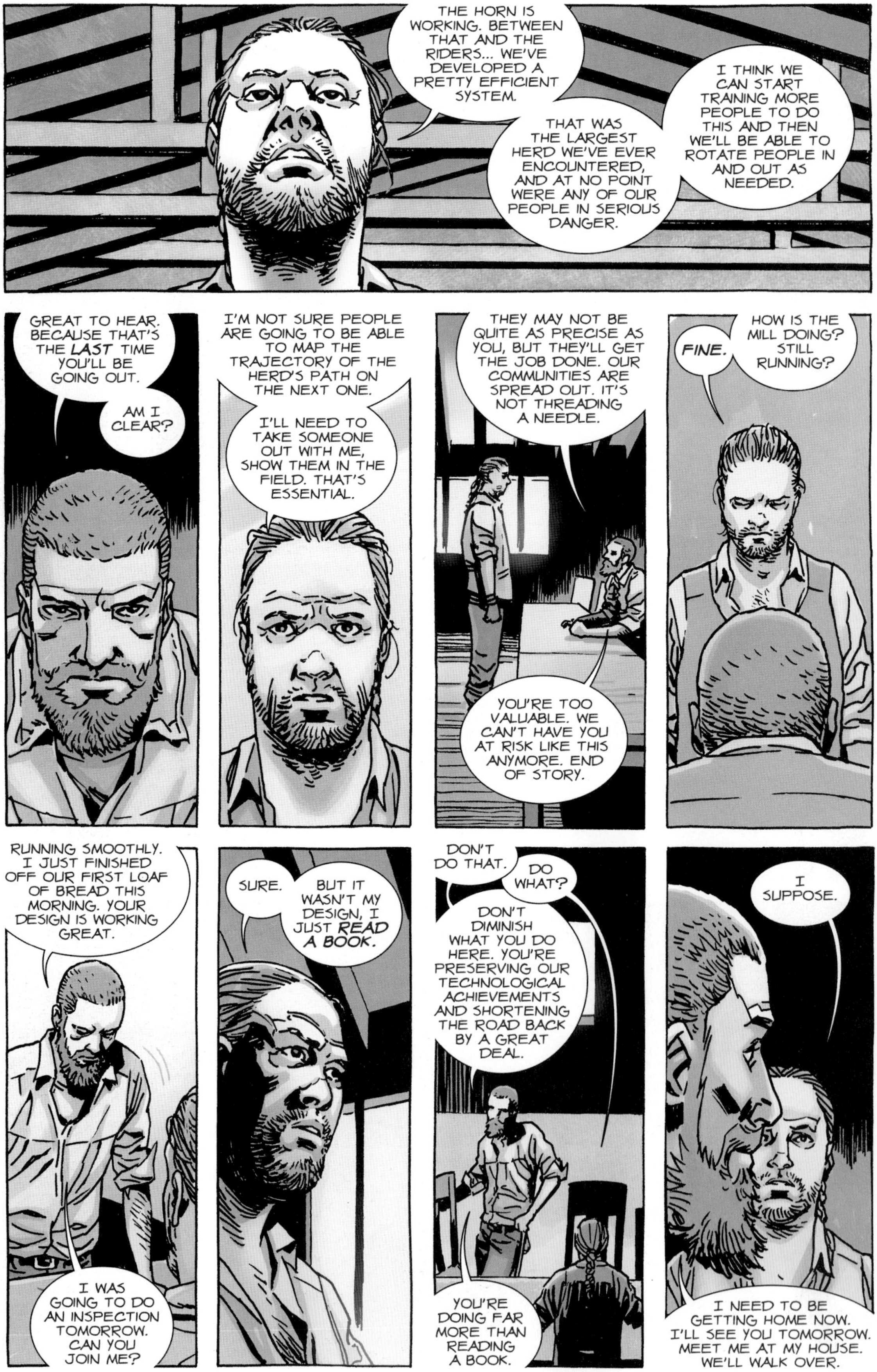

THE HORN IS WORKING. BETWEEN THAT AND THE RIDERS... WE'VE DEVELOPED A PRETTY EFFICIENT SYSTEM.
THAT WAS THE LARGEST HERD WE'VE EVER ENCOUNTERED, AND AT NO POINT WERE ANY OF OUR PEOPLE IN SERIOUS DANGER.
I THINK WE CAN START TRAINING MORE PEOPLE TO DO THIS AND THEN WE'LL BE ABLE TO ROTATE PEOPLE IN AND OUT AS NEEDED.
GREAT TO HEAR. BECAUSE THAT'S THE LAST TIME YOU'LL BE GOING OUT.
AM I CLEAR?
I'M NOT SURE PEOPLE ARE GOING TO BE ABLE TO MAP THE TRAJECTORY OF THE HERD'S PATH ON THE NEXT ONE.
I'LL NEED TO TAKE SOMEONE OUT WITH ME, SHOW THEM IN THE FIELD. THAT'S ESSENTIAL.
THEY MAY NOT BE QUITE AS PRECISE AS YOU, BUT THEY'LL GET THE JOB DONE. OUR COMMUNITIES ARE SPREAD OUT. IT'S NOT THREADING A NEEDLE.
YOU'RE TOO VALUABLE. WE CAN'T HAVE YOU AT RISK LIKE THIS ANYMORE. END OF STORY.
FINE.
HOW IS THE MILL DOING? STILL RUNNING?
RUNNING SMOOTHLY. I JUST FINISHED OFF OUR FIRST LOAF OF BREAD THIS MORNING. YOUR DESIGN IS WORKING GREAT.
I WAS GOING TO DO AN INSPECTION TOMORROW. CAN YOU JOIN ME?
SURE.
BUT IT WASN'T MY DESIGN, I JUST READ A BOOK.
DON'T DO THAT.
DO WHAT?
DON'T DIMINISH WHAT YOU DO HERE. YOU'RE PRESERVING OUR TECHNOLOGICAL ACHIEVEMENTS AND SHORTENING THE ROAD BACK BY A GREAT DEAL.
YOU'RE DOING FAR MORE THAN READING A BOOK.
I SUPPOSE.
I NEED TO BE GETTING HOME NOW. I'LL SEE YOU TOMORROW. MEET ME AT MY HOUSE. WE'LL WALK OVER.

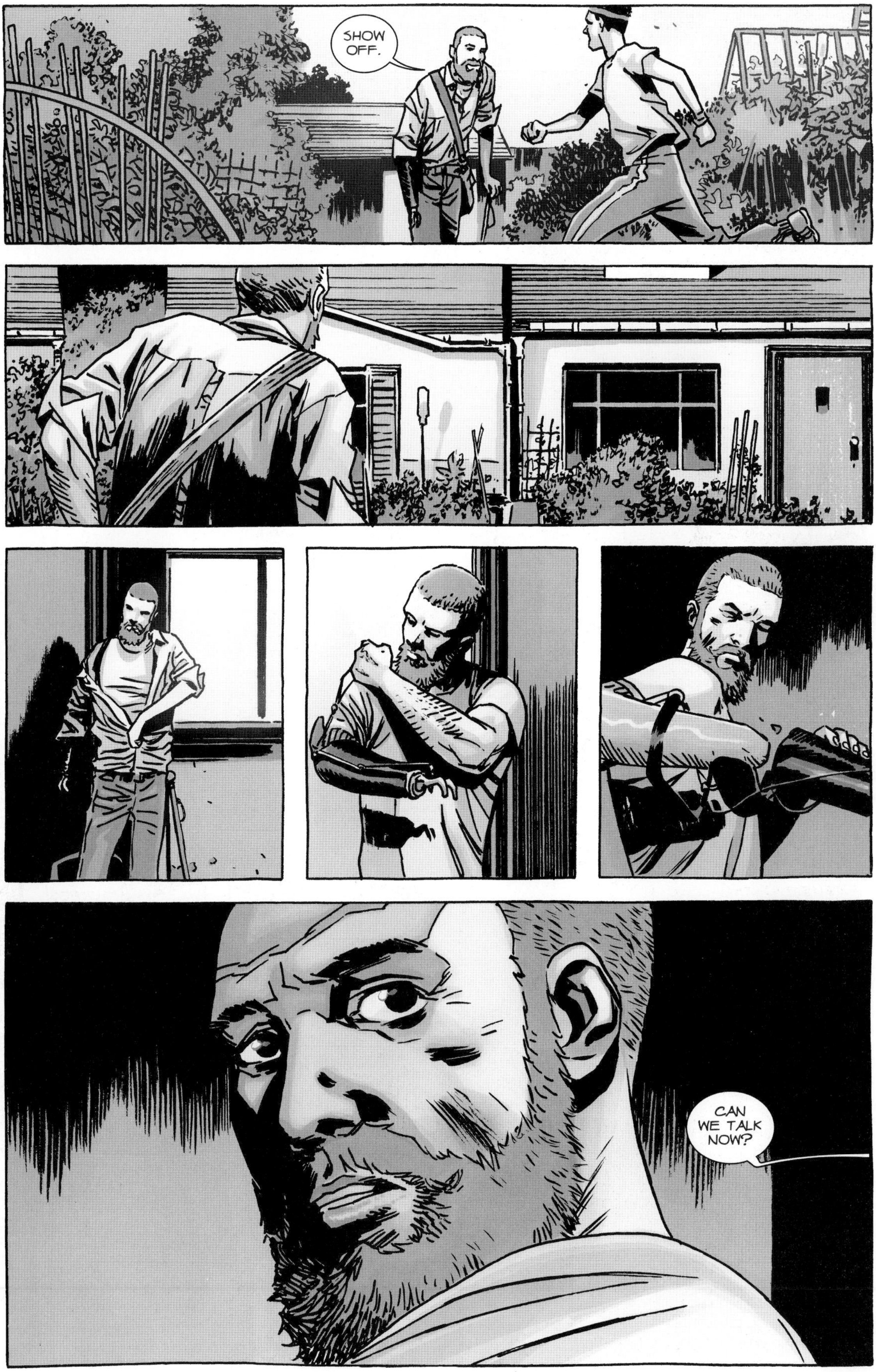
SHOW OFF.
CAN WE TALK NOW?

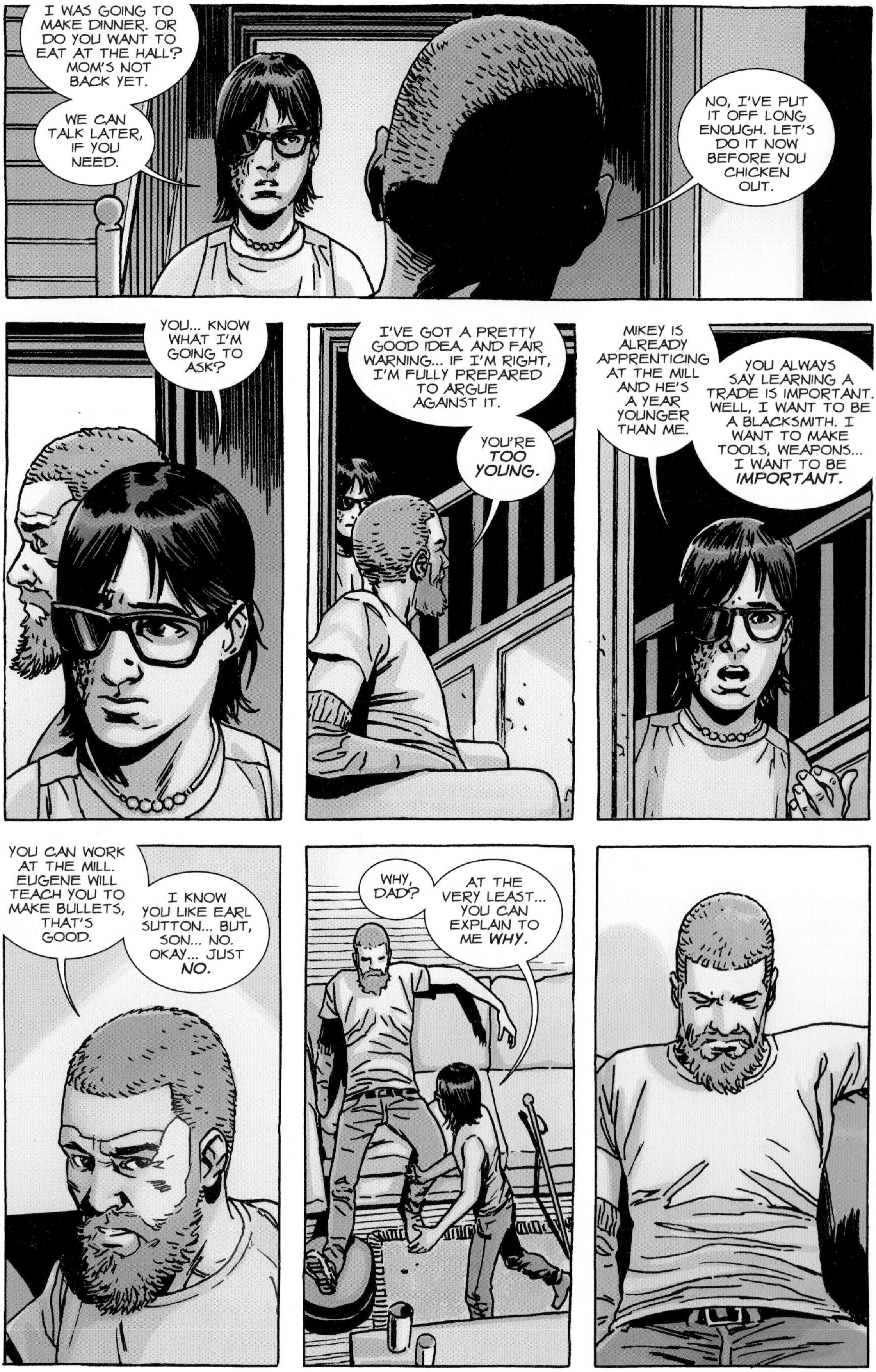
I WAS GOING TO MAKE DINNER. OR DO YOU WANT TO EAT AT THE HALL? MOM'S NOT BACK YET.
WE CAN TALK LATER, IF YOU NEED.
NO, I'VE PUT IT OFF LONG ENOUGH. LET'S DO IT NOW BEFORE YOU CHICKEN OUT.
YOU... KNOW WHAT I'M GOING TO ASK?
I'VE GOT A PRETTY GOOD IDEA AND FAIR WARNING... IF I'M RIGHT, I'M FULLY PREPARED TO ARGUE AGAINST IT.
YOU'RE TOO YOUNG.
MIKEY IS ALREADY APPRENTICING AT THE MILL AND HE'S A YEAR YOUNGER THAN ME.
YOU ALWAYS SAY LEARNING A TRADE IS IMPORTANT. WELL, I WANT TO BE A BLACKSMITH. I WANT TO MAKE TOOLS, WEAPONS... I WANT TO BE IMPORTANT.
YOU CAN WORK AT THE MILL. EUGENE WILL TEACH YOU TO MAKE BULLETS, THAT'S GOOD.
I KNOW YOU LIKE EARL SUTTON... BUT, SON... NO. OKAY... JUST NO.
WHY, DAD?
AT THE VERY LEAST... YOU CAN EXPLAIN TO ME WHY.

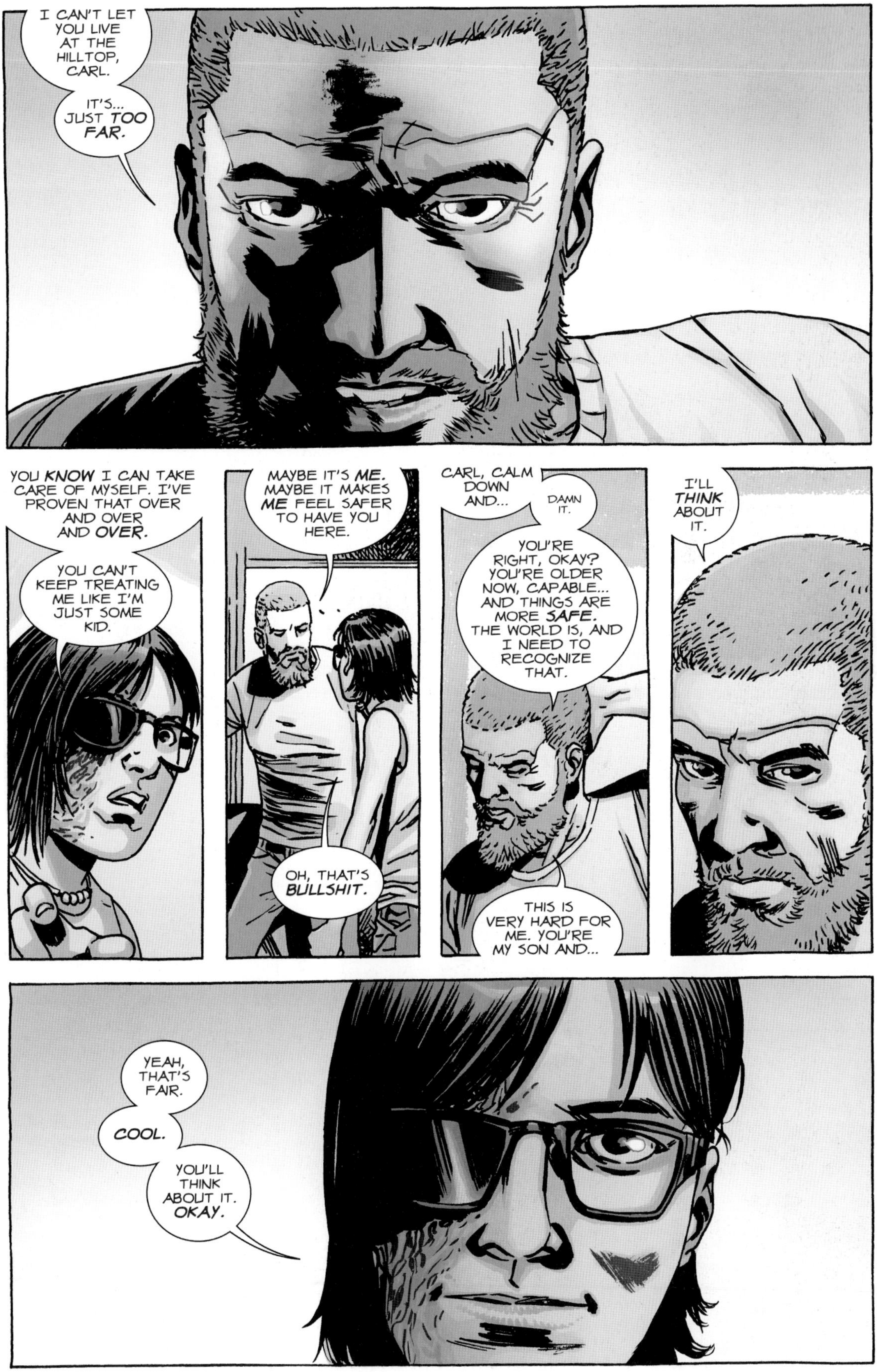
I CAN'T LET YOU LIVE AT THE HILLTOP, CARL.
IT'S... JUST **TOO FAR.**
YOU **KNOW** I CAN TAKE CARE OF MYSELF. I'VE PROVEN THAT OVER AND OVER AND **OVER.**
YOU CAN'T KEEP TREATING ME LIKE I'M JUST SOME KID.
MAYBE IT'S **ME.** MAYBE IT MAKES **ME** FEEL SAFER TO HAVE YOU HERE.
OH, THAT'S **BULLSHIT.**
CARL, CALM DOWN AND...
DAMN IT.
YOU'RE RIGHT, OKAY? YOU'RE OLDER NOW, CAPABLE... AND THINGS ARE MORE **SAFE.** THE WORLD IS, AND I NEED TO RECOGNIZE THAT.
THIS IS VERY HARD FOR ME. YOU'RE MY SON AND...
I'LL **THINK** ABOUT IT.
YEAH, THAT'S FAIR.
COOL.
YOU'LL THINK ABOUT IT. **OKAY.**

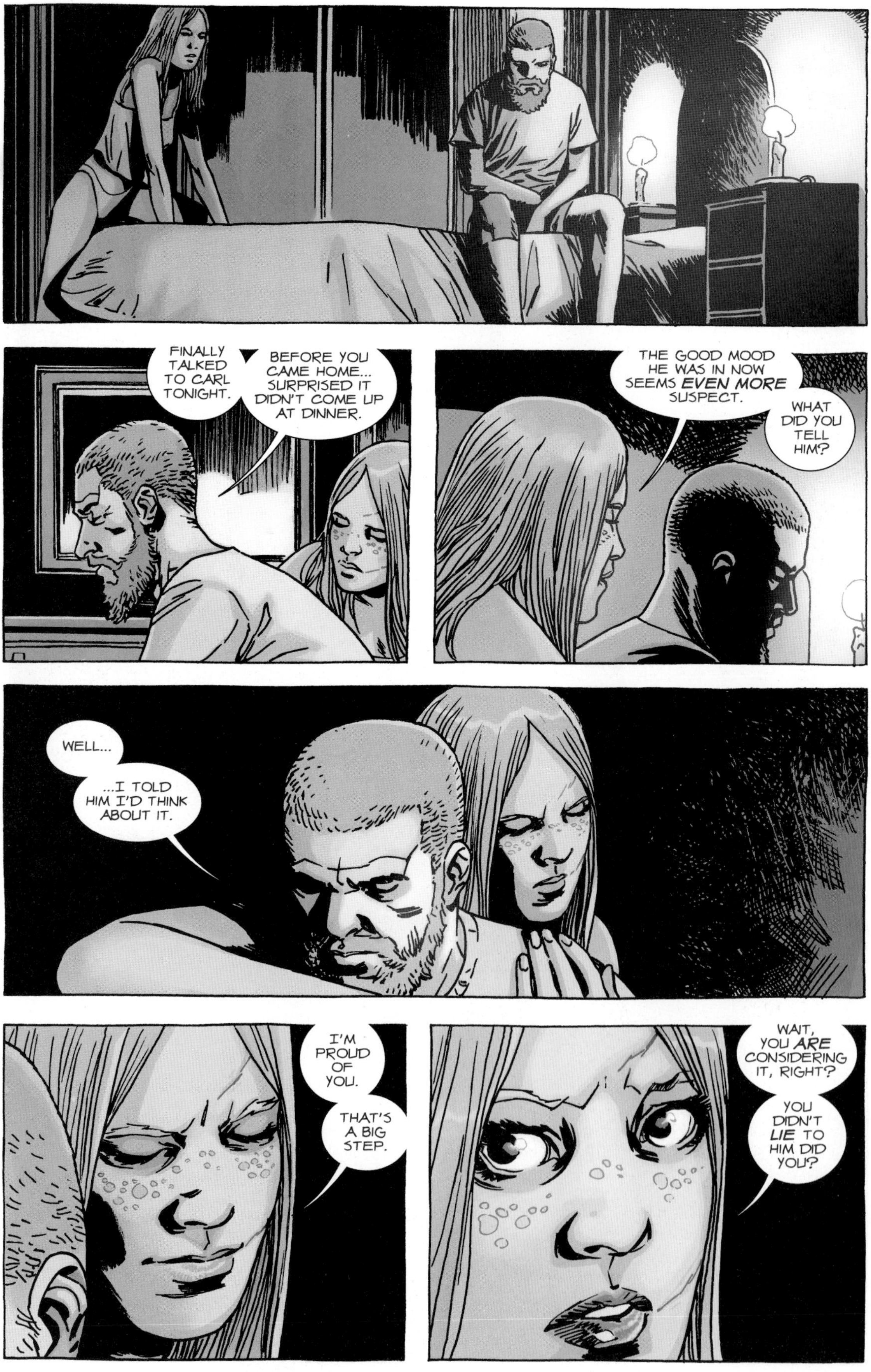
FINALLY TALKED TO CARL TONIGHT.
BEFORE YOU CAME HOME... SURPRISED IT DIDN'T COME UP AT DINNER.
THE GOOD MOOD HE WAS IN NOW SEEMS **EVEN MORE** SUSPECT.
WHAT DID YOU TELL HIM?
WELL...
...I TOLD HIM I'D THINK ABOUT IT.
I'M PROUD OF YOU.
THAT'S A BIG STEP.
WAIT, YOU **ARE** CONSIDERING IT, RIGHT?
YOU DIDN'T **LIE** TO HIM DID YOU?

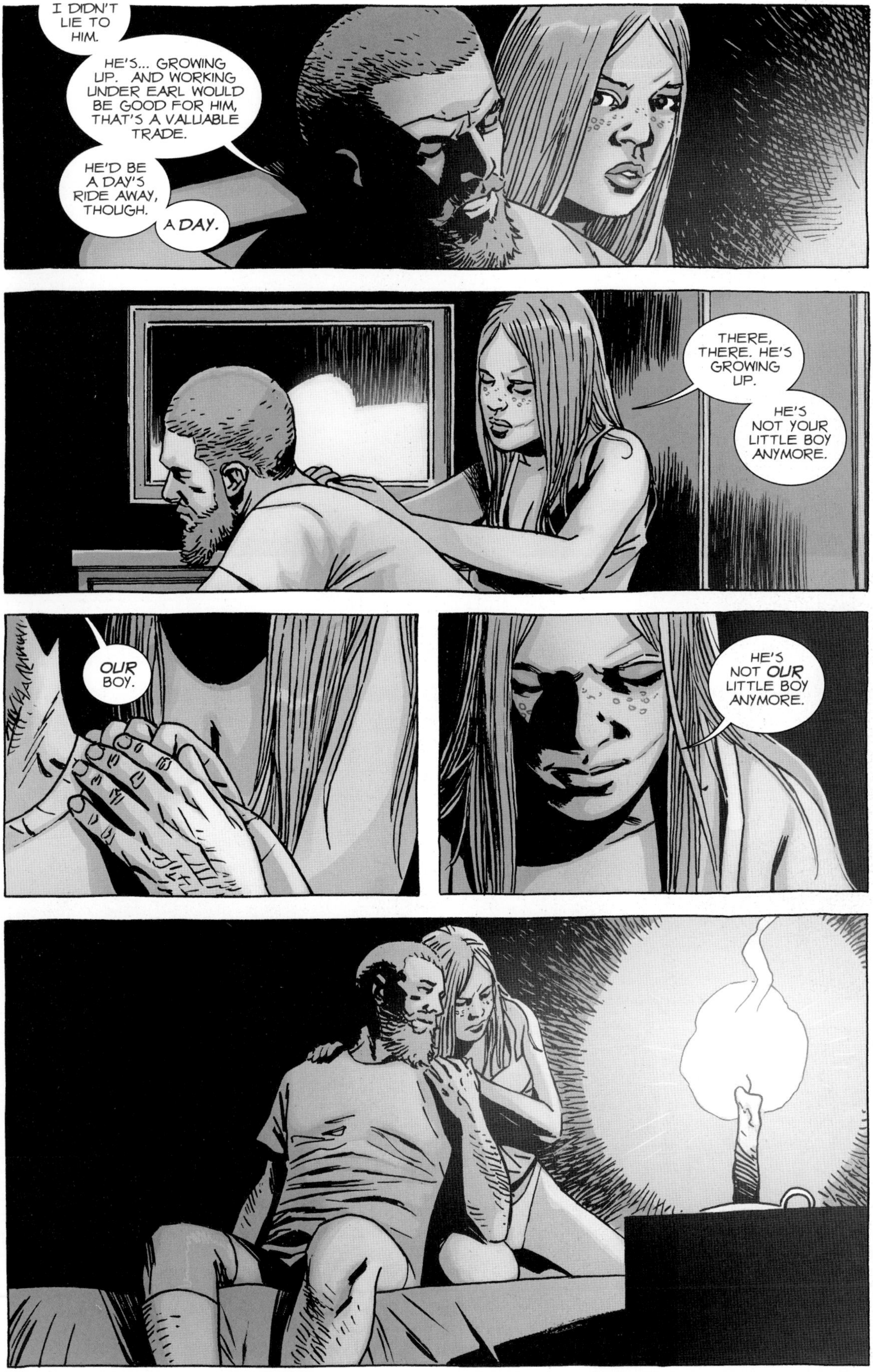
I DIDN'T LIE TO HIM.
HE'S... GROWING UP. AND WORKING UNDER EARL WOULD BE GOOD FOR HIM, THAT'S A VALUABLE TRADE.
HE'D BE A DAY'S RIDE AWAY, THOUGH.
A *DAY.*
THERE, THERE. HE'S GROWING UP.
HE'S NOT YOUR LITTLE BOY ANYMORE.
OUR BOY.
HE'S NOT *OUR* LITTLE BOY ANYMORE.

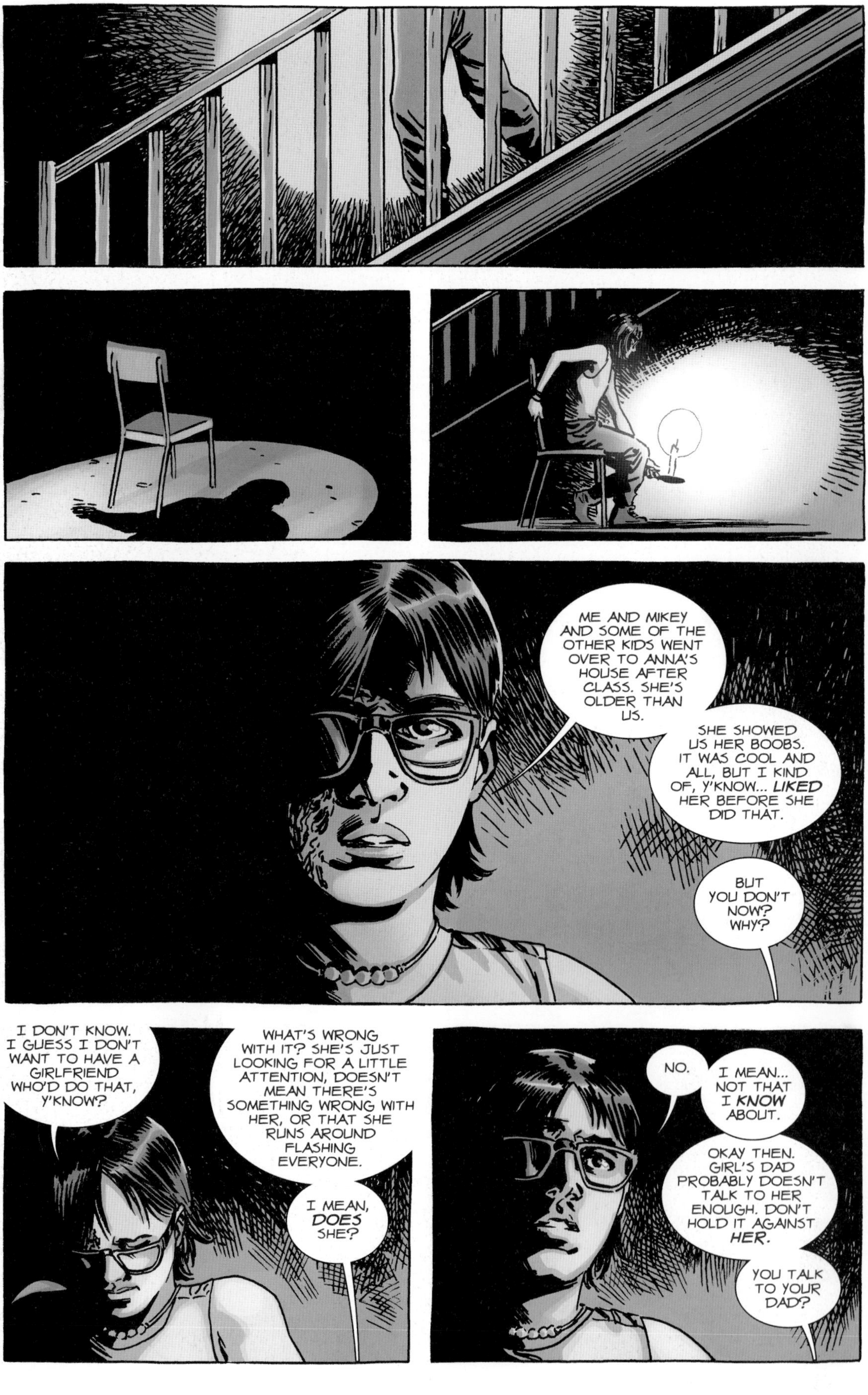
ME AND MIKEY AND SOME OF THE OTHER KIDS WENT OVER TO ANNA'S HOUSE AFTER CLASS. SHE'S OLDER THAN US.
SHE SHOWED US HER BOOBS. IT WAS COOL AND ALL, BUT I KIND OF, Y'KNOW... *LIKED* HER BEFORE SHE DID THAT.
BUT YOU DON'T NOW? WHY?
I DON'T KNOW. I GUESS I DON'T WANT TO HAVE A GIRLFRIEND WHO'D DO THAT, Y'KNOW?
WHAT'S WRONG WITH IT? SHE'S JUST LOOKING FOR A LITTLE ATTENTION, DOESN'T MEAN THERE'S SOMETHING WRONG WITH HER, OR THAT SHE RUNS AROUND FLASHING EVERYONE.
I MEAN, *DOES* SHE?
NO.
I MEAN... NOT THAT I *KNOW* ABOUT.
OKAY THEN. GIRL'S DAD PROBABLY DOESN'T TALK TO HER ENOUGH. DON'T HOLD IT AGAINST *HER*.
YOU TALK TO YOUR DAD?

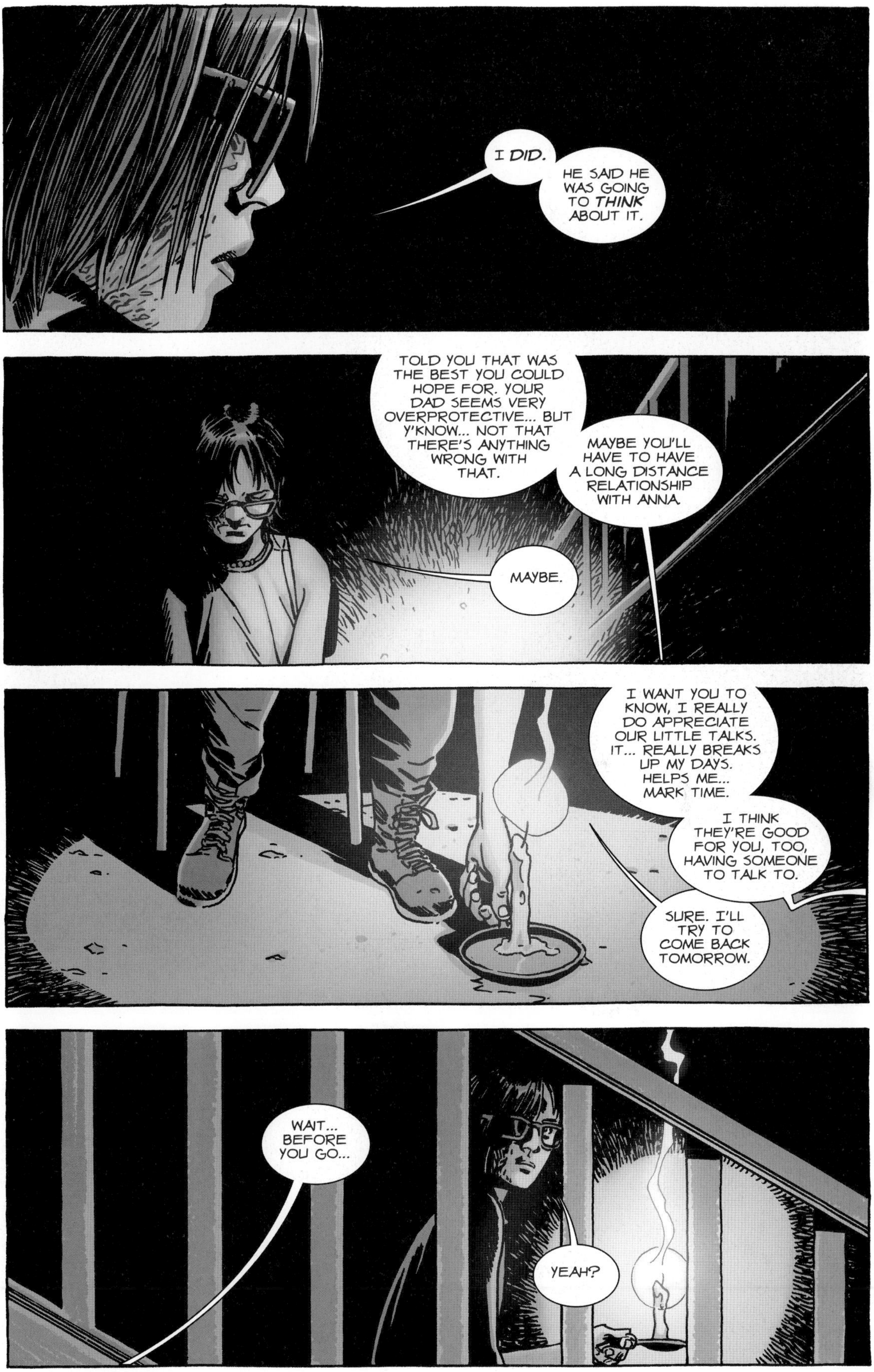
I DID.
HE SAID HE WAS GOING TO *THINK* ABOUT IT.
TOLD YOU THAT WAS THE BEST YOU COULD HOPE FOR. YOUR DAD SEEMS VERY OVERPROTECTIVE... BUT Y'KNOW... NOT THAT THERE'S ANYTHING WRONG WITH THAT.
MAYBE YOU'LL HAVE TO HAVE A LONG DISTANCE RELATIONSHIP WITH ANNA.
MAYBE.
I WANT YOU TO KNOW, I REALLY DO APPRECIATE OUR LITTLE TALKS. IT... REALLY BREAKS UP MY DAYS. HELPS ME... MARK TIME.
I THINK THEY'RE GOOD FOR YOU, TOO, HAVING SOMEONE TO TALK TO.
SURE. I'LL TRY TO COME BACK TOMORROW.
WAIT... BEFORE YOU GO...
YEAH?

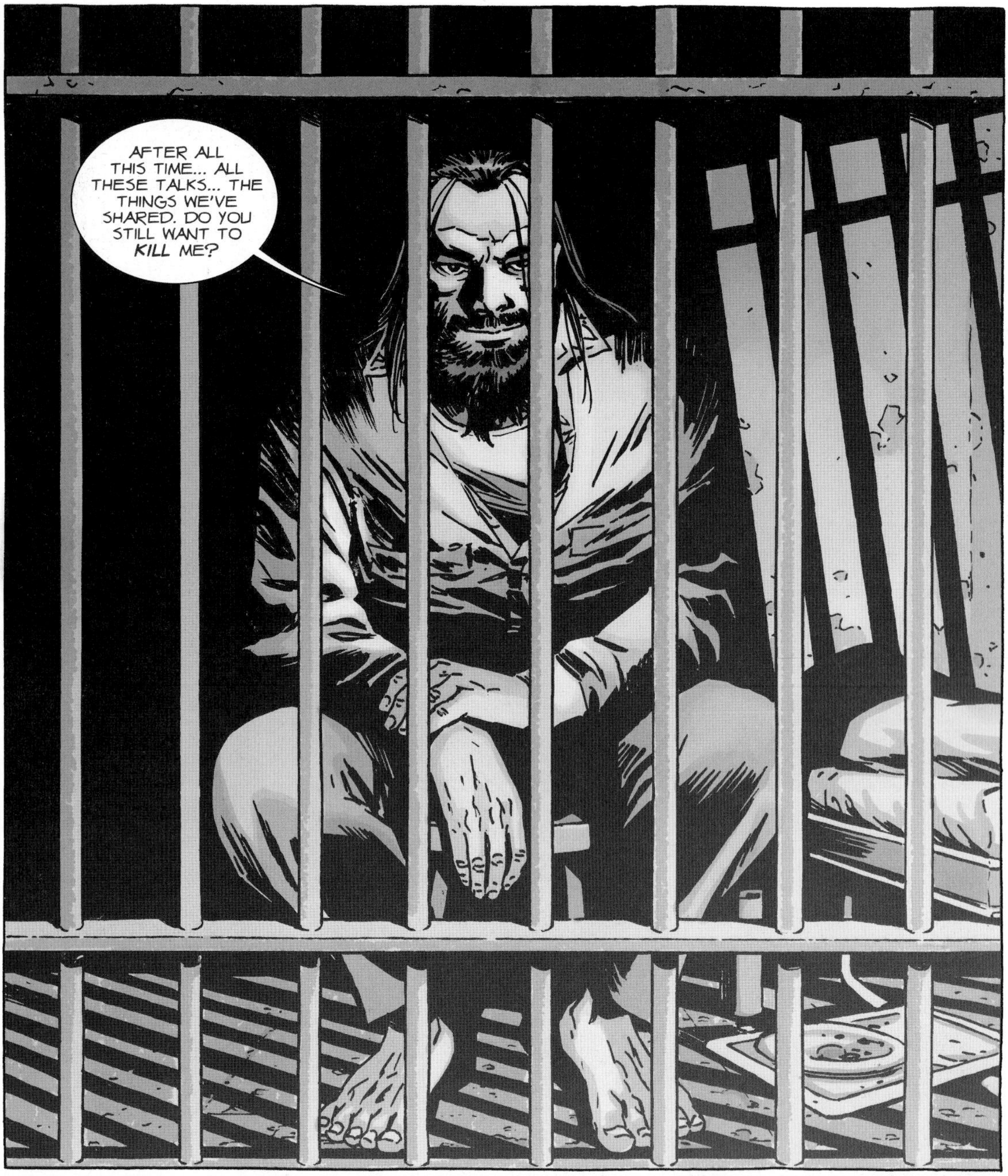
AFTER ALL THIS TIME... ALL THESE TALKS... THE THINGS WE'VE SHARED. DO YOU STILL WANT TO *KILL* ME?

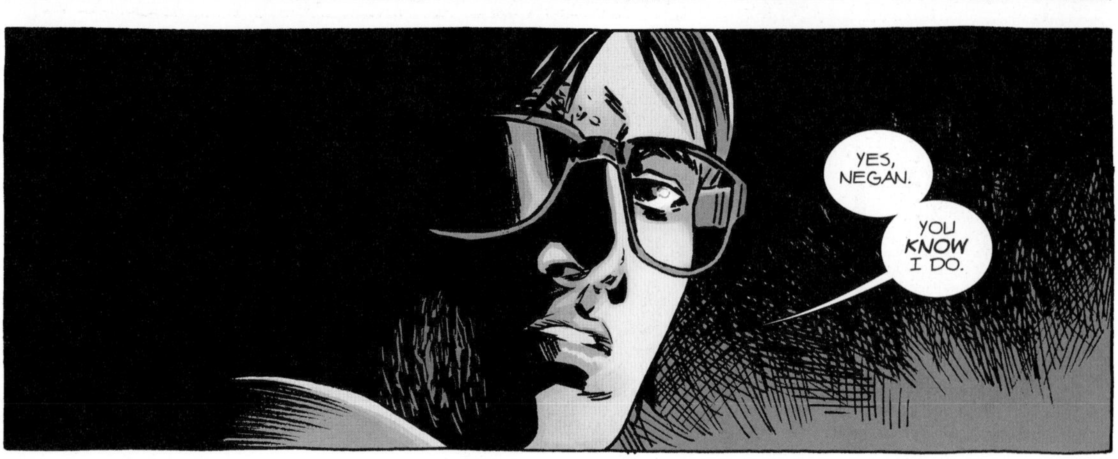
YES, NEGAN.
YOU *KNOW* I DO.

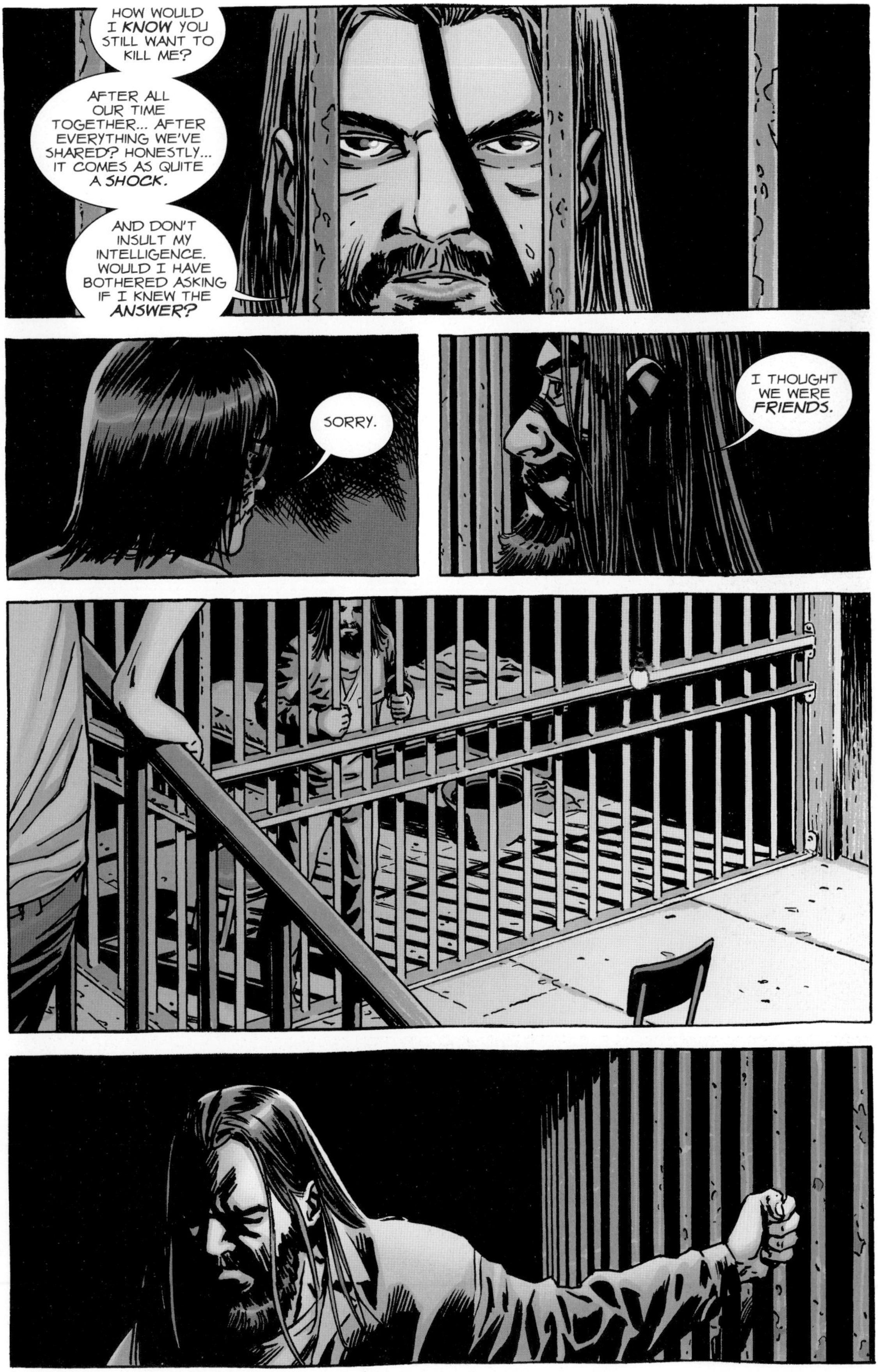
HOW WOULD I KNOW YOU STILL WANT TO KILL ME?
AFTER ALL OUR TIME TOGETHER... AFTER EVERYTHING WE'VE SHARED? HONESTLY... IT COMES AS QUITE A SHOCK.
AND DON'T INSULT MY INTELLIGENCE. WOULD I HAVE BOTHERED ASKING IF I KNEW THE ANSWER?
SORRY.
I THOUGHT WE WERE FRIENDS.

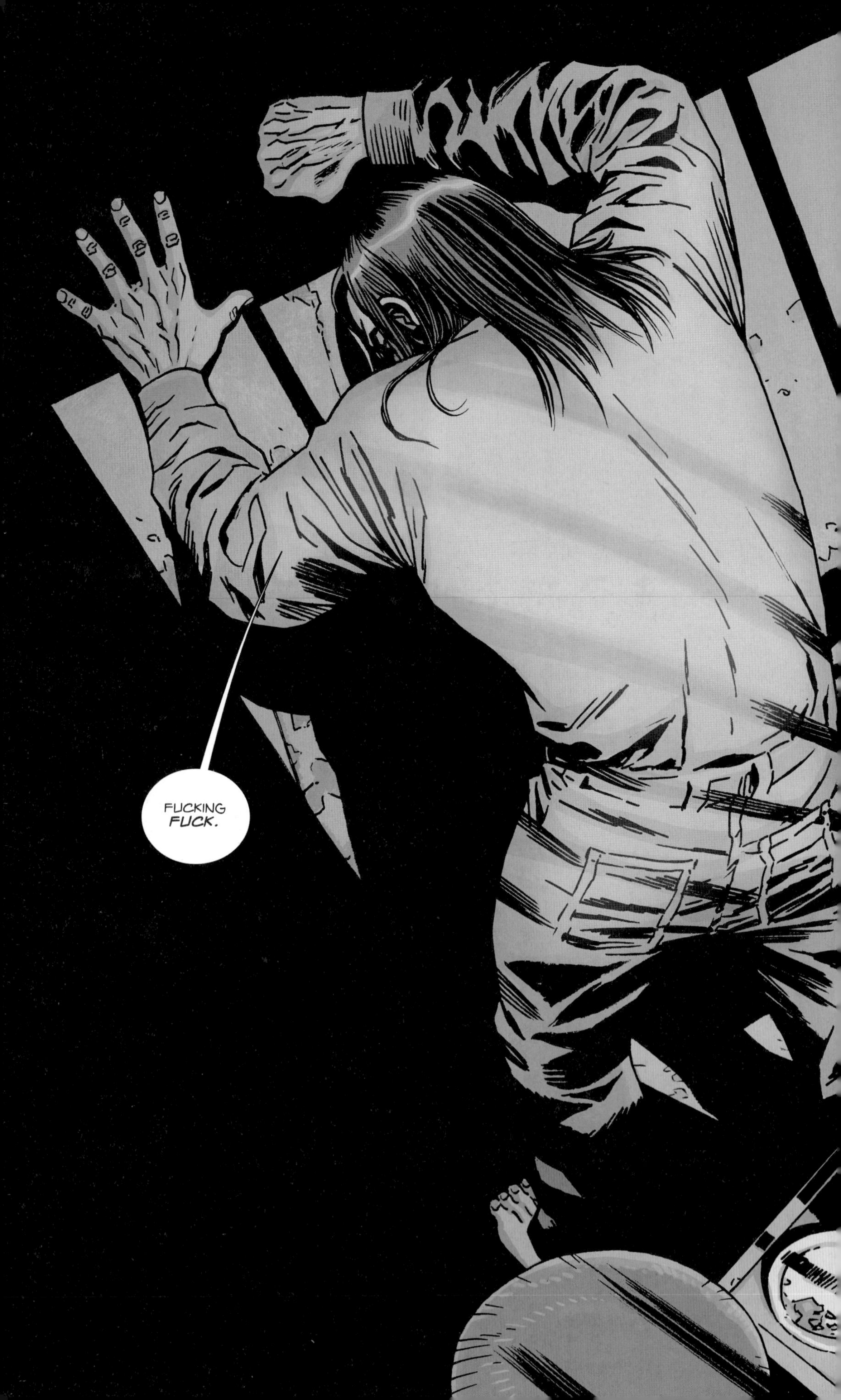
FUCKING FUCK.

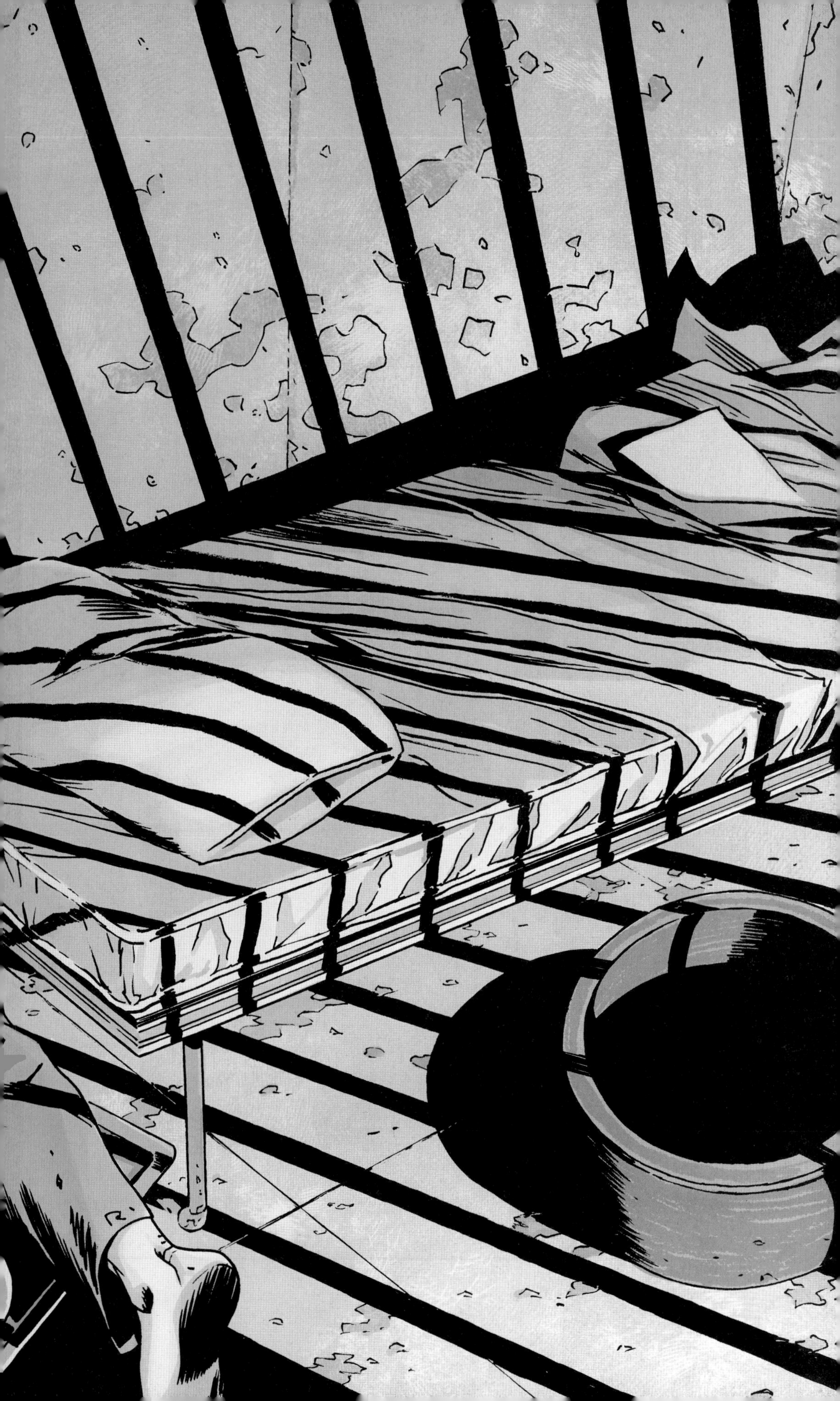

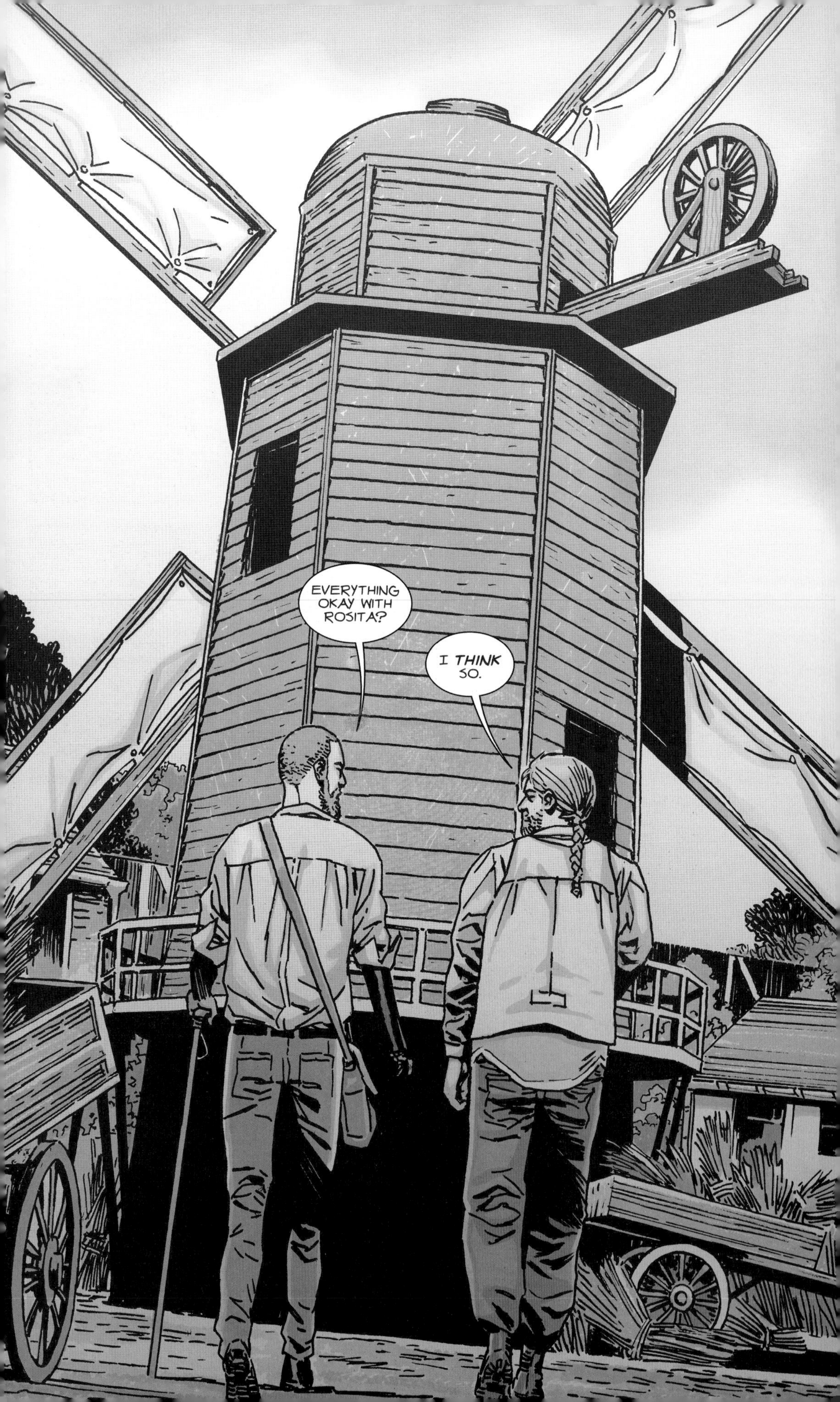
EVERYTHING OKAY WITH ROSITA?
I THINK SO.

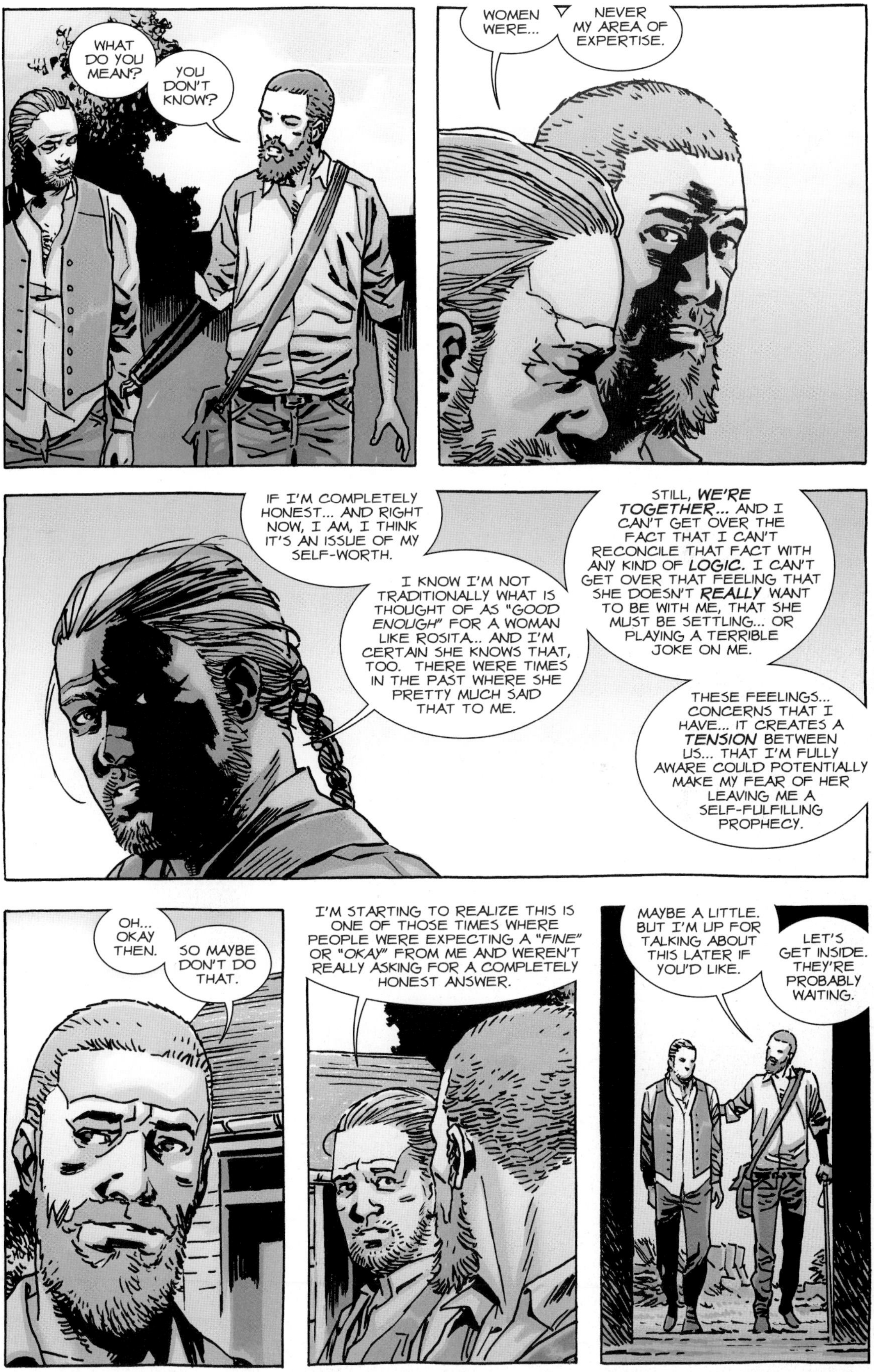
WHAT DO YOU MEAN?
YOU DON'T KNOW?
WOMEN WERE...
NEVER MY AREA OF EXPERTISE.
IF I'M COMPLETELY HONEST... AND RIGHT NOW, I AM, I THINK IT'S AN ISSUE OF MY SELF-WORTH.
I KNOW I'M NOT TRADITIONALLY WHAT IS THOUGHT OF AS "GOOD ENOUGH" FOR A WOMAN LIKE ROSITA.. AND I'M CERTAIN SHE KNOWS THAT, TOO. THERE WERE TIMES IN THE PAST WHERE SHE PRETTY MUCH SAID THAT TO ME.
STILL, WE'RE TOGETHER... AND I CAN'T GET OVER THE FACT THAT I CAN'T RECONCILE THAT FACT WITH ANY KIND OF LOGIC. I CAN'T GET OVER THAT FEELING THAT SHE DOESN'T REALLY WANT TO BE WITH ME, THAT SHE MUST BE SETTLING... OR PLAYING A TERRIBLE JOKE ON ME.
THESE FEELINGS... CONCERNS THAT I HAVE... IT CREATES A TENSION BETWEEN US... THAT I'M FULLY AWARE COULD POTENTIALLY MAKE MY FEAR OF HER LEAVING ME A SELF-FULFILLING PROPHECY.
OH... OKAY THEN.
SO MAYBE DON'T DO THAT.
I'M STARTING TO REALIZE THIS IS ONE OF THOSE TIMES WHERE PEOPLE WERE EXPECTING A "FINE" OR "OKAY" FROM ME AND WEREN'T REALLY ASKING FOR A COMPLETELY HONEST ANSWER.
MAYBE A LITTLE. BUT I'M UP FOR TALKING ABOUT THIS LATER IF YOU'D LIKE.
LET'S GET INSIDE. THEY'RE PROBABLY WAITING.

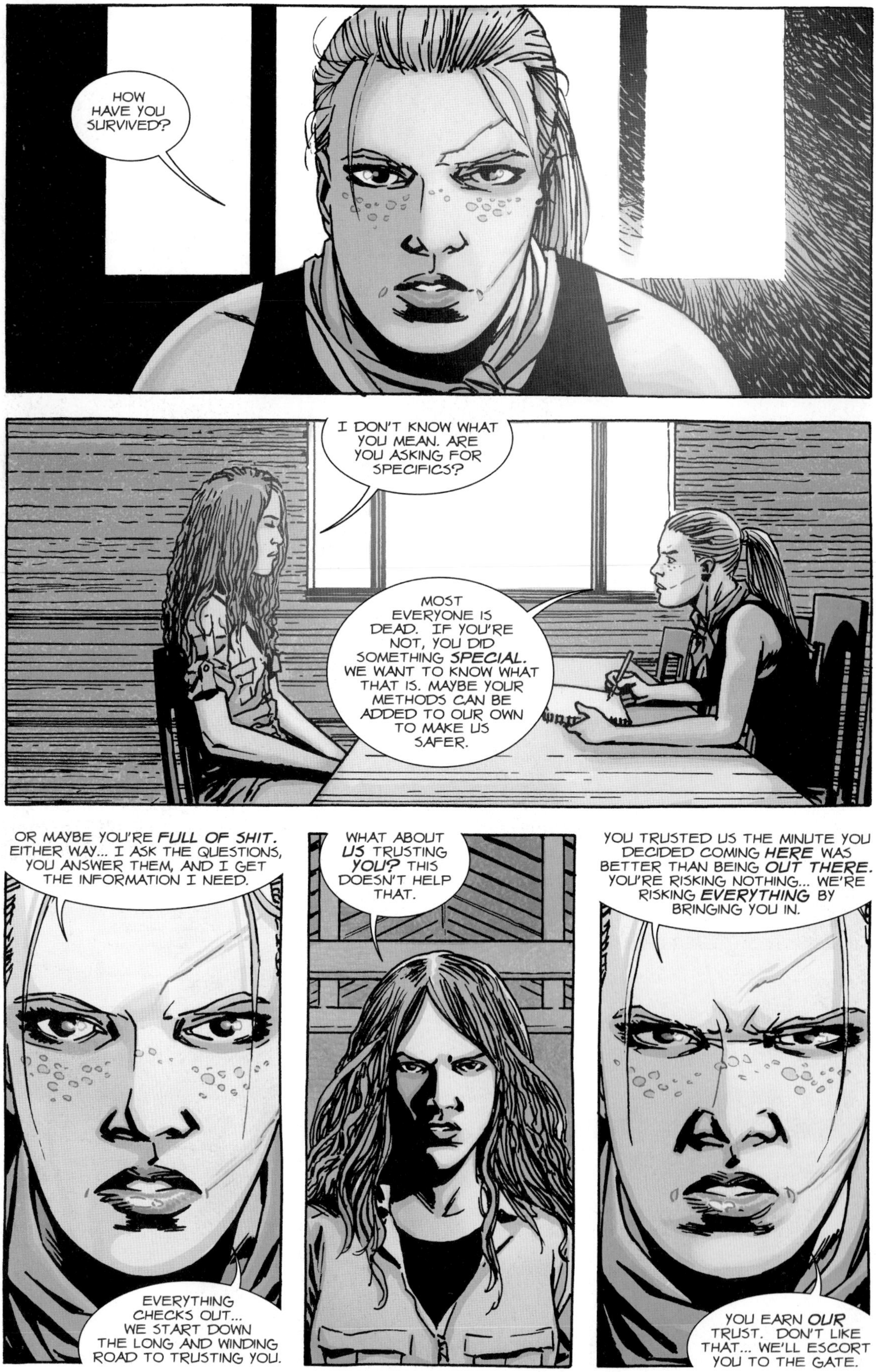
HOW HAVE YOU SURVIVED?
I DON'T KNOW WHAT YOU MEAN. ARE YOU ASKING FOR SPECIFICS?
MOST EVERYONE IS DEAD. IF YOU'RE NOT, YOU DID SOMETHING SPECIAL. WE WANT TO KNOW WHAT THAT IS. MAYBE YOUR METHODS CAN BE ADDED TO OUR OWN TO MAKE US SAFER.
OR MAYBE YOU'RE FULL OF SHIT. EITHER WAY... I ASK THE QUESTIONS, YOU ANSWER THEM, AND I GET THE INFORMATION I NEED.
EVERYTHING CHECKS OUT... WE START DOWN THE LONG AND WINDING ROAD TO TRUSTING YOU.
WHAT ABOUT US TRUSTING YOU? THIS DOESN'T HELP THAT.
YOU TRUSTED US THE MINUTE YOU DECIDED COMING HERE WAS BETTER THAN BEING OUT THERE. YOU'RE RISKING NOTHING... WE'RE RISKING EVERYTHING BY BRINGING YOU IN.
YOU EARN OUR TRUST. DON'T LIKE THAT... WE'LL ESCORT YOU TO THE GATE.

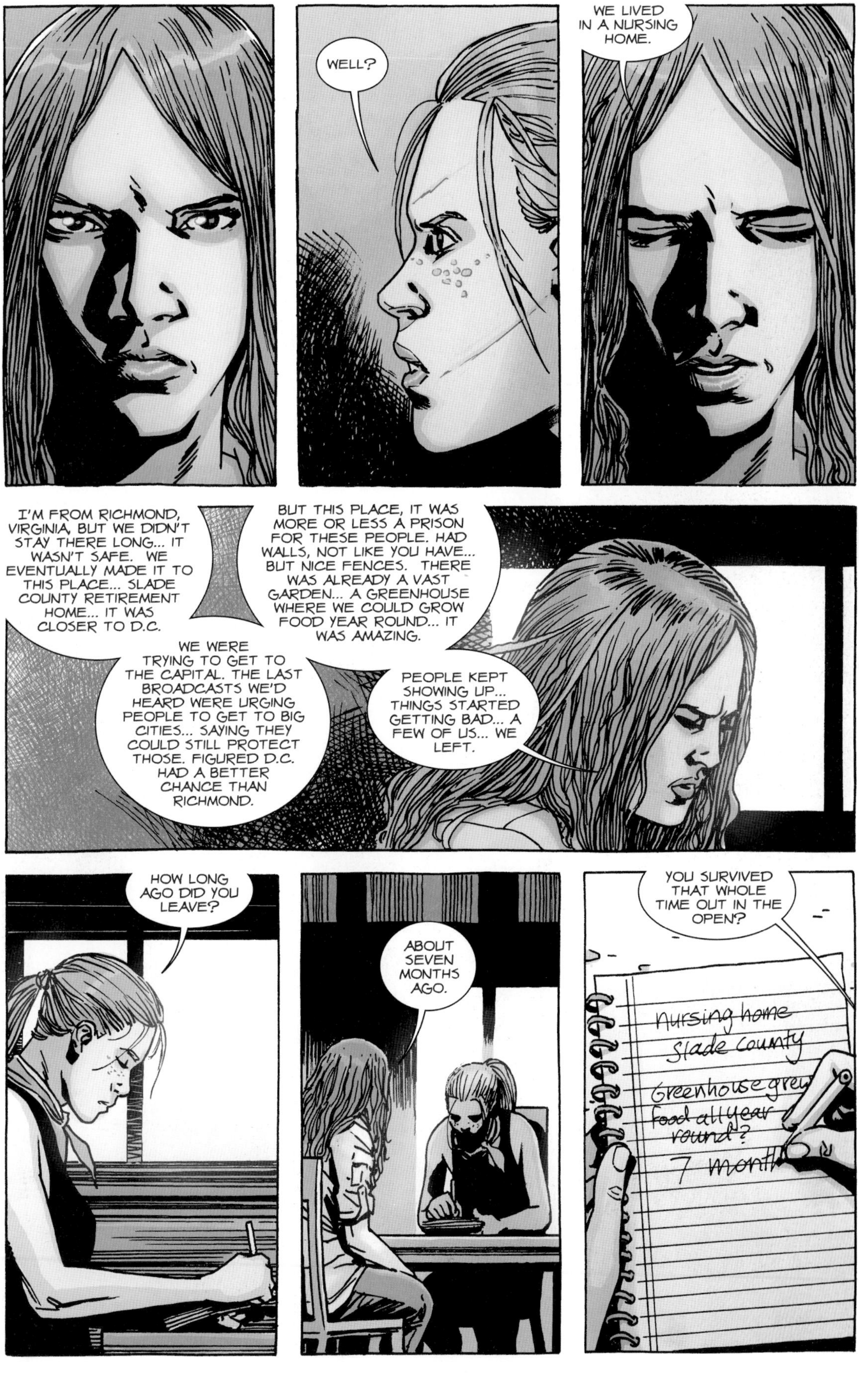

WELL?
WE LIVED IN A NURSING HOME.
I'M FROM RICHMOND, VIRGINIA, BUT WE DIDN'T STAY THERE LONG... IT WASN'T SAFE. WE EVENTUALLY MADE IT TO THIS PLACE... SLADE COUNTY RETIREMENT HOME... IT WAS CLOSER TO D.C.
WE WERE TRYING TO GET TO THE CAPITAL. THE LAST BROADCASTS WE'D HEARD WERE URGING PEOPLE TO GET TO BIG CITIES... SAYING THEY COULD STILL PROTECT THOSE. FIGURED D.C. HAD A BETTER CHANCE THAN RICHMOND.
BUT THIS PLACE, IT WAS MORE OR LESS A PRISON FOR THESE PEOPLE. HAD WALLS, NOT LIKE YOU HAVE... BUT NICE FENCES. THERE WAS ALREADY A VAST GARDEN... A GREENHOUSE WHERE WE COULD GROW FOOD YEAR ROUND... IT WAS AMAZING.
PEOPLE KEPT SHOWING UP... THINGS STARTED GETTING BAD... A FEW OF US... WE LEFT.
HOW LONG AGO DID YOU LEAVE?
ABOUT SEVEN MONTHS AGO.
YOU SURVIVED THAT WHOLE TIME OUT IN THE OPEN?
nursing home
slade county
Greenhouse grew
food all year
round?
7 month

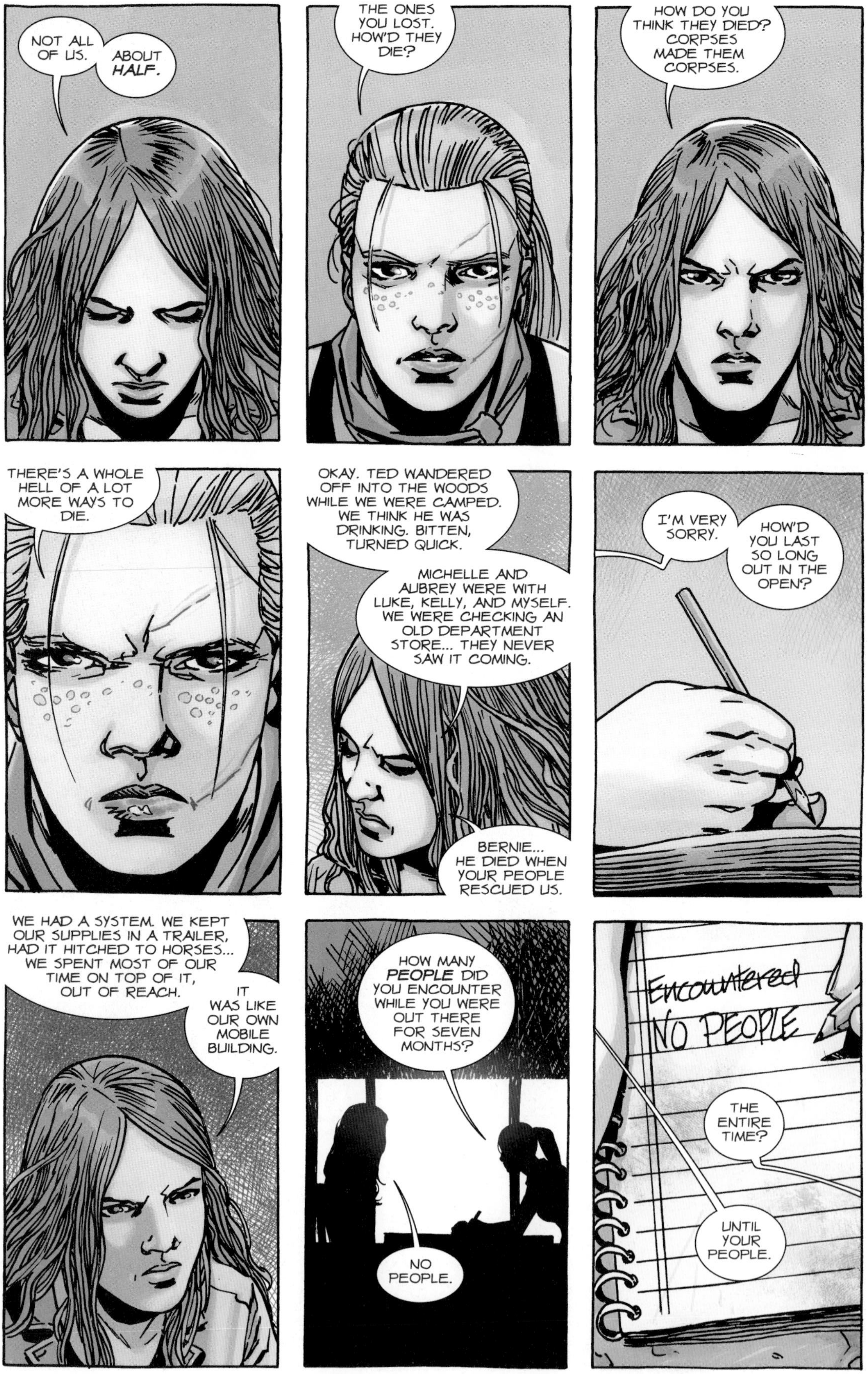
NOT ALL OF US.
ABOUT HALF.
THE ONES YOU LOST. HOW'D THEY DIE?
HOW DO YOU THINK THEY DIED? CORPSES MADE THEM CORPSES.
THERE'S A WHOLE HELL OF A LOT MORE WAYS TO DIE.
OKAY. TED WANDERED OFF INTO THE WOODS WHILE WE WERE CAMPED. WE THINK HE WAS DRINKING. BITTEN, TURNED QUICK.
MICHELLE AND AUBREY WERE WITH LUKE, KELLY, AND MYSELF. WE WERE CHECKING AN OLD DEPARTMENT STORE... THEY NEVER SAW IT COMING.
BERNIE... HE DIED WHEN YOUR PEOPLE RESCUED US.
I'M VERY SORRY.
HOW'D YOU LAST SO LONG OUT IN THE OPEN?
WE HAD A SYSTEM. WE KEPT OUR SUPPLIES IN A TRAILER, HAD IT HITCHED TO HORSES... WE SPENT MOST OF OUR TIME ON TOP OF IT, OUT OF REACH.
IT WAS LIKE OUR OWN MOBILE BUILDING.
HOW MANY PEOPLE DID YOU ENCOUNTER WHILE YOU WERE OUT THERE FOR SEVEN MONTHS?
NO PEOPLE.
Encountered
NO PEOPLE
THE ENTIRE TIME?
UNTIL YOUR PEOPLE.

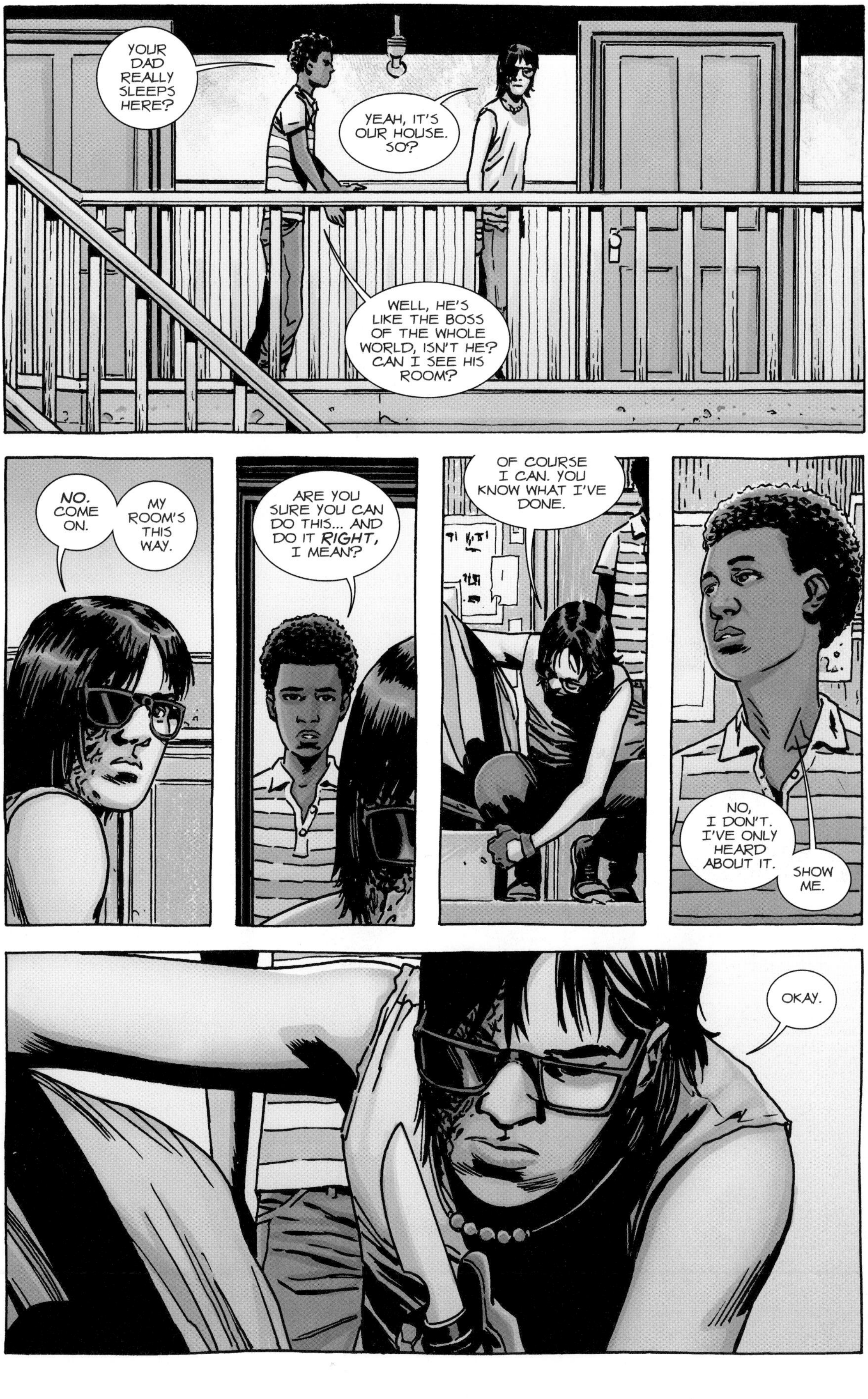
YOUR DAD REALLY SLEEPS HERE?
YEAH, IT'S OUR HOUSE. SO?
WELL, HE'S LIKE THE BOSS OF THE WHOLE WORLD, ISN'T HE? CAN I SEE HIS ROOM?
NO. COME ON.
MY ROOM'S THIS WAY.
ARE YOU SURE YOU CAN DO THIS... AND DO IT *RIGHT*, I MEAN?
OF COURSE I CAN. YOU KNOW WHAT I'VE DONE.
NO, I DON'T. I'VE ONLY HEARD ABOUT IT.
SHOW ME.
OKAY.

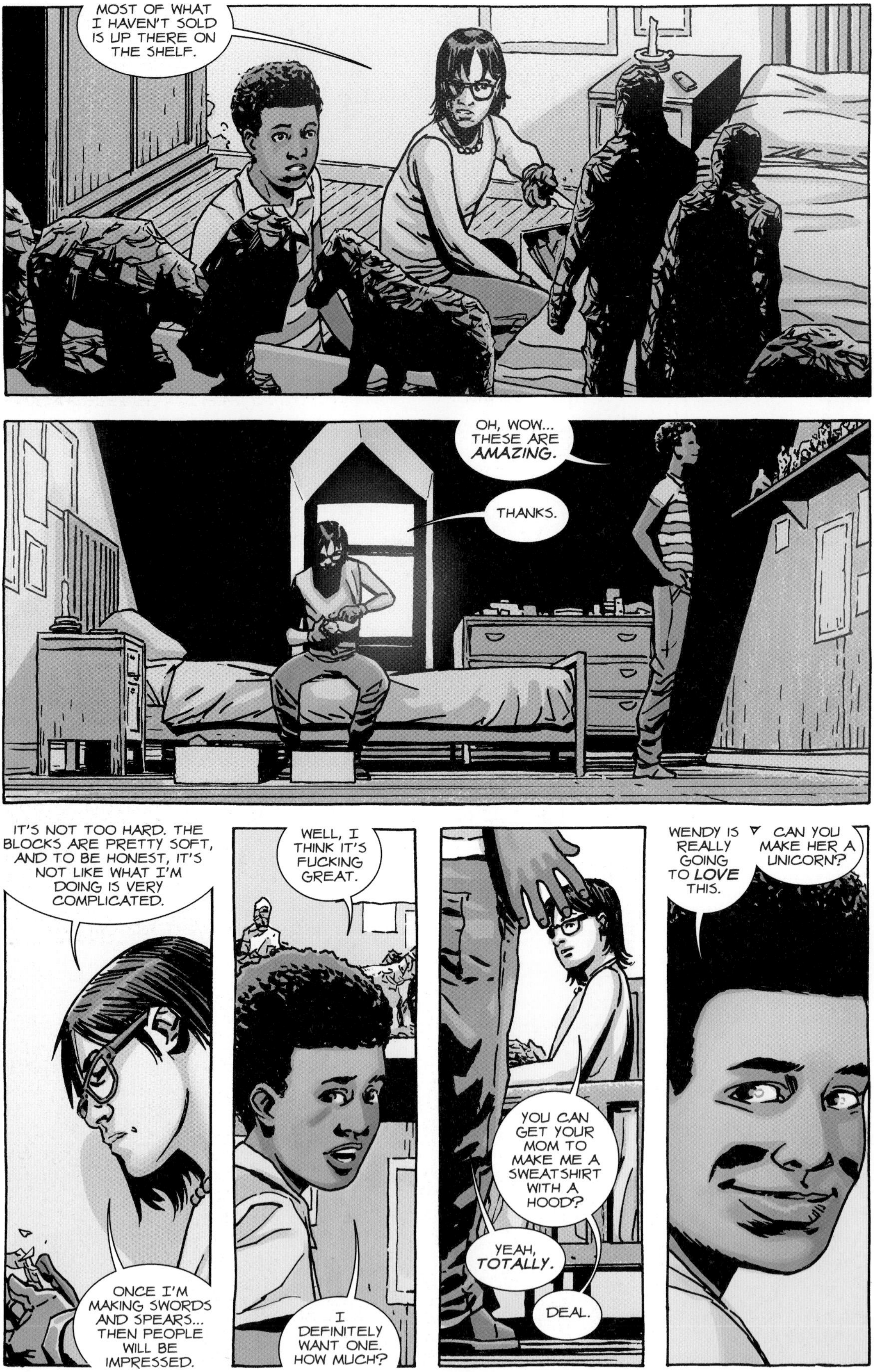

MOST OF WHAT I HAVEN'T SOLD IS UP THERE ON THE SHELF.
OH, WOW... THESE ARE *AMAZING*.
THANKS.
IT'S NOT TOO HARD. THE BLOCKS ARE PRETTY SOFT, AND TO BE HONEST, IT'S NOT LIKE WHAT I'M DOING IS VERY COMPLICATED.
ONCE I'M MAKING SWORDS AND SPEARS... THEN PEOPLE WILL BE IMPRESSED.
WELL, I THINK IT'S FUCKING GREAT.
I DEFINITELY WANT ONE. HOW MUCH?
YOU CAN GET YOUR MOM TO MAKE ME A SWEATSHIRT WITH A HOOD?
YEAH, *TOTALLY*.
DEAL.
WENDY IS REALLY GOING TO *LOVE* THIS.
CAN YOU MAKE HER A UNICORN?

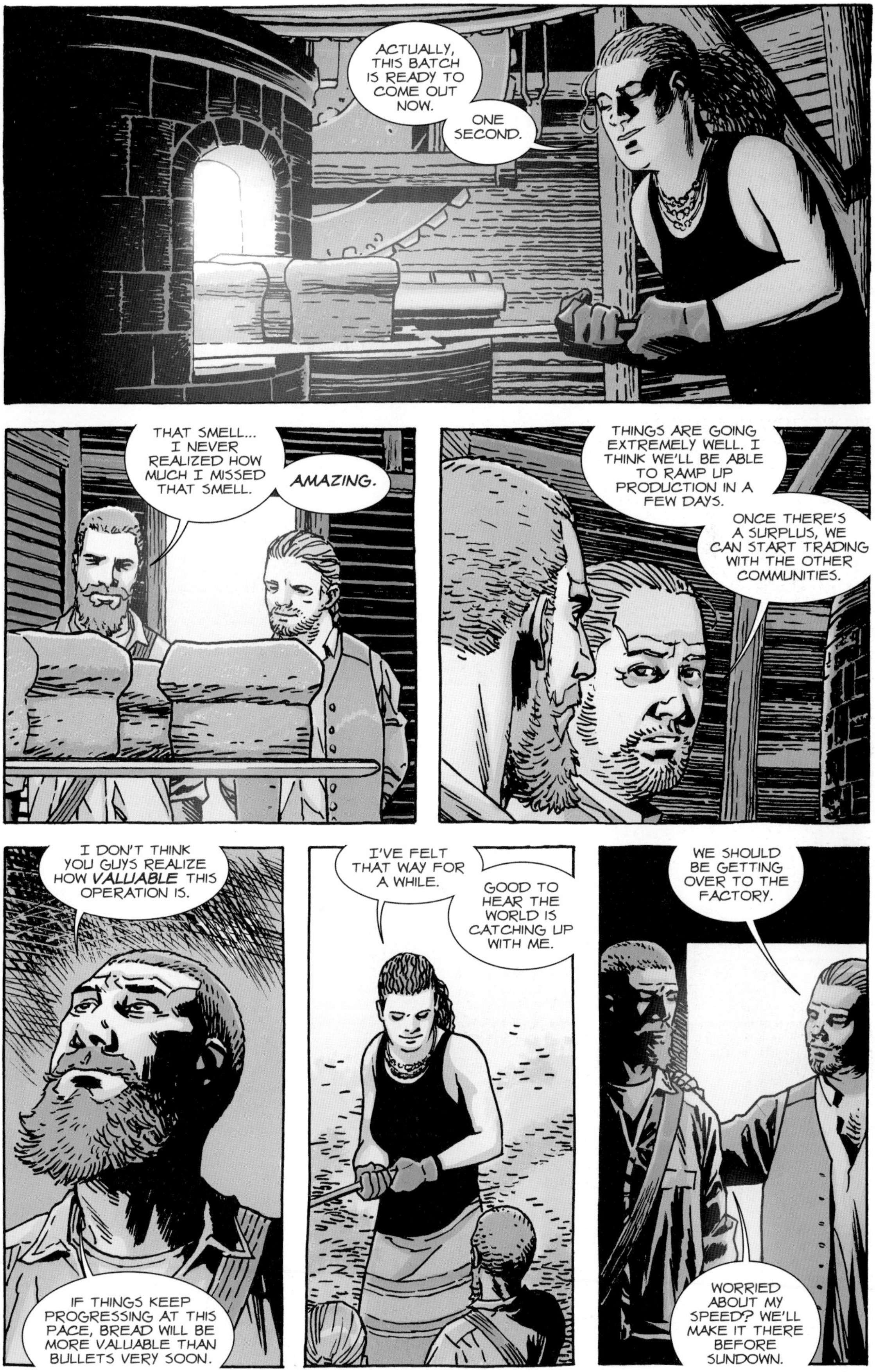
ACTUALLY, THIS BATCH IS READY TO COME OUT NOW.
ONE SECOND.
THAT SMELL... I NEVER REALIZED HOW MUCH I MISSED THAT SMELL.
AMAZING.
THINGS ARE GOING EXTREMELY WELL. I THINK WE'LL BE ABLE TO RAMP UP PRODUCTION IN A FEW DAYS.
ONCE THERE'S A SURPLUS, WE CAN START TRADING WITH THE OTHER COMMUNITIES.
I DON'T THINK YOU GUYS REALIZE HOW VALUABLE THIS OPERATION IS.
IF THINGS KEEP PROGRESSING AT THIS PACE, BREAD WILL BE MORE VALUABLE THAN BULLETS VERY SOON.
I'VE FELT THAT WAY FOR A WHILE.
GOOD TO HEAR THE WORLD IS CATCHING UP WITH ME.
WE SHOULD BE GETTING OVER TO THE FACTORY.
WORRIED ABOUT MY SPEED? WE'LL MAKE IT THERE BEFORE SUNDOWN.

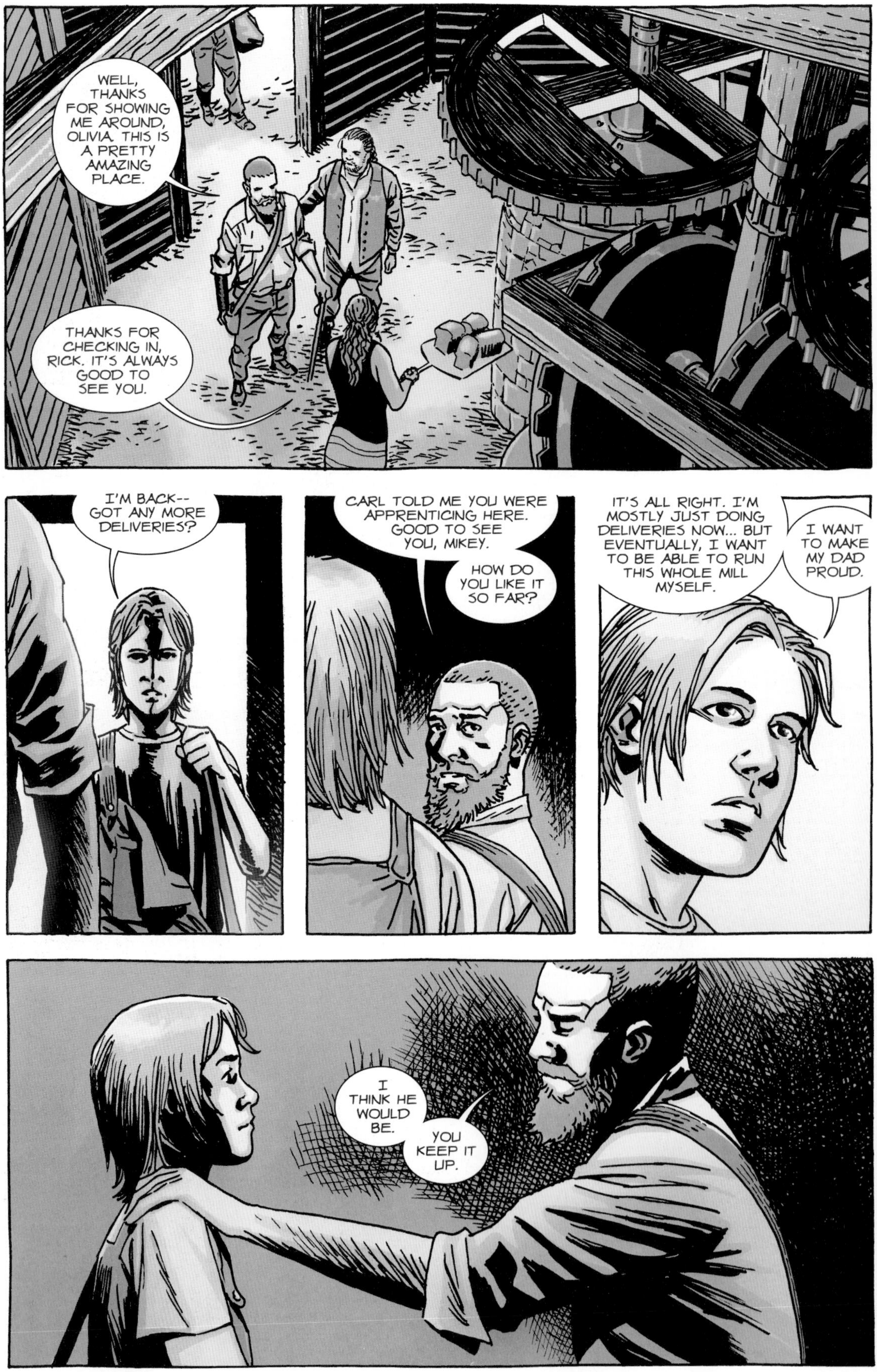

WELL, THANKS FOR SHOWING ME AROUND, OLIVIA. THIS IS A PRETTY AMAZING PLACE.
THANKS FOR CHECKING IN, RICK. IT'S ALWAYS GOOD TO SEE YOU.
I'M BACK-- GOT ANY MORE DELIVERIES?
CARL TOLD ME YOU WERE APPRENTICING HERE. GOOD TO SEE YOU, MIKEY.
HOW DO YOU LIKE IT SO FAR?
IT'S ALL RIGHT. I'M MOSTLY JUST DOING DELIVERIES NOW... BUT EVENTUALLY, I WANT TO BE ABLE TO RUN THIS WHOLE MILL MYSELF.
I WANT TO MAKE MY DAD PROUD.
I THINK HE WOULD BE.
YOU KEEP IT UP.

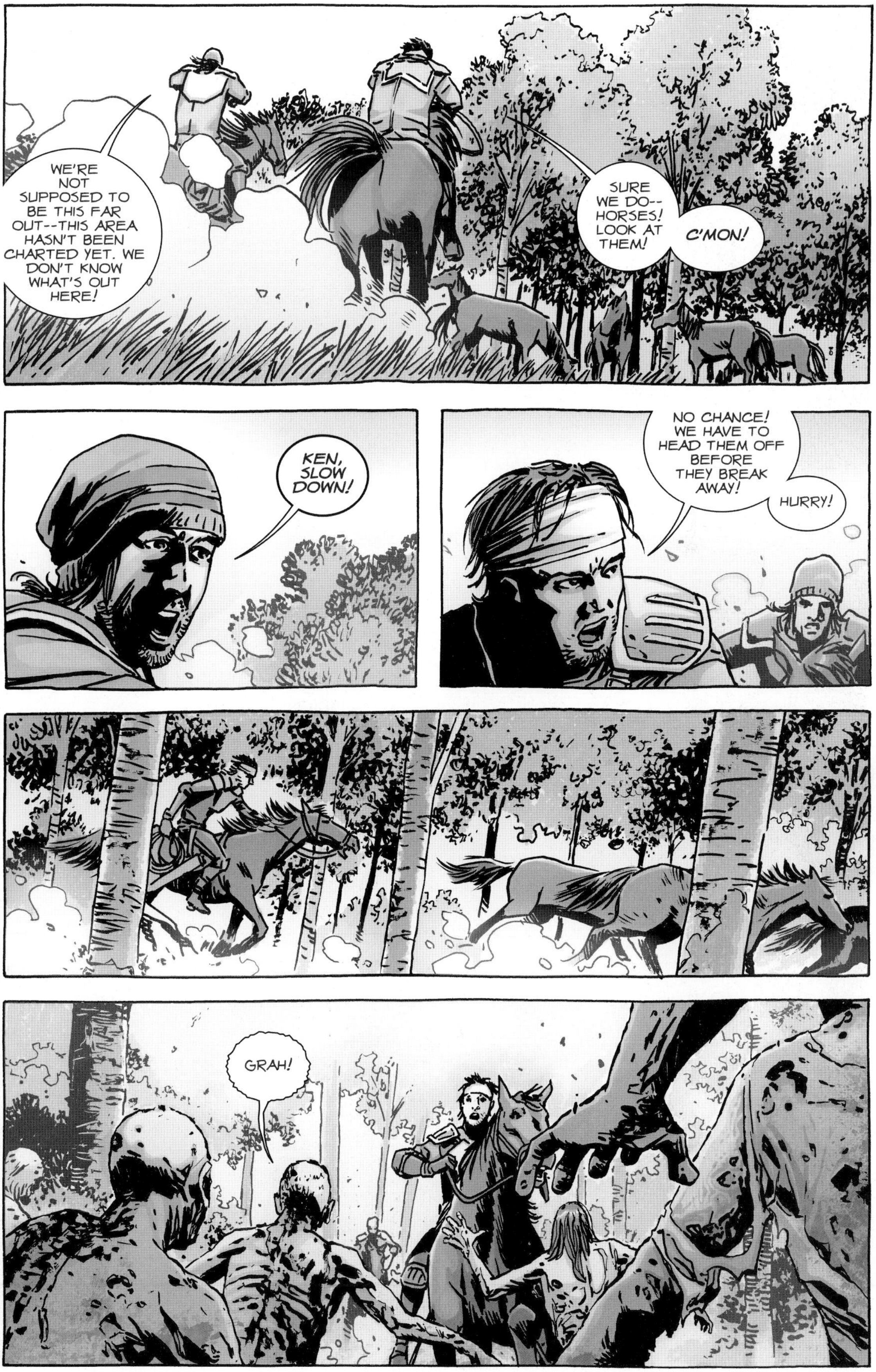
WE'RE NOT SUPPOSED TO BE THIS FAR OUT--THIS AREA HASN'T BEEN CHARTED YET. WE DON'T KNOW WHAT'S OUT HERE!
SURE WE DO--HORSES! LOOK AT THEM!
C'MON!
KEN, SLOW DOWN!
NO CHANCE! WE HAVE TO HEAD THEM OFF BEFORE THEY BREAK AWAY!
HURRY!
GRAH!

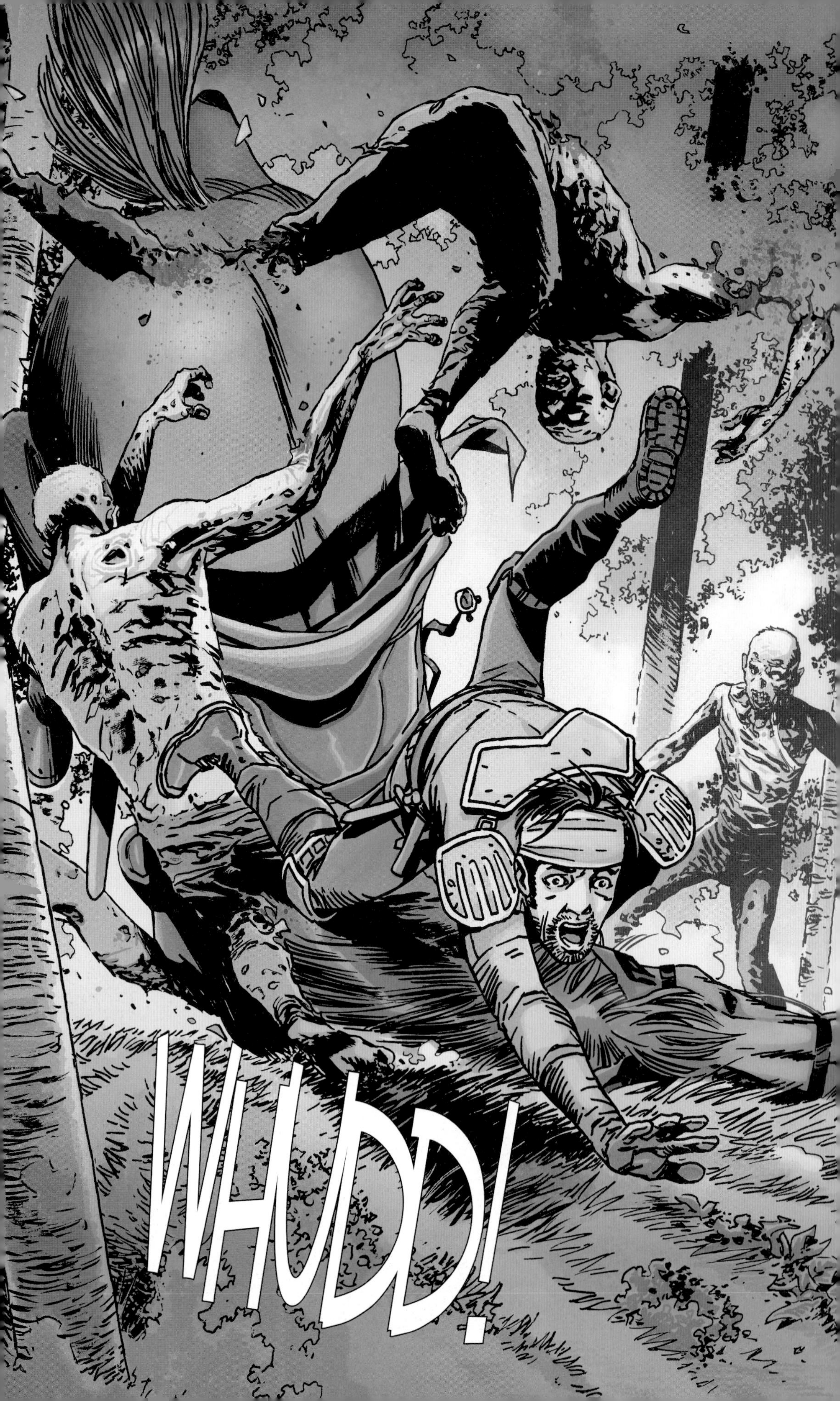
WHUDD!

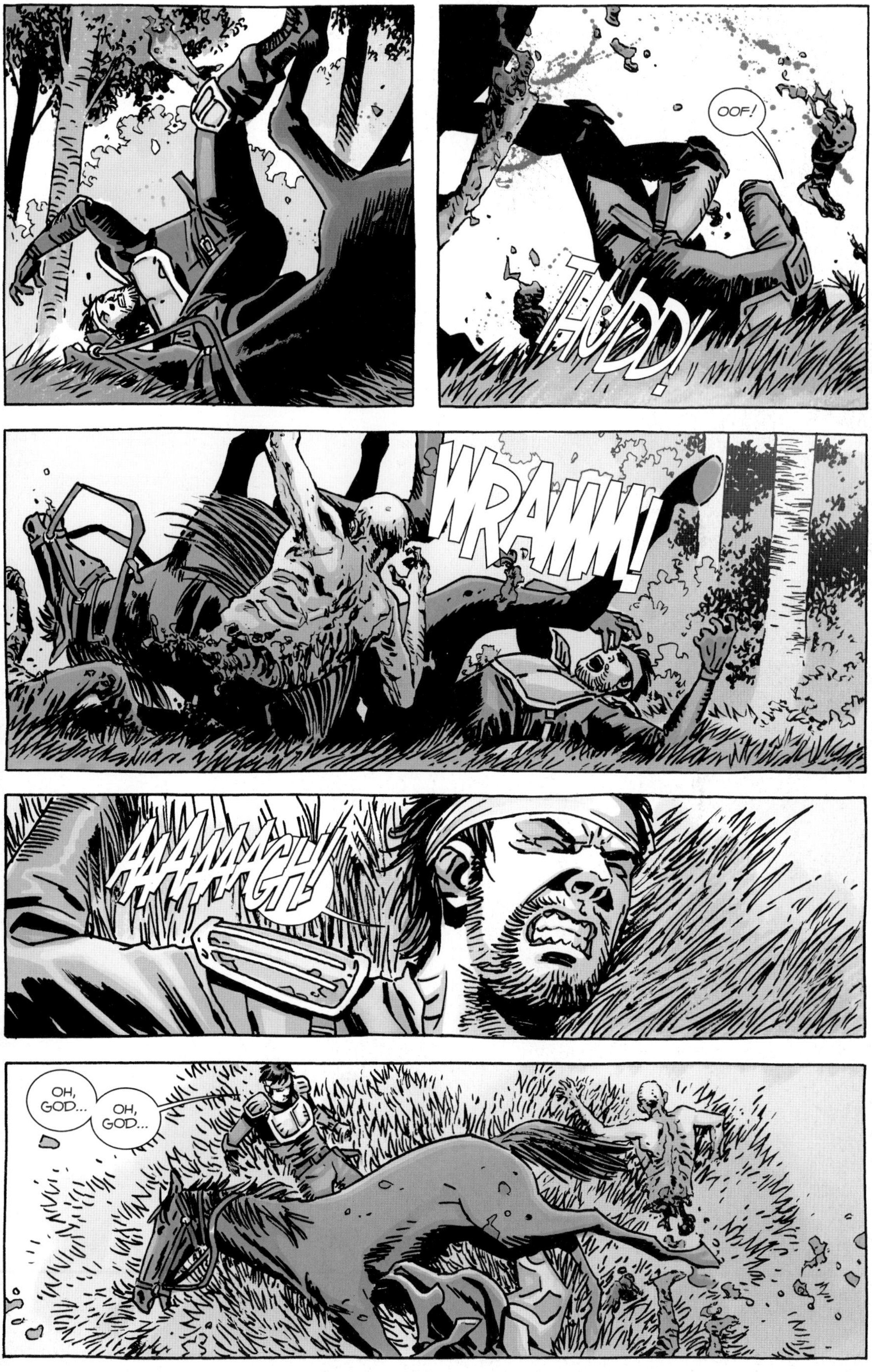
OOF!
THUDD!
WRAMM!
AAAAAAGH!
OH, GOD...
OH, GOD...

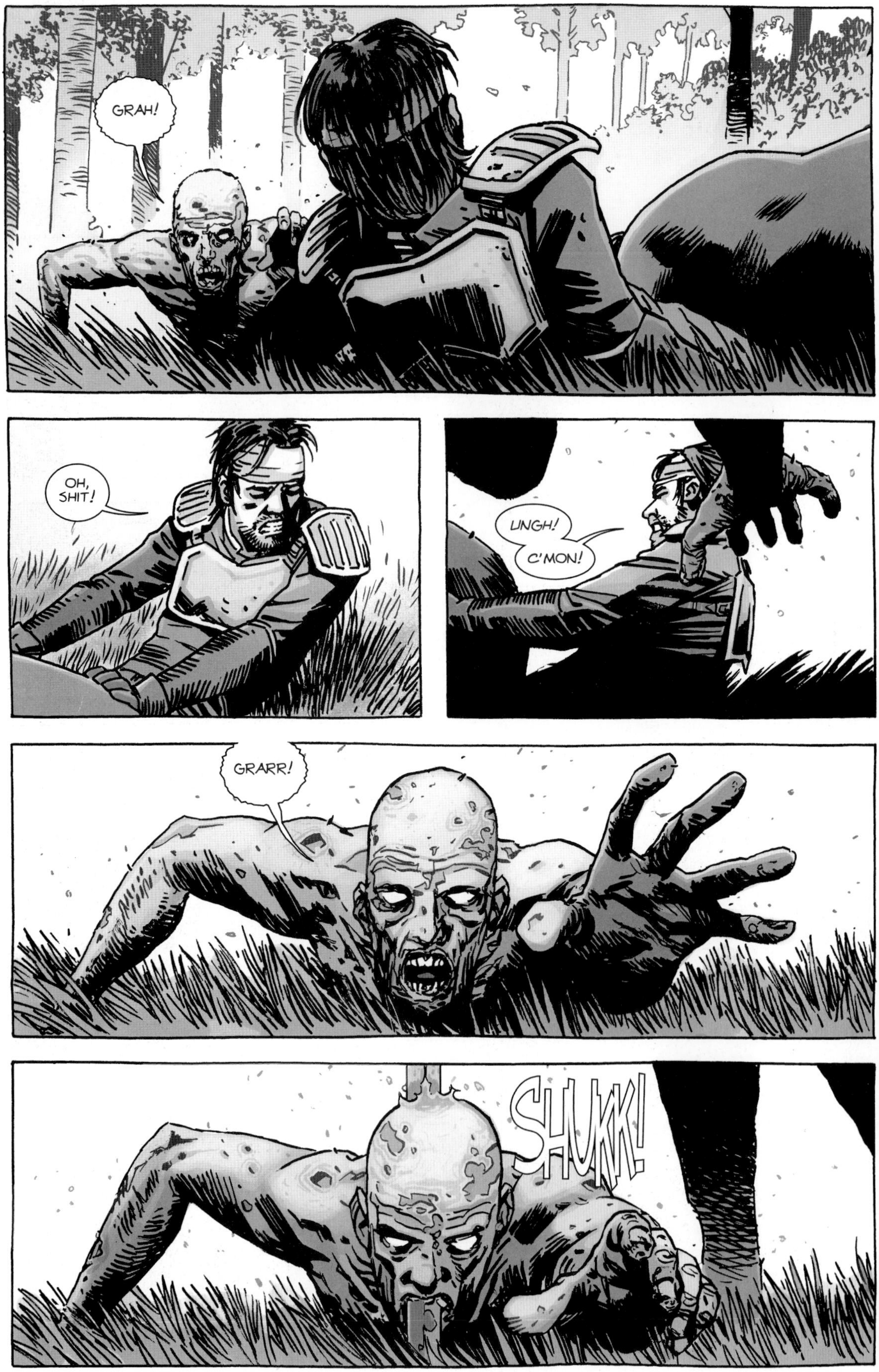
GRAH!
OH, SHIT!
UNGH!
C'MON!
GRARR!
SHUKK!

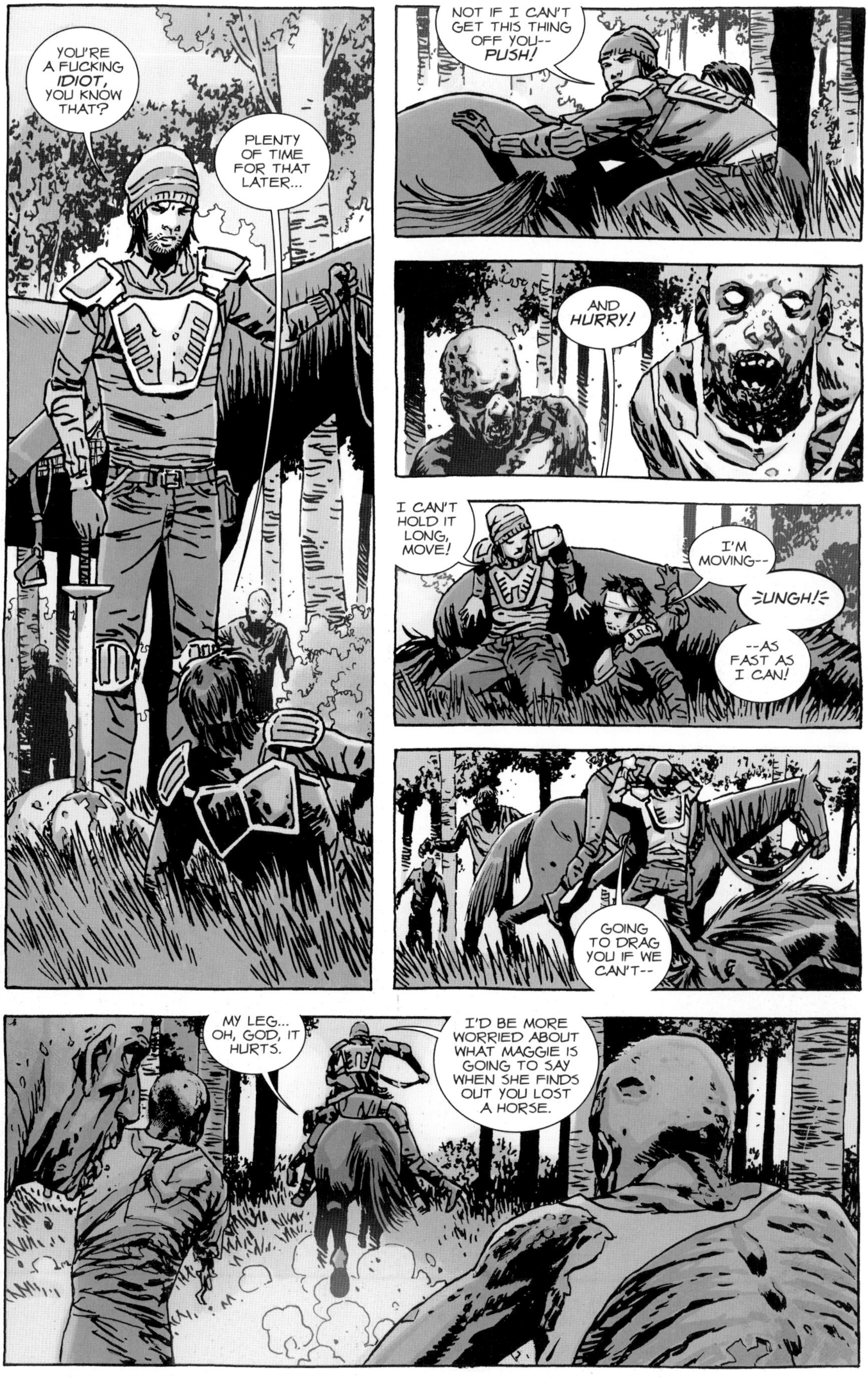
YOU'RE A FUCKING IDIOT, YOU KNOW THAT?
PLENTY OF TIME FOR THAT LATER...
NOT IF I CAN'T GET THIS THING OFF YOU-- PUSH!
AND HURRY!
I CAN'T HOLD IT LONG, MOVE!
I'M MOVING--
UNGH!
--AS FAST AS I CAN!
GOING TO DRAG YOU IF WE CAN'T--
MY LEG... OH, GOD, IT HURTS.
I'D BE MORE WORRIED ABOUT WHAT MAGGIE IS GOING TO SAY WHEN SHE FINDS OUT YOU LOST A HORSE.

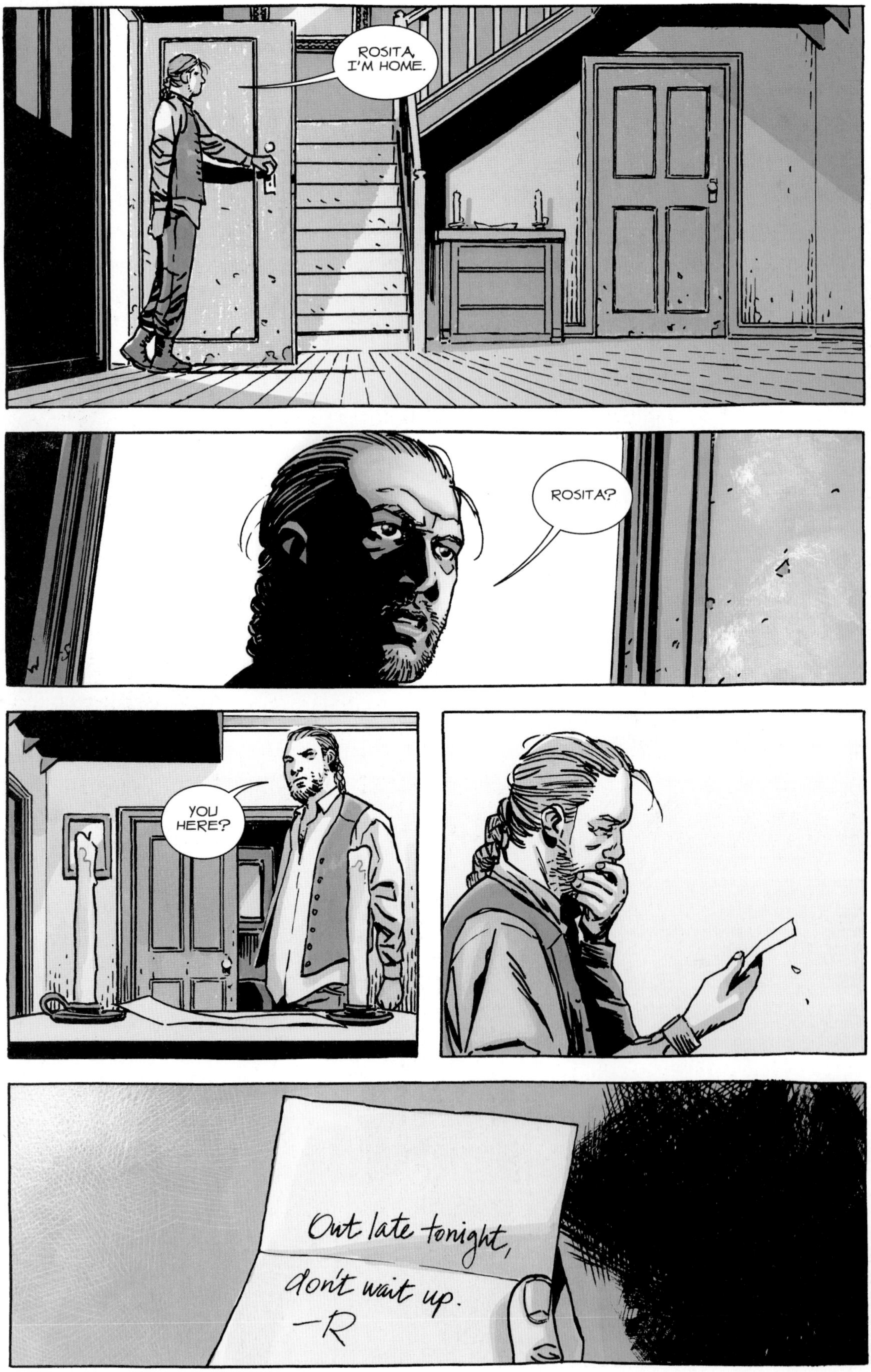
ROSITA, I'M HOME.
ROSITA?
YOU HERE?
Out late tonight, don't wait up. -R

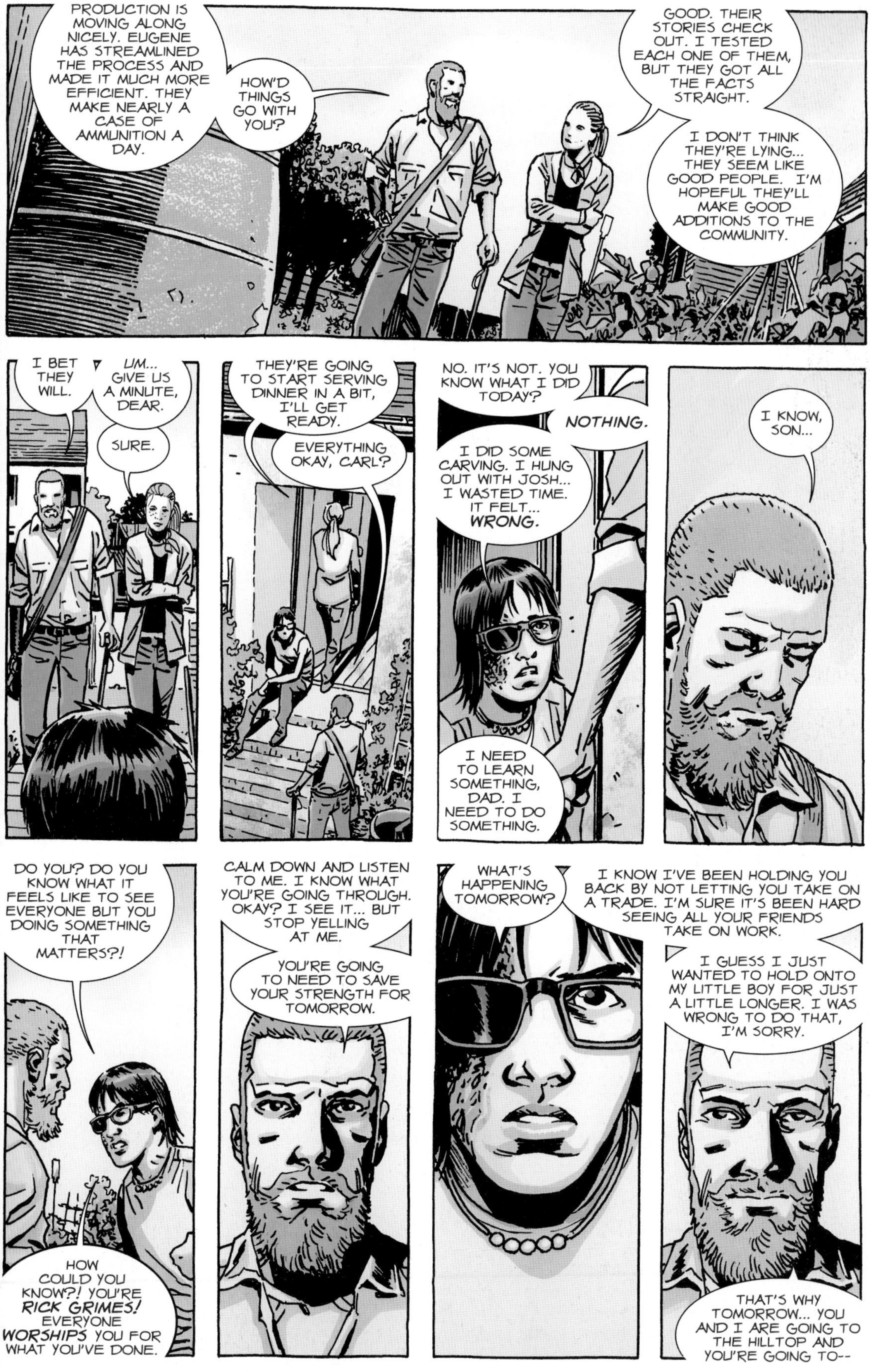

PRODUCTION IS MOVING ALONG NICELY. EUGENE HAS STREAMLINED THE PROCESS AND MADE IT MUCH MORE EFFICIENT. THEY MAKE NEARLY A CASE OF AMMUNITION A DAY.
HOW'D THINGS GO WITH YOU?
GOOD. THEIR STORIES CHECK OUT. I TESTED EACH ONE OF THEM, BUT THEY GOT ALL THE FACTS STRAIGHT.
I DON'T THINK THEY'RE LYING... THEY SEEM LIKE GOOD PEOPLE. I'M HOPEFUL THEY'LL MAKE GOOD ADDITIONS TO THE COMMUNITY.
I BET THEY WILL.
UM... GIVE US A MINUTE, DEAR.
SURE.
THEY'RE GOING TO START SERVING DINNER IN A BIT, I'LL GET READY.
EVERYTHING OKAY, CARL?
NO. IT'S NOT. YOU KNOW WHAT I DID TODAY?
NOTHING.
I DID SOME CARVING. I HUNG OUT WITH JOSH... I WASTED TIME. IT FELT... WRONG.
I NEED TO LEARN SOMETHING, DAD. I NEED TO DO SOMETHING.
I KNOW, SON...
DO YOU? DO YOU KNOW WHAT IT FEELS LIKE TO SEE EVERYONE BUT YOU DOING SOMETHING THAT MATTERS?!
HOW COULD YOU KNOW?! YOU'RE RICK GRIMES! EVERYONE WORSHIPS YOU FOR WHAT YOU'VE DONE.
CALM DOWN AND LISTEN TO ME. I KNOW WHAT YOU'RE GOING THROUGH. OKAY? I SEE IT... BUT STOP YELLING AT ME.
YOU'RE GOING TO NEED TO SAVE YOUR STRENGTH FOR TOMORROW.
WHAT'S HAPPENING TOMORROW?
I KNOW I'VE BEEN HOLDING YOU BACK BY NOT LETTING YOU TAKE ON A TRADE. I'M SURE IT'S BEEN HARD SEEING ALL YOUR FRIENDS TAKE ON WORK.
I GUESS I JUST WANTED TO HOLD ONTO MY LITTLE BOY FOR JUST A LITTLE LONGER. I WAS WRONG TO DO THAT, I'M SORRY.
THAT'S WHY TOMORROW... YOU AND I ARE GOING TO THE HILLTOP AND YOU'RE GOING TO--

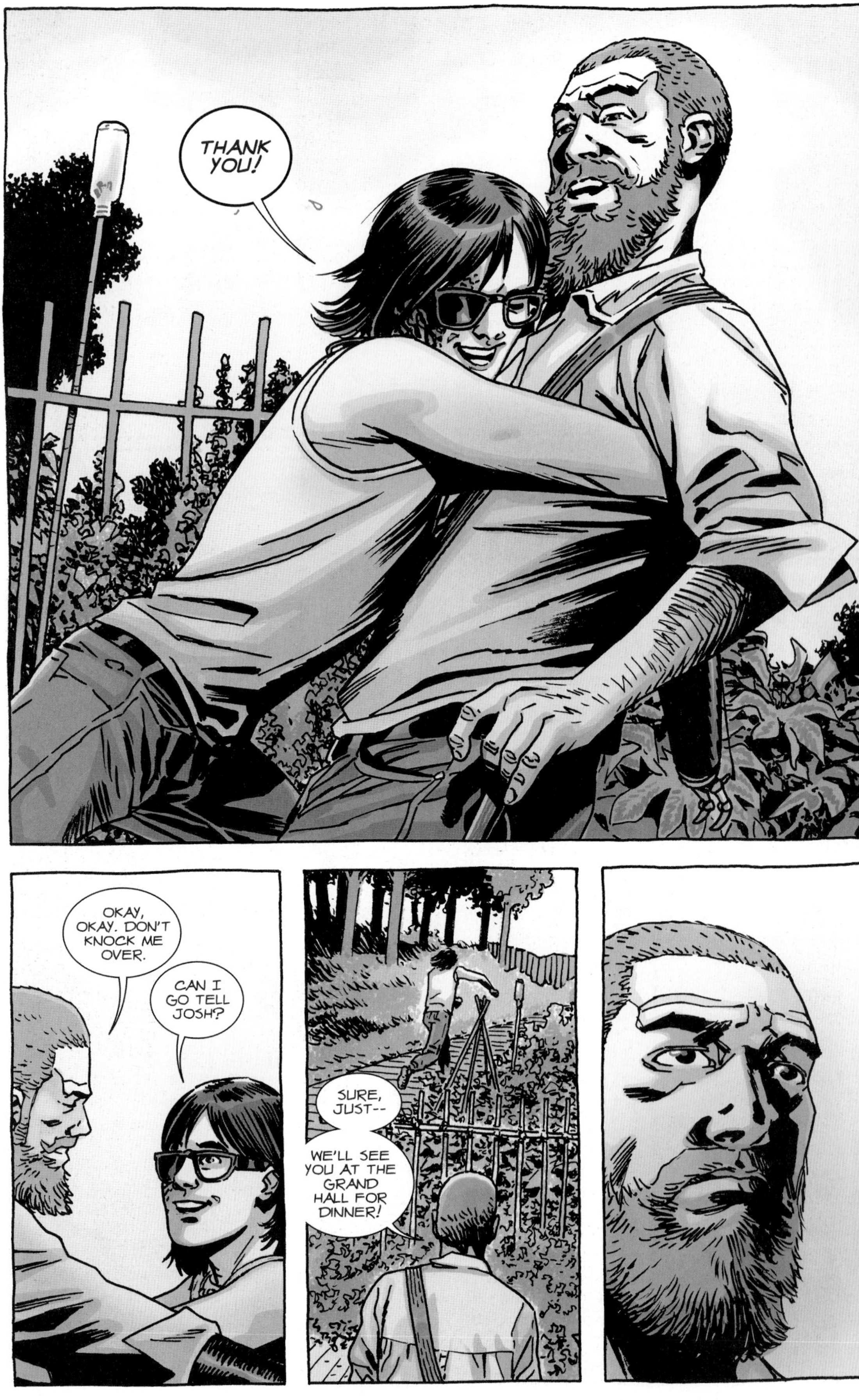
THANK YOU!
OKAY, OKAY. DON'T KNOCK ME OVER.
CAN I GO TELL JOSH?
SURE, JUST--
WE'LL SEE YOU AT THE GRAND HALL FOR DINNER!

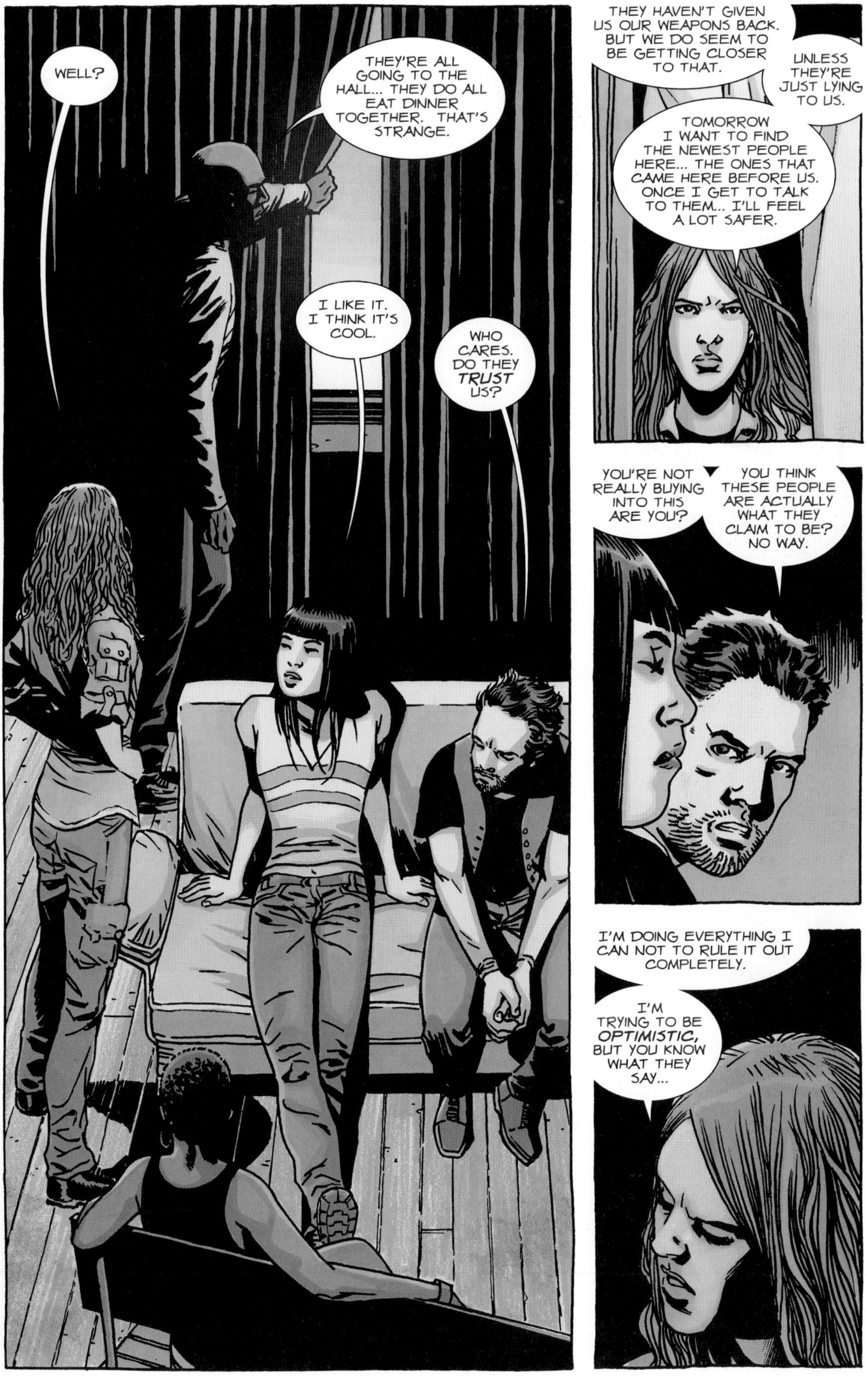
WELL?
THEY'RE ALL GOING TO THE HALL... THEY DO ALL EAT DINNER TOGETHER. THAT'S STRANGE.
I LIKE IT. I THINK IT'S COOL.
WHO CARES. DO THEY *TRUST* US?
THEY HAVEN'T GIVEN US OUR WEAPONS BACK. BUT WE DO SEEM TO BE GETTING CLOSER TO THAT.
UNLESS THEY'RE JUST LYING TO US.
TOMORROW I WANT TO FIND THE NEWEST PEOPLE HERE... THE ONES THAT CAME HERE BEFORE US. ONCE I GET TO TALK TO THEM... I'LL FEEL A LOT SAFER.
YOU'RE NOT REALLY BUYING INTO THIS ARE YOU?
YOU THINK THESE PEOPLE ARE ACTUALLY WHAT THEY CLAIM TO BE? NO WAY.
I'M DOING EVERYTHING I CAN NOT TO RULE IT OUT COMPLETELY.
I'M TRYING TO BE *OPTIMISTIC*, BUT YOU KNOW WHAT THEY SAY...

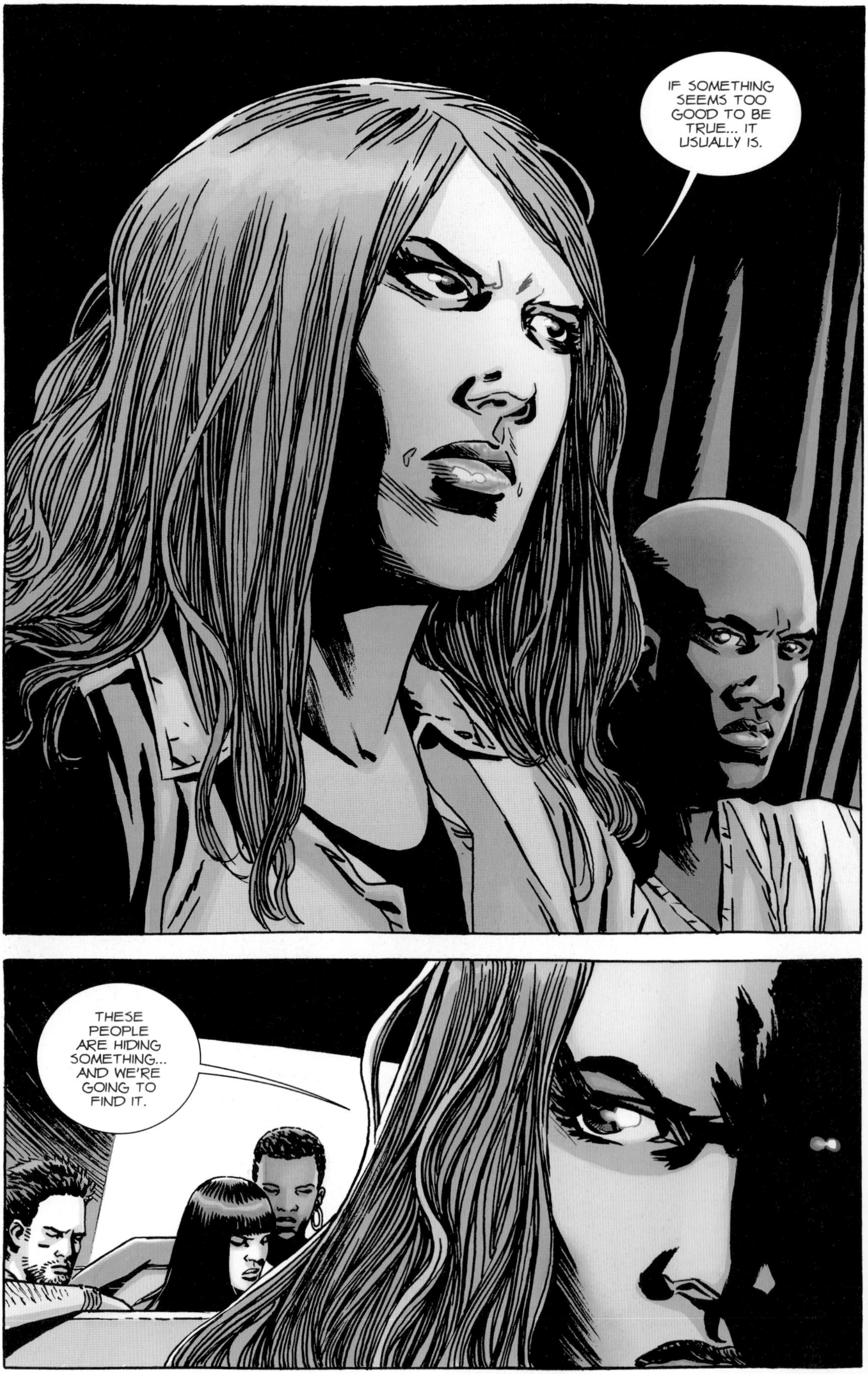
IF SOMETHING SEEMS TOO GOOD TO BE TRUE... IT USUALLY IS.
THESE PEOPLE ARE HIDING SOMETHING... AND WE'RE GOING TO FIND IT.

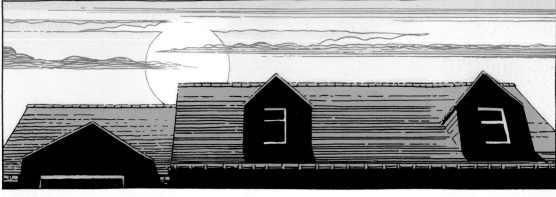

EVERYTHING OKAY?

NERVOUS?

NOT AT ALL.

I JUST... IT'S *WEIRD.* I NEVER THOUGHT I'D HAVE ENOUGH STUFF TO FILL *TWO* DUFFLE BAGS.

DON'T FEEL LIKE YOU HAVE TO TAKE *EVERYTHING.* IT'S NOT LIKE WE NEED THE ROOM.

AND IT MIGHT BE A WHILE, AND IT MIGHT WELL BE YOU VISITING WITH YOUR WIFE AND KIDS... BUT YOU'LL BE BACK.

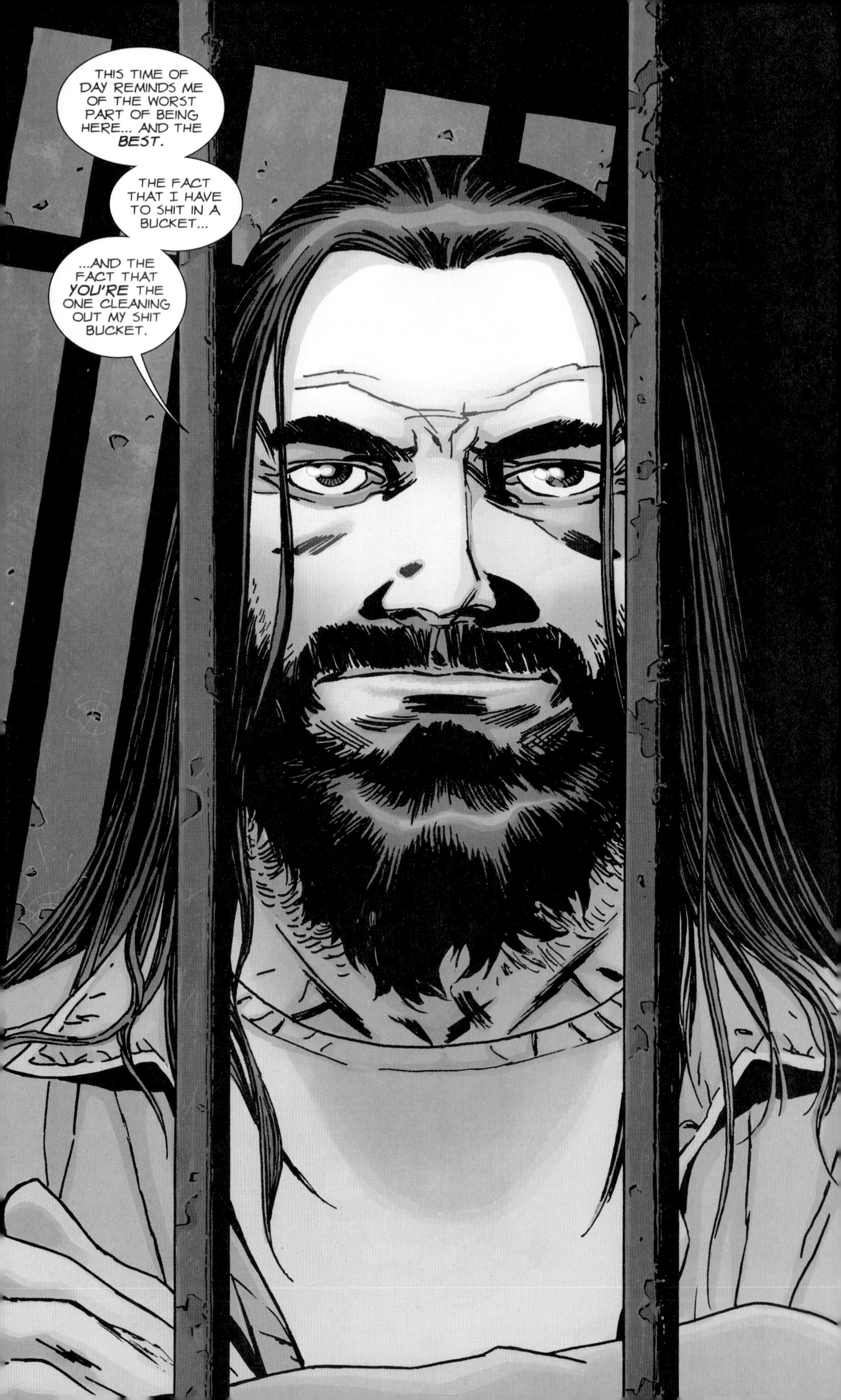
THIS TIME OF DAY REMINDS ME OF THE WORST PART OF BEING HERE... AND THE *BEST.*
THE FACT THAT I HAVE TO SHIT IN A BUCKET...
...AND THE FACT THAT *YOU'RE* THE ONE CLEANING OUT MY SHIT BUCKET.

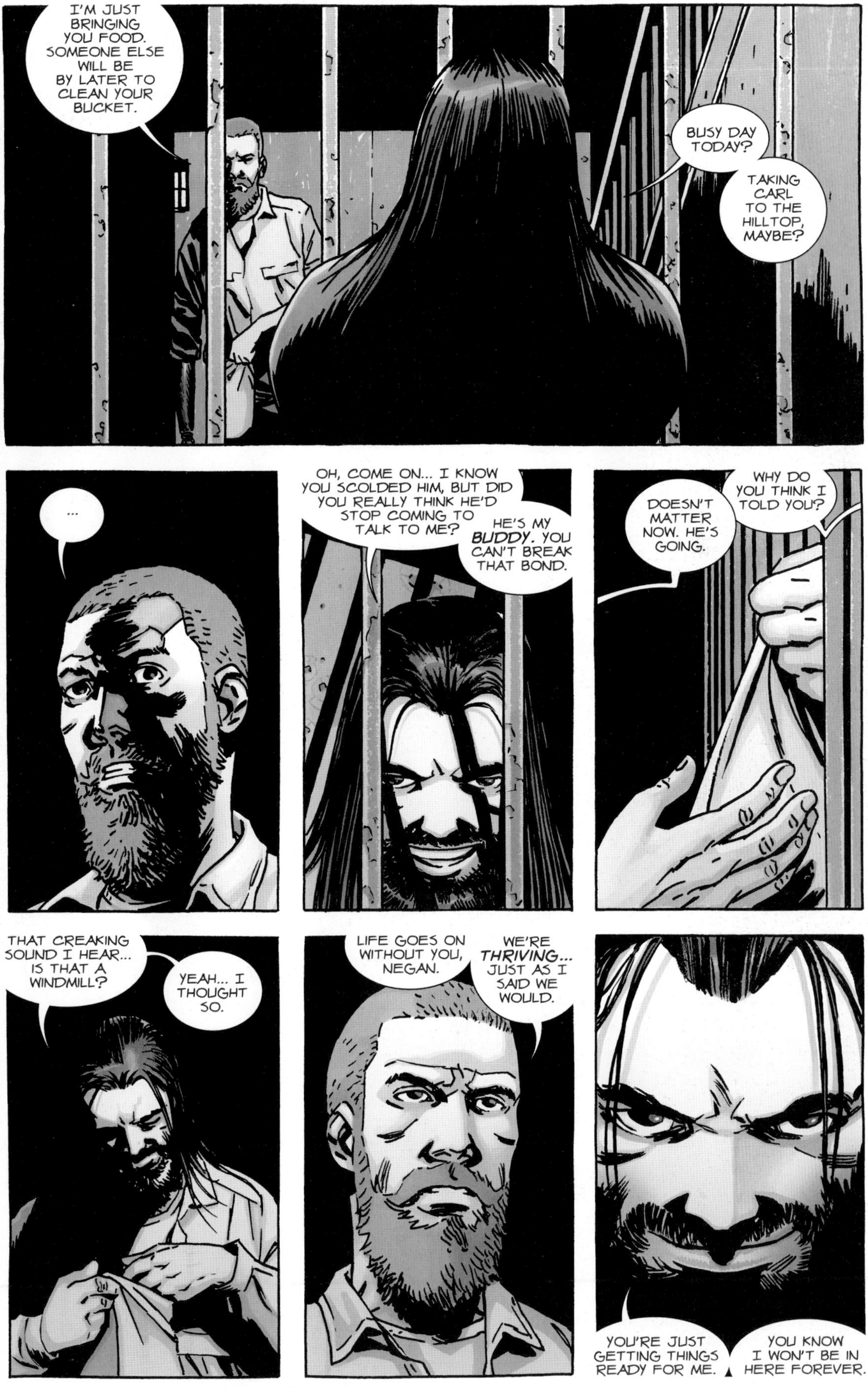
I'M JUST BRINGING YOU FOOD. SOMEONE ELSE WILL BE BY LATER TO CLEAN YOUR BUCKET.
BUSY DAY TODAY?
TAKING CARL TO THE HILLTOP, MAYBE?
...
OH, COME ON... I KNOW YOU SCOLDED HIM, BUT DID YOU REALLY THINK HE'D STOP COMING TO TALK TO ME?
HE'S MY BUDDY. YOU CAN'T BREAK THAT BOND.
DOESN'T MATTER NOW. HE'S GOING.
WHY DO YOU THINK I TOLD YOU?
THAT CREAKING SOUND I HEAR... IS THAT A WINDMILL?
YEAH... I THOUGHT SO.
LIFE GOES ON WITHOUT YOU, NEGAN.
WE'RE THRIVING... JUST AS I SAID WE WOULD.
YOU'RE JUST GETTING THINGS READY FOR ME.
YOU KNOW I WON'T BE IN HERE FOREVER.

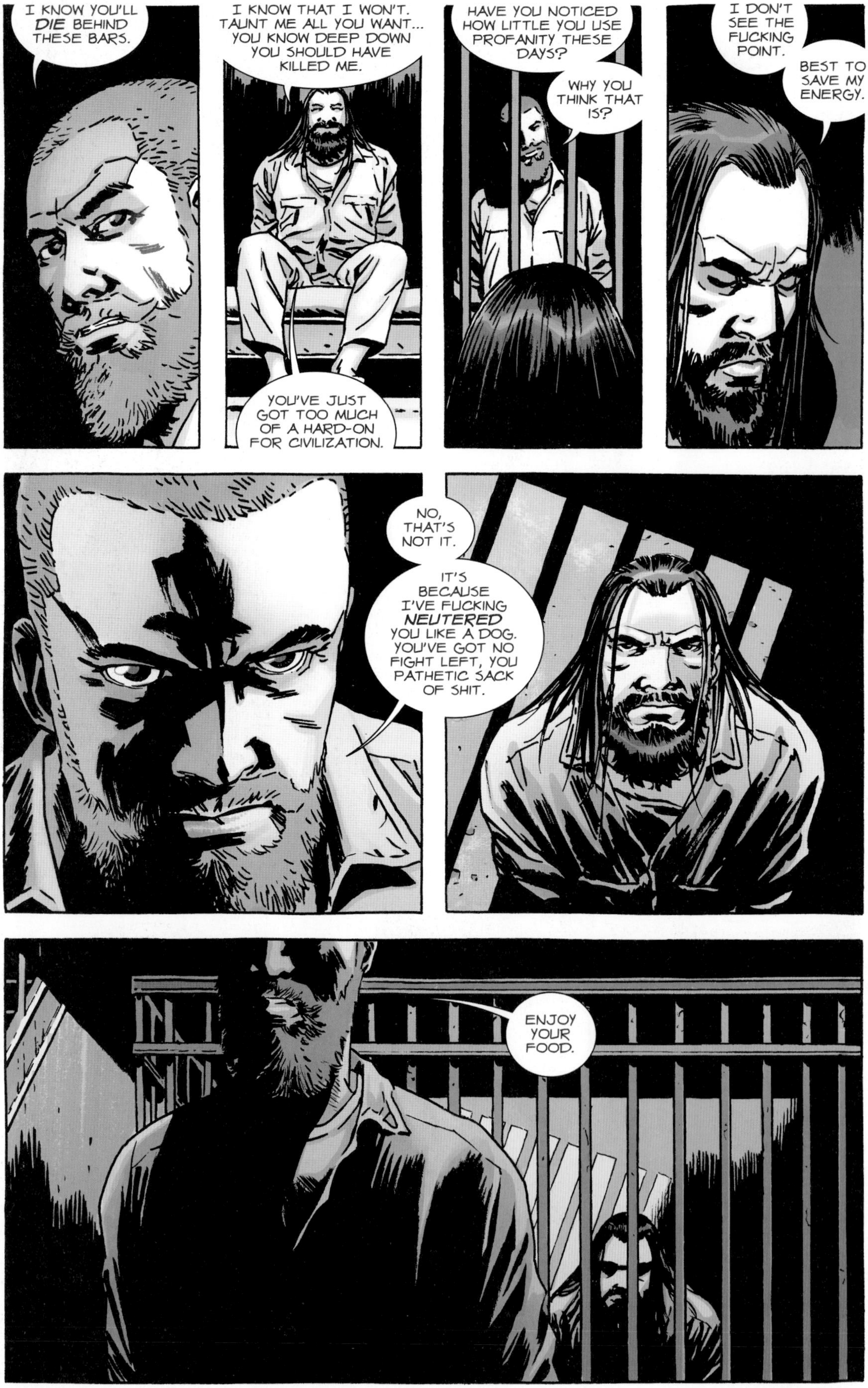
I KNOW YOU'LL DIE BEHIND THESE BARS.
I KNOW THAT I WON'T. TAUNT ME ALL YOU WANT... YOU KNOW DEEP DOWN YOU SHOULD HAVE KILLED ME.
YOU'VE JUST GOT TOO MUCH OF A HARD-ON FOR CIVILIZATION.
HAVE YOU NOTICED HOW LITTLE YOU USE PROFANITY THESE DAYS?
WHY YOU THINK THAT IS?
I DON'T SEE THE FUCKING POINT.
BEST TO SAVE MY ENERGY.
NO, THAT'S NOT IT.
IT'S BECAUSE I'VE FUCKING NEUTERED YOU LIKE A DOG. YOU'VE GOT NO FIGHT LEFT, YOU PATHETIC SACK OF SHIT.
ENJOY YOUR FOOD.

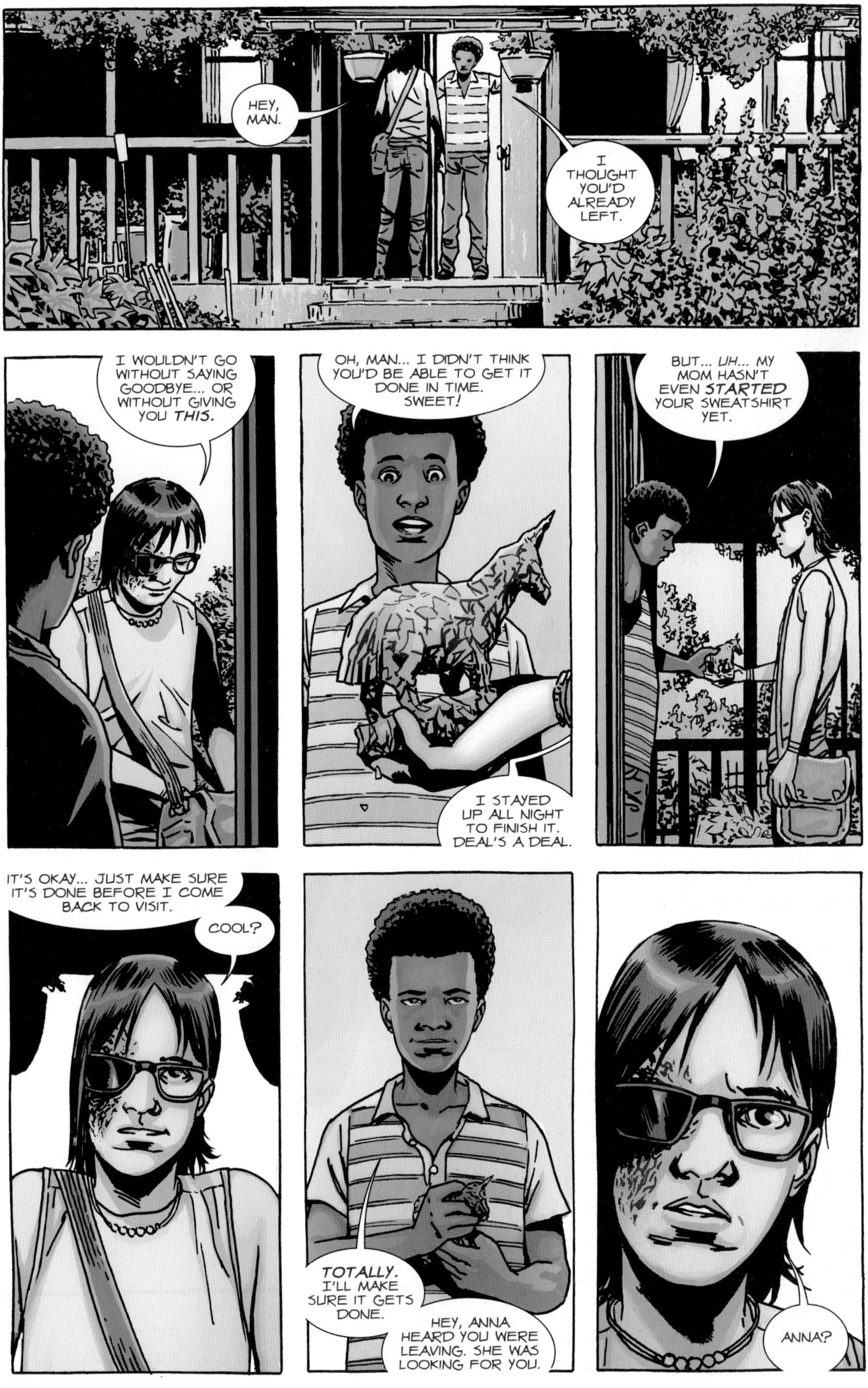
HEY, MAN.
I THOUGHT YOU'D ALREADY LEFT.
I WOULDN'T GO WITHOUT SAYING GOODBYE... OR WITHOUT GIVING YOU THIS.
OH, MAN... I DIDN'T THINK YOU'D BE ABLE TO GET IT DONE IN TIME. SWEET!
I STAYED UP ALL NIGHT TO FINISH IT. DEAL'S A DEAL.
BUT... UH... MY MOM HASN'T EVEN STARTED YOUR SWEATSHIRT YET.
IT'S OKAY... JUST MAKE SURE IT'S DONE BEFORE I COME BACK TO VISIT.
COOL?
TOTALLY. I'LL MAKE SURE IT GETS DONE.
HEY, ANNA HEARD YOU WERE LEAVING. SHE WAS LOOKING FOR YOU.
ANNA?

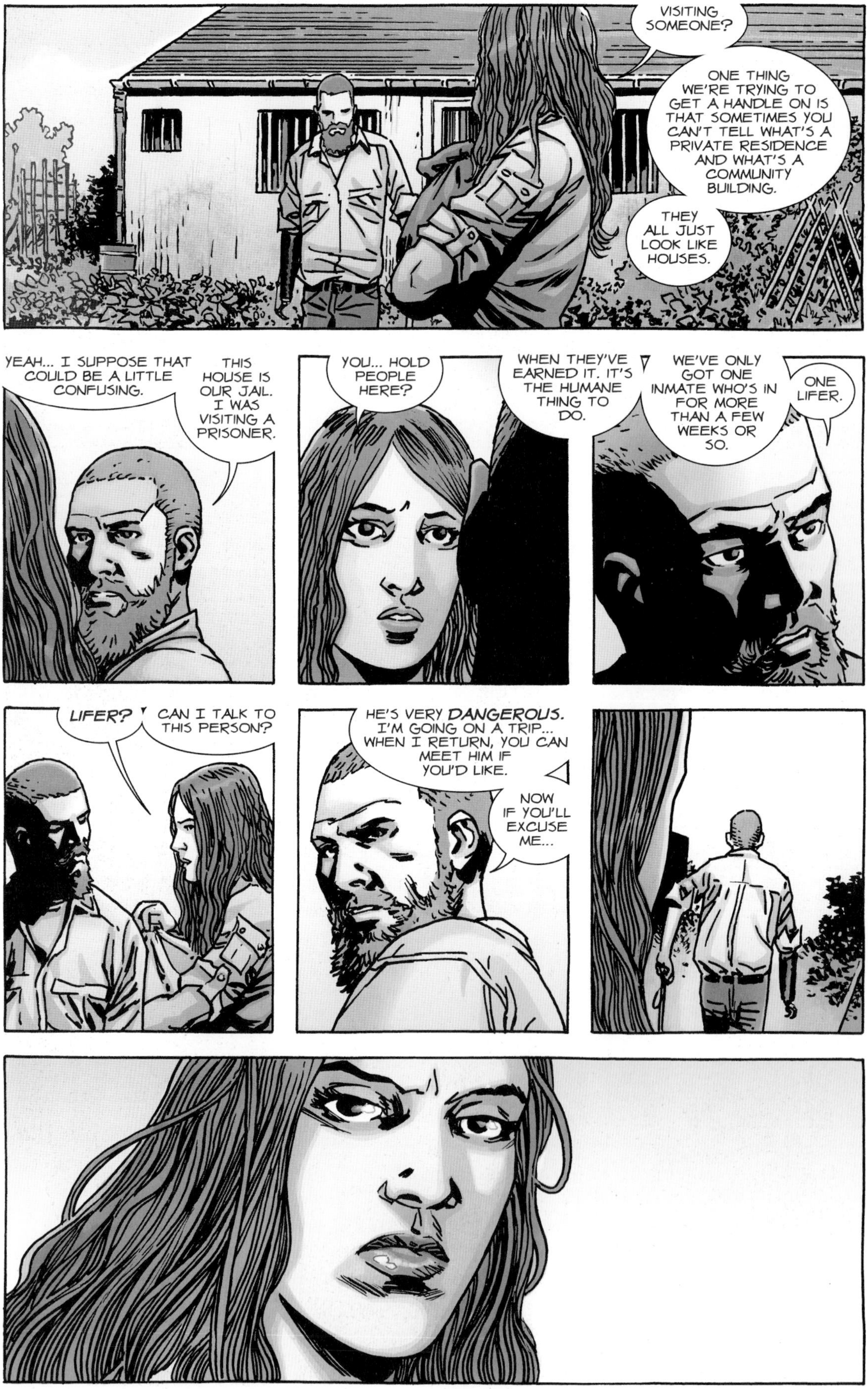

VISITING SOMEONE?
ONE THING WE'RE TRYING TO GET A HANDLE ON IS THAT SOMETIMES YOU CAN'T TELL WHAT'S A PRIVATE RESIDENCE AND WHAT'S A COMMUNITY BUILDING.
THEY ALL JUST LOOK LIKE HOUSES.
YEAH... I SUPPOSE THAT COULD BE A LITTLE CONFUSING.
THIS HOUSE IS OUR JAIL. I WAS VISITING A PRISONER.
YOU... HOLD PEOPLE HERE?
WHEN THEY'VE EARNED IT. IT'S THE HUMANE THING TO DO.
WE'VE ONLY GOT ONE INMATE WHO'S IN FOR MORE THAN A FEW WEEKS OR SO.
ONE LIFER.
LIFER?
CAN I TALK TO THIS PERSON?
HE'S VERY DANGEROUS. I'M GOING ON A TRIP... WHEN I RETURN, YOU CAN MEET HIM IF YOU'D LIKE.
NOW IF YOU'LL EXCUSE ME...

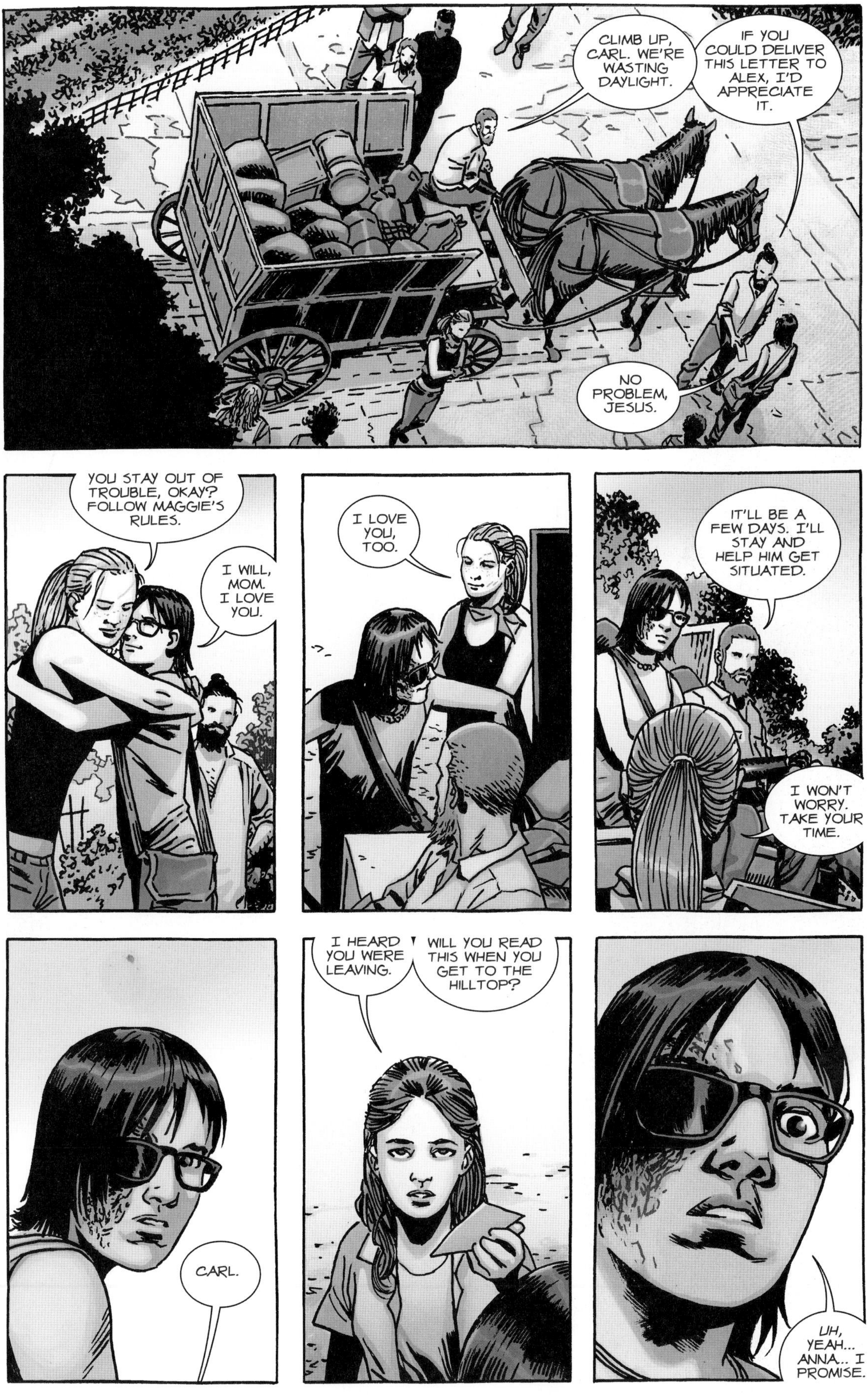
CLIMB UP, CARL. WE'RE WASTING DAYLIGHT.
IF YOU COULD DELIVER THIS LETTER TO ALEX, I'D APPRECIATE IT.
NO PROBLEM, JESUS.
YOU STAY OUT OF TROUBLE, OKAY? FOLLOW MAGGIE'S RULES.
I WILL, MOM. I LOVE YOU.
I LOVE YOU, TOO.
IT'LL BE A FEW DAYS. I'LL STAY AND HELP HIM GET SITUATED.
I WON'T WORRY. TAKE YOUR TIME.
CARL.
I HEARD YOU WERE LEAVING.
WILL YOU READ THIS WHEN YOU GET TO THE HILLTOP?
UH, YEAH... ANNA... I PROMISE.

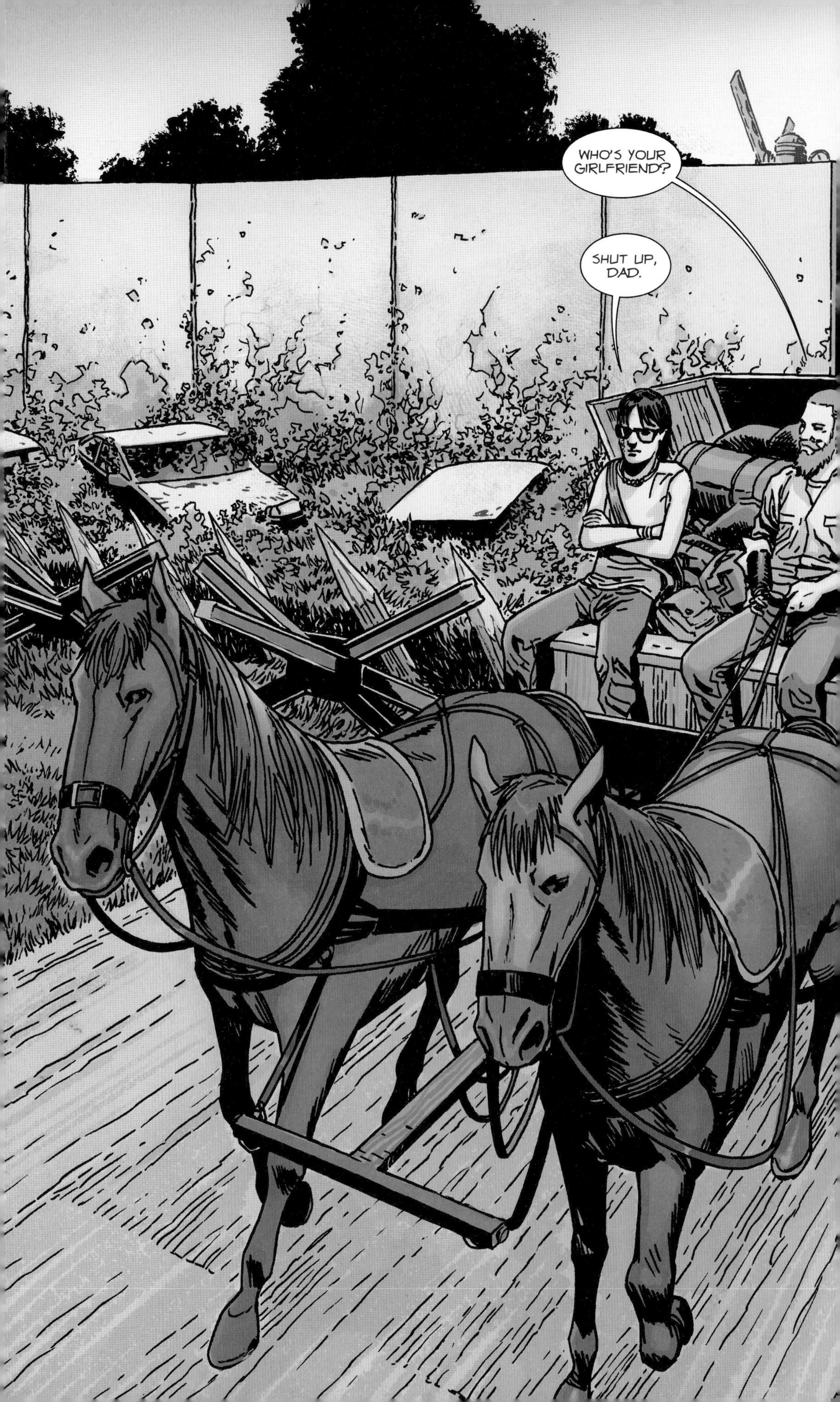
WHO'S YOUR GIRLFRIEND?
SHUT UP, DAD.

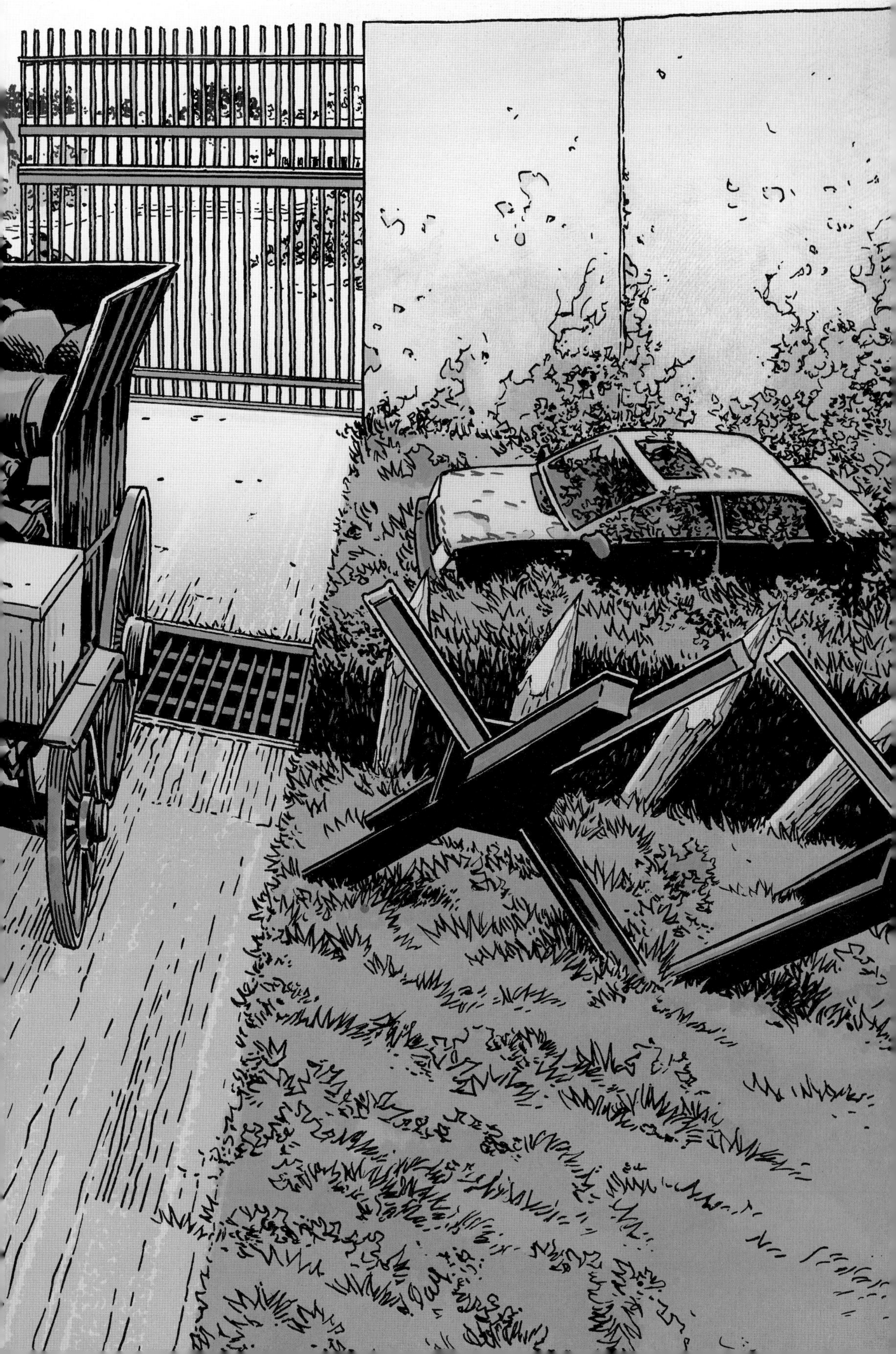

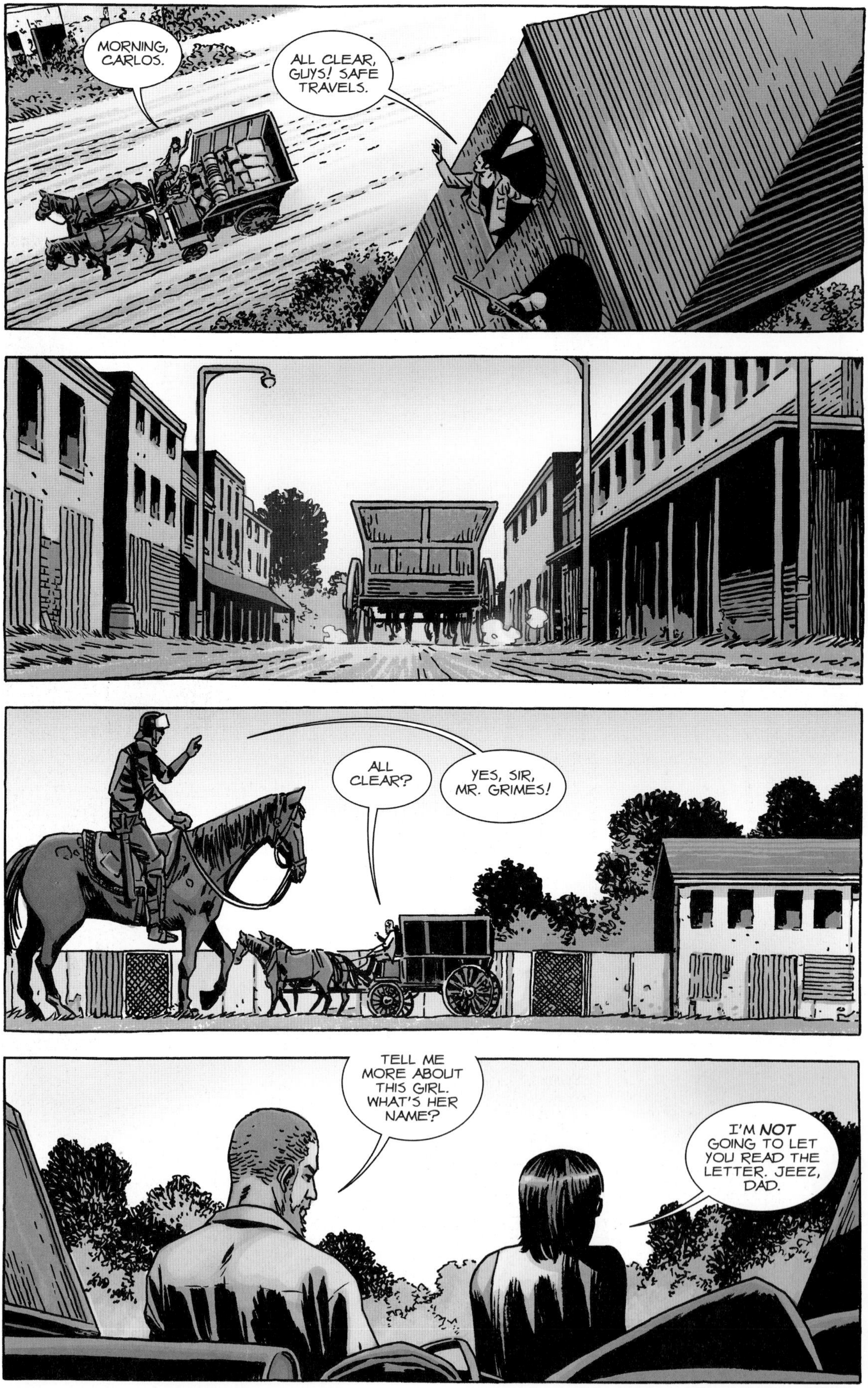
MORNING, CARLOS.
ALL CLEAR, GUYS! SAFE TRAVELS.
ALL CLEAR?
YES, SIR, MR. GRIMES!
TELL ME MORE ABOUT THIS GIRL. WHAT'S HER NAME?
I'M NOT GOING TO LET YOU READ THE LETTER. JEEZ, DAD.

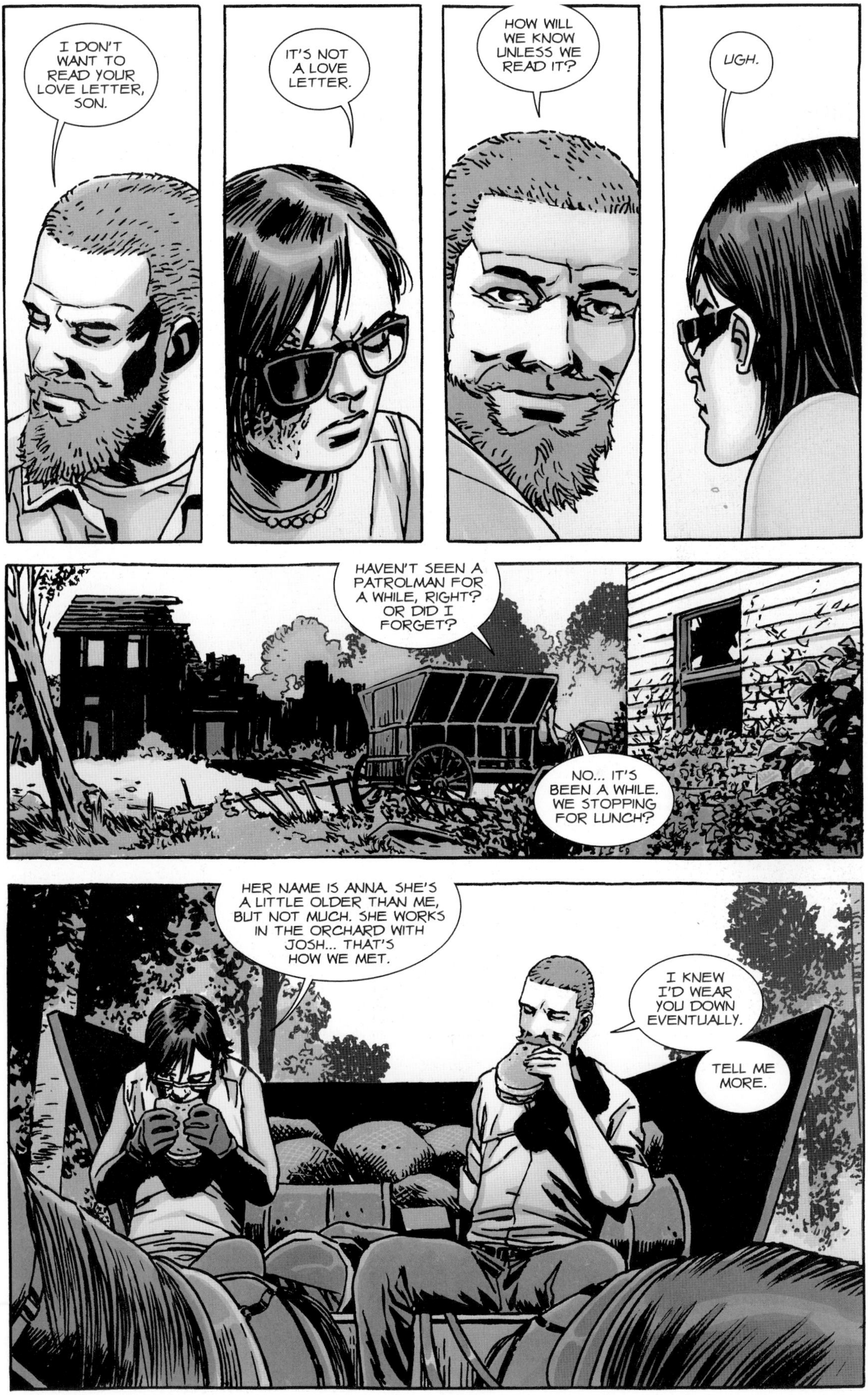

I DON'T WANT TO READ YOUR LOVE LETTER, SON.
IT'S NOT A LOVE LETTER.
HOW WILL WE KNOW UNLESS WE READ IT?
UGH.
HAVEN'T SEEN A PATROLMAN FOR A WHILE, RIGHT? OR DID I FORGET?
NO... IT'S BEEN A WHILE. WE STOPPING FOR LUNCH?
HER NAME IS ANNA. SHE'S A LITTLE OLDER THAN ME, BUT NOT MUCH. SHE WORKS IN THE ORCHARD WITH JOSH... THAT'S HOW WE MET.
I KNEW I'D WEAR YOU DOWN EVENTUALLY.
TELL ME MORE.

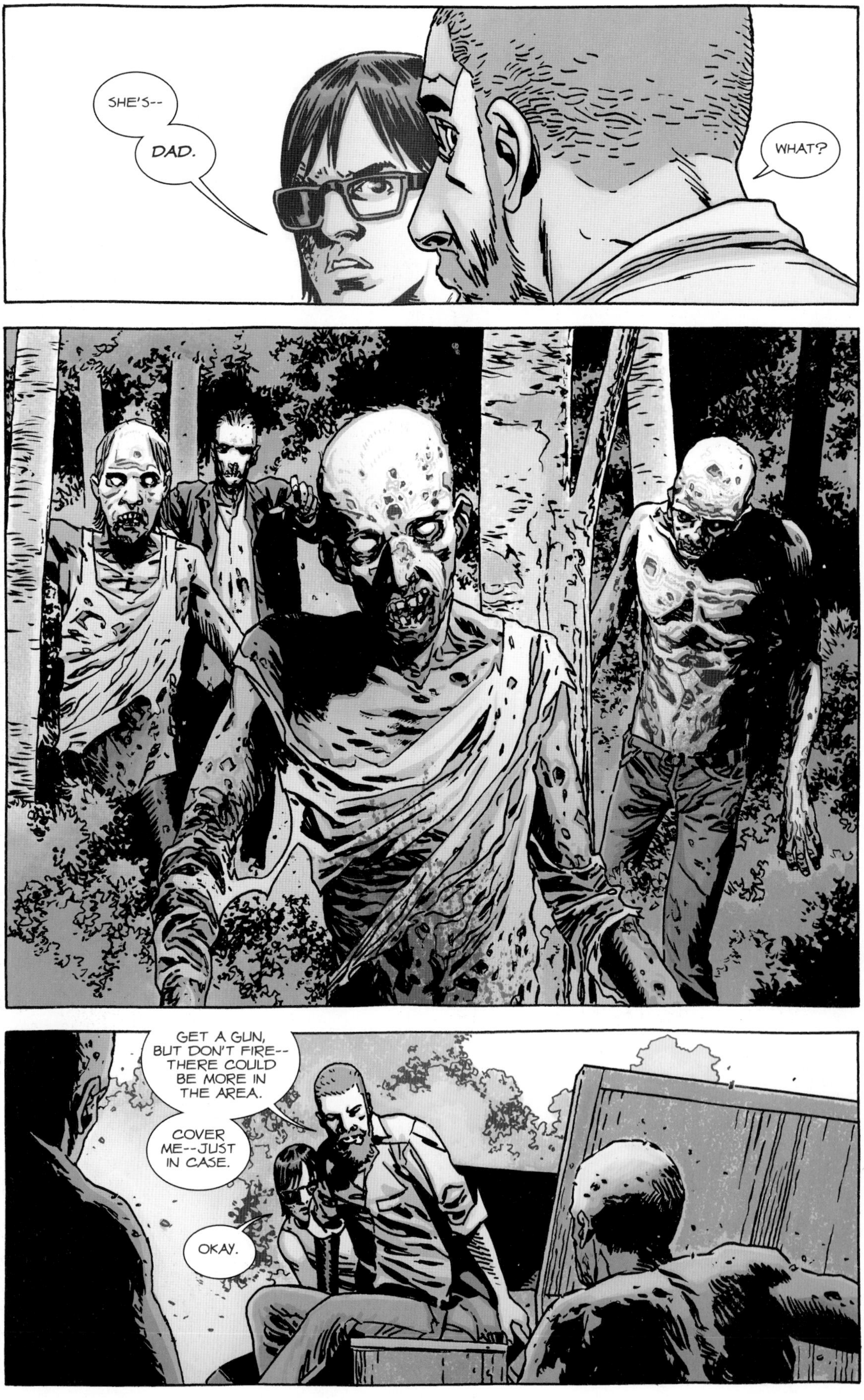
SHE'S--
DAD.
WHAT?
GET A GUN, BUT DON'T FIRE-- THERE COULD BE MORE IN THE AREA.
COVER ME--JUST IN CASE.
OKAY.

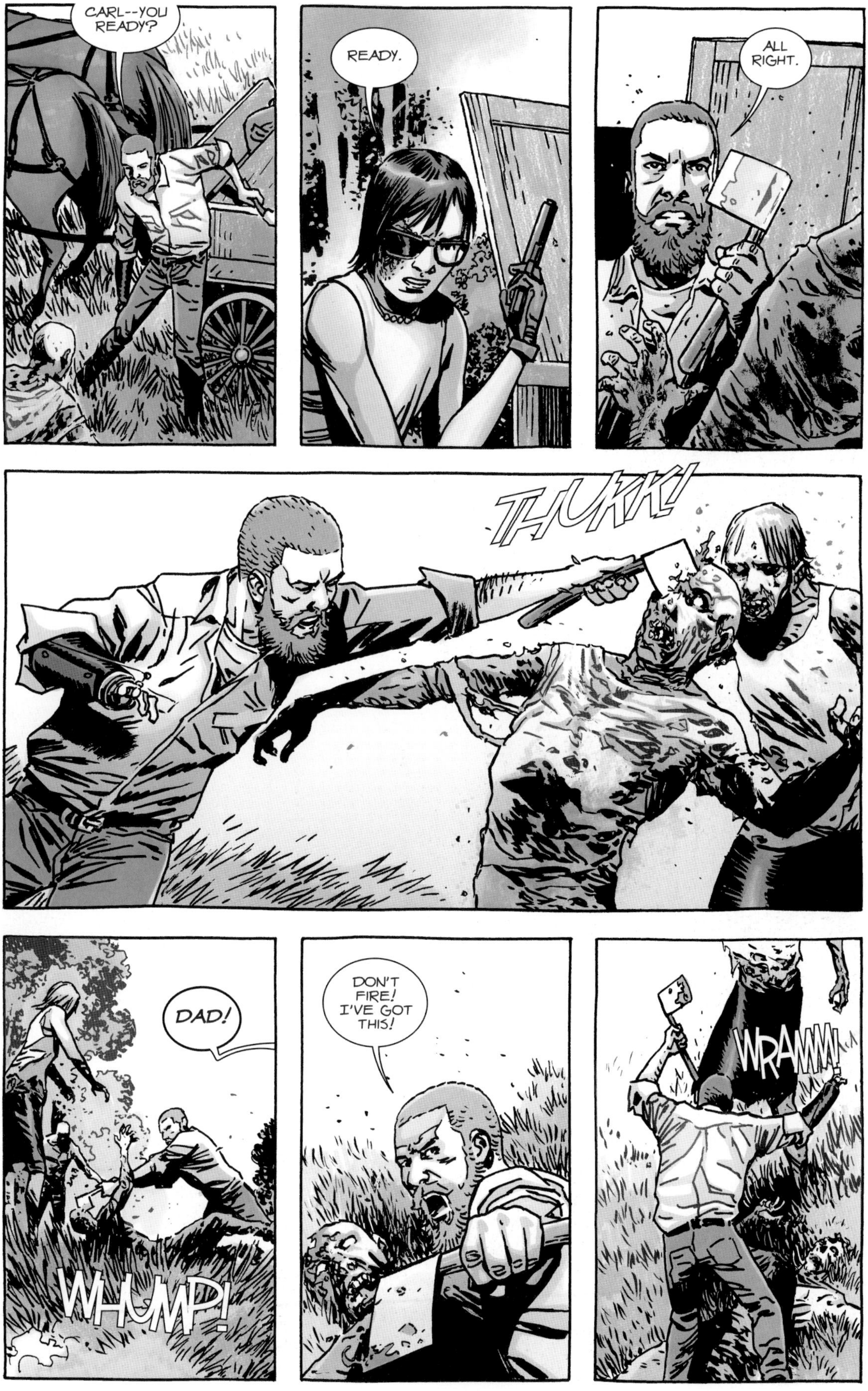
CARL--YOU READY?
READY.
ALL RIGHT.
THUKK!
DAD!
WHUMP!
DON'T FIRE! I'VE GOT THIS!
WRAMM!

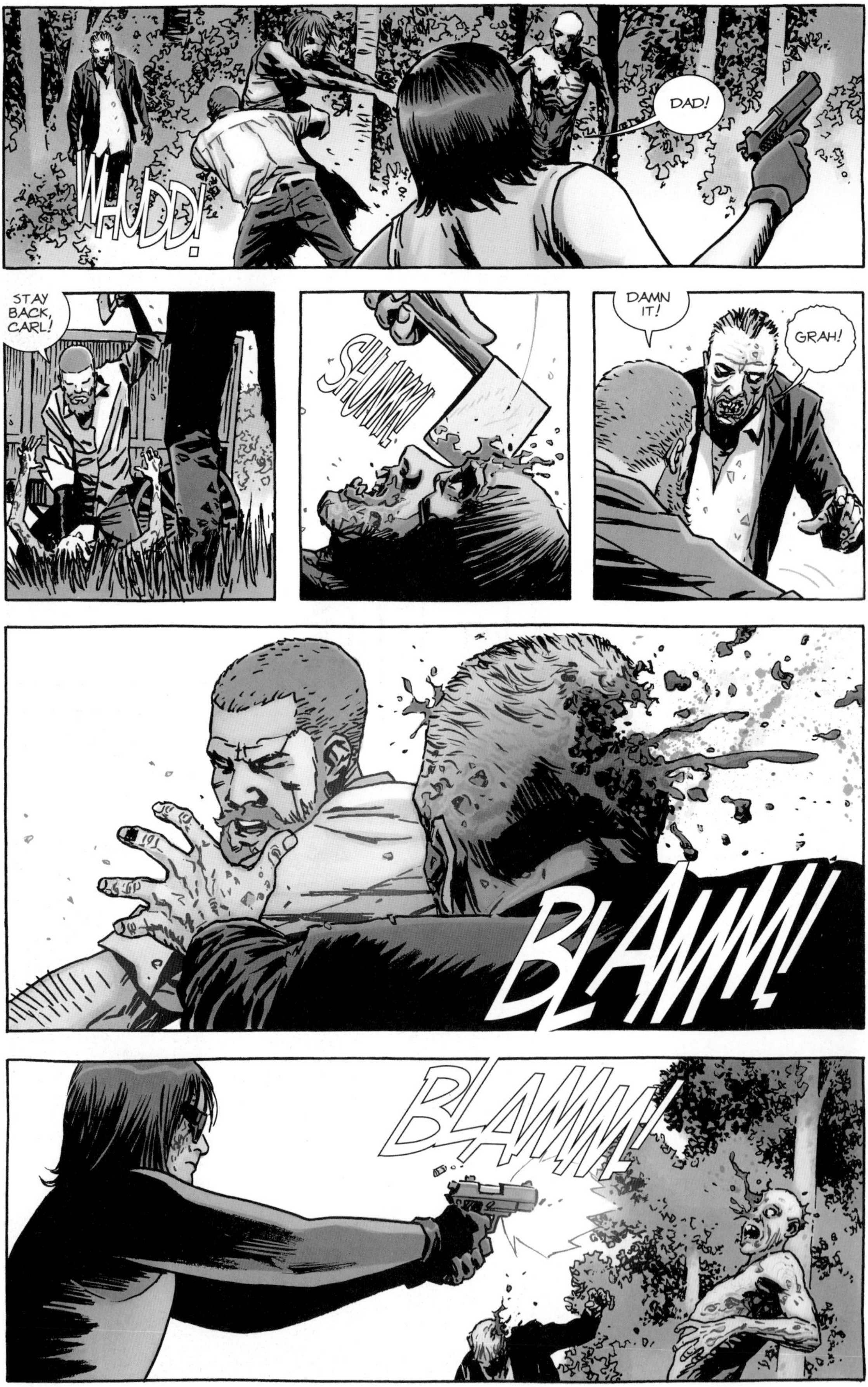

WHUDD!
DAD!
STAY BACK, CARL!
SHUNKK!
DAMN IT!
GRAH!
BLAMM!
BLAMM!

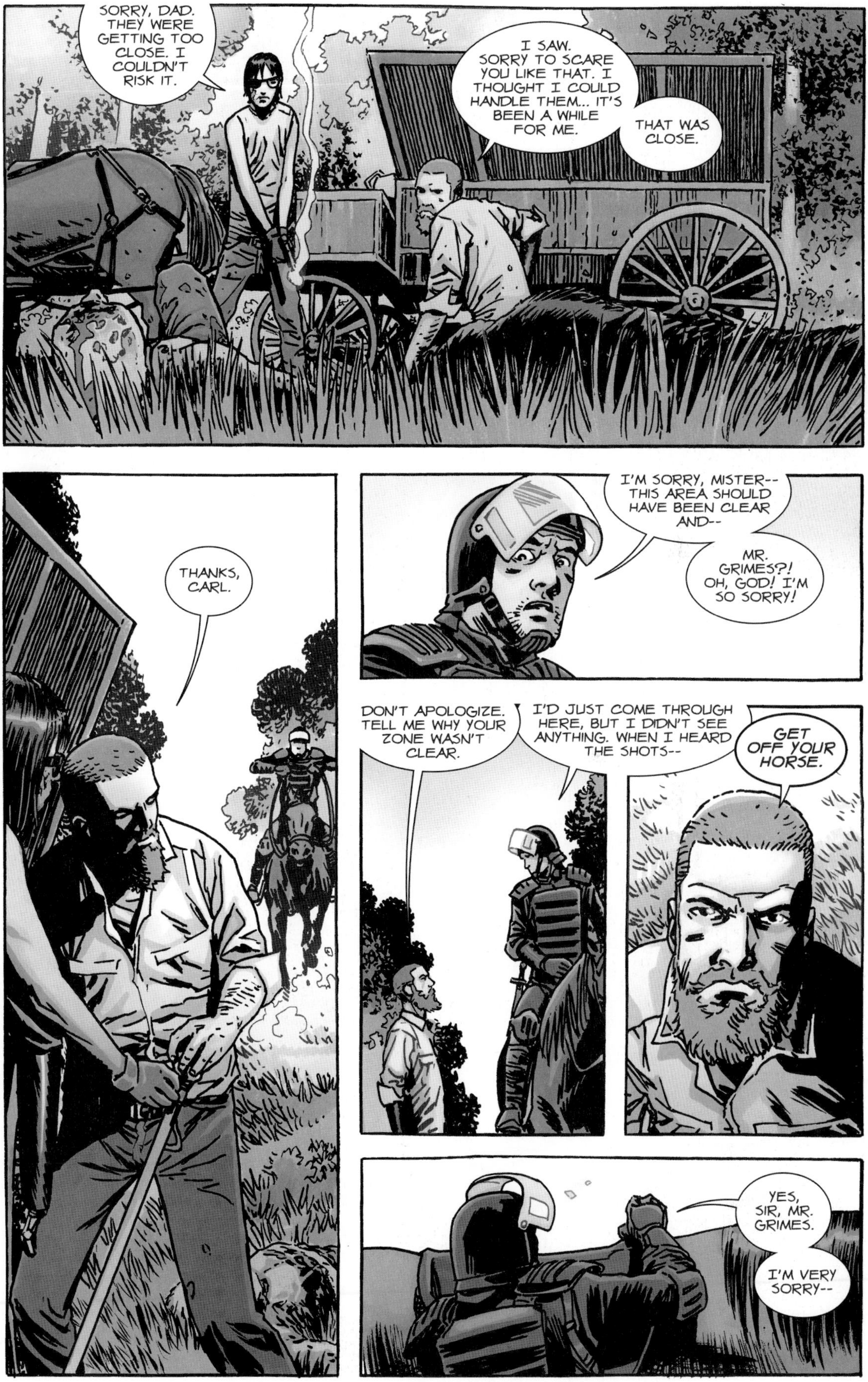
SORRY, DAD. THEY WERE GETTING TOO CLOSE. I COULDN'T RISK IT.
I SAW. SORRY TO SCARE YOU LIKE THAT. I THOUGHT I COULD HANDLE THEM... IT'S BEEN A WHILE FOR ME.
THAT WAS CLOSE.
THANKS, CARL.
I'M SORRY, MISTER-- THIS AREA SHOULD HAVE BEEN CLEAR AND--
MR. GRIMES?! OH, GOD! I'M SO SORRY!
DON'T APOLOGIZE. TELL ME WHY YOUR ZONE WASN'T CLEAR.
I'D JUST COME THROUGH HERE, BUT I DIDN'T SEE ANYTHING. WHEN I HEARD THE SHOTS--
GET OFF YOUR HORSE.
YES, SIR, MR. GRIMES.
I'M VERY SORRY--

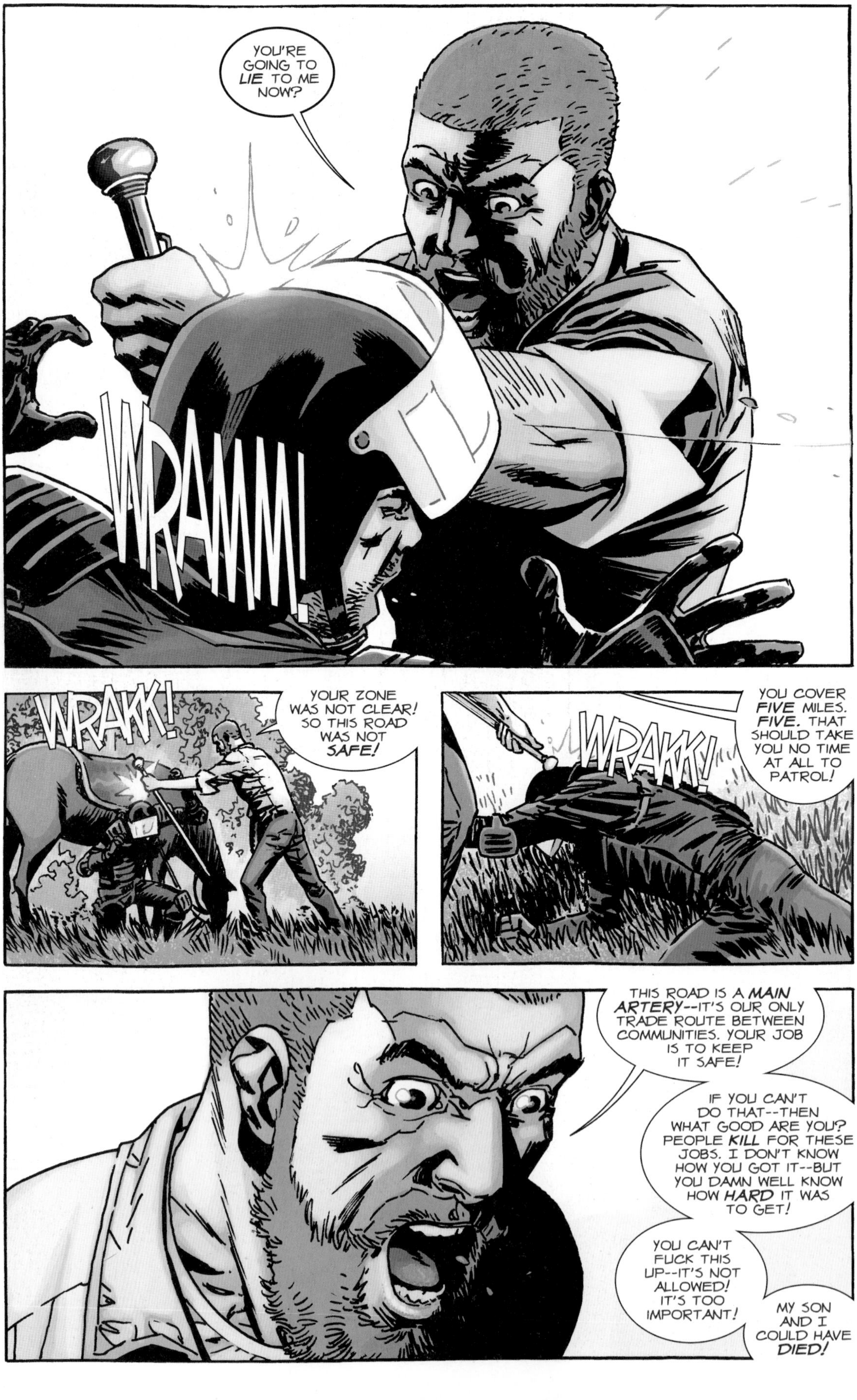

YOU'RE GOING TO LIE TO ME NOW?
WRAMM!
WRAKK!
YOUR ZONE WAS NOT CLEAR! SO THIS ROAD WAS NOT SAFE!
YOU COVER FIVE MILES. FIVE. THAT SHOULD TAKE YOU NO TIME AT ALL TO PATROL!
WRAKK!
THIS ROAD IS A MAIN ARTERY--IT'S OUR ONLY TRADE ROUTE BETWEEN COMMUNITIES. YOUR JOB IS TO KEEP IT SAFE!
IF YOU CAN'T DO THAT--THEN WHAT GOOD ARE YOU? PEOPLE KILL FOR THESE JOBS. I DON'T KNOW HOW YOU GOT IT--BUT YOU DAMN WELL KNOW HOW HARD IT WAS TO GET!
YOU CAN'T FUCK THIS UP--IT'S NOT ALLOWED! IT'S TOO IMPORTANT!
MY SON AND I COULD HAVE DIED!

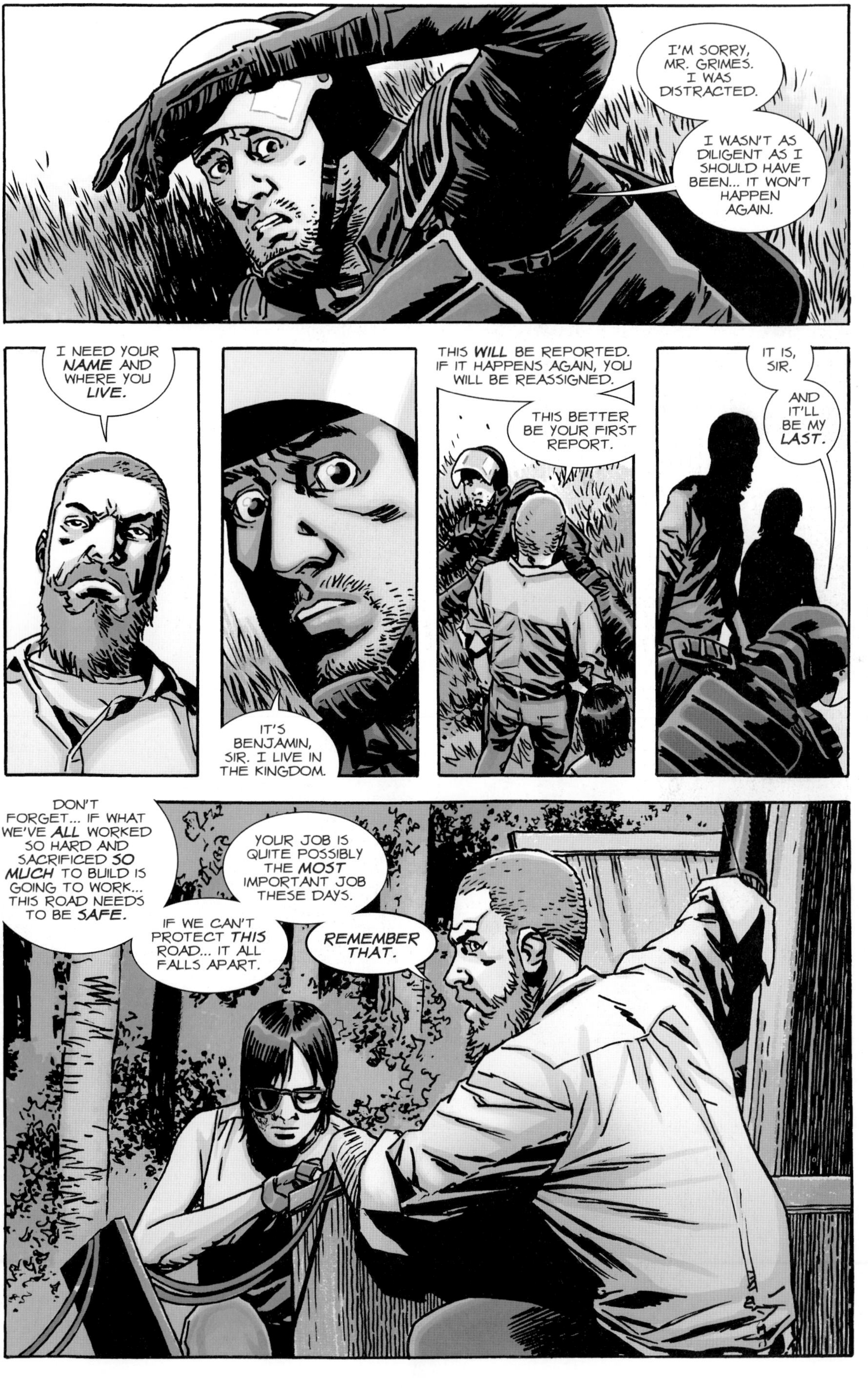
I'M SORRY, MR. GRIMES. I WAS DISTRACTED.
I WASN'T AS DILIGENT AS I SHOULD HAVE BEEN... IT WON'T HAPPEN AGAIN.
I NEED YOUR NAME AND WHERE YOU LIVE.
IT'S BENJAMIN, SIR. I LIVE IN THE KINGDOM.
THIS WILL BE REPORTED. IF IT HAPPENS AGAIN, YOU WILL BE REASSIGNED.
THIS BETTER BE YOUR FIRST REPORT.
IT IS, SIR.
AND IT'LL BE MY LAST.
DON'T FORGET... IF WHAT WE'VE ALL WORKED SO HARD AND SACRIFICED SO MUCH TO BUILD IS GOING TO WORK... THIS ROAD NEEDS TO BE SAFE.
IF WE CAN'T PROTECT THIS ROAD... IT ALL FALLS APART.
YOUR JOB IS QUITE POSSIBLY THE MOST IMPORTANT JOB THESE DAYS.
REMEMBER THAT.

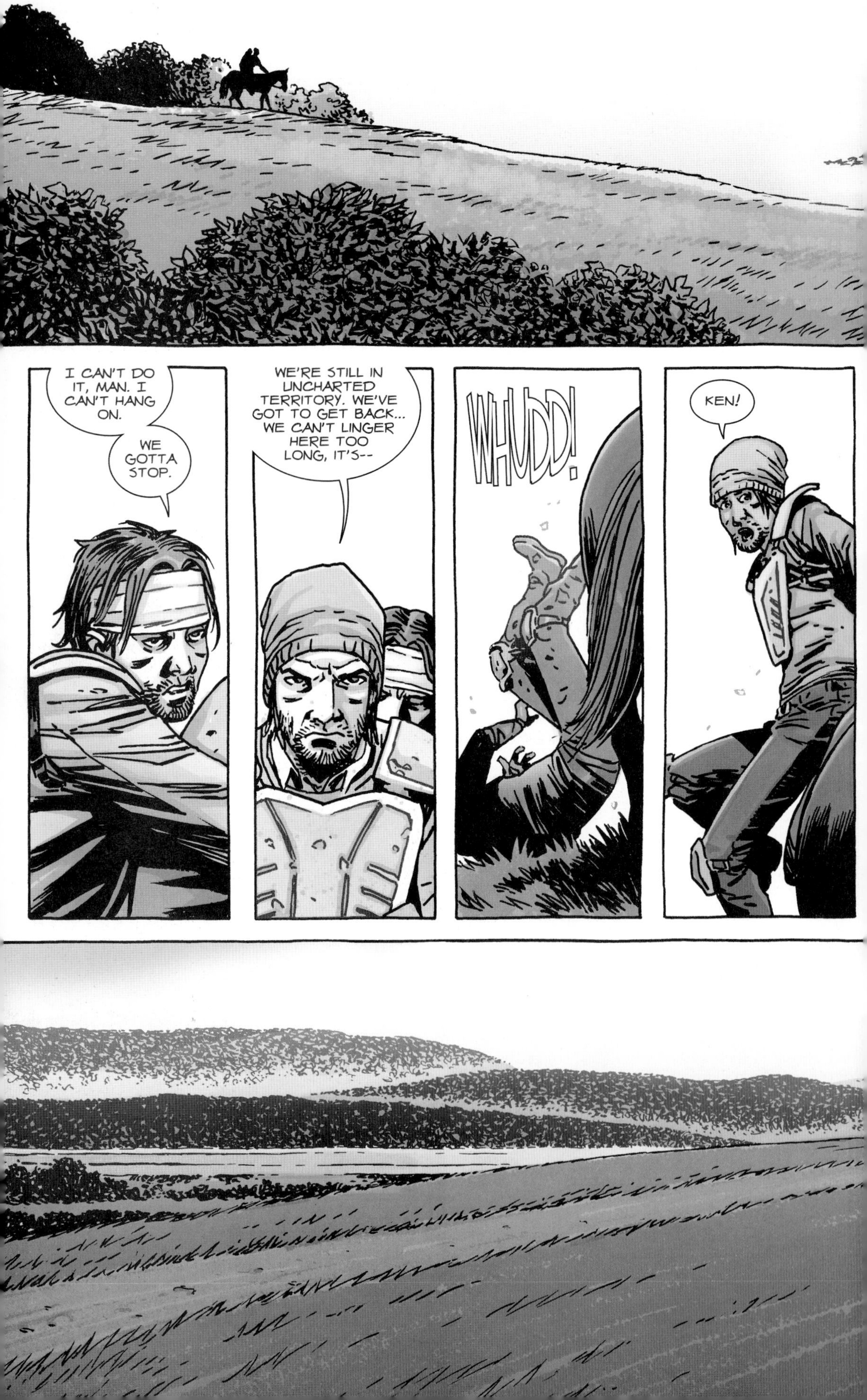

I CAN'T DO IT, MAN. I CAN'T HANG ON.
WE GOTTA STOP.
WE'RE STILL IN UNCHARTED TERRITORY. WE'VE GOT TO GET BACK... WE CAN'T LINGER HERE TOO LONG, IT'S--
WHUDD!
KEN!

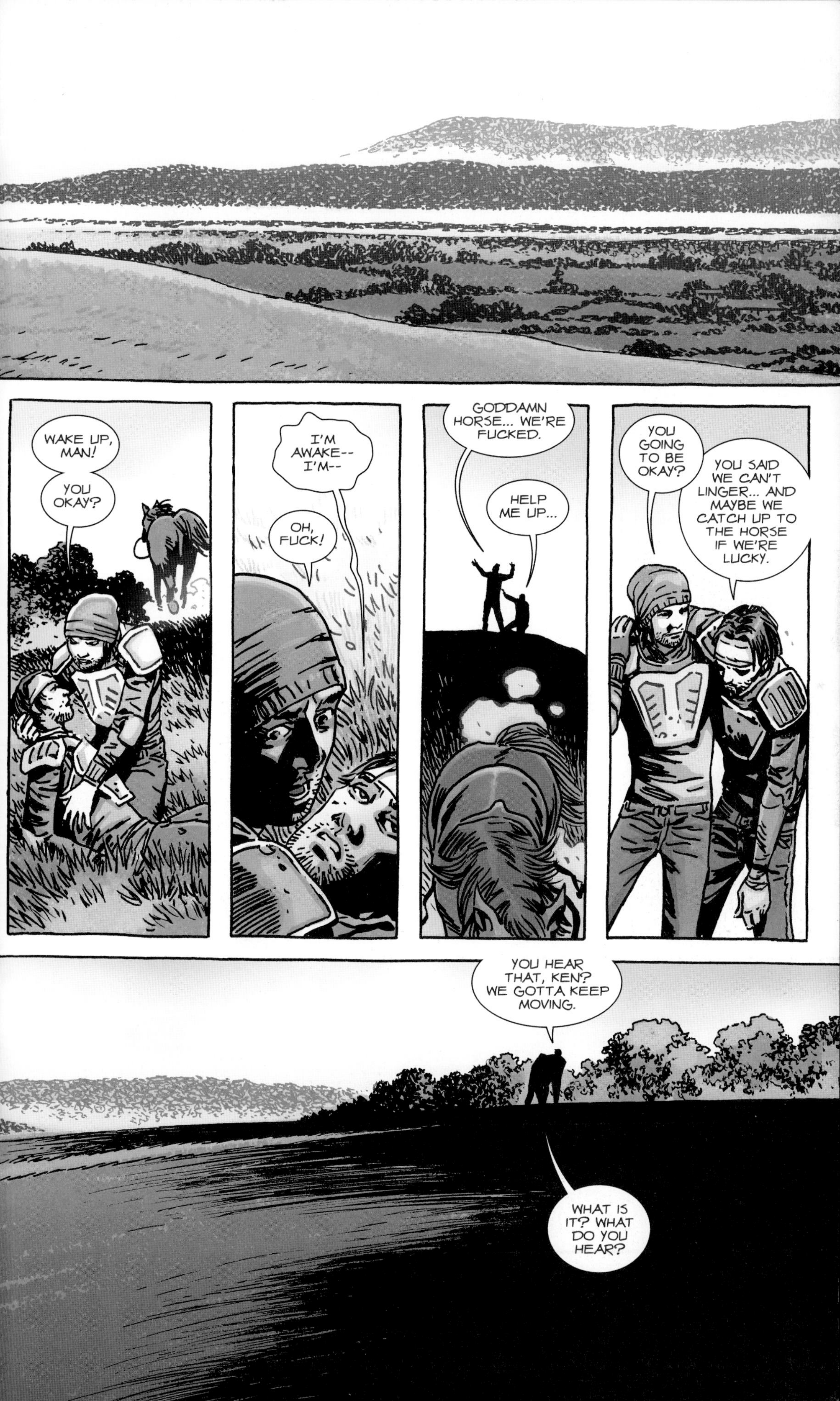
WAKE UP, MAN!
YOU OKAY?
I'M AWAKE-- I'M--
OH, FUCK!
GODDAMN HORSE... WE'RE FUCKED.
HELP ME UP...
YOU GOING TO BE OKAY?
YOU SAID WE CAN'T LINGER... AND MAYBE WE CATCH UP TO THE HORSE IF WE'RE LUCKY.
YOU HEAR THAT, KEN? WE GOTTA KEEP MOVING.
WHAT IS IT? WHAT DO YOU HEAR?

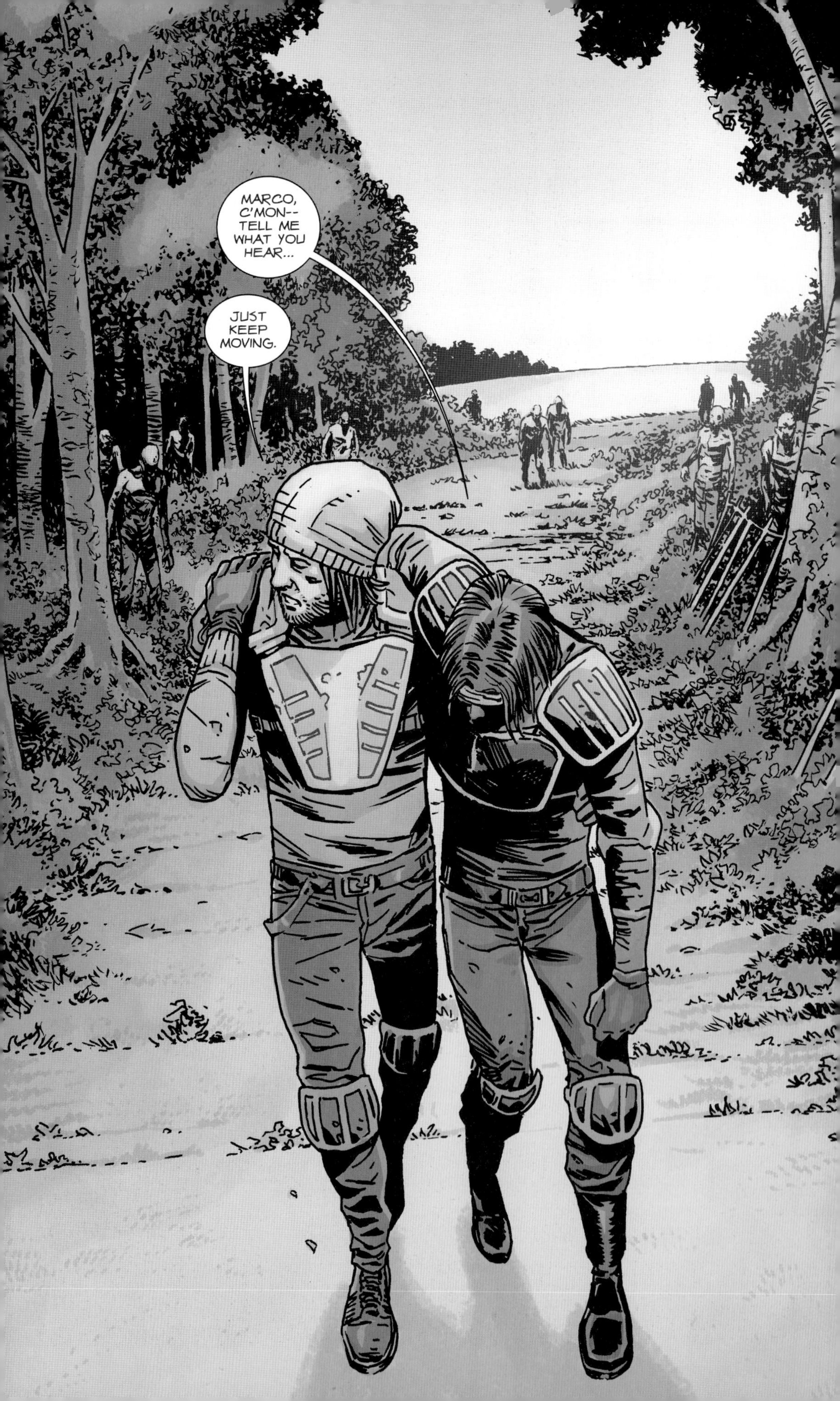
MARCO, C'MON-- TELL ME WHAT YOU HEAR...
JUST KEEP MOVING.

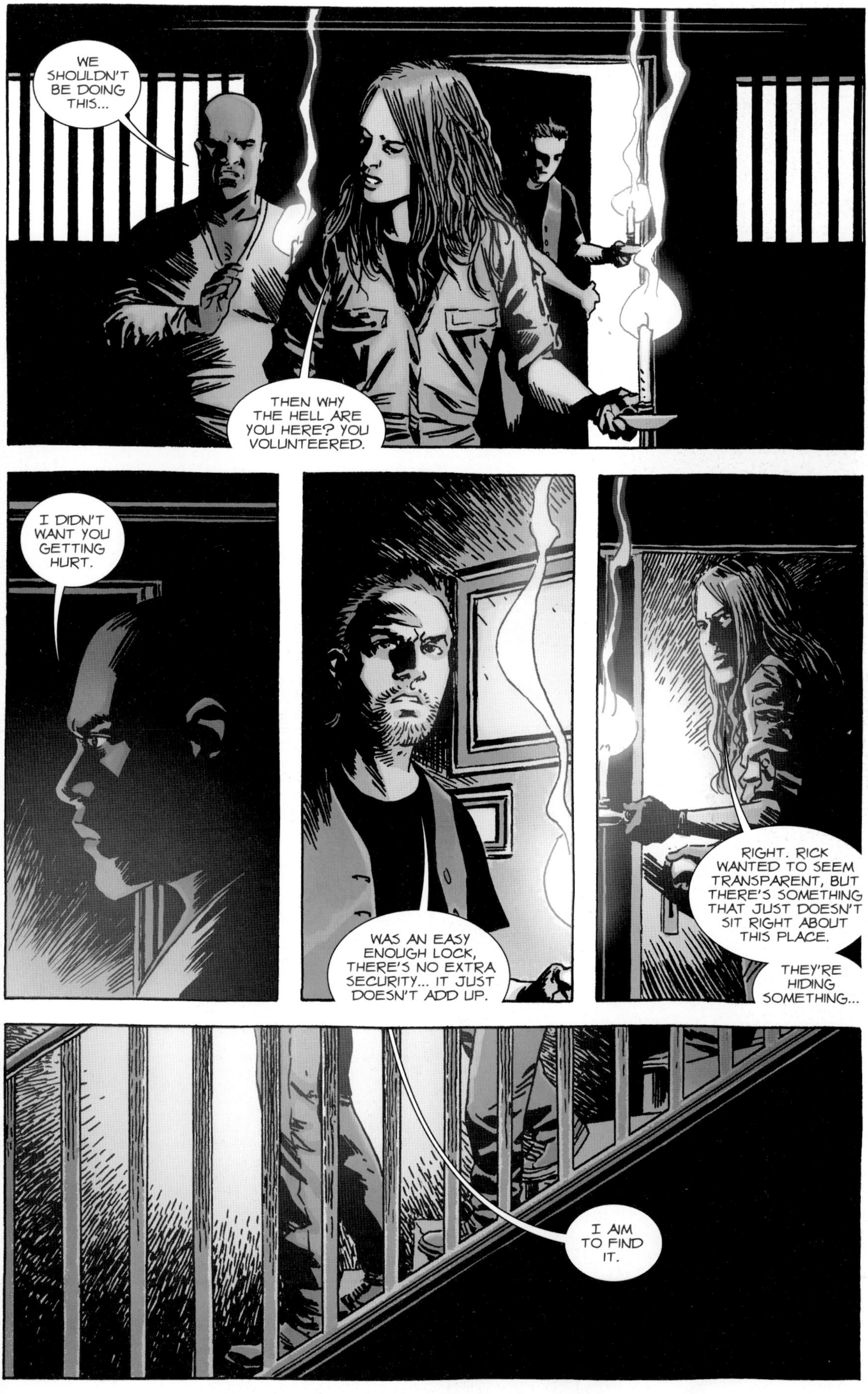
WE SHOULDN'T BE DOING THIS...
THEN WHY THE HELL ARE YOU HERE? YOU VOLUNTEERED.
I DIDN'T WANT YOU GETTING HURT.
WAS AN EASY ENOUGH LOCK, THERE'S NO EXTRA SECURITY... IT JUST DOESN'T ADD UP.
RIGHT. RICK WANTED TO SEEM TRANSPARENT, BUT THERE'S SOMETHING THAT JUST DOESN'T SIT RIGHT ABOUT THIS PLACE.
THEY'RE HIDING SOMETHING...
I AIM TO FIND IT.

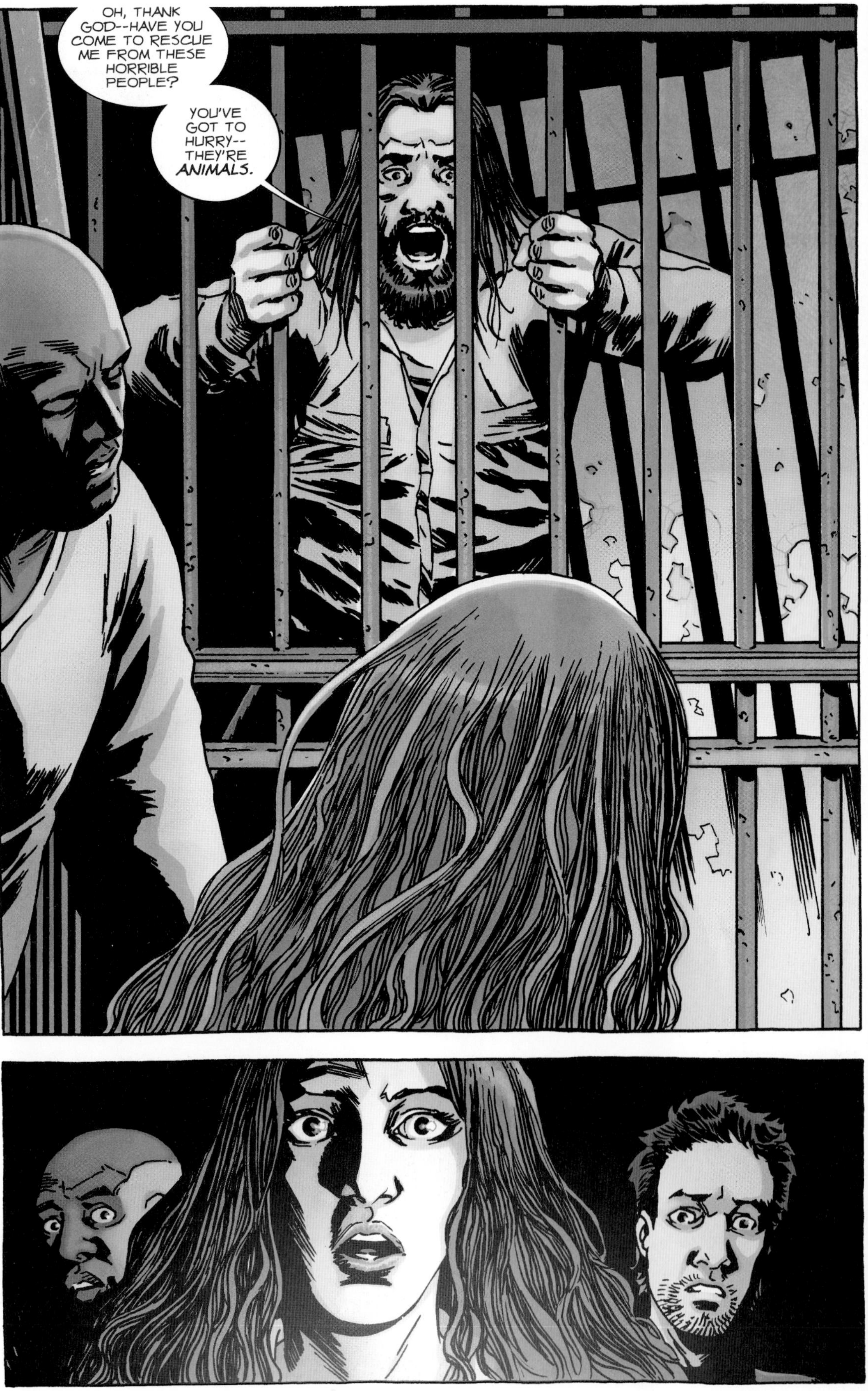
OH, THANK GOD--HAVE YOU COME TO RESCUE ME FROM THESE HORRIBLE PEOPLE?
YOU'VE GOT TO HURRY--THEY'RE ANIMALS.

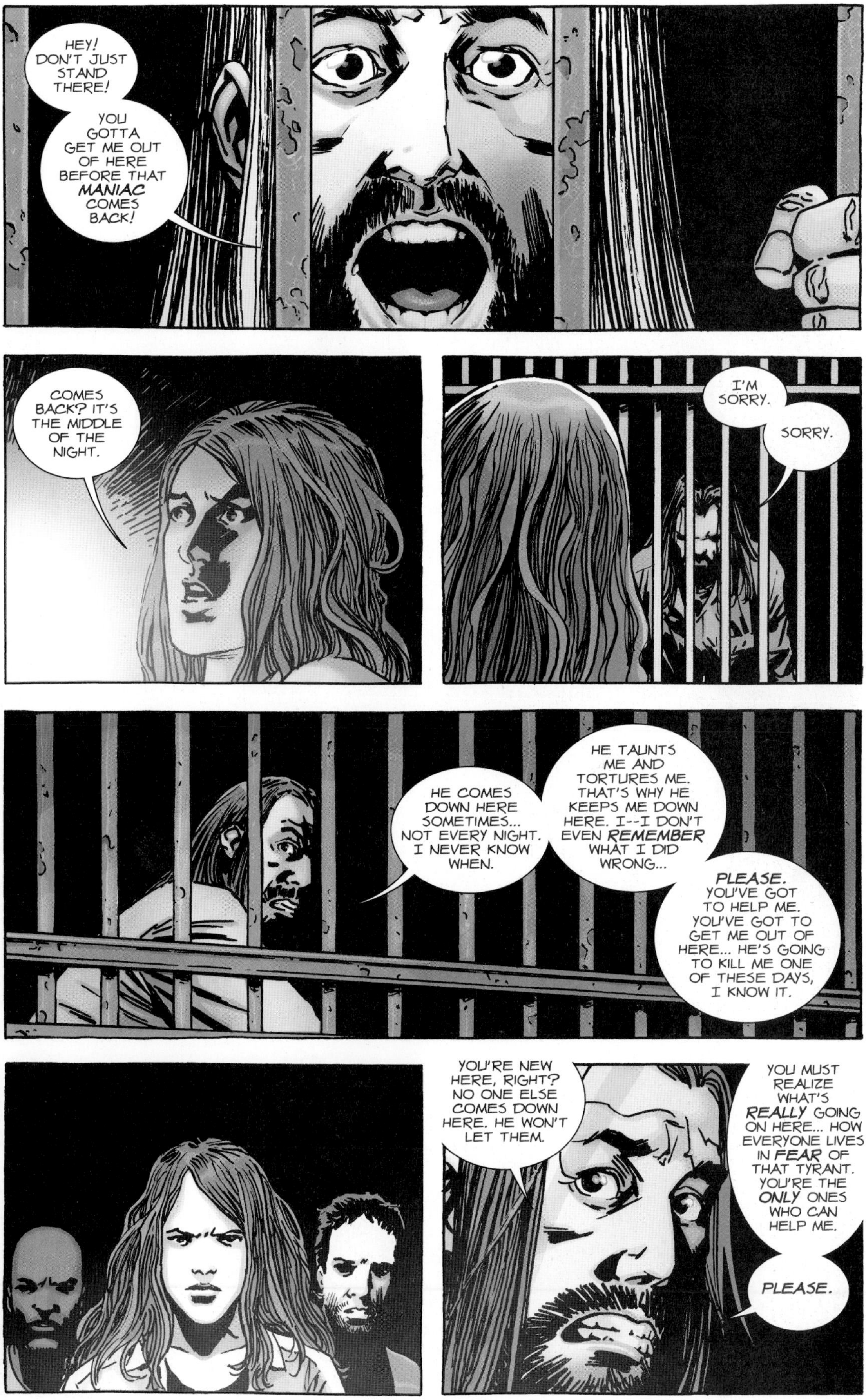
HEY! DON'T JUST STAND THERE!
YOU GOTTA GET ME OUT OF HERE BEFORE THAT MANIAC COMES BACK!
COMES BACK? IT'S THE MIDDLE OF THE NIGHT.
I'M SORRY.
SORRY.
HE COMES DOWN HERE SOMETIMES... NOT EVERY NIGHT. I NEVER KNOW WHEN.
HE TAUNTS ME AND TORTURES ME. THAT'S WHY HE KEEPS ME DOWN HERE. I--I DON'T EVEN REMEMBER WHAT I DID WRONG...
PLEASE. YOU'VE GOT TO HELP ME. YOU'VE GOT TO GET ME OUT OF HERE... HE'S GOING TO KILL ME ONE OF THESE DAYS, I KNOW IT.
YOU'RE NEW HERE, RIGHT? NO ONE ELSE COMES DOWN HERE. HE WON'T LET THEM.
YOU MUST REALIZE WHAT'S REALLY GOING ON HERE... HOW EVERYONE LIVES IN FEAR OF THAT TYRANT. YOU'RE THE ONLY ONES WHO CAN HELP ME.
PLEASE.

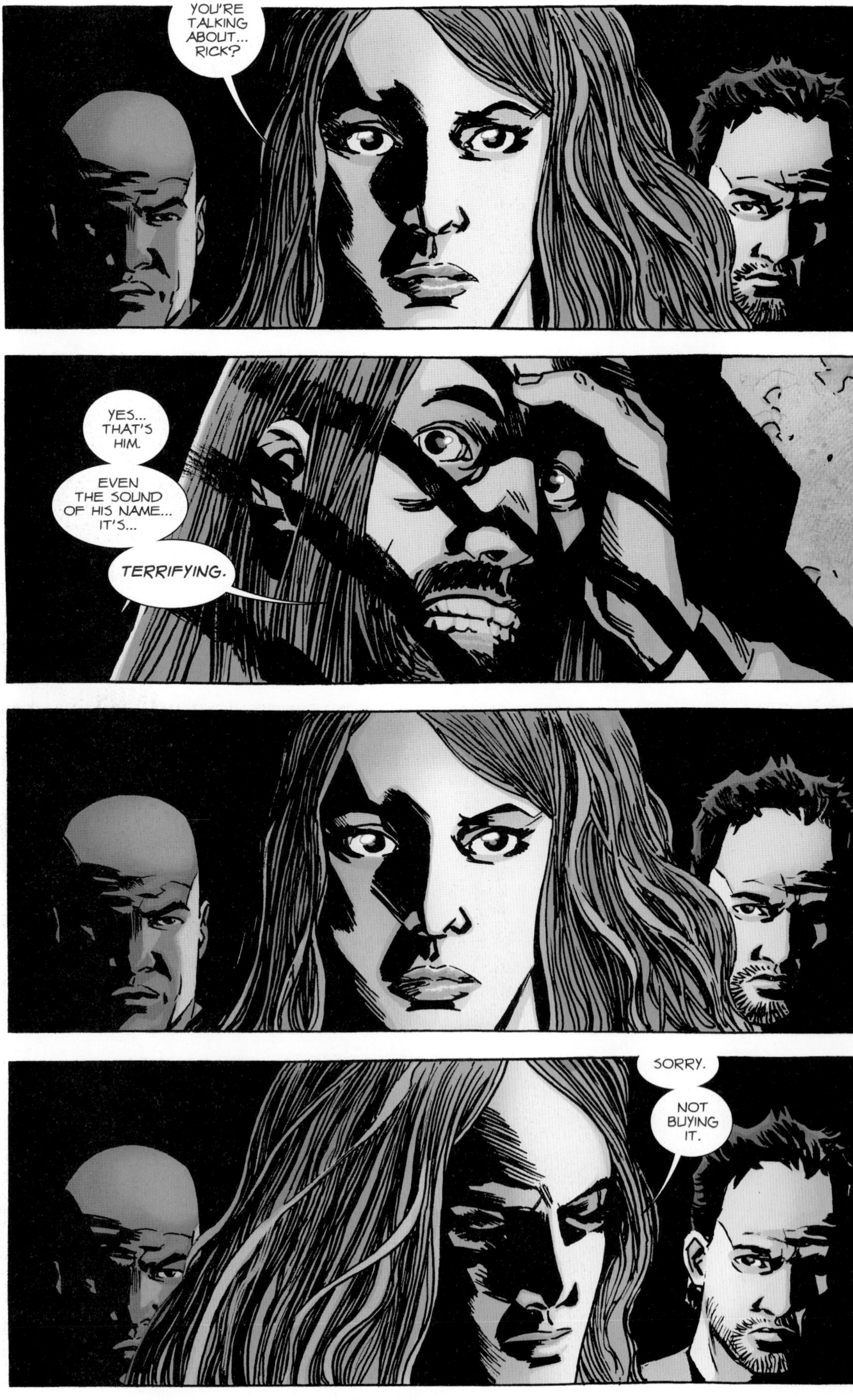
YOU'RE TALKING ABOUT... RICK?
YES... THAT'S HIM.
EVEN THE SOUND OF HIS NAME... IT'S...
TERRIFYING.
SORRY.
NOT BUYING IT.

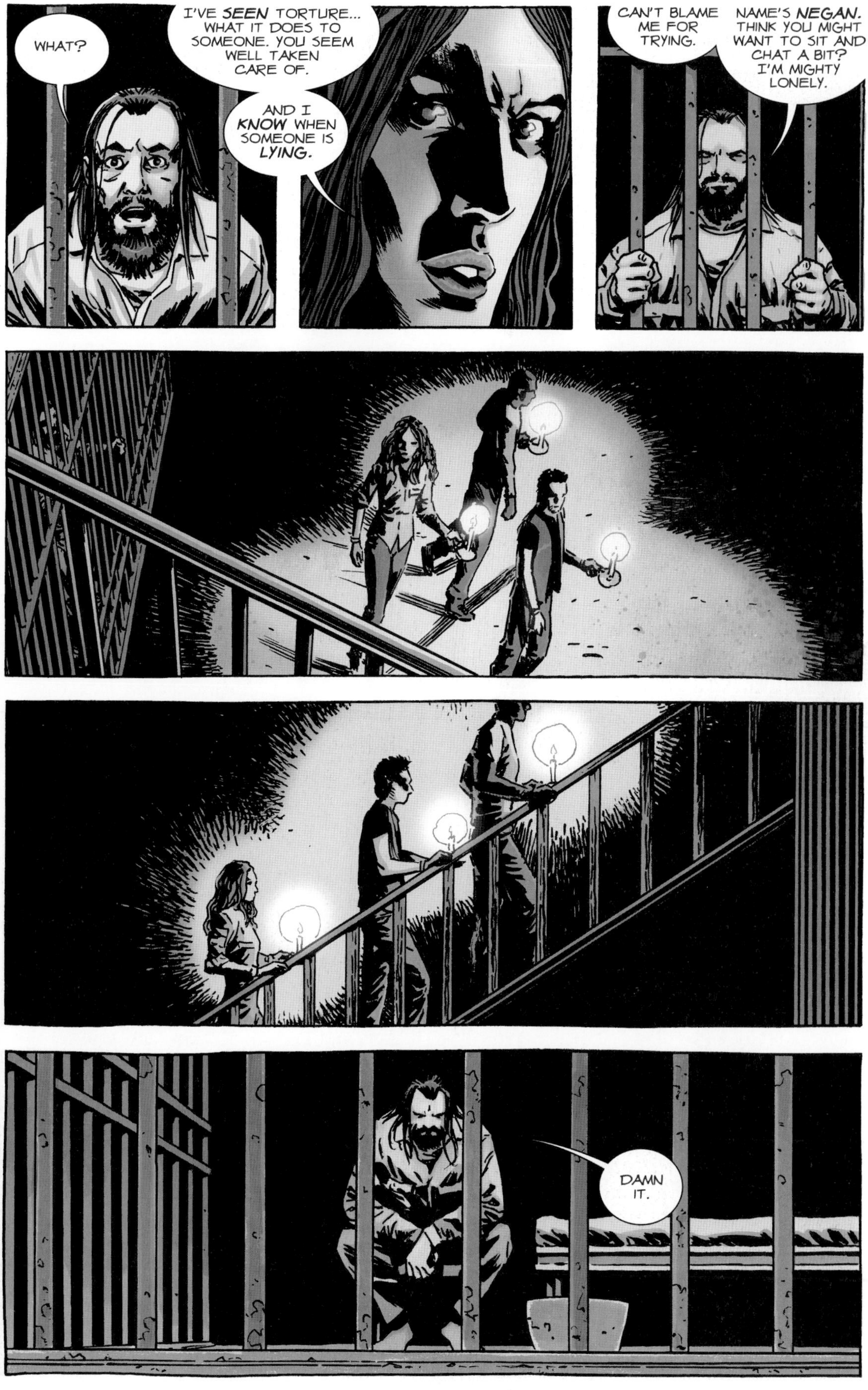
WHAT?
I'VE SEEN TORTURE... WHAT IT DOES TO SOMEONE. YOU SEEM WELL TAKEN CARE OF.
AND I KNOW WHEN SOMEONE IS LYING.
CAN'T BLAME ME FOR TRYING.
NAME'S NEGAN. THINK YOU MIGHT WANT TO SIT AND CHAT A BIT? I'M MIGHTY LONELY.
DAMN IT.

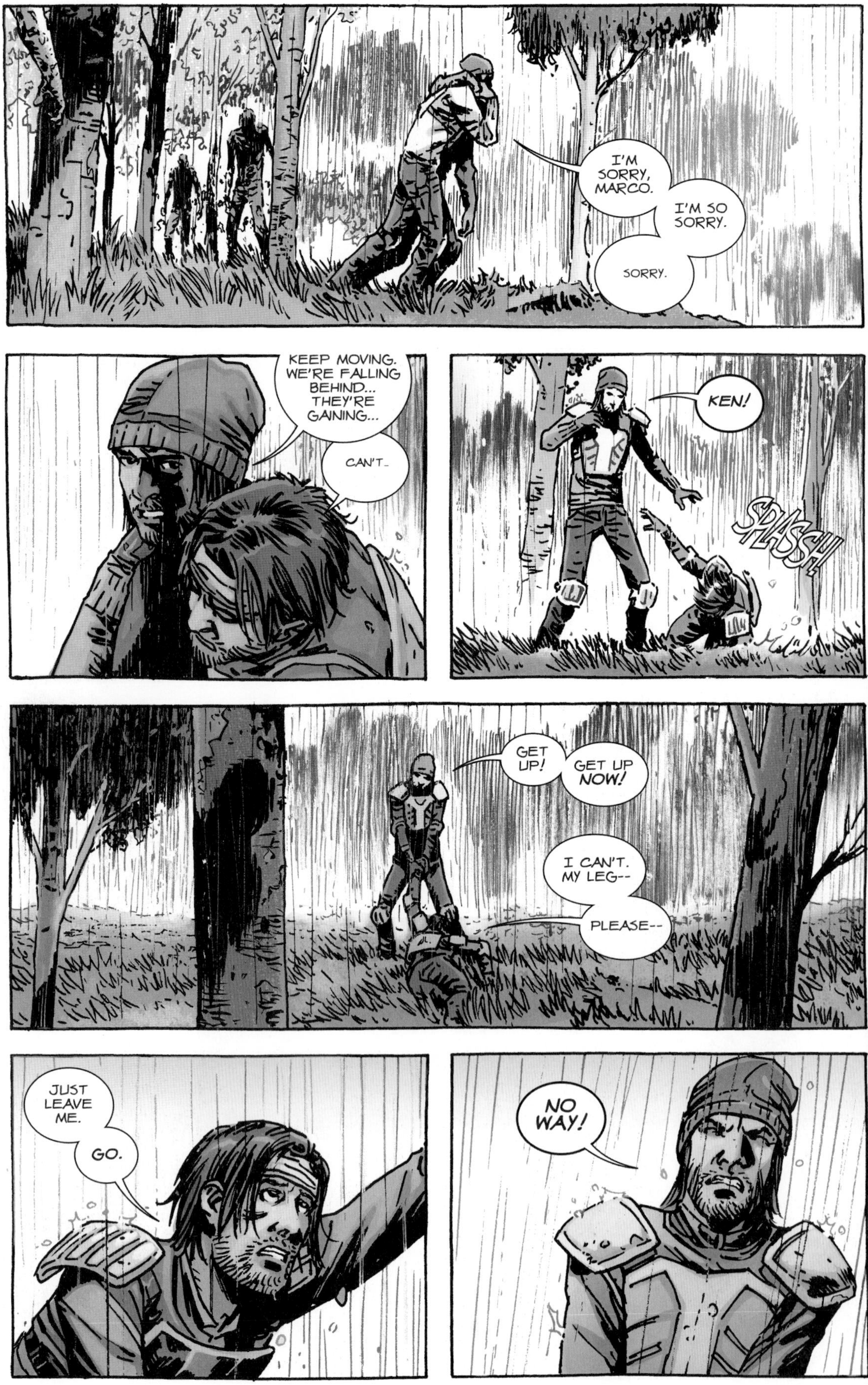
I'M SORRY, MARCO.
I'M SO SORRY.
SORRY.
KEEP MOVING. WE'RE FALLING BEHIND... THEY'RE GAINING...
CAN'T...
KEN!
SPLASSH!
GET UP!
GET UP NOW!
I CAN'T. MY LEG--
PLEASE--
JUST LEAVE ME.
GO.
NO WAY!

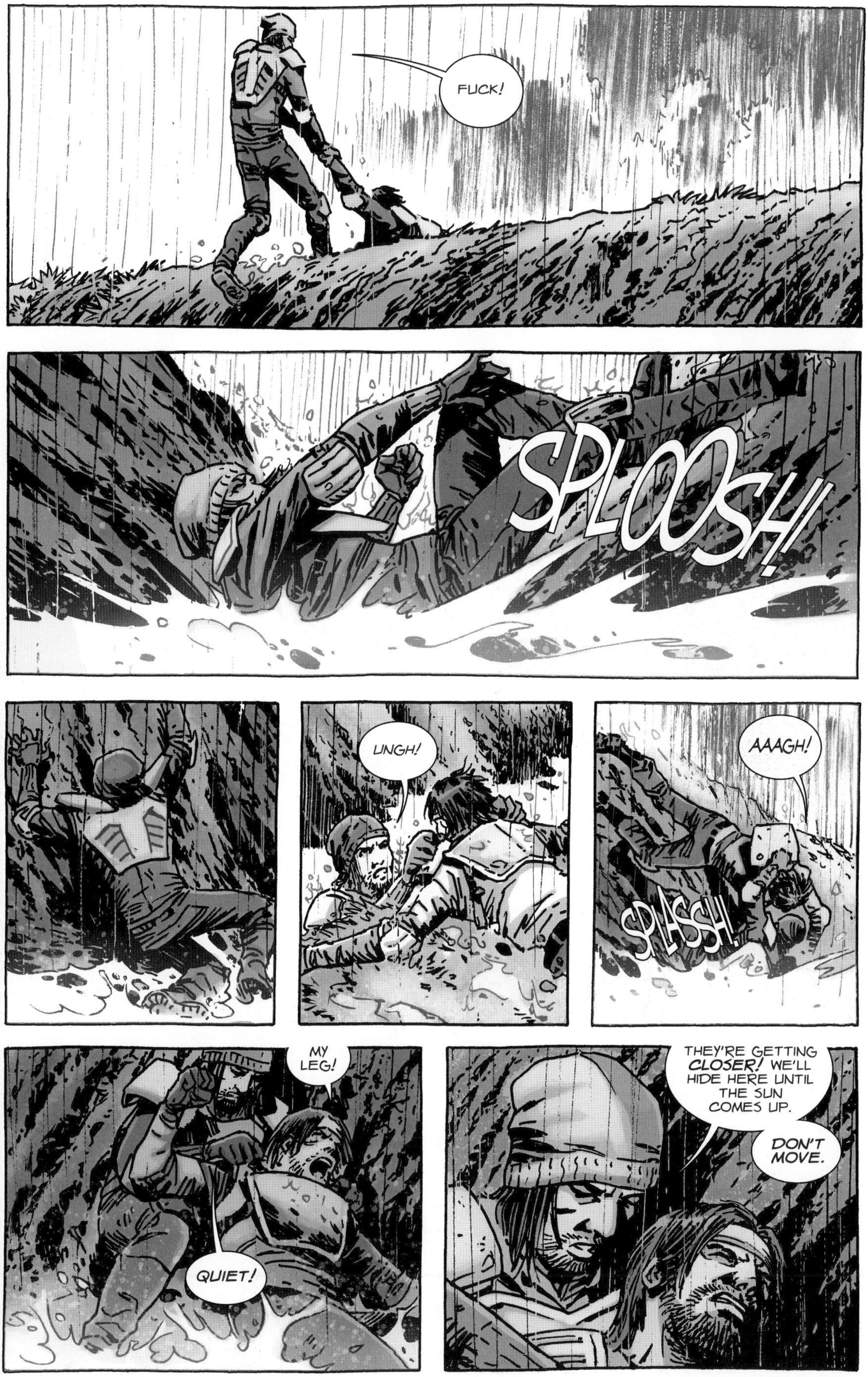
FUCK!
SPLOOSH!!
UNGH!
AAAGH!
SPLASSH!
MY LEG!
QUIET!
THEY'RE GETTING CLOSER! WE'LL HIDE HERE UNTIL THE SUN COMES UP.
DON'T MOVE.

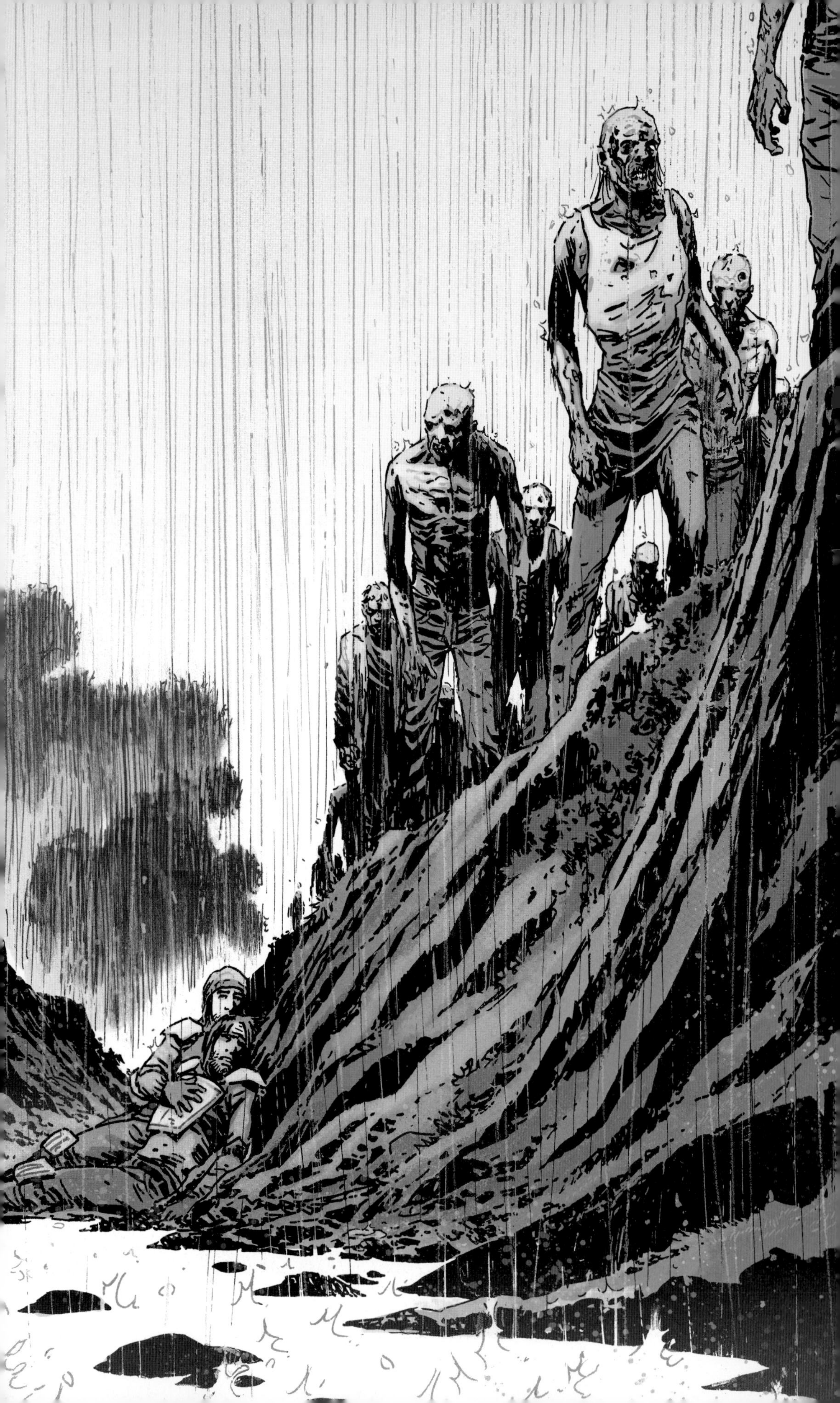

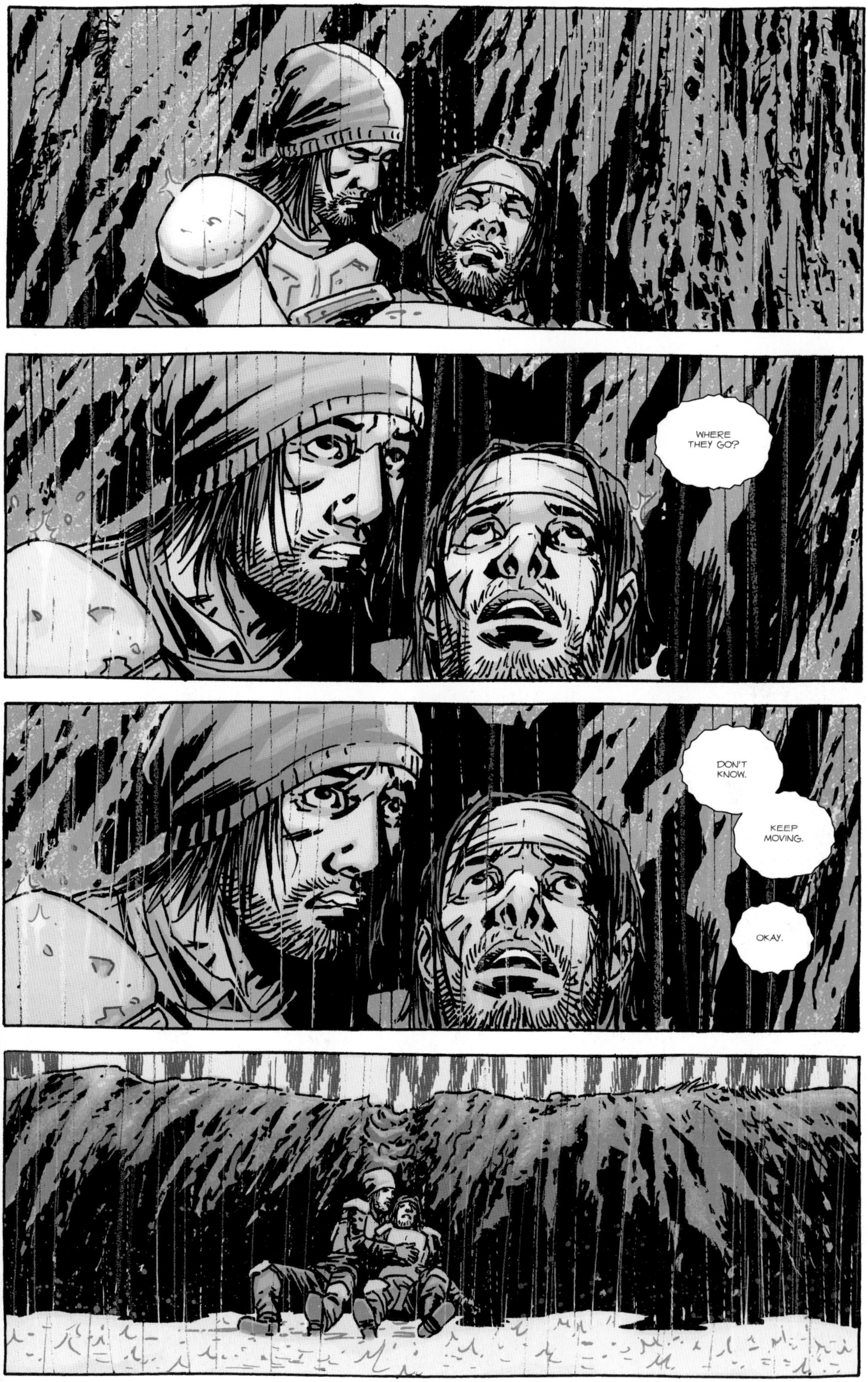
WHERE THEY GO?
DON'T KNOW.
KEEP MOVING.
OKAY.

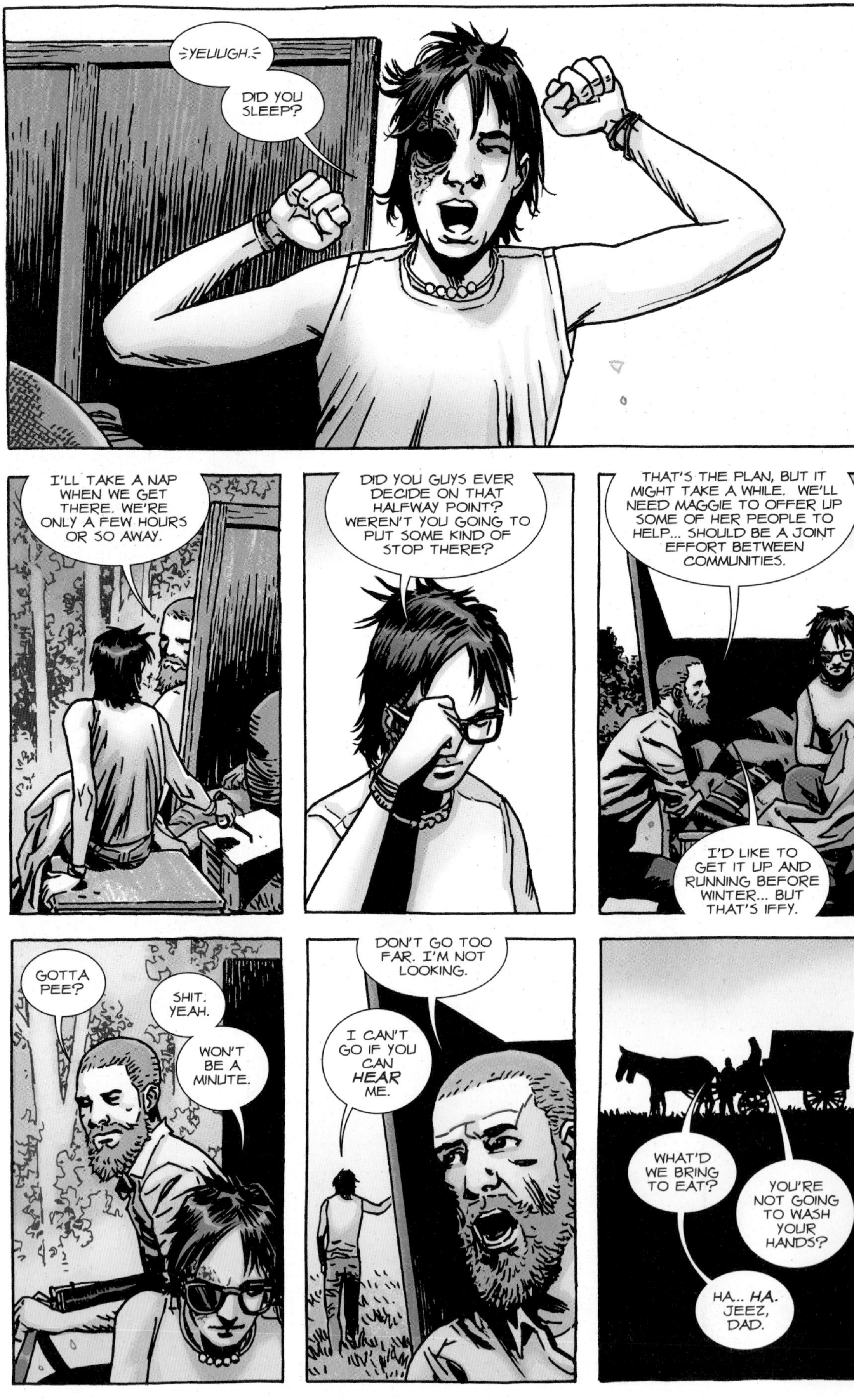
YEUUGH.
DID YOU SLEEP?
I'LL TAKE A NAP WHEN WE GET THERE. WE'RE ONLY A FEW HOURS OR SO AWAY.
DID YOU GUYS EVER DECIDE ON THAT HALFWAY POINT? WEREN'T YOU GOING TO PUT SOME KIND OF STOP THERE?
THAT'S THE PLAN, BUT IT MIGHT TAKE A WHILE. WE'LL NEED MAGGIE TO OFFER UP SOME OF HER PEOPLE TO HELP... SHOULD BE A JOINT EFFORT BETWEEN COMMUNITIES.
I'D LIKE TO GET IT UP AND RUNNING BEFORE WINTER... BUT THAT'S IFFY.
GOTTA PEE?
SHIT. YEAH.
WON'T BE A MINUTE.
DON'T GO TOO FAR. I'M NOT LOOKING.
I CAN'T GO IF YOU CAN HEAR ME.
WHAT'D WE BRING TO EAT?
YOU'RE NOT GOING TO WASH YOUR HANDS?
HA... HA. JEEZ, DAD.

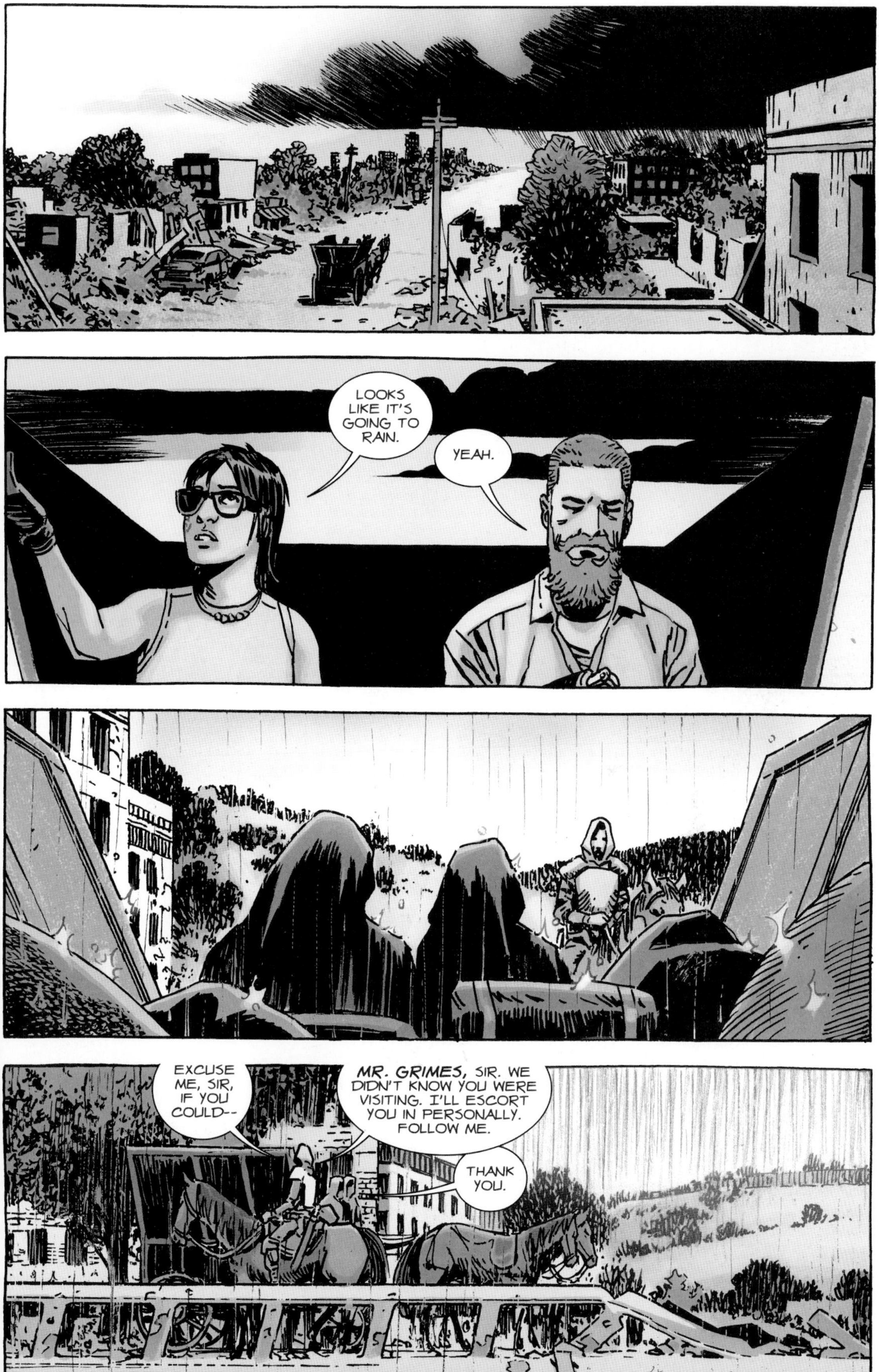
LOOKS LIKE IT'S GOING TO RAIN.
YEAH.
EXCUSE ME, SIR, IF YOU COULD--
MR. GRIMES, SIR. WE DIDN'T KNOW YOU WERE VISITING. I'LL ESCORT YOU IN PERSONALLY. FOLLOW ME.
THANK YOU.

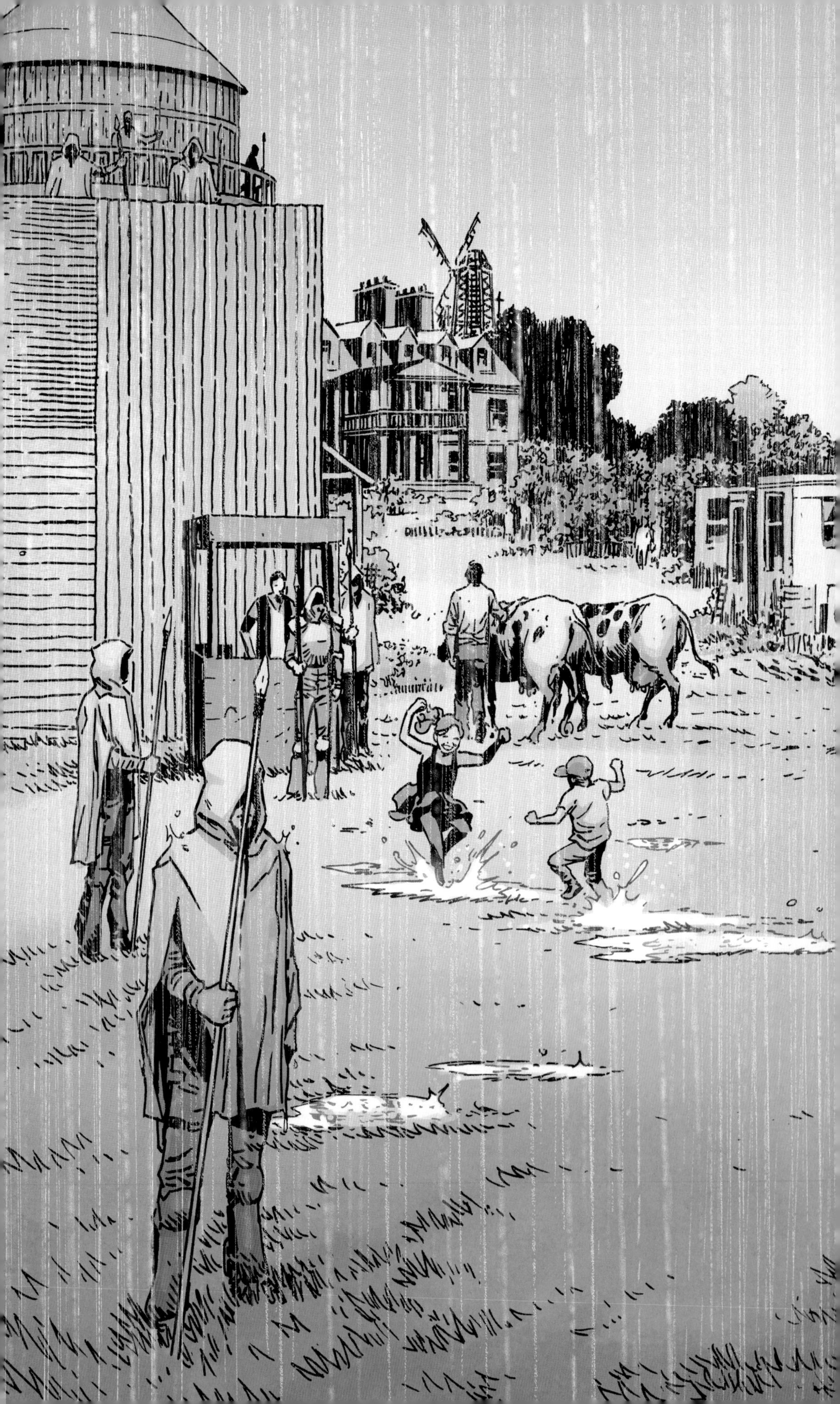

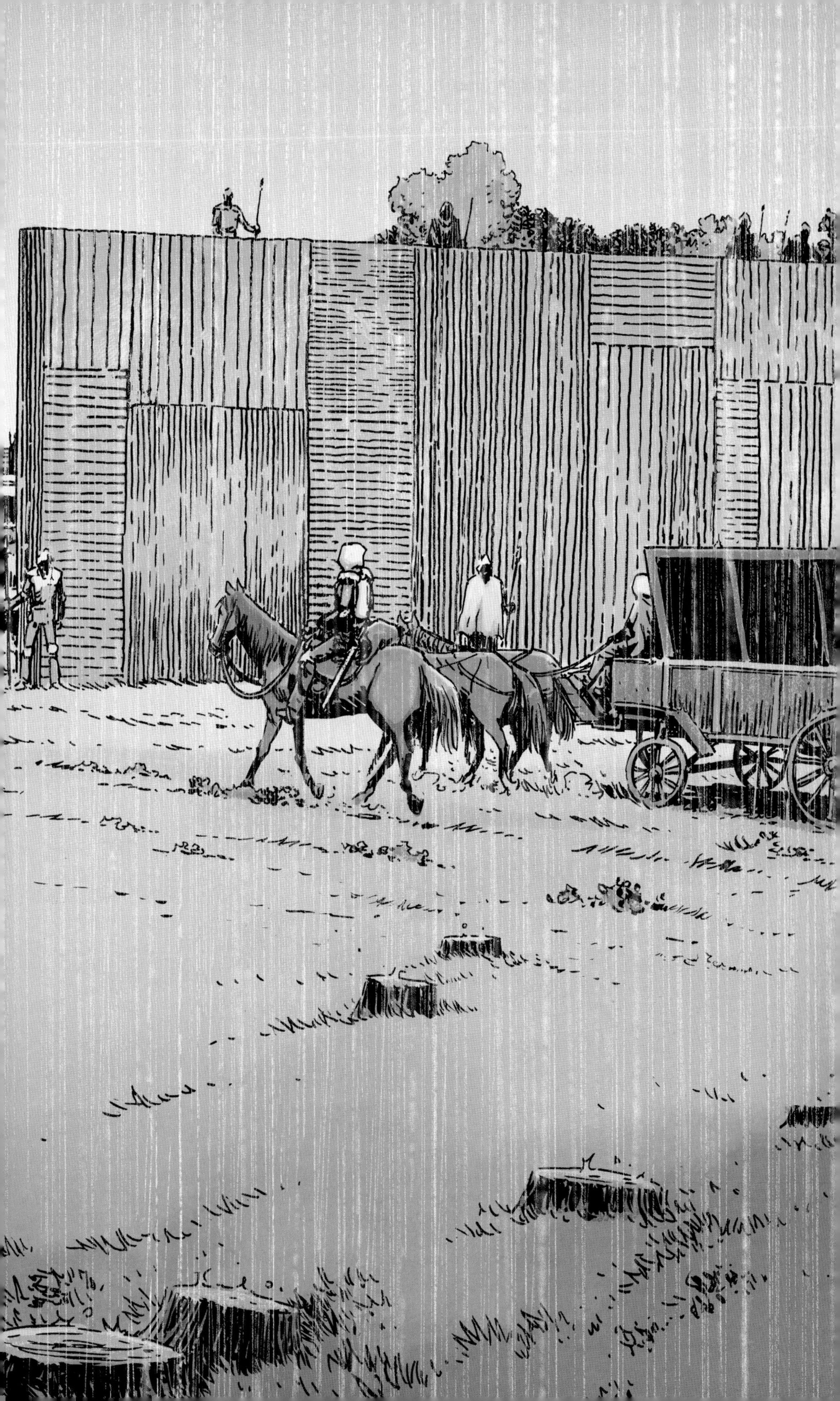

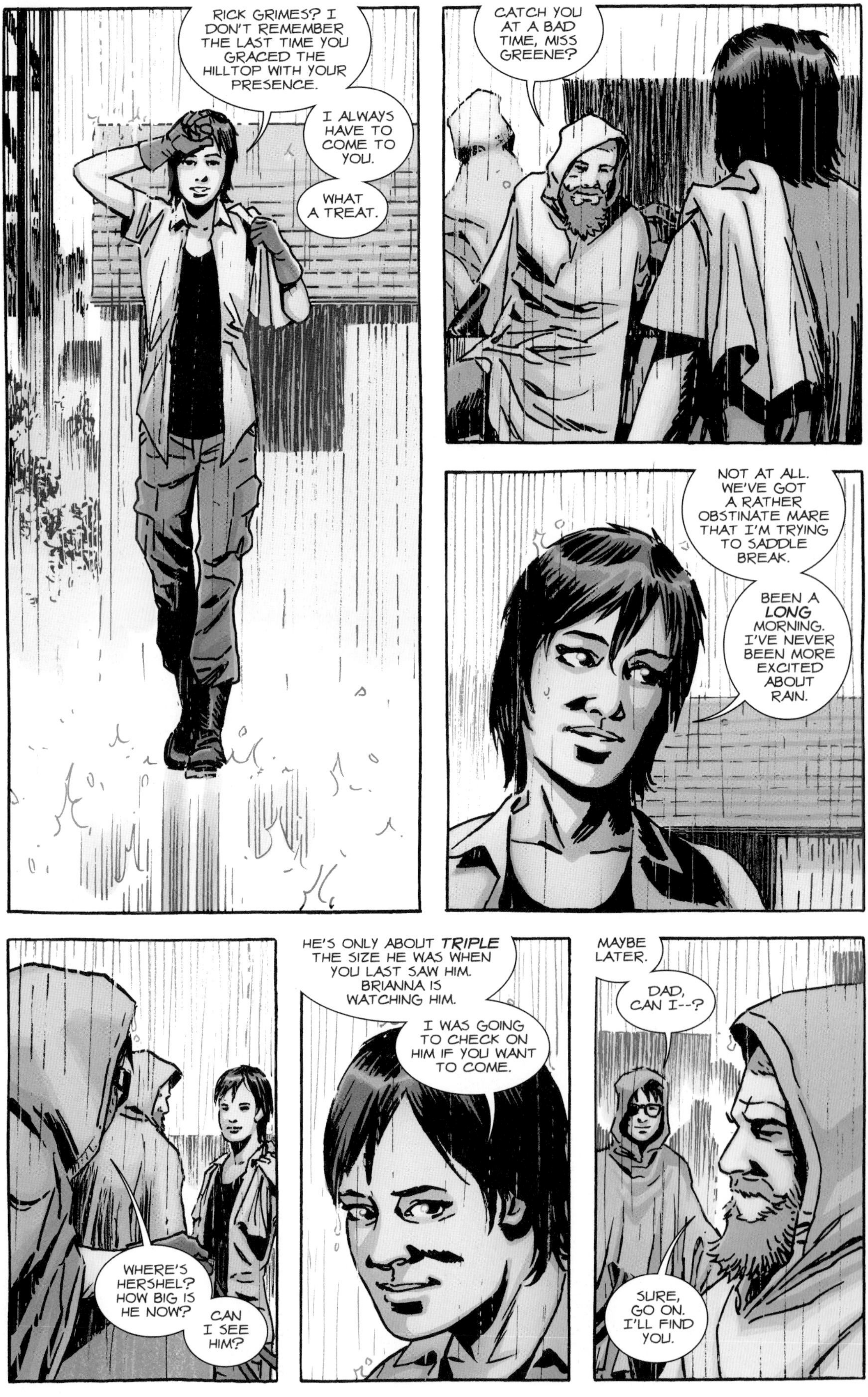
RICK GRIMES? I DON'T REMEMBER THE LAST TIME YOU GRACED THE HILLTOP WITH YOUR PRESENCE.
I ALWAYS HAVE TO COME TO YOU.
WHAT A TREAT.
CATCH YOU AT A BAD TIME, MISS GREENE?
NOT AT ALL. WE'VE GOT A RATHER OBSTINATE MARE THAT I'M TRYING TO SADDLE BREAK.
BEEN A *LONG* MORNING. I'VE NEVER BEEN MORE EXCITED ABOUT RAIN.
WHERE'S HERSHEL? HOW BIG IS HE NOW?
CAN I SEE HIM?
HE'S ONLY ABOUT *TRIPLE* THE SIZE HE WAS WHEN YOU LAST SAW HIM. BRIANNA IS WATCHING HIM.
I WAS GOING TO CHECK ON HIM IF YOU WANT TO COME.
DAD, CAN I--?
SURE, GO ON. I'LL FIND YOU.
MAYBE LATER.

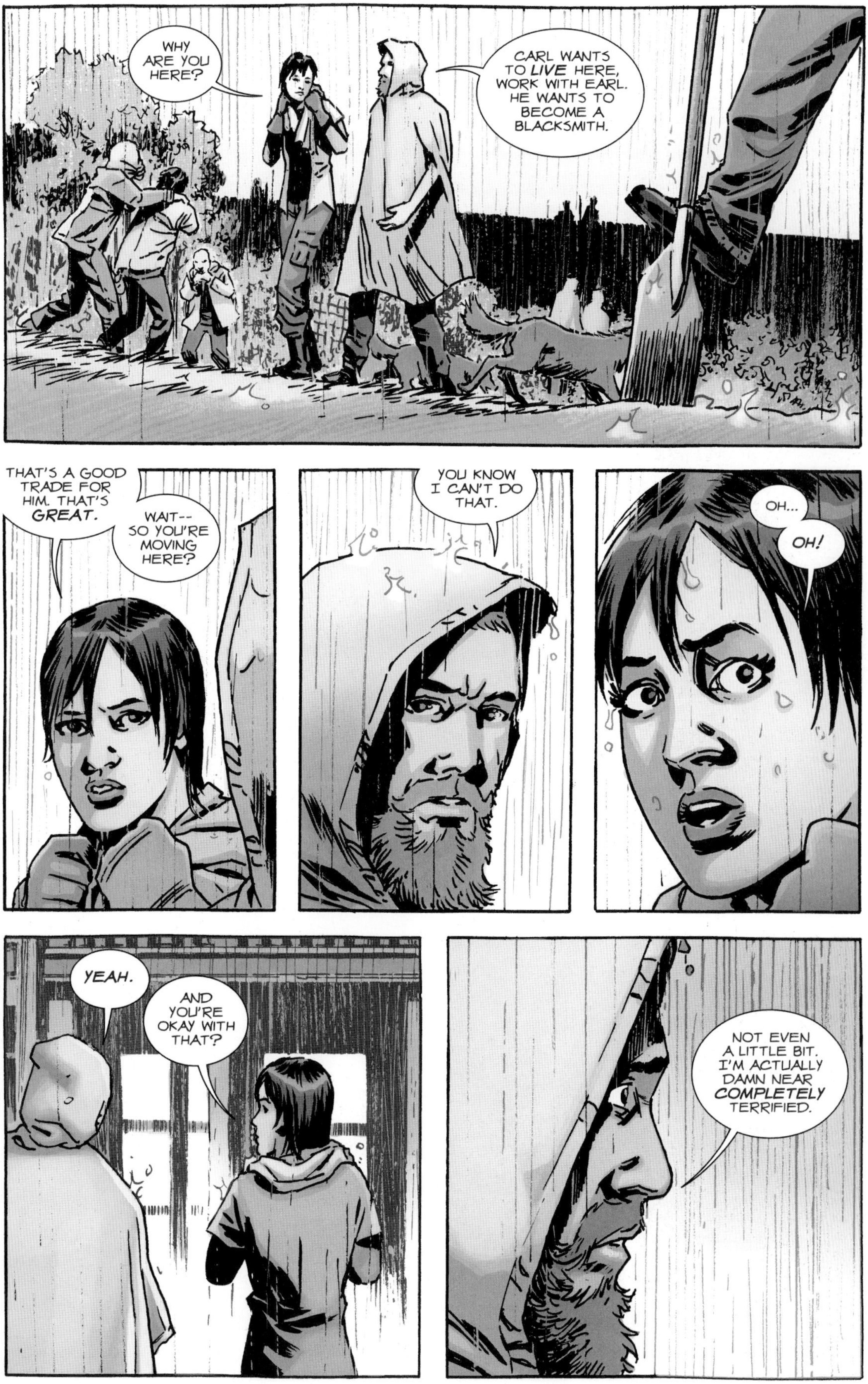
WHY ARE YOU HERE?
CARL WANTS TO LIVE HERE, WORK WITH EARL. HE WANTS TO BECOME A BLACKSMITH.
THAT'S A GOOD TRADE FOR HIM. THAT'S GREAT.
WAIT-- SO YOU'RE MOVING HERE?
YOU KNOW I CAN'T DO THAT.
OH...
OH!
YEAH.
AND YOU'RE OKAY WITH THAT?
NOT EVEN A LITTLE BIT. I'M ACTUALLY DAMN NEAR COMPLETELY TERRIFIED.

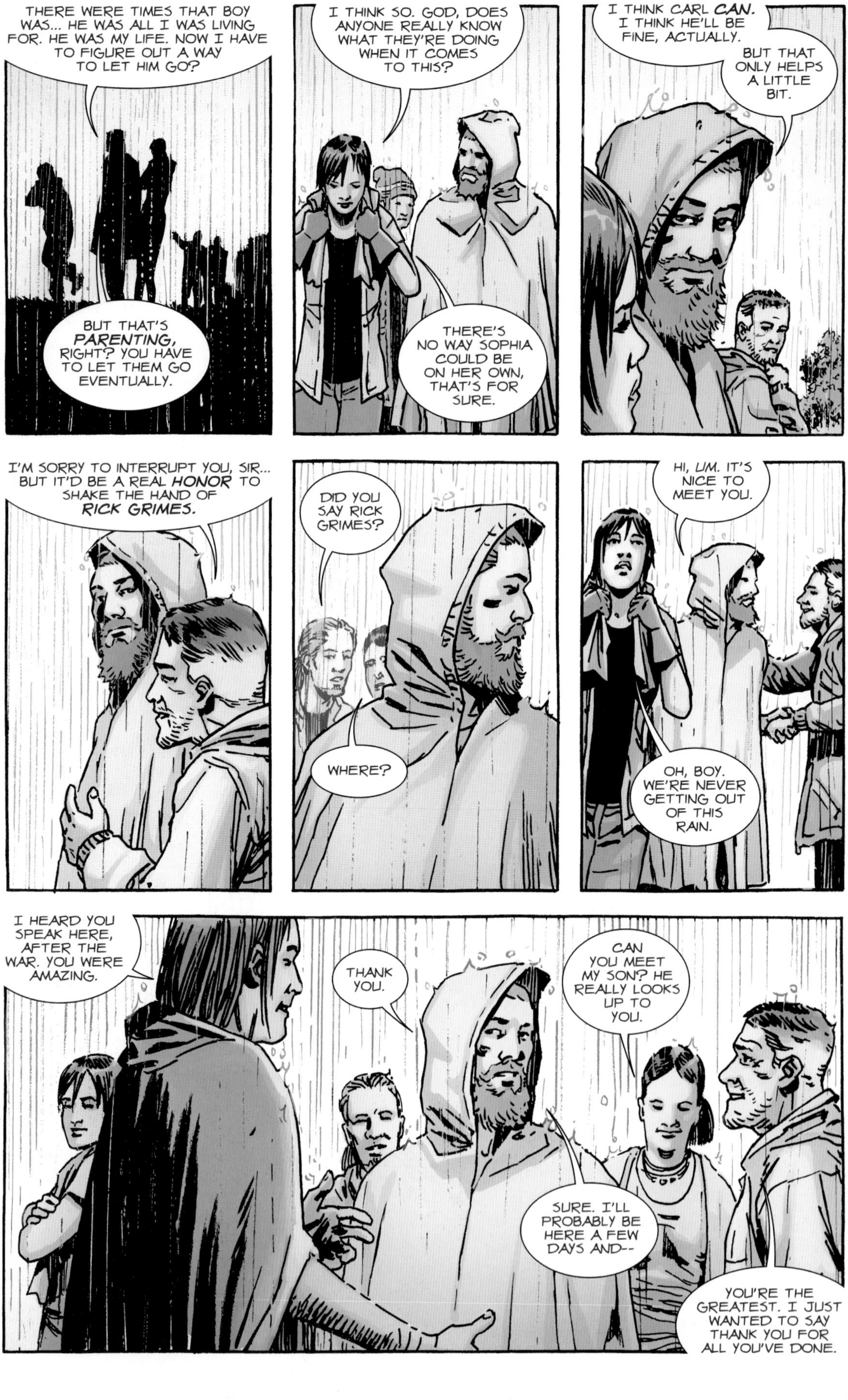
THERE WERE TIMES THAT BOY WAS... HE WAS ALL I WAS LIVING FOR. HE WAS MY LIFE. NOW I HAVE TO FIGURE OUT A WAY TO LET HIM GO?
BUT THAT'S *PARENTING,* RIGHT? YOU HAVE TO LET THEM GO EVENTUALLY.
I THINK SO. GOD, DOES ANYONE REALLY KNOW WHAT THEY'RE DOING WHEN IT COMES TO THIS?
THERE'S NO WAY SOPHIA COULD BE ON HER OWN, THAT'S FOR SURE.
I THINK CARL **CAN.** I THINK HE'LL BE FINE, ACTUALLY.
BUT THAT ONLY HELPS A LITTLE BIT.
I'M SORRY TO INTERRUPT YOU, SIR... BUT IT'D BE A REAL *HONOR* TO SHAKE THE HAND OF *RICK GRIMES.*
DID YOU SAY RICK GRIMES?
WHERE?
HI, *UM.* IT'S NICE TO MEET YOU.
OH, BOY. WE'RE NEVER GETTING OUT OF THIS RAIN.
I HEARD YOU SPEAK HERE, AFTER THE WAR. YOU WERE AMAZING.
THANK YOU.
CAN YOU MEET MY SON? HE REALLY LOOKS UP TO YOU.
SURE. I'LL PROBABLY BE HERE A FEW DAYS AND--
YOU'RE THE GREATEST. I JUST WANTED TO SAY THANK YOU FOR ALL YOU'VE DONE.

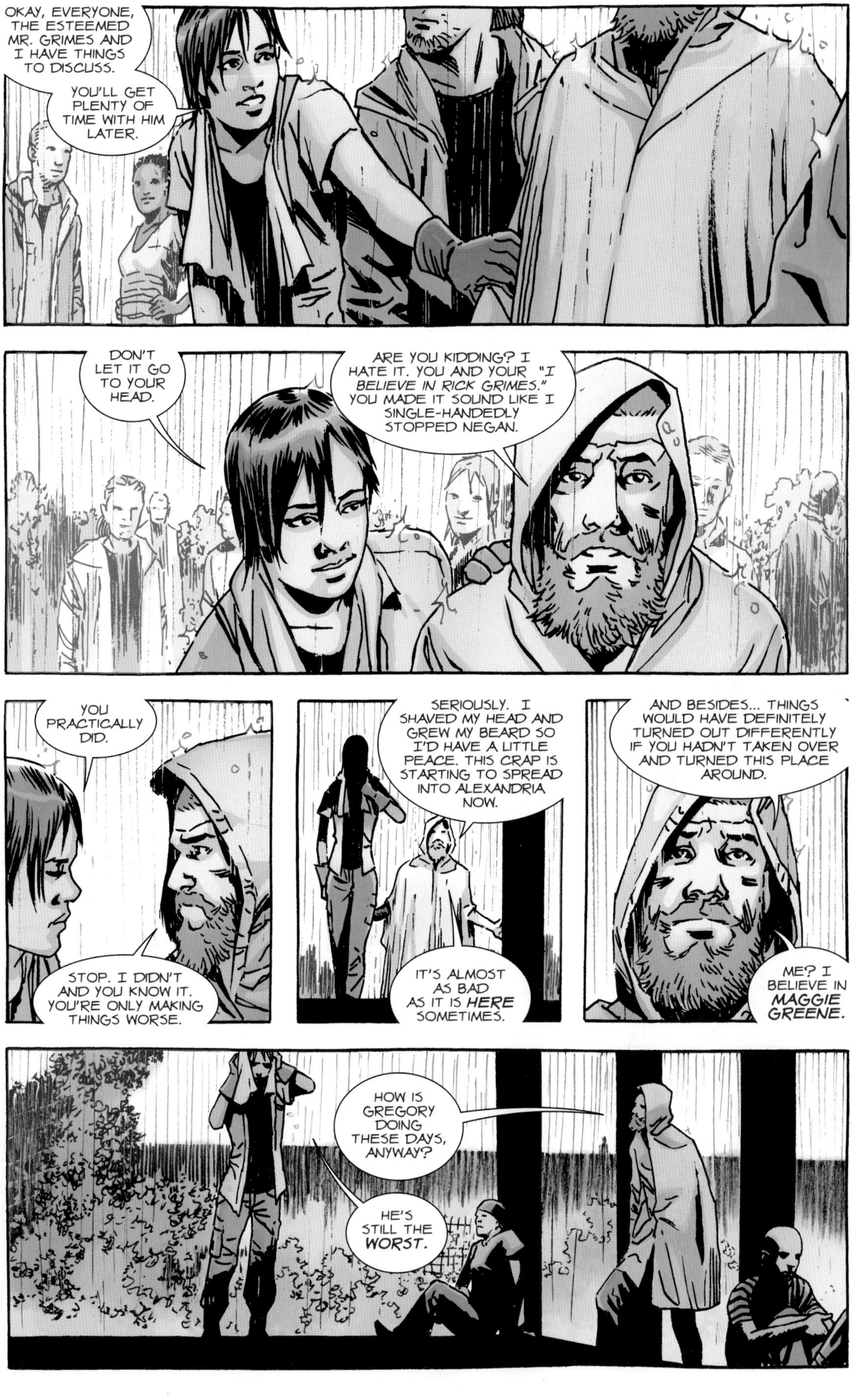
OKAY, EVERYONE, THE ESTEEMED MR. GRIMES AND I HAVE THINGS TO DISCUSS.
YOU'LL GET PLENTY OF TIME WITH HIM LATER.
DON'T LET IT GO TO YOUR HEAD.
ARE YOU KIDDING? I HATE IT. YOU AND YOUR "I BELIEVE IN RICK GRIMES." YOU MADE IT SOUND LIKE I SINGLE-HANDEDLY STOPPED NEGAN.
YOU PRACTICALLY DID.
STOP. I DIDN'T AND YOU KNOW IT. YOU'RE ONLY MAKING THINGS WORSE.
SERIOUSLY. I SHAVED MY HEAD AND GREW MY BEARD SO I'D HAVE A LITTLE PEACE. THIS CRAP IS STARTING TO SPREAD INTO ALEXANDRIA NOW.
IT'S ALMOST AS BAD AS IT IS HERE SOMETIMES.
AND BESIDES... THINGS WOULD HAVE DEFINITELY TURNED OUT DIFFERENTLY IF YOU HADN'T TAKEN OVER AND TURNED THIS PLACE AROUND.
ME? I BELIEVE IN MAGGIE GREENE.
HOW IS GREGORY DOING THESE DAYS, ANYWAY?
HE'S STILL THE WORST.

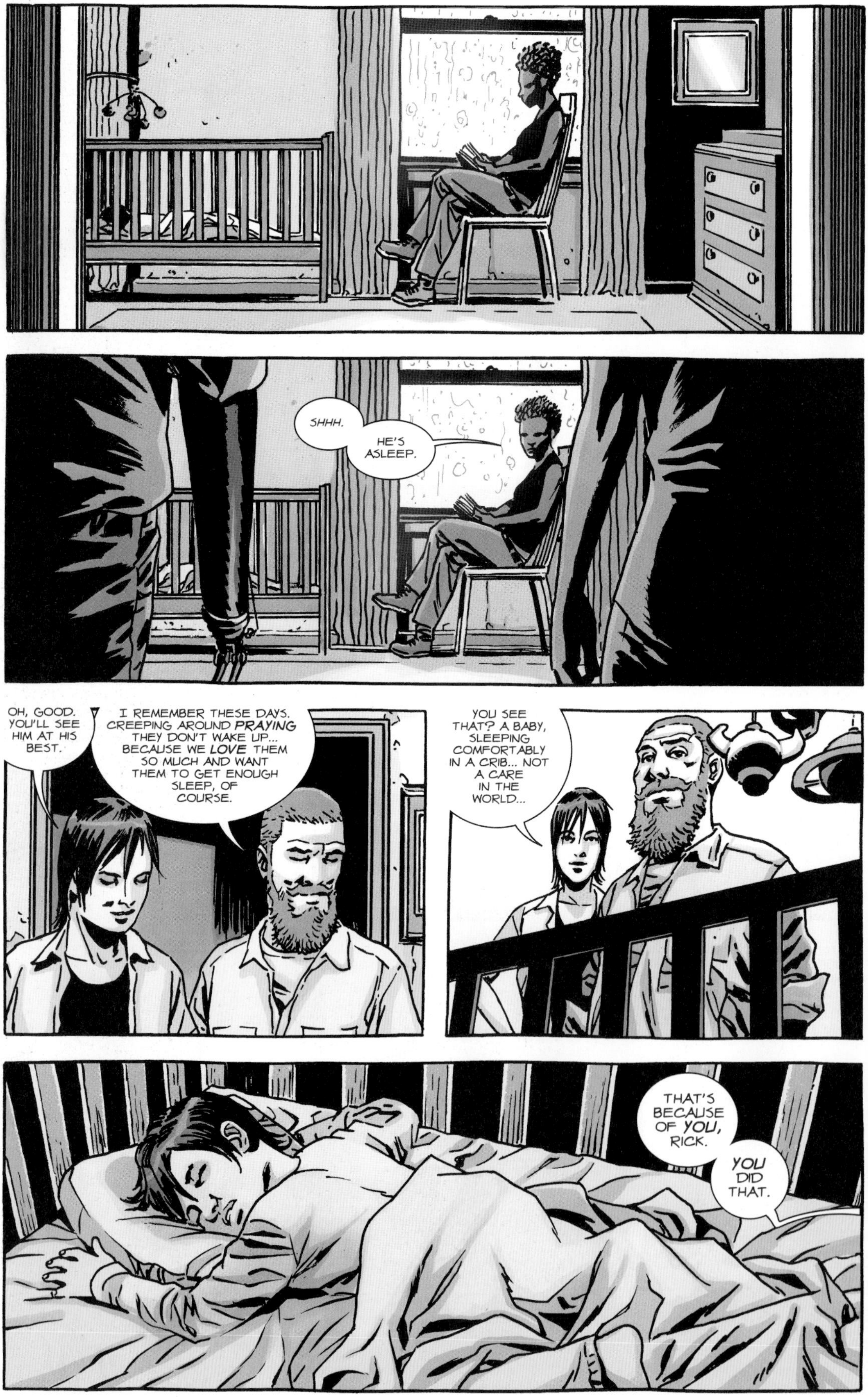
SHHH.
HE'S ASLEEP.
OH, GOOD. YOU'LL SEE HIM AT HIS BEST.
I REMEMBER THESE DAYS. CREEPING AROUND PRAYING THEY DON'T WAKE UP... BECAUSE WE LOVE THEM SO MUCH AND WANT THEM TO GET ENOUGH SLEEP, OF COURSE.
YOU SEE THAT? A BABY, SLEEPING COMFORTABLY IN A CRIB... NOT A CARE IN THE WORLD...
THAT'S BECAUSE OF YOU, RICK.
YOU DID THAT.

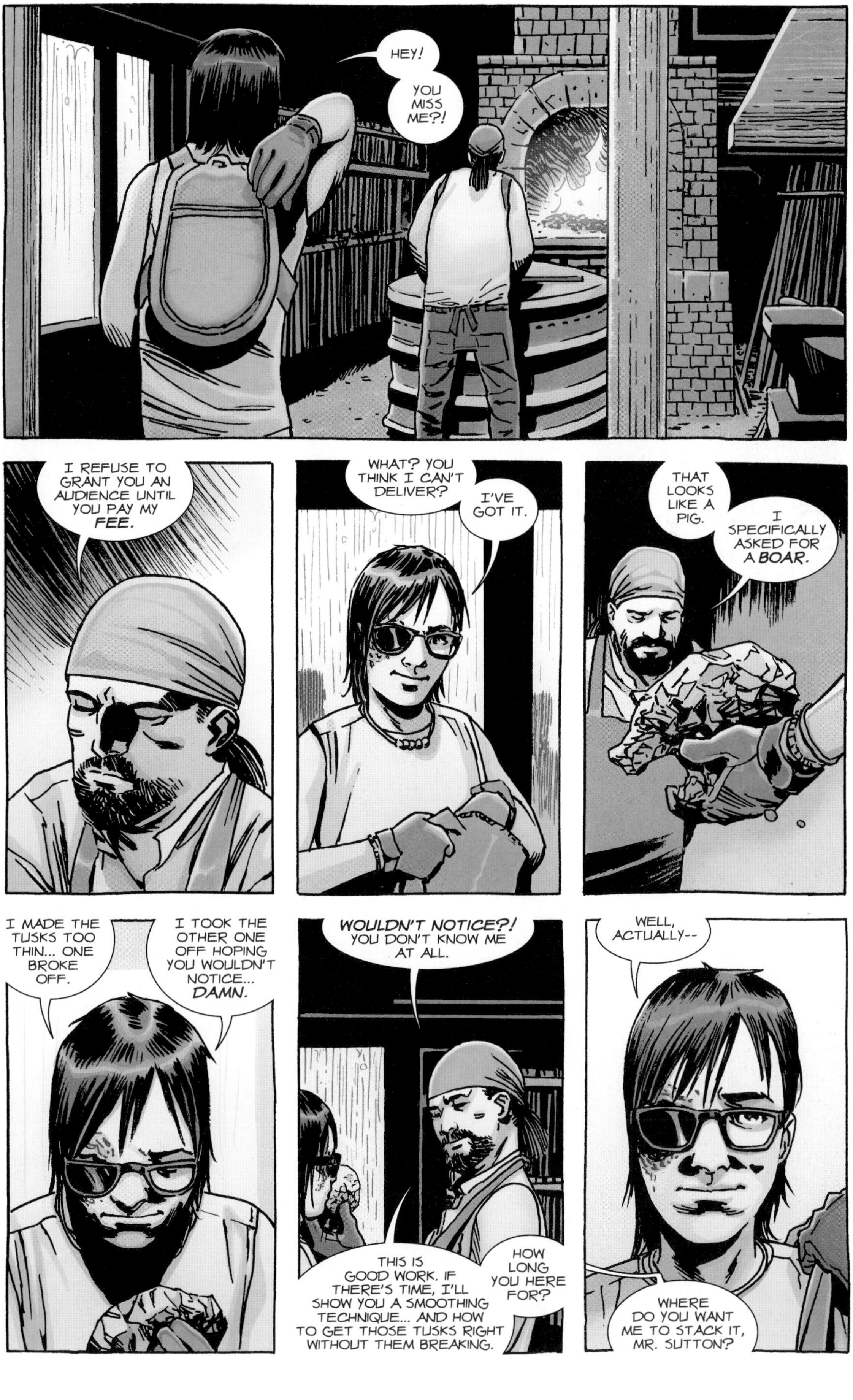
HEY!
YOU MISS ME?!
I REFUSE TO GRANT YOU AN AUDIENCE UNTIL YOU PAY MY FEE.
WHAT? YOU THINK I CAN'T DELIVER?
I'VE GOT IT.
THAT LOOKS LIKE A PIG.
I SPECIFICALLY ASKED FOR A BOAR.
I MADE THE TUSKS TOO THIN... ONE BROKE OFF.
I TOOK THE OTHER ONE OFF HOPING YOU WOULDN'T NOTICE... DAMN.
WOULDN'T NOTICE?! YOU DON'T KNOW ME AT ALL.
THIS IS GOOD WORK. IF THERE'S TIME, I'LL SHOW YOU A SMOOTHING TECHNIQUE... AND HOW TO GET THOSE TUSKS RIGHT WITHOUT THEM BREAKING.
HOW LONG YOU HERE FOR?
WELL, ACTUALLY--
WHERE DO YOU WANT ME TO STACK IT, MR. SUTTON?

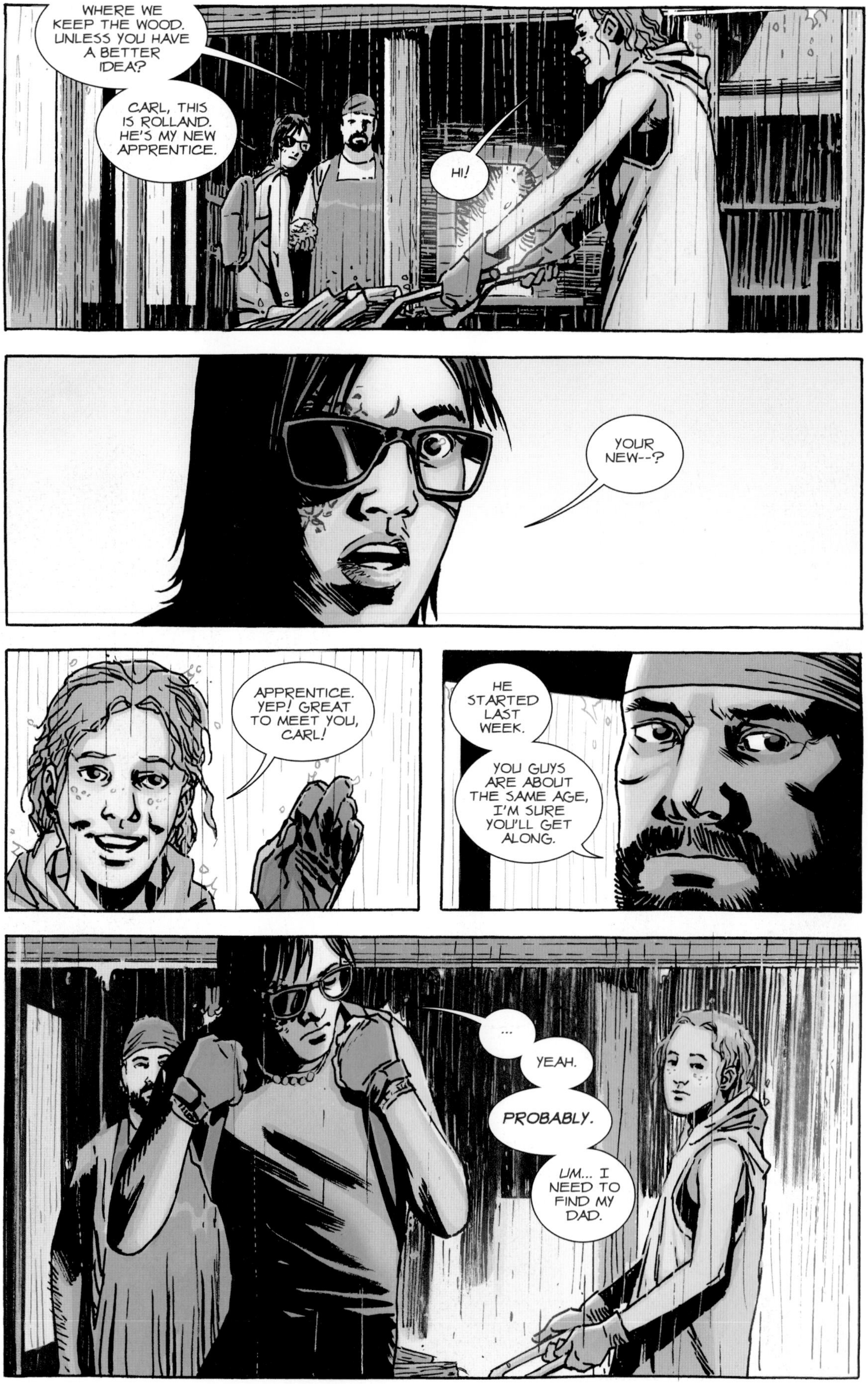
WHERE WE KEEP THE WOOD. UNLESS YOU HAVE A BETTER IDEA?
CARL, THIS IS ROLLAND. HE'S MY NEW APPRENTICE.
HI!
YOUR NEW--?
APPRENTICE. YEP! GREAT TO MEET YOU, CARL!
HE STARTED LAST WEEK.
YOU GUYS ARE ABOUT THE SAME AGE, I'M SURE YOU'LL GET ALONG.
...
YEAH.
PROBABLY.
UM... I NEED TO FIND MY DAD.

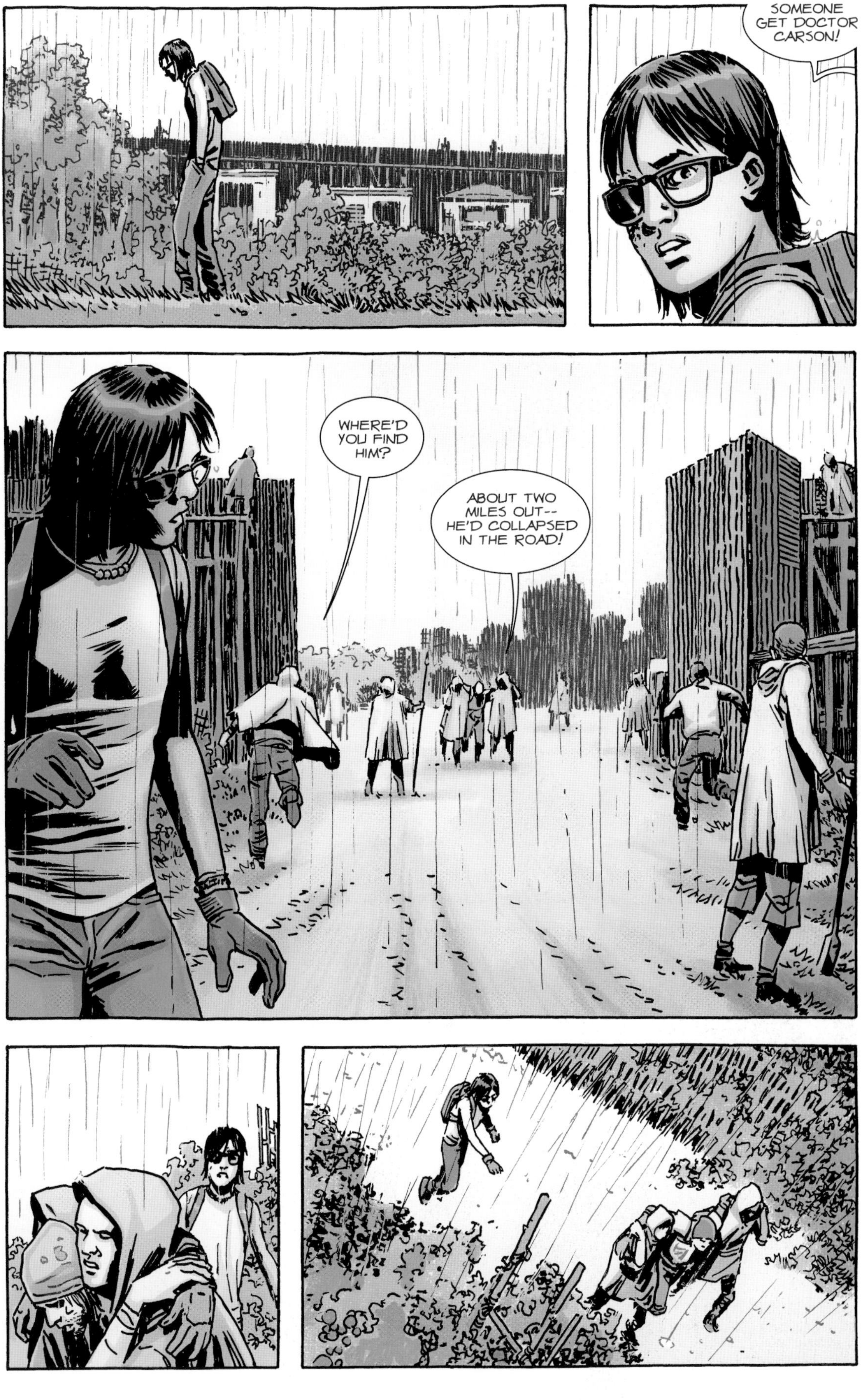
SOMEONE GET DOCTOR CARSON!
WHERE'D YOU FIND HIM?
ABOUT TWO MILES OUT-- HE'D COLLAPSED IN THE ROAD!

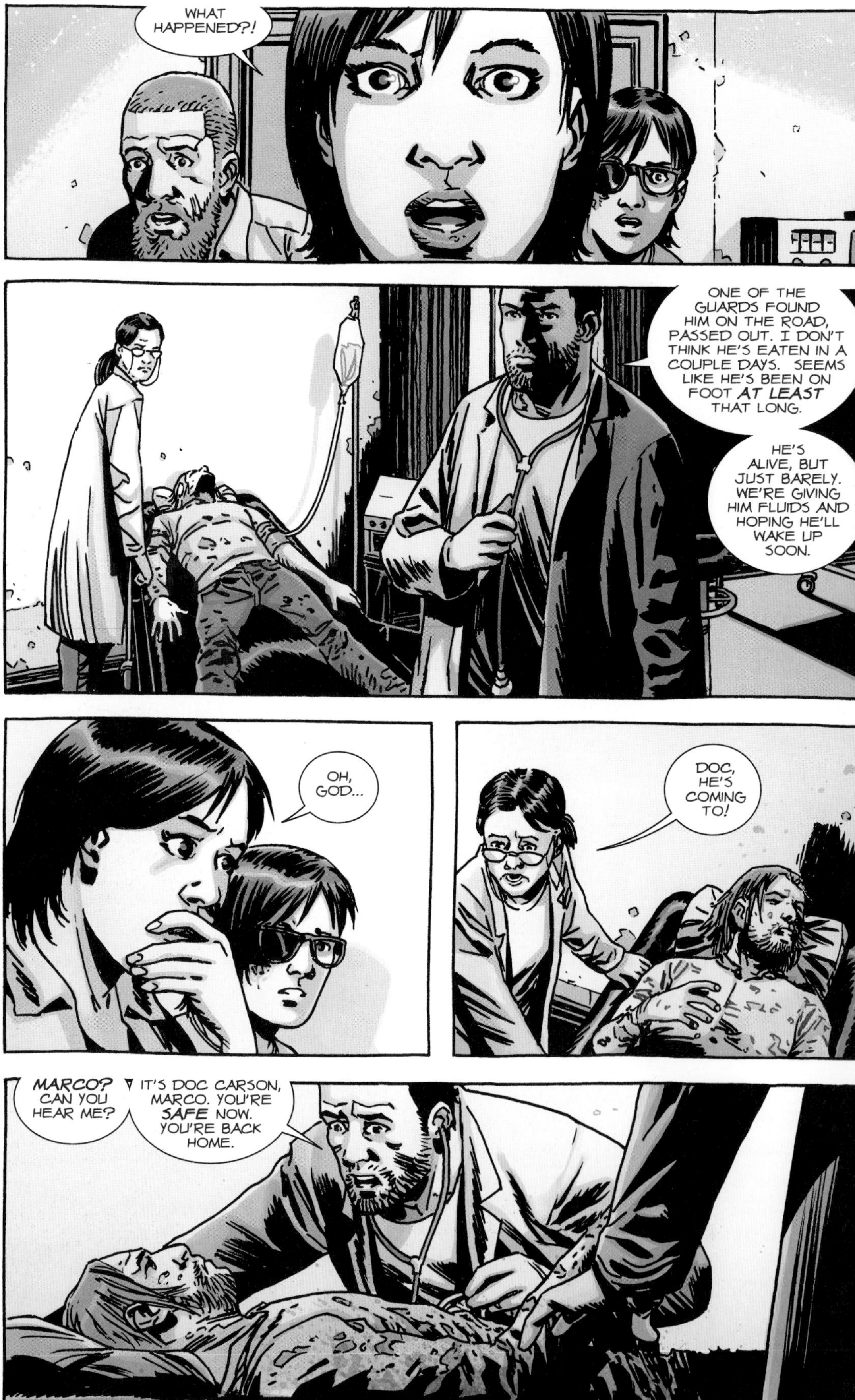
WHAT HAPPENED?!
ONE OF THE GUARDS FOUND HIM ON THE ROAD, PASSED OUT. I DON'T THINK HE'S EATEN IN A COUPLE DAYS. SEEMS LIKE HE'S BEEN ON FOOT AT LEAST THAT LONG.
HE'S ALIVE, BUT JUST BARELY. WE'RE GIVING HIM FLUIDS AND HOPING HE'LL WAKE UP SOON.
OH, GOD...
DOC, HE'S COMING TO!
MARCO? CAN YOU HEAR ME?
IT'S DOC CARSON, MARCO. YOU'RE SAFE NOW. YOU'RE BACK HOME.

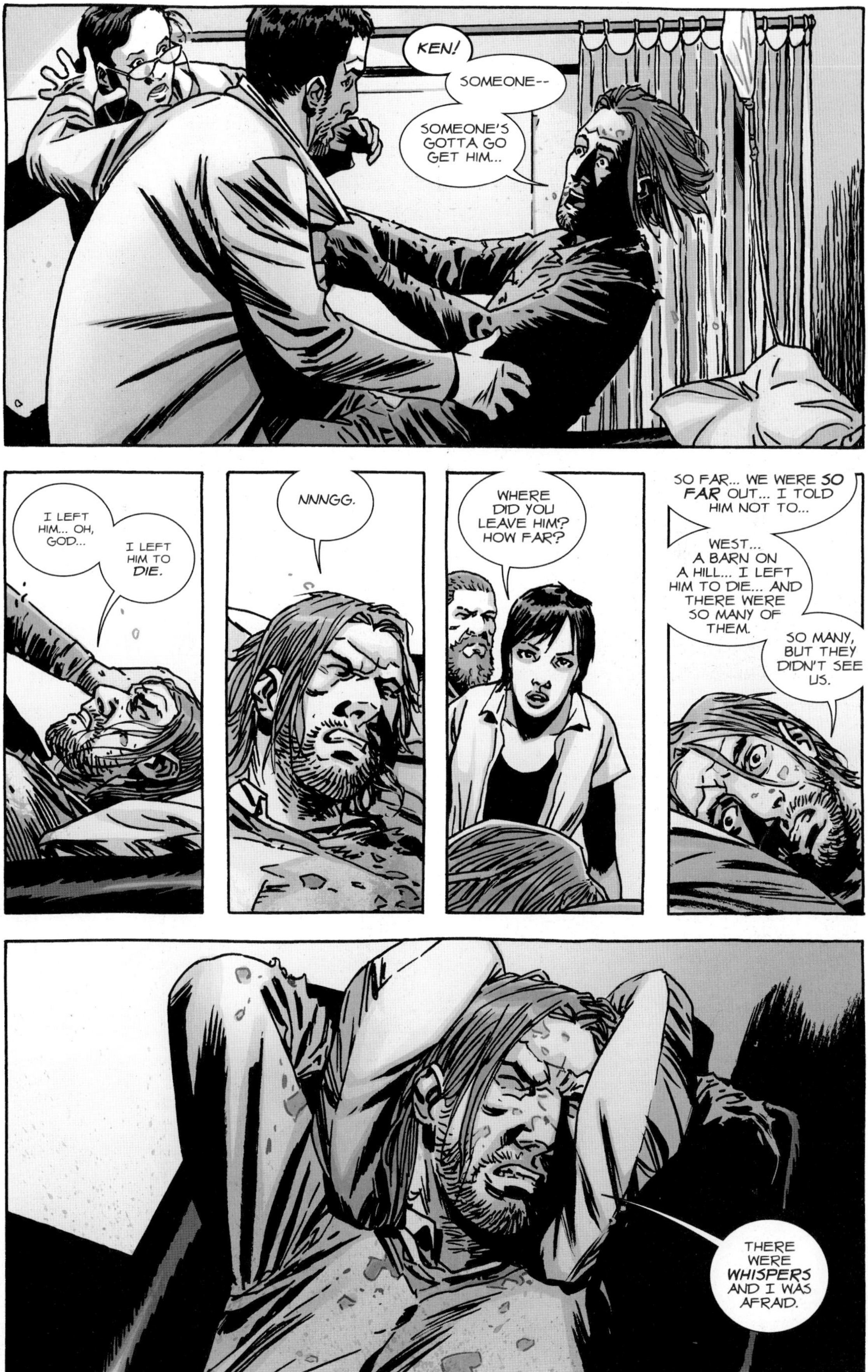
KEN!
SOMEONE--
SOMEONE'S GOTTA GO GET HIM...
I LEFT HIM... OH, GOD...
I LEFT HIM TO DIE.
NNNGG.
WHERE DID YOU LEAVE HIM? HOW FAR?
SO FAR... WE WERE SO FAR OUT... I TOLD HIM NOT TO...
WEST... A BARN ON A HILL... I LEFT HIM TO DIE... AND THERE WERE SO MANY OF THEM.
SO MANY, BUT THEY DIDN'T SEE US.
THERE WERE WHISPERS AND I WAS AFRAID.

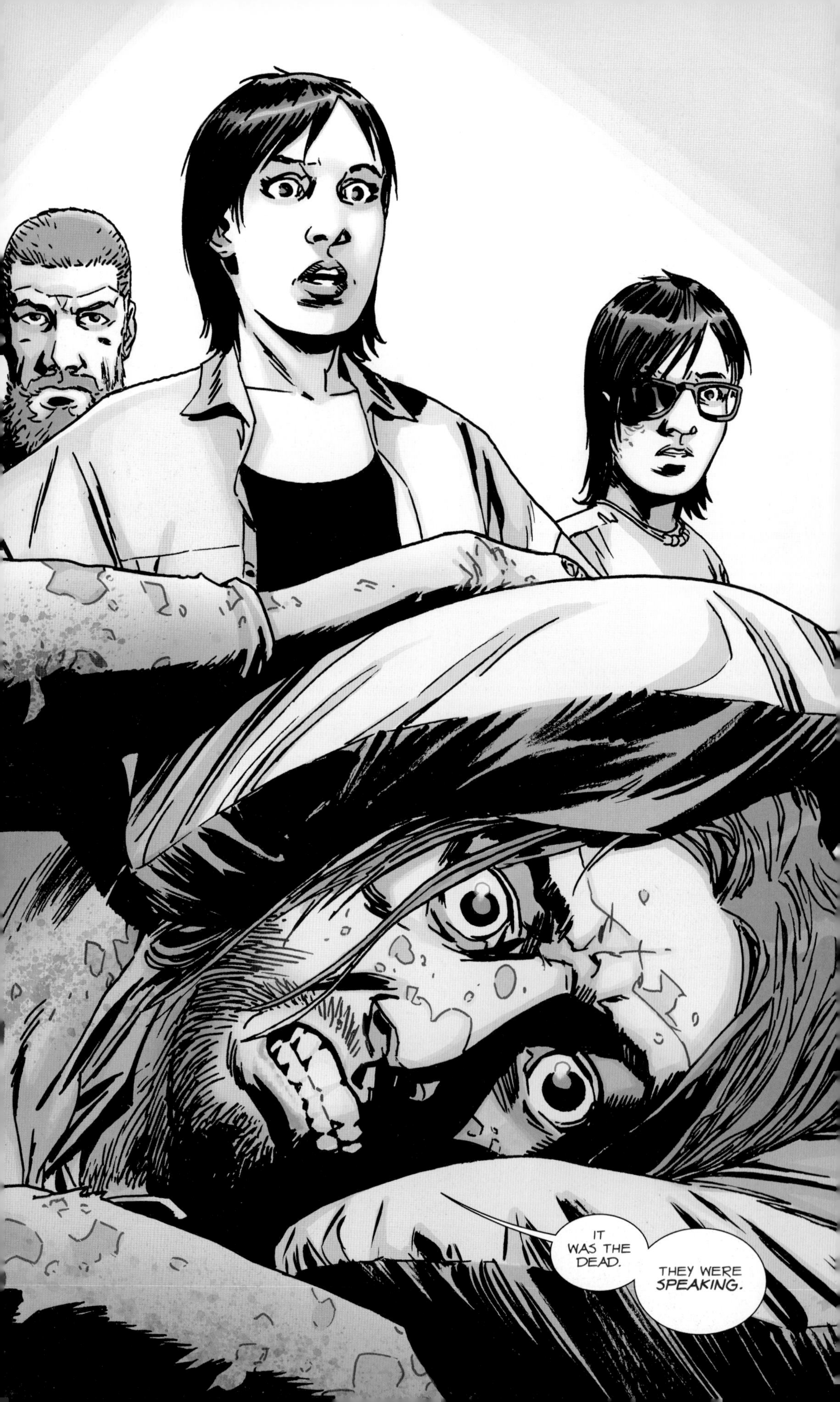

IT WAS THE DEAD.
THEY WERE *SPEAKING.*

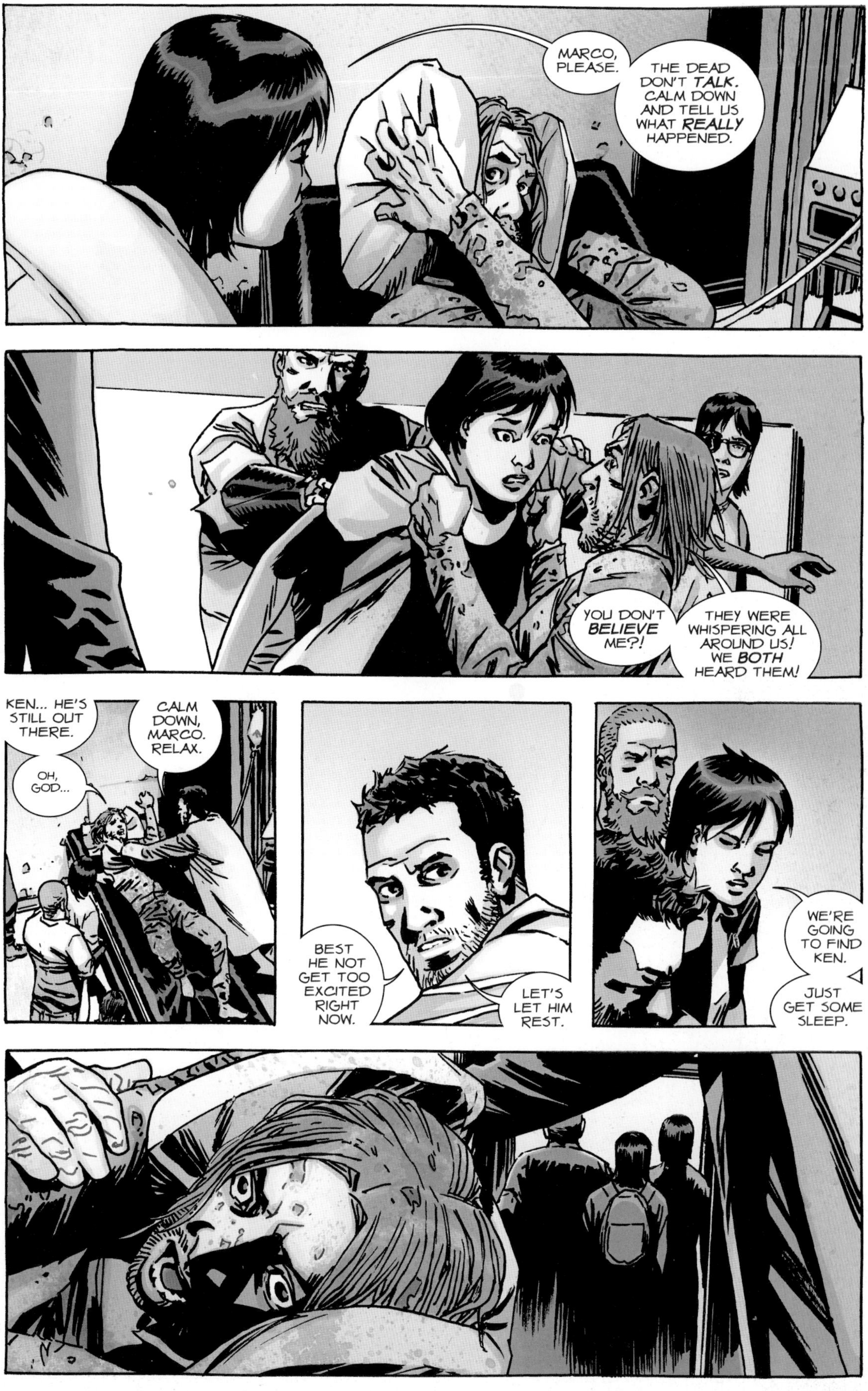

MARCO, PLEASE.
THE DEAD DON'T TALK. CALM DOWN AND TELL US WHAT REALLY HAPPENED.
YOU DON'T BELIEVE ME?!
THEY WERE WHISPERING ALL AROUND US! WE BOTH HEARD THEM!
KEN... HE'S STILL OUT THERE.
CALM DOWN, MARCO. RELAX.
OH, GOD...
BEST HE NOT GET TOO EXCITED RIGHT NOW.
LET'S LET HIM REST.
WE'RE GOING TO FIND KEN.
JUST GET SOME SLEEP.

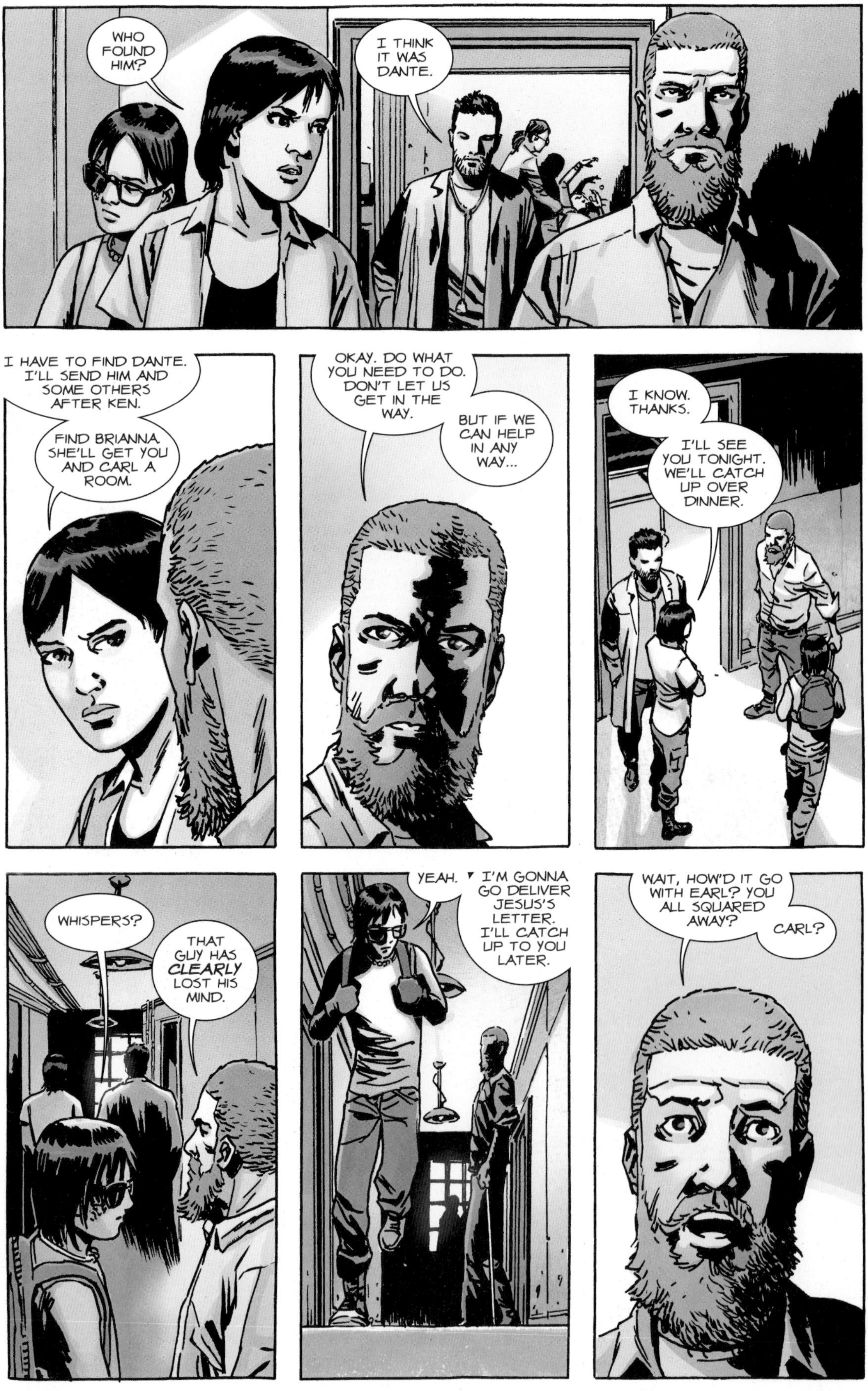
WHO FOUND HIM?
I THINK IT WAS DANTE.
I HAVE TO FIND DANTE. I'LL SEND HIM AND SOME OTHERS AFTER KEN.
FIND BRIANNA. SHE'LL GET YOU AND CARL A ROOM.
OKAY. DO WHAT YOU NEED TO DO. DON'T LET US GET IN THE WAY.
BUT IF WE CAN HELP IN ANY WAY...
I KNOW. THANKS.
I'LL SEE YOU TONIGHT. WE'LL CATCH UP OVER DINNER.
WHISPERS?
THAT GUY HAS CLEARLY LOST HIS MIND.
YEAH.
I'M GONNA GO DELIVER JESUS'S LETTER. I'LL CATCH UP TO YOU LATER.
WAIT, HOW'D IT GO WITH EARL? YOU ALL SQUARED AWAY?
CARL?

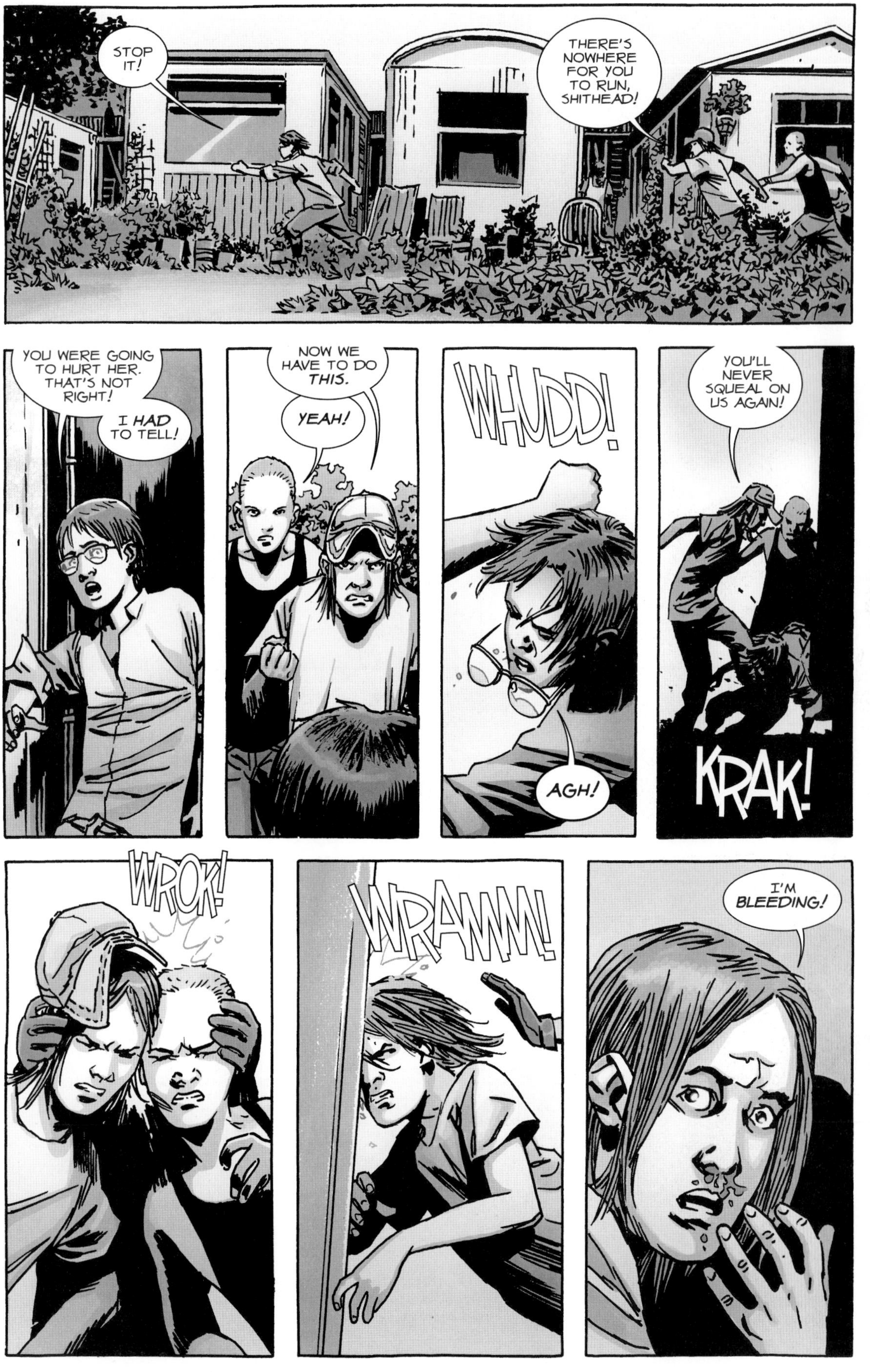
STOP IT!
THERE'S NOWHERE FOR YOU TO RUN, SHITHEAD!
YOU WERE GOING TO HURT HER. THAT'S NOT RIGHT!
I HAD TO TELL!
NOW WE HAVE TO DO THIS.
YEAH!
WHUDD!
AGH!
YOU'LL NEVER SQUEAL ON US AGAIN!
KRAK!
WROK!
WRAMM!
I'M BLEEDING!

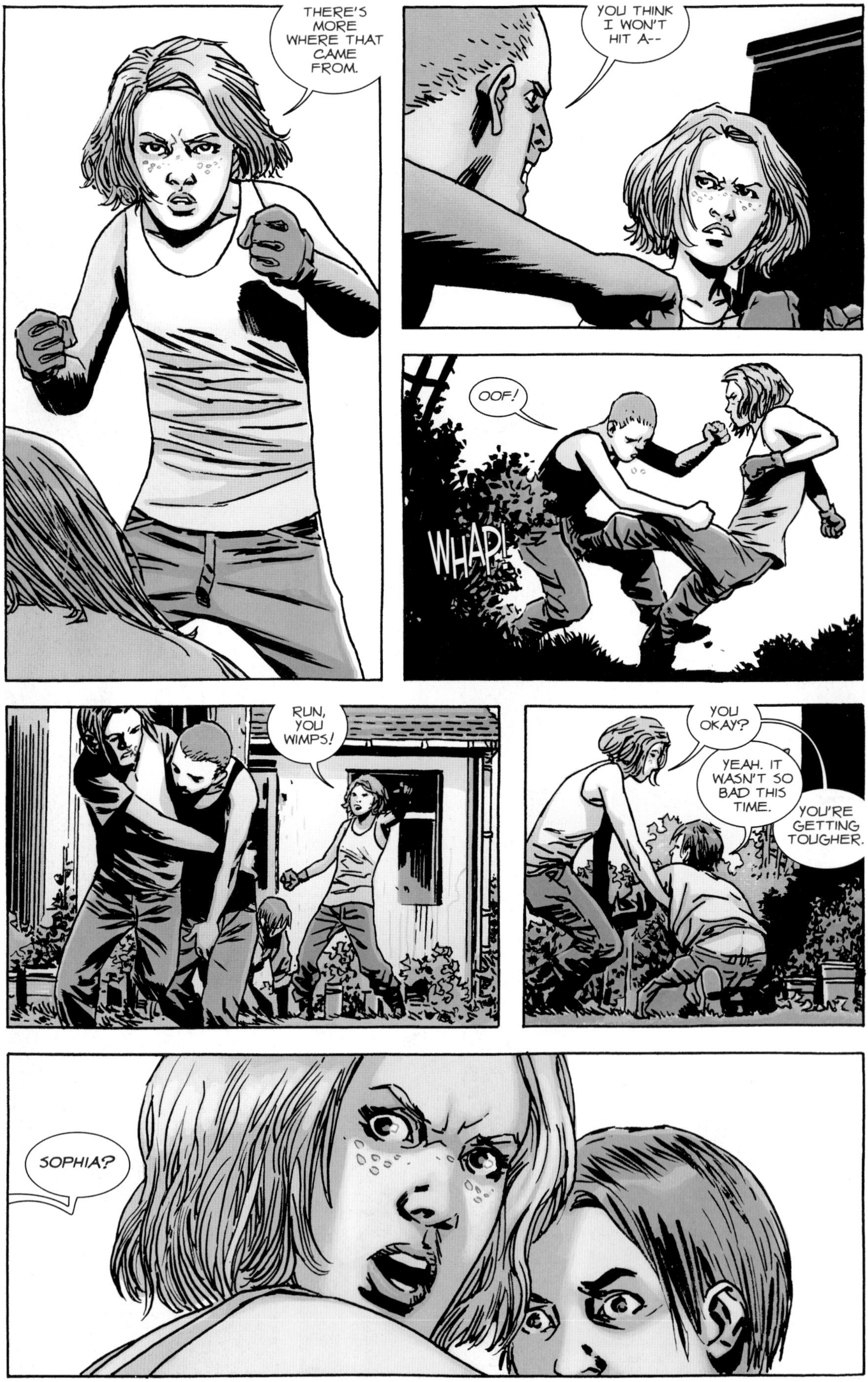
THERE'S MORE WHERE THAT CAME FROM.
YOU THINK I WON'T HIT A--
OOF!
WHAP!
RUN, YOU WIMPS!
YOU OKAY?
YEAH. IT WASN'T SO BAD THIS TIME.
YOU'RE GETTING TOUGHER.
SOPHIA?

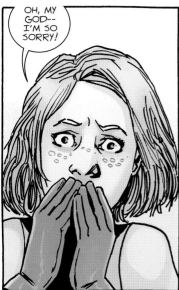

OH, MY GOD-- I'M SO SORRY!

NICE TO SEE *YOU*, TOO.

CRAP, I THOUGHT YOU WERE... I'M SORRY.

IT'S OKAY... IT'S NOT LIKE I'VE ONLY GOT ONE GOOD EYE LEFT OR ANYTHING.

OKAY... NOW YOU'RE LAYING IT ON A LITTLE THICK.

YOU SHOULD HAVE BEEN ABLE TO DODGE THAT, RIGHT? THE GREAT CARL GRIMES... *SUCKER-PUNCHED* BY A GIRL.

I'M NOT REALLY KNOWN FOR MY FISTFIGHTS.

I'M TRYING TO DELIVER A LETTER FOR A FRIEND. DO YOU KNOW WHERE ALEX LIVES?

YEAH, COME ON. THIS WAY.

CATCH YOU LATER, BRIAN.

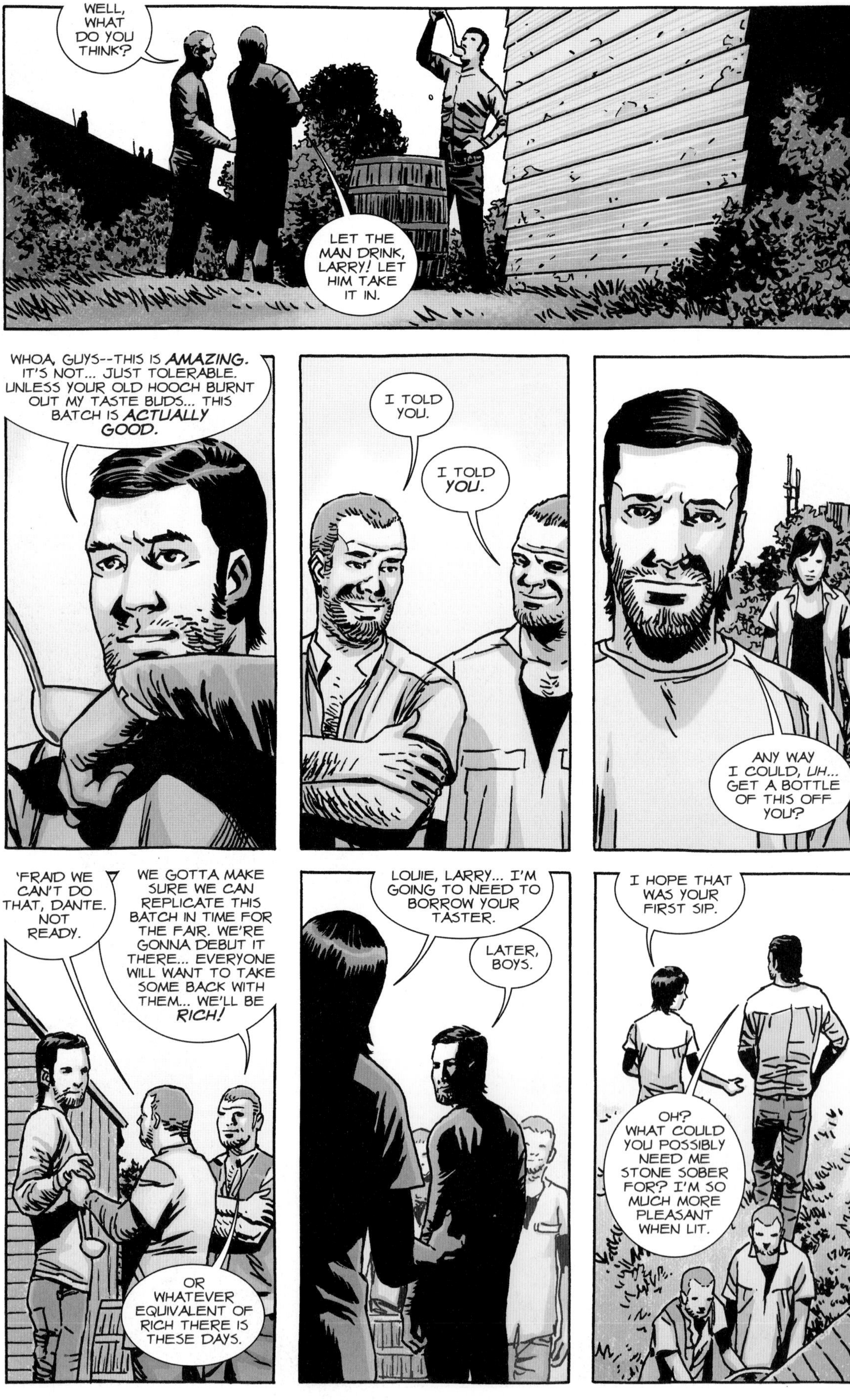
WELL, WHAT DO YOU THINK?
LET THE MAN DRINK, LARRY! LET HIM TAKE IT IN.
WHOA, GUYS--THIS IS AMAZING. IT'S NOT... JUST TOLERABLE. UNLESS YOUR OLD HOOCH BURNT OUT MY TASTE BUDS... THIS BATCH IS ACTUALLY GOOD.
I TOLD YOU.
I TOLD YOU.
ANY WAY I COULD, UH... GET A BOTTLE OF THIS OFF YOU?
'FRAID WE CAN'T DO THAT, DANTE. NOT READY.
WE GOTTA MAKE SURE WE CAN REPLICATE THIS BATCH IN TIME FOR THE FAIR. WE'RE GONNA DEBUT IT THERE... EVERYONE WILL WANT TO TAKE SOME BACK WITH THEM... WE'LL BE RICH!
OR WHATEVER EQUIVALENT OF RICH THERE IS THESE DAYS.
LOUIE, LARRY... I'M GOING TO NEED TO BORROW YOUR TASTER.
LATER, BOYS.
I HOPE THAT WAS YOUR FIRST SIP.
OH? WHAT COULD YOU POSSIBLY NEED ME STONE SOBER FOR? I'M SO MUCH MORE PLEASANT WHEN LIT.

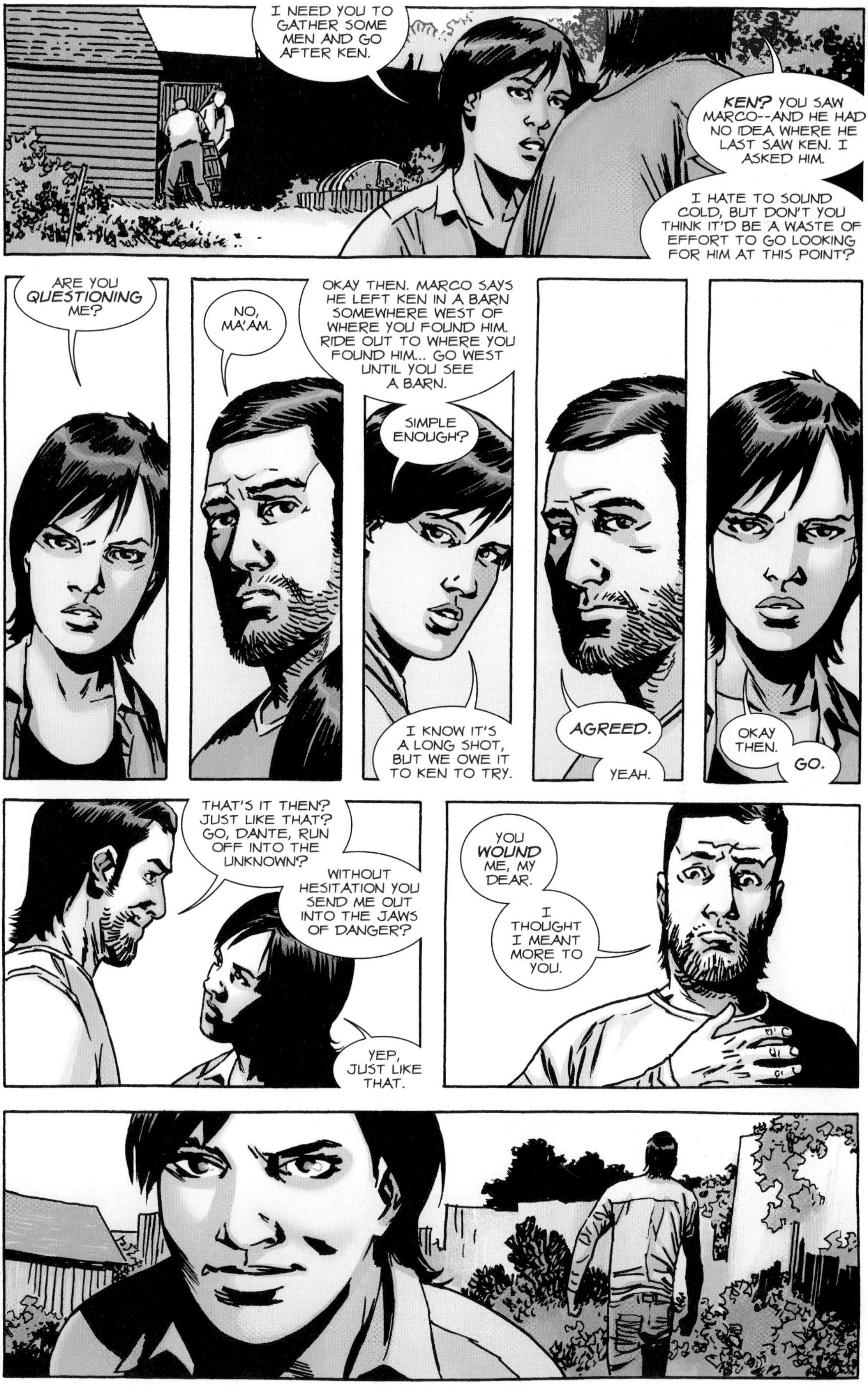
I NEED YOU TO GATHER SOME MEN AND GO AFTER KEN.
KEN? YOU SAW MARCO--AND HE HAD NO IDEA WHERE HE LAST SAW KEN. I ASKED HIM.
I HATE TO SOUND COLD, BUT DON'T YOU THINK IT'D BE A WASTE OF EFFORT TO GO LOOKING FOR HIM AT THIS POINT?
ARE YOU QUESTIONING ME?
NO, MA'AM.
OKAY THEN. MARCO SAYS HE LEFT KEN IN A BARN SOMEWHERE WEST OF WHERE YOU FOUND HIM. RIDE OUT TO WHERE YOU FOUND HIM... GO WEST UNTIL YOU SEE A BARN.
SIMPLE ENOUGH?
I KNOW IT'S A LONG SHOT, BUT WE OWE IT TO KEN TO TRY.
AGREED.
YEAH.
OKAY THEN.
GO.
THAT'S IT THEN? JUST LIKE THAT? GO, DANTE, RUN OFF INTO THE UNKNOWN?
WITHOUT HESITATION YOU SEND ME OUT INTO THE JAWS OF DANGER?
YEP, JUST LIKE THAT.
YOU WOUND ME, MY DEAR.
I THOUGHT I MEANT MORE TO YOU.

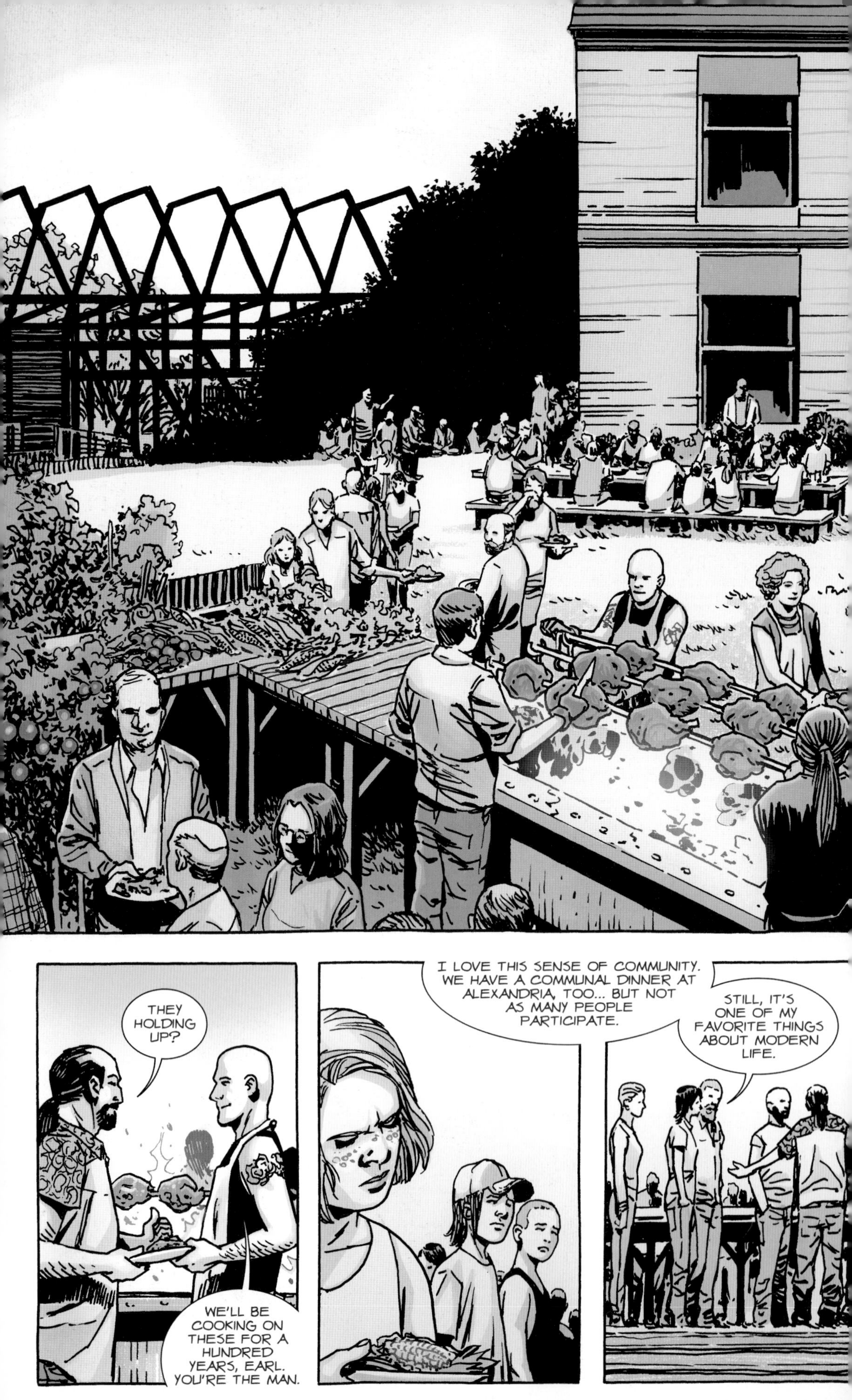
THEY HOLDING UP?
WE'LL BE COOKING ON THESE FOR A HUNDRED YEARS, EARL. YOU'RE THE MAN.
I LOVE THIS SENSE OF COMMUNITY. WE HAVE A COMMUNAL DINNER AT ALEXANDRIA, TOO... BUT NOT AS MANY PEOPLE PARTICIPATE.
STILL, IT'S ONE OF MY FAVORITE THINGS ABOUT MODERN LIFE.

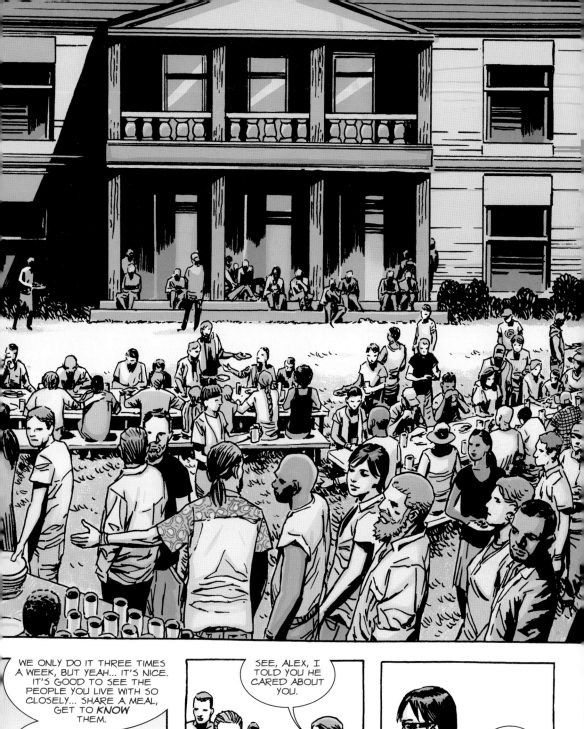

WE ONLY DO IT THREE TIMES A WEEK, BUT YEAH... IT'S NICE. IT'S GOOD TO SEE THE PEOPLE YOU LIVE WITH SO CLOSELY... SHARE A MEAL, GET TO *KNOW* THEM.

I STILL DON'T KNOW *EVERYONE* HERE. THAT BUGS ME, BUT I'LL GET THERE.

SEE, ALEX, I TOLD YOU HE CARED ABOUT YOU.

CARL?

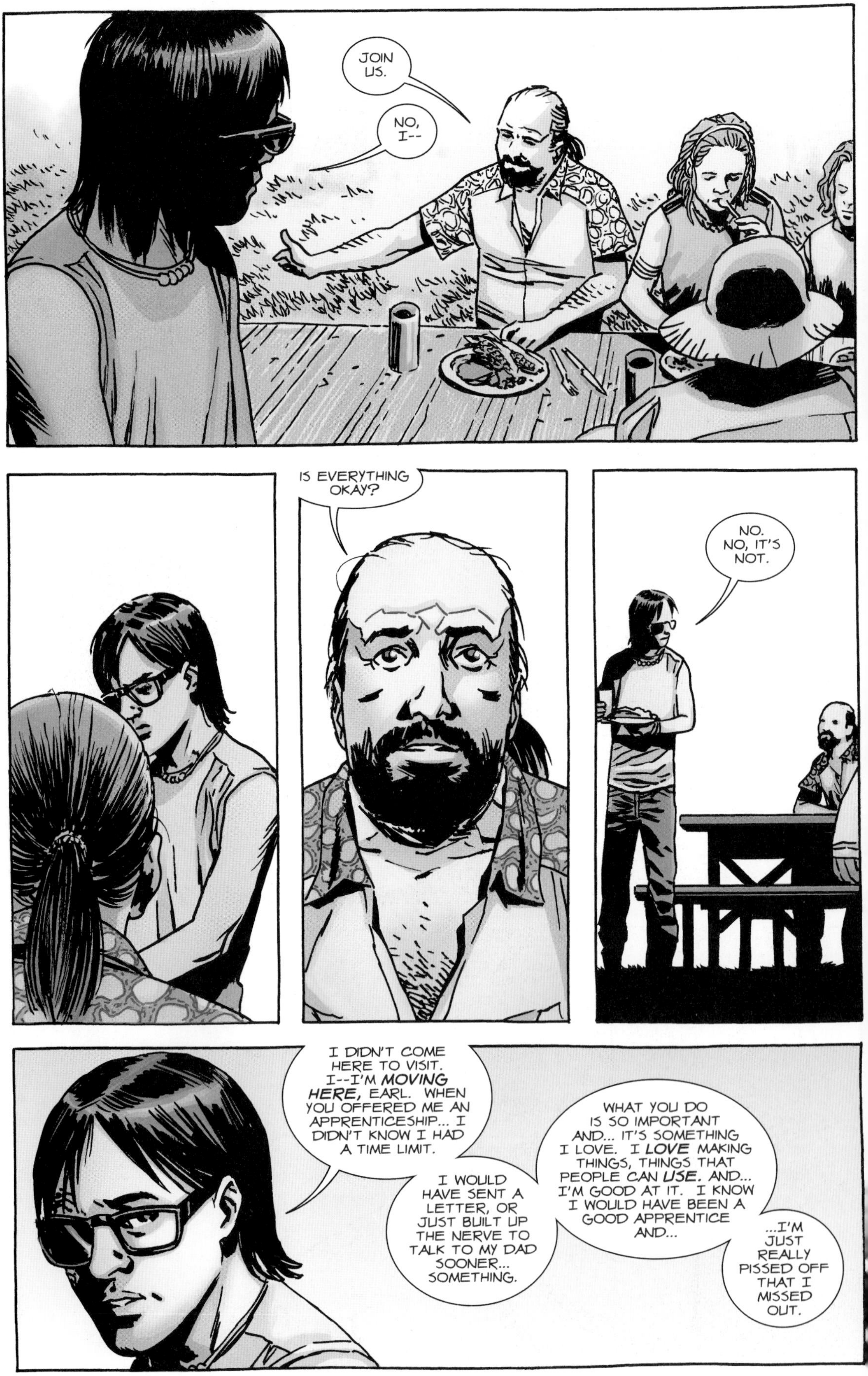
JOIN US.
NO, I--
IS EVERYTHING OKAY?
NO. NO, IT'S NOT.
I DIDN'T COME HERE TO VISIT. I--I'M MOVING HERE, EARL. WHEN YOU OFFERED ME AN APPRENTICESHIP... I DIDN'T KNOW I HAD A TIME LIMIT.
I WOULD HAVE SENT A LETTER, OR JUST BUILT UP THE NERVE TO TALK TO MY DAD SOONER... SOMETHING.
WHAT YOU DO IS SO IMPORTANT AND... IT'S SOMETHING I LOVE. I LOVE MAKING THINGS, THINGS THAT PEOPLE CAN USE. AND... I'M GOOD AT IT. I KNOW I WOULD HAVE BEEN A GOOD APPRENTICE AND...
...I'M JUST REALLY PISSED OFF THAT I MISSED OUT.

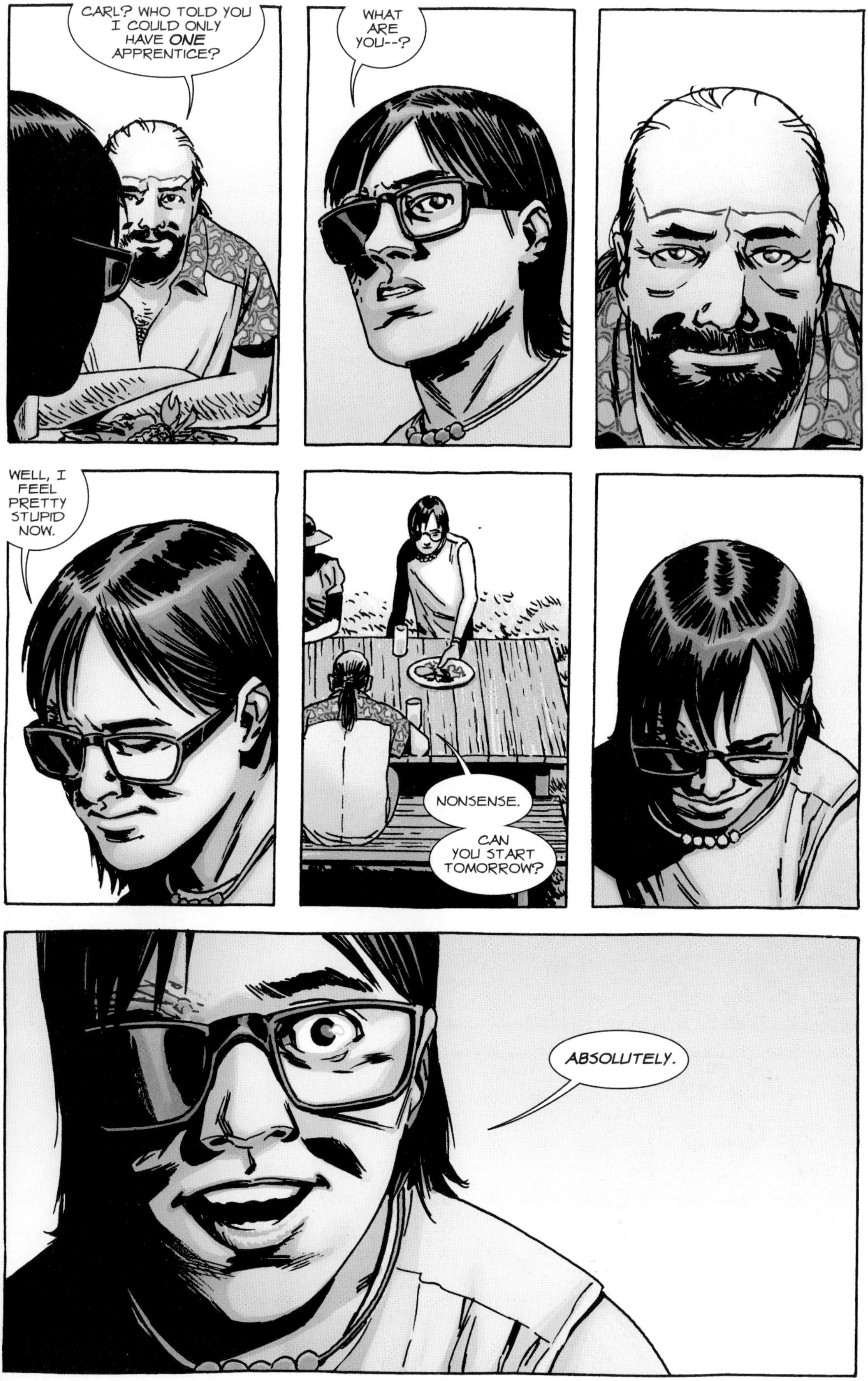
CARL? WHO TOLD YOU I COULD ONLY HAVE ONE APPRENTICE?
WHAT ARE YOU--?
WELL, I FEEL PRETTY STUPID NOW.
NONSENSE.
CAN YOU START TOMORROW?
ABSOLUTELY.

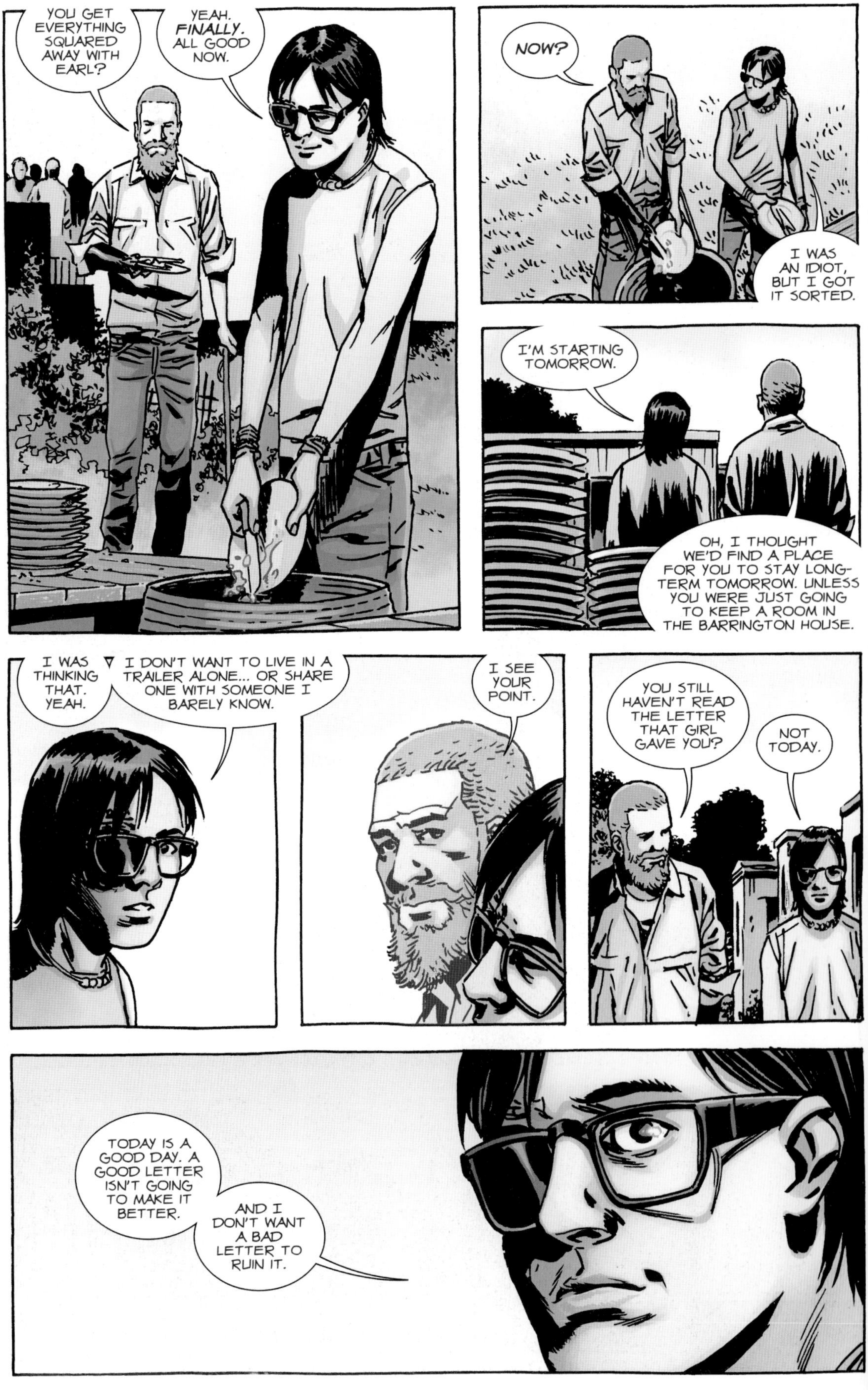
YOU GET EVERYTHING SQUARED AWAY WITH EARL?
YEAH. FINALLY. ALL GOOD NOW.
NOW?
I WAS AN IDIOT, BUT I GOT IT SORTED.
I'M STARTING TOMORROW.
OH, I THOUGHT WE'D FIND A PLACE FOR YOU TO STAY LONG-TERM TOMORROW. UNLESS YOU WERE JUST GOING TO KEEP A ROOM IN THE BARRINGTON HOUSE.
I WAS THINKING THAT. YEAH.
I DON'T WANT TO LIVE IN A TRAILER ALONE... OR SHARE ONE WITH SOMEONE I BARELY KNOW.
I SEE YOUR POINT.
YOU STILL HAVEN'T READ THE LETTER THAT GIRL GAVE YOU?
NOT TODAY.
TODAY IS A GOOD DAY. A GOOD LETTER ISN'T GOING TO MAKE IT BETTER.
AND I DON'T WANT A BAD LETTER TO RUIN IT.

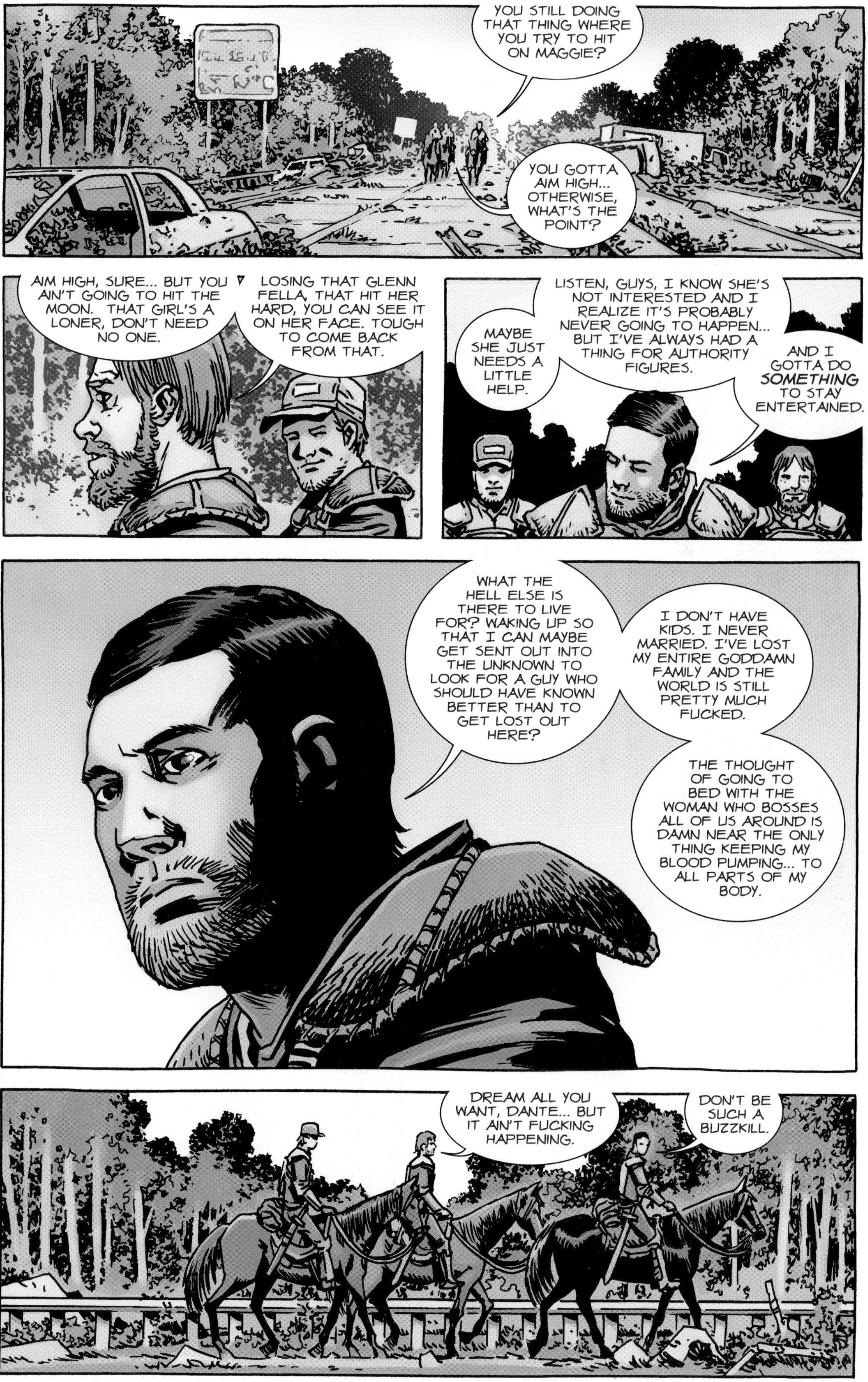
YOU STILL DOING THAT THING WHERE YOU TRY TO HIT ON MAGGIE?
YOU GOTTA AIM HIGH... OTHERWISE, WHAT'S THE POINT?
AIM HIGH, SURE... BUT YOU AIN'T GOING TO HIT THE MOON. THAT GIRL'S A LONER, DON'T NEED NO ONE.
LOSING THAT GLENN FELLA, THAT HIT HER HARD, YOU CAN SEE IT ON HER FACE. TOUGH TO COME BACK FROM THAT.
MAYBE SHE JUST NEEDS A LITTLE HELP.
LISTEN, GUYS, I KNOW SHE'S NOT INTERESTED AND I REALIZE IT'S PROBABLY NEVER GOING TO HAPPEN... BUT I'VE ALWAYS HAD A THING FOR AUTHORITY FIGURES.
AND I GOTTA DO SOMETHING TO STAY ENTERTAINED.
WHAT THE HELL ELSE IS THERE TO LIVE FOR? WAKING UP SO THAT I CAN MAYBE GET SENT OUT INTO THE UNKNOWN TO LOOK FOR A GUY WHO SHOULD HAVE KNOWN BETTER THAN TO GET LOST OUT HERE?
I DON'T HAVE KIDS. I NEVER MARRIED. I'VE LOST MY ENTIRE GODDAMN FAMILY AND THE WORLD IS STILL PRETTY MUCH FUCKED.
THE THOUGHT OF GOING TO BED WITH THE WOMAN WHO BOSSES ALL OF US AROUND IS DAMN NEAR THE ONLY THING KEEPING MY BLOOD PUMPING... TO ALL PARTS OF MY BODY.
DREAM ALL YOU WANT, DANTE... BUT IT AIN'T FUCKING HAPPENING.
DON'T BE SUCH A BUZZKILL.

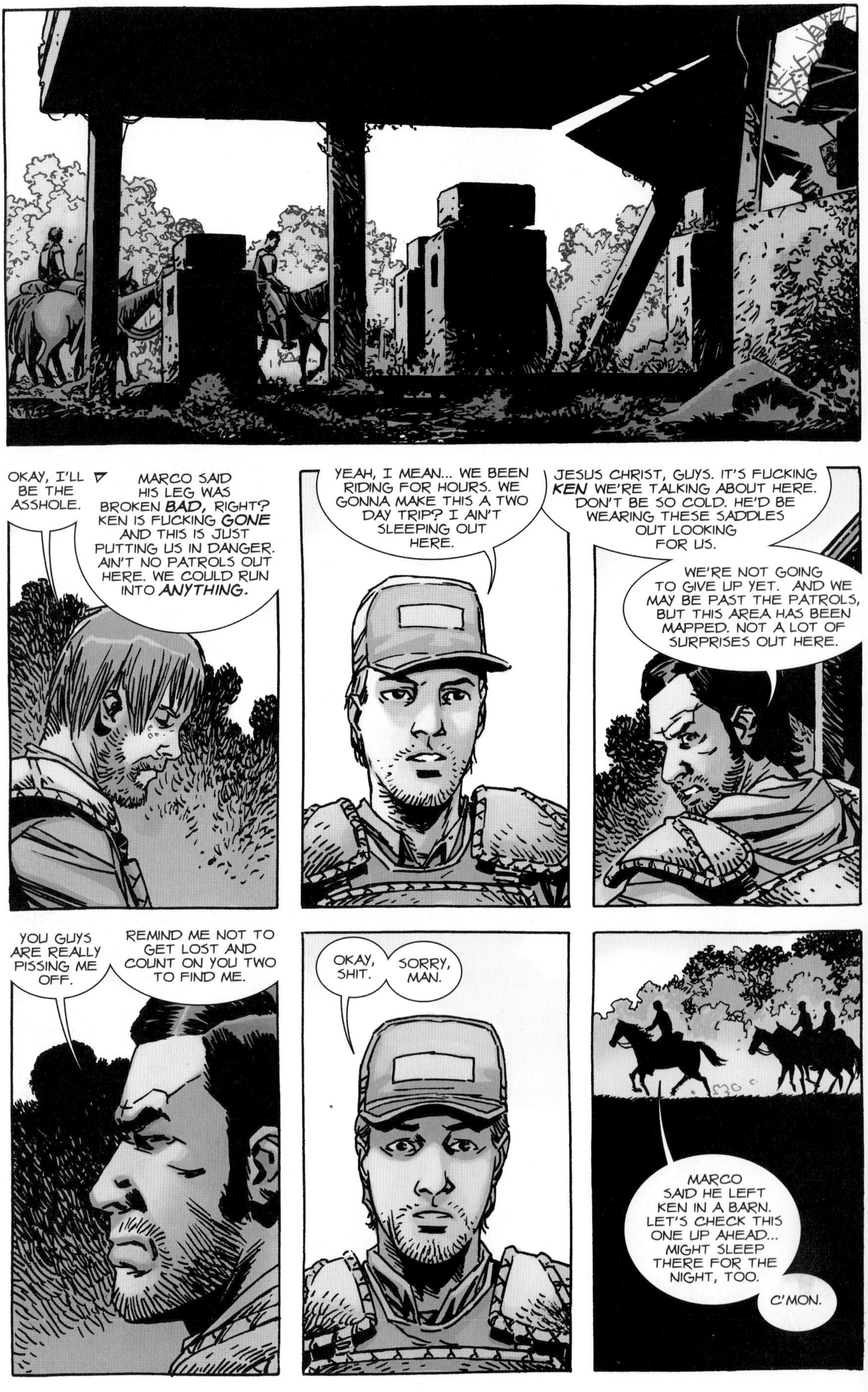

OKAY, I'LL BE THE ASSHOLE.
MARCO SAID HIS LEG WAS BROKEN BAD, RIGHT? KEN IS FUCKING GONE AND THIS IS JUST PUTTING US IN DANGER. AIN'T NO PATROLS OUT HERE. WE COULD RUN INTO ANYTHING.
YEAH, I MEAN... WE BEEN RIDING FOR HOURS. WE GONNA MAKE THIS A TWO DAY TRIP? I AIN'T SLEEPING OUT HERE.
JESUS CHRIST, GUYS. IT'S FUCKING KEN WE'RE TALKING ABOUT HERE. DON'T BE SO COLD. HE'D BE WEARING THESE SADDLES OUT LOOKING FOR US.
WE'RE NOT GOING TO GIVE UP YET. AND WE MAY BE PAST THE PATROLS, BUT THIS AREA HAS BEEN MAPPED. NOT A LOT OF SURPRISES OUT HERE.
YOU GUYS ARE REALLY PISSING ME OFF.
REMIND ME NOT TO GET LOST AND COUNT ON YOU TWO TO FIND ME.
OKAY, SHIT.
SORRY, MAN.
MARCO SAID HE LEFT KEN IN A BARN. LET'S CHECK THIS ONE UP AHEAD... MIGHT SLEEP THERE FOR THE NIGHT, TOO.
C'MON.

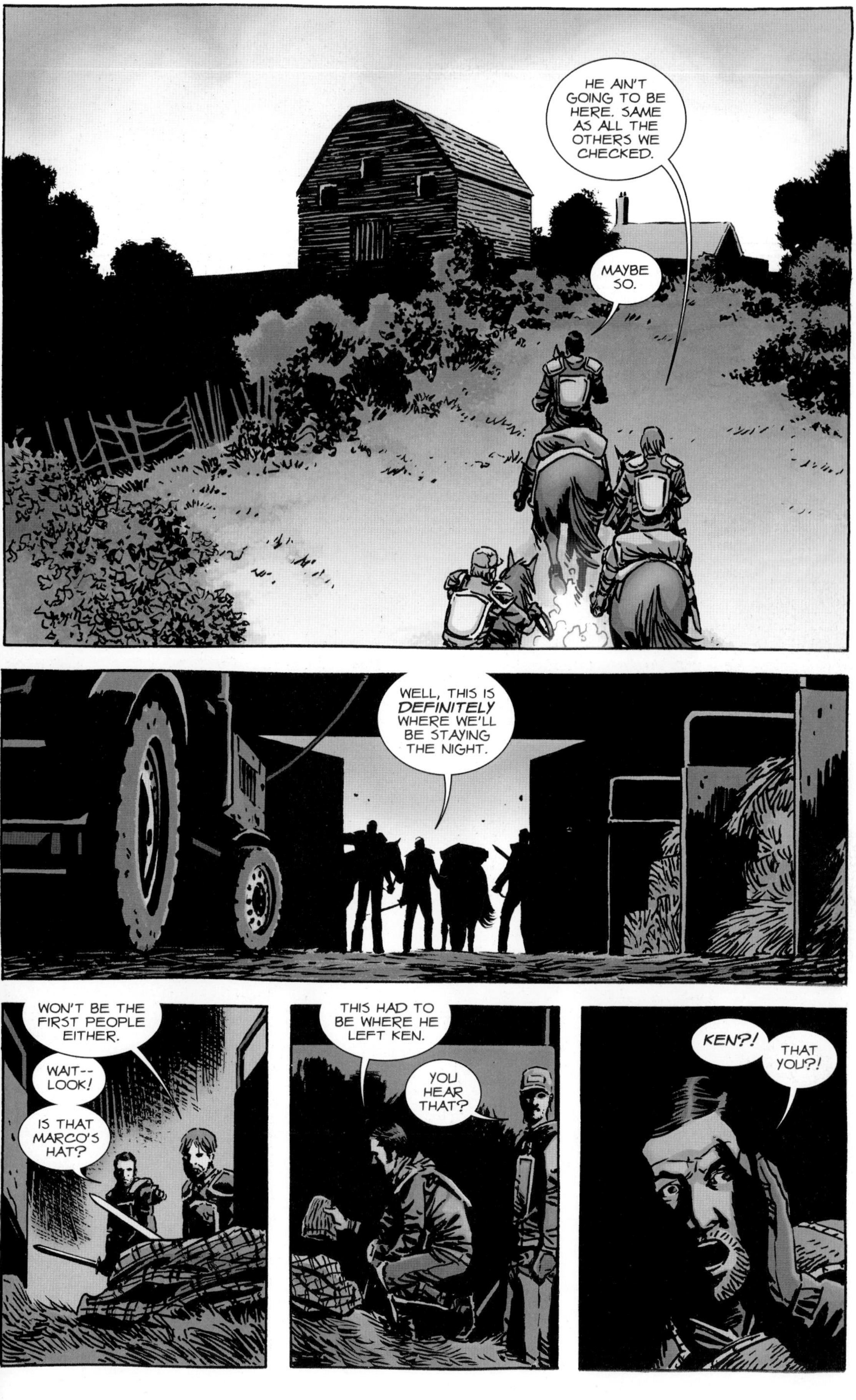
HE AIN'T GOING TO BE HERE. SAME AS ALL THE OTHERS WE CHECKED.
MAYBE SO.
WELL, THIS IS *DEFINITELY* WHERE WE'LL BE STAYING THE NIGHT.
WON'T BE THE FIRST PEOPLE EITHER.
WAIT-- LOOK!
IS THAT MARCO'S HAT?
THIS HAD TO BE WHERE HE LEFT KEN.
YOU HEAR THAT?
KEN?!
THAT YOU?!

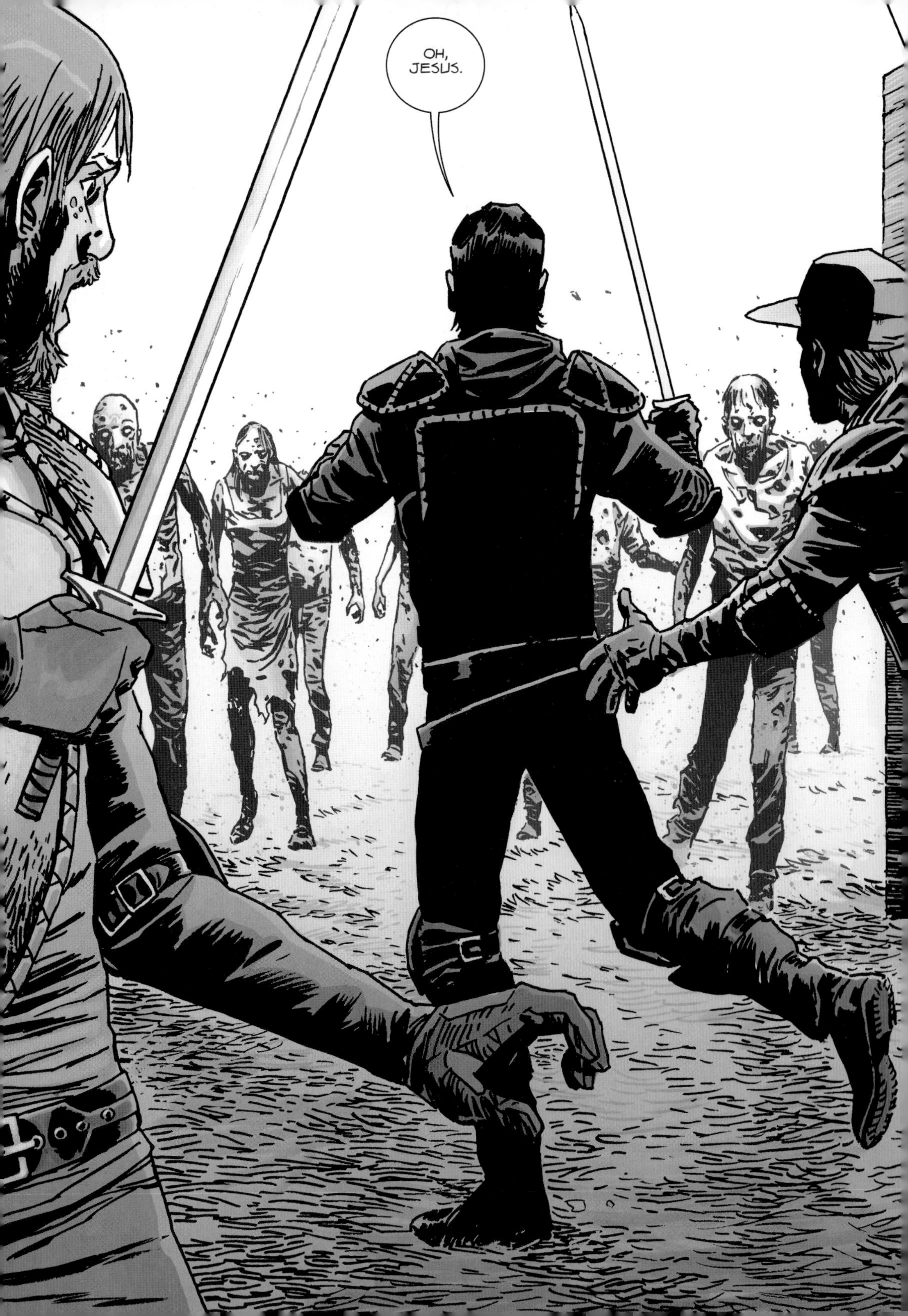
OH, JESUS.

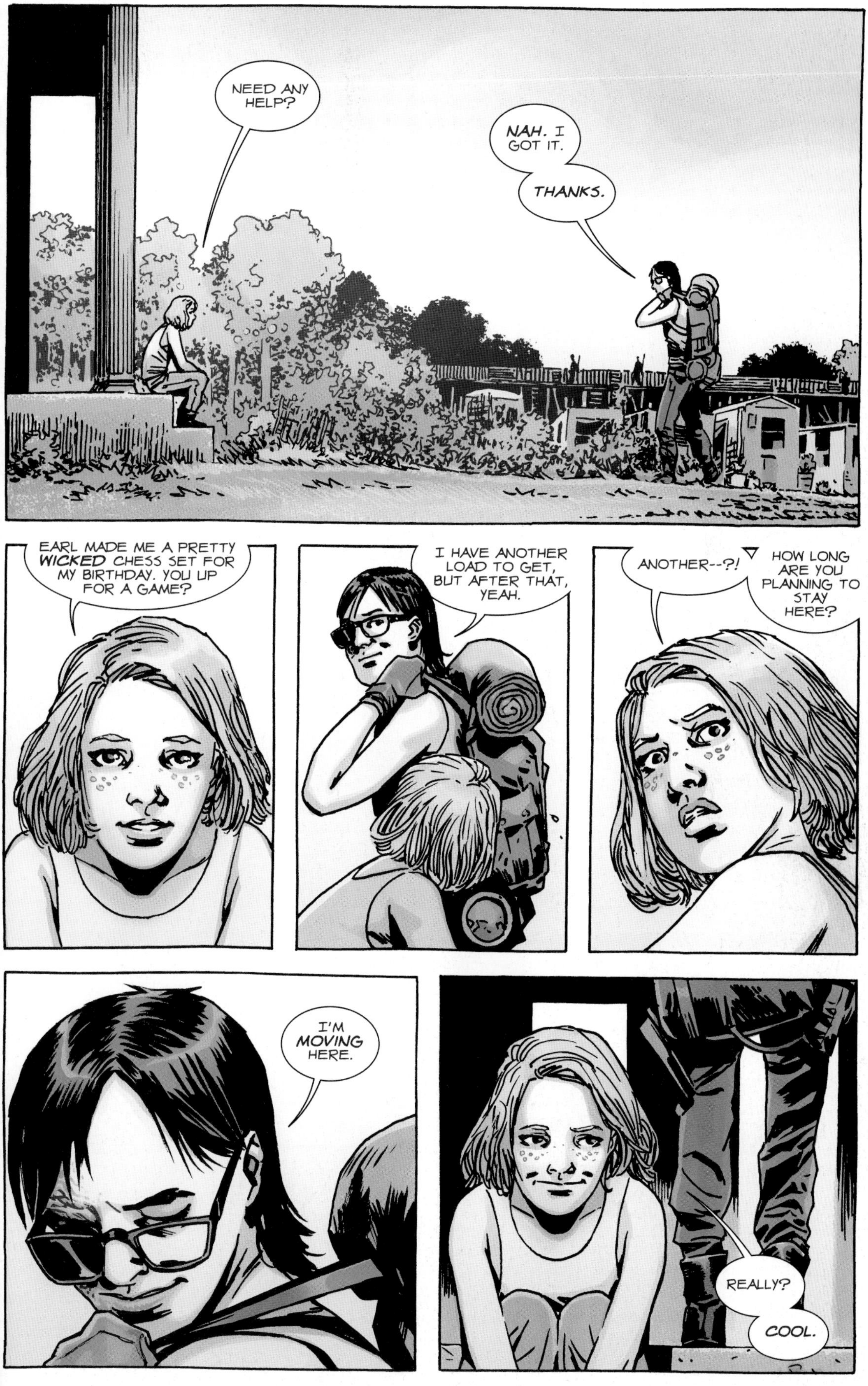
NEED ANY HELP?
NAH. I GOT IT.
THANKS.
EARL MADE ME A PRETTY WICKED CHESS SET FOR MY BIRTHDAY. YOU UP FOR A GAME?
I HAVE ANOTHER LOAD TO GET, BUT AFTER THAT, YEAH.
ANOTHER--?!
HOW LONG ARE YOU PLANNING TO STAY HERE?
I'M MOVING HERE.
REALLY?
COOL.

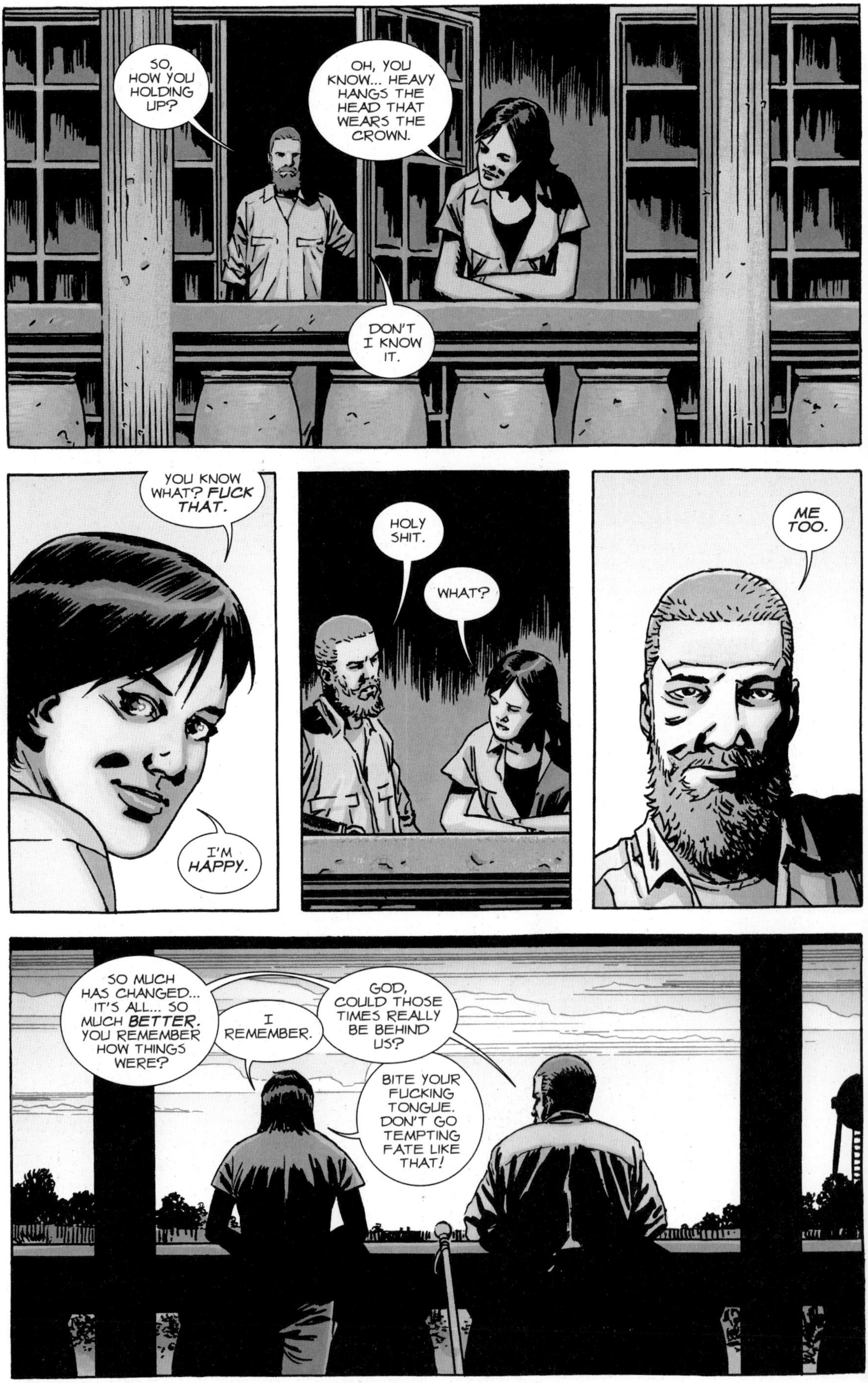
SO, HOW YOU HOLDING UP?
OH, YOU KNOW... HEAVY HANGS THE HEAD THAT WEARS THE CROWN.
DON'T I KNOW IT.
YOU KNOW WHAT? *FUCK THAT.*
I'M *HAPPY.*
HOLY SHIT.
WHAT?
ME TOO.
SO MUCH HAS CHANGED... IT'S ALL... SO MUCH *BETTER*. YOU REMEMBER HOW THINGS WERE?
I REMEMBER.
GOD, COULD THOSE TIMES REALLY BE BEHIND US?
BITE YOUR FUCKING TONGUE. DON'T GO TEMPTING FATE LIKE THAT!

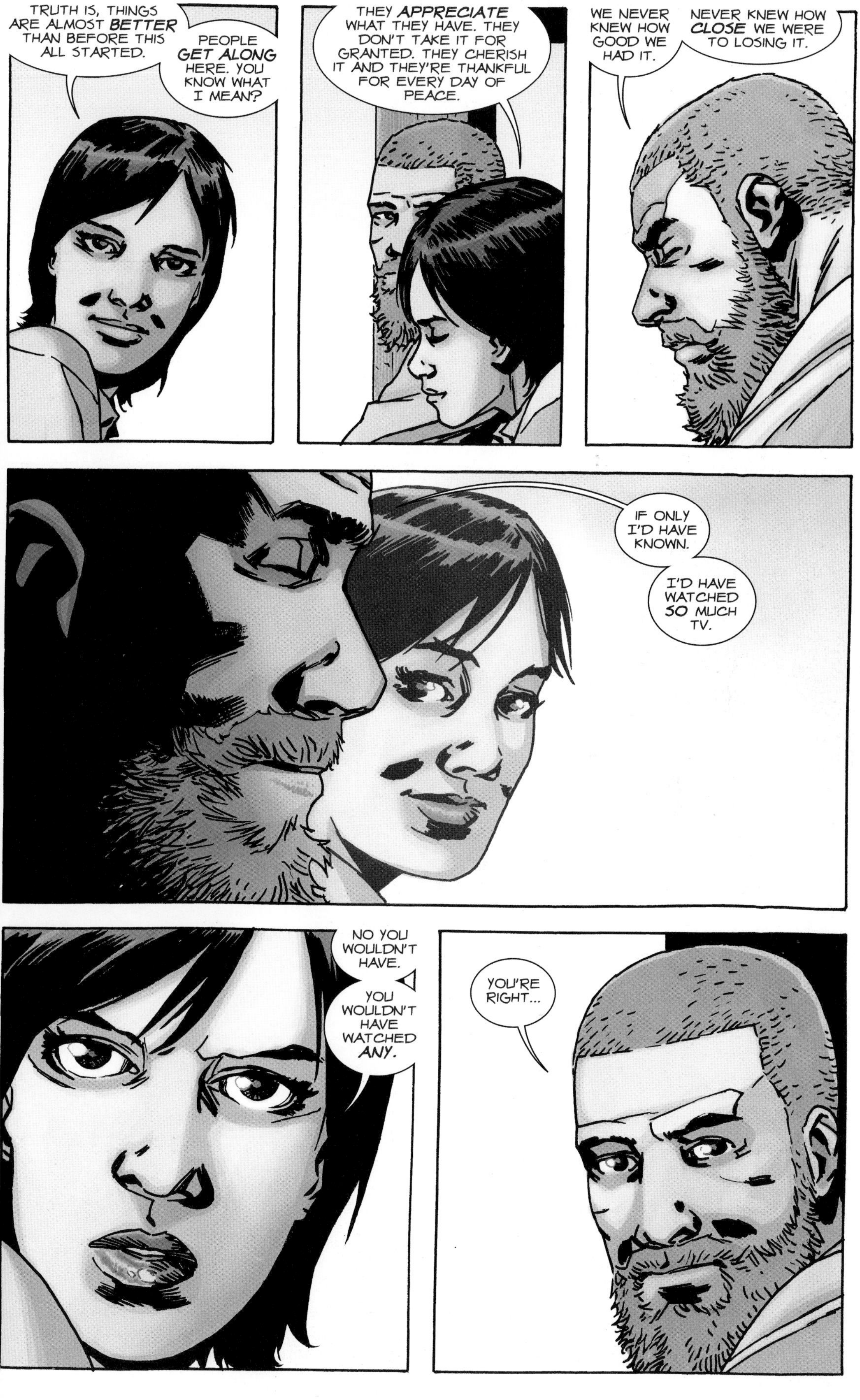
TRUTH IS, THINGS ARE ALMOST BETTER THAN BEFORE THIS ALL STARTED.
PEOPLE GET ALONG HERE. YOU KNOW WHAT I MEAN?
THEY APPRECIATE WHAT THEY HAVE. THEY DON'T TAKE IT FOR GRANTED. THEY CHERISH IT AND THEY'RE THANKFUL FOR EVERY DAY OF PEACE.
WE NEVER KNEW HOW GOOD WE HAD IT.
NEVER KNEW HOW CLOSE WE WERE TO LOSING IT.
IF ONLY I'D HAVE KNOWN.
I'D HAVE WATCHED SO MUCH TV.
NO YOU WOULDN'T HAVE.
YOU WOULDN'T HAVE WATCHED ANY.
YOU'RE RIGHT...

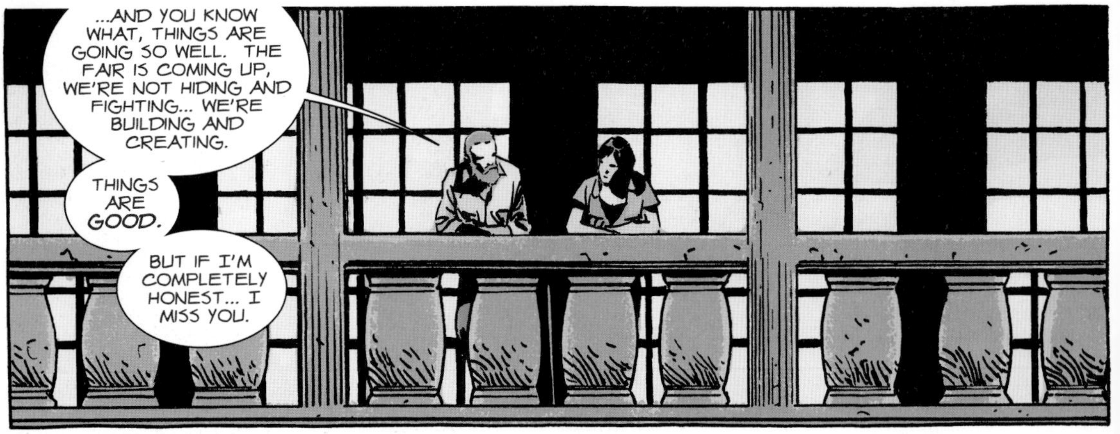
...AND YOU KNOW WHAT, THINGS ARE GOING SO WELL. THE FAIR IS COMING UP, WE'RE NOT HIDING AND FIGHTING... WE'RE BUILDING AND CREATING.
THINGS ARE *GOOD.*
BUT IF I'M COMPLETELY HONEST... I MISS YOU.

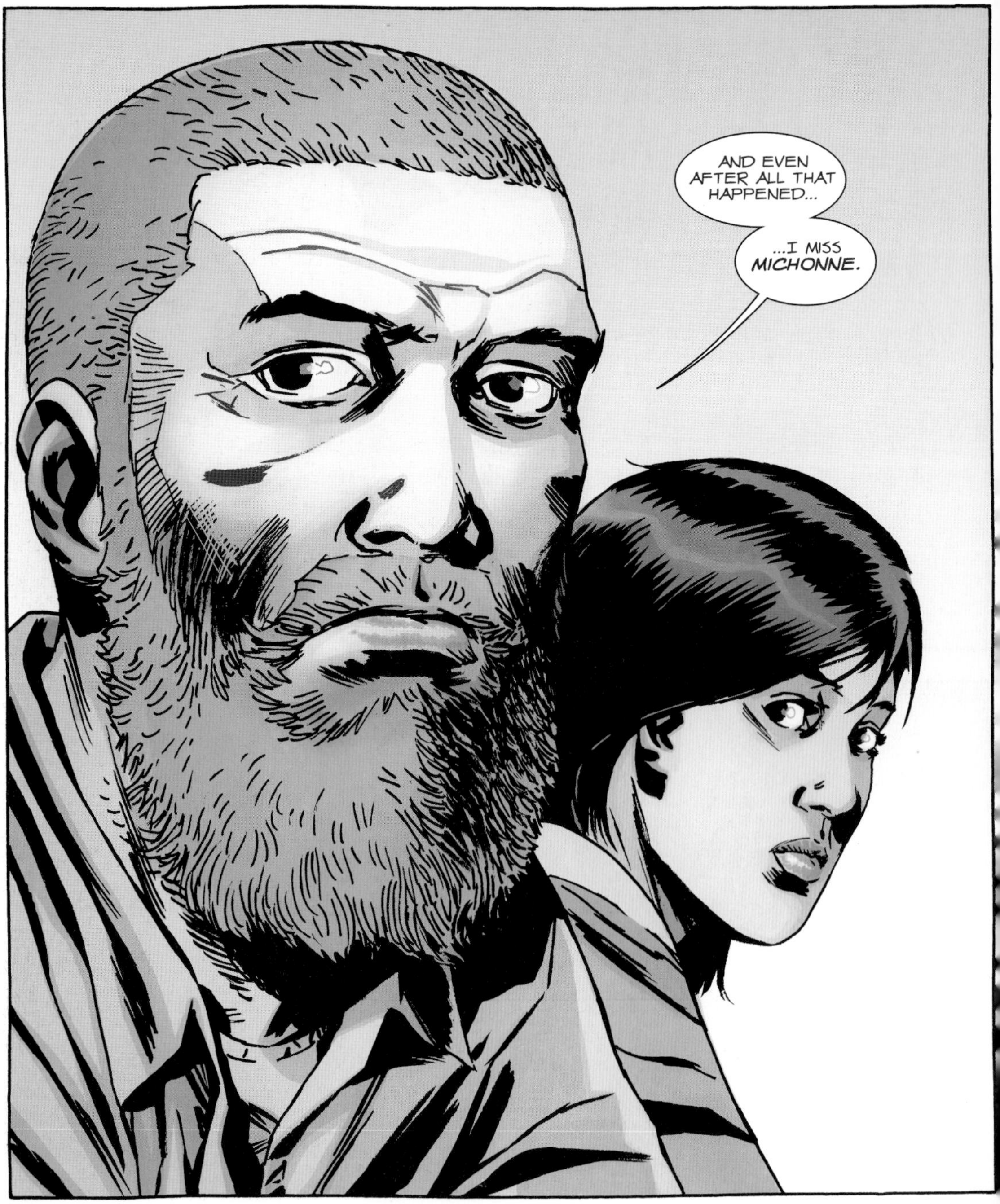
AND EVEN AFTER ALL THAT HAPPENED...
...I MISS *MICHONNE.*

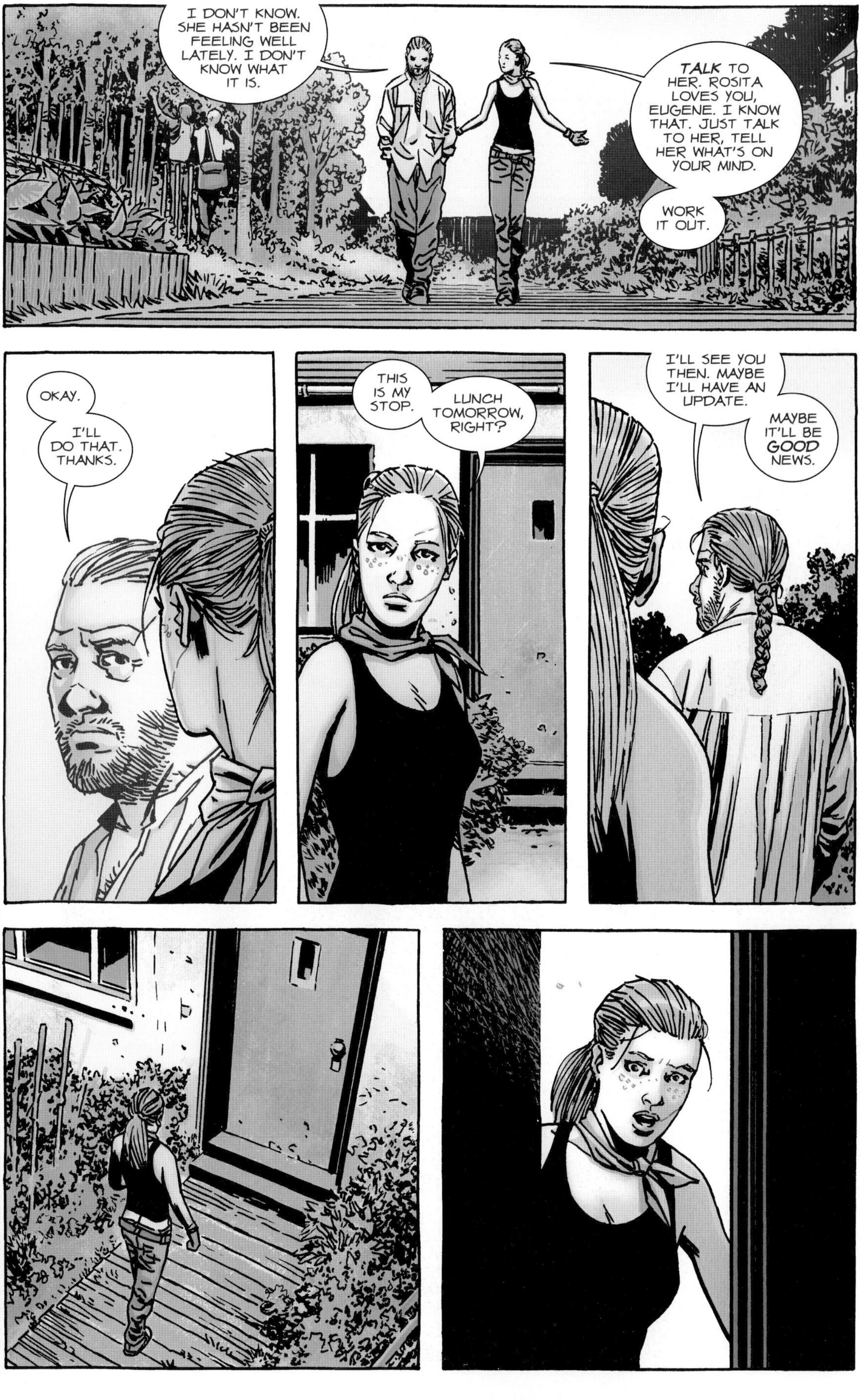
I DON'T KNOW. SHE HASN'T BEEN FEELING WELL LATELY. I DON'T KNOW WHAT IT IS.
TALK TO HER. ROSITA LOVES YOU, EUGENE. I KNOW THAT. JUST TALK TO HER, TELL HER WHAT'S ON YOUR MIND.
WORK IT OUT.
OKAY.
I'LL DO THAT. THANKS.
THIS IS MY STOP.
LUNCH TOMORROW, RIGHT?
I'LL SEE YOU THEN. MAYBE I'LL HAVE AN UPDATE.
MAYBE IT'LL BE *GOOD* NEWS.

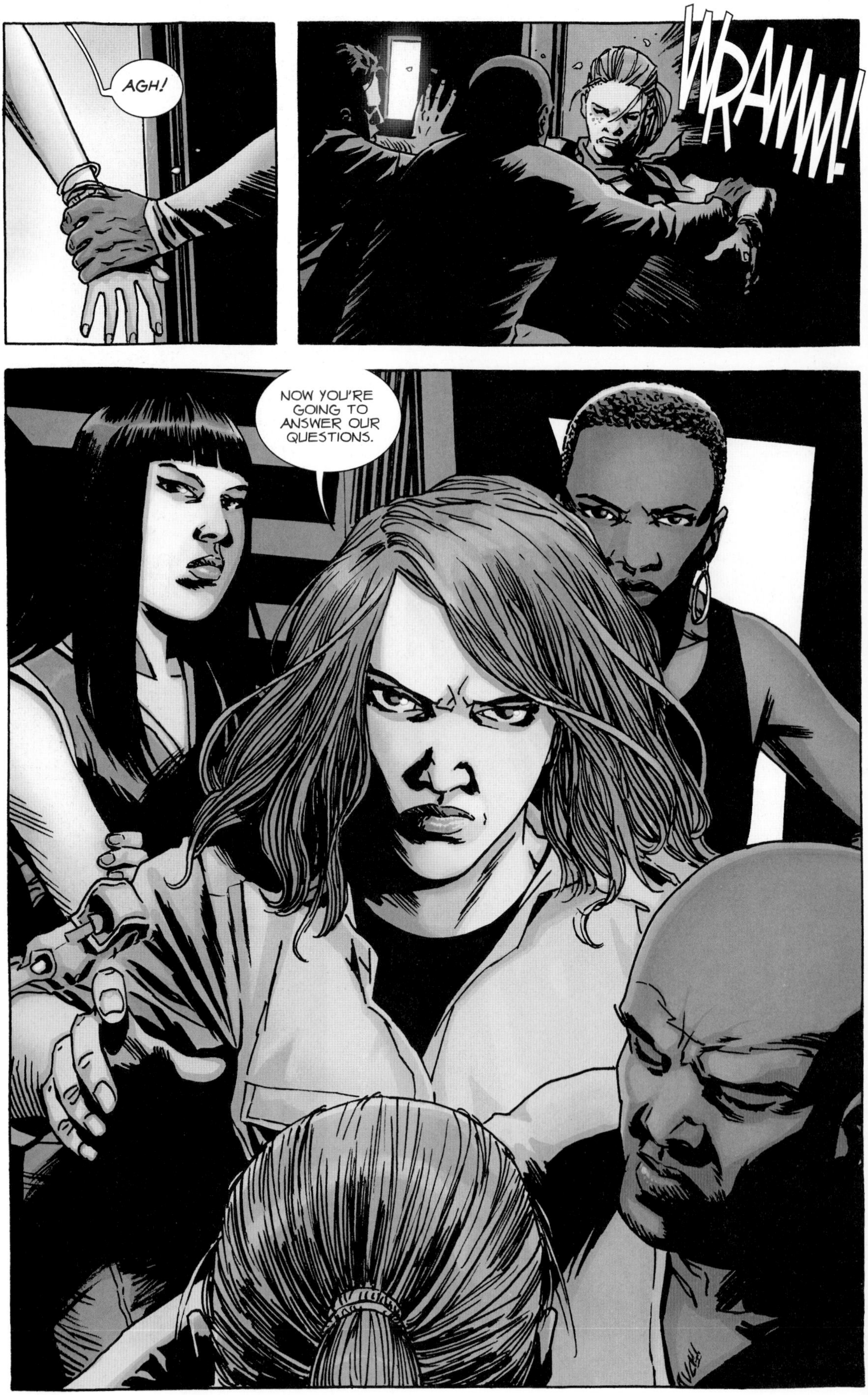
AGH!
WRAMM!
NOW YOU'RE GOING TO ANSWER OUR QUESTIONS.

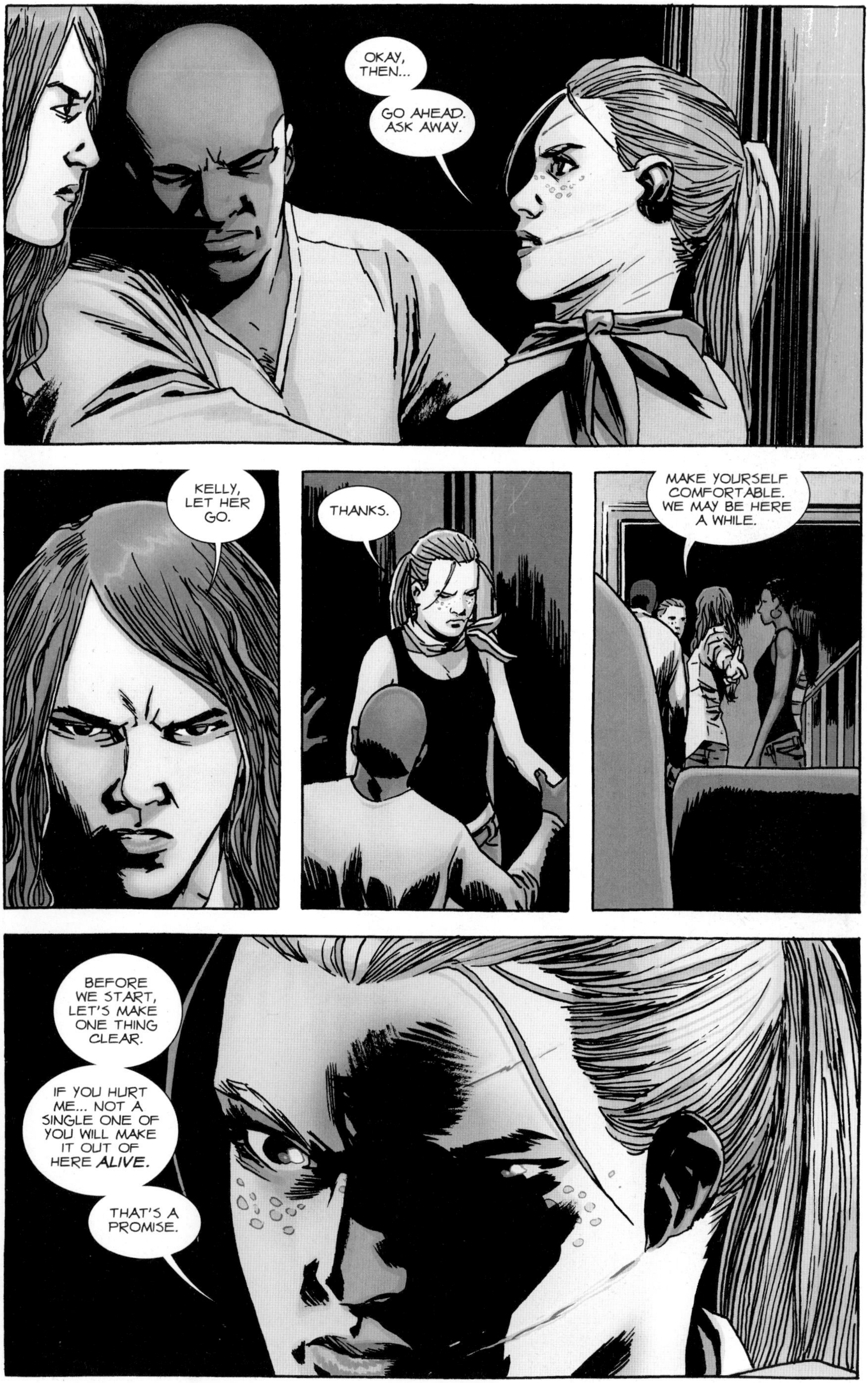
OKAY, THEN...
GO AHEAD. ASK AWAY.
KELLY, LET HER GO.
THANKS.
MAKE YOURSELF COMFORTABLE. WE MAY BE HERE A WHILE.
BEFORE WE START, LET'S MAKE ONE THING CLEAR.
IF YOU HURT ME... NOT A SINGLE ONE OF YOU WILL MAKE IT OUT OF HERE *ALIVE.*
THAT'S A PROMISE.

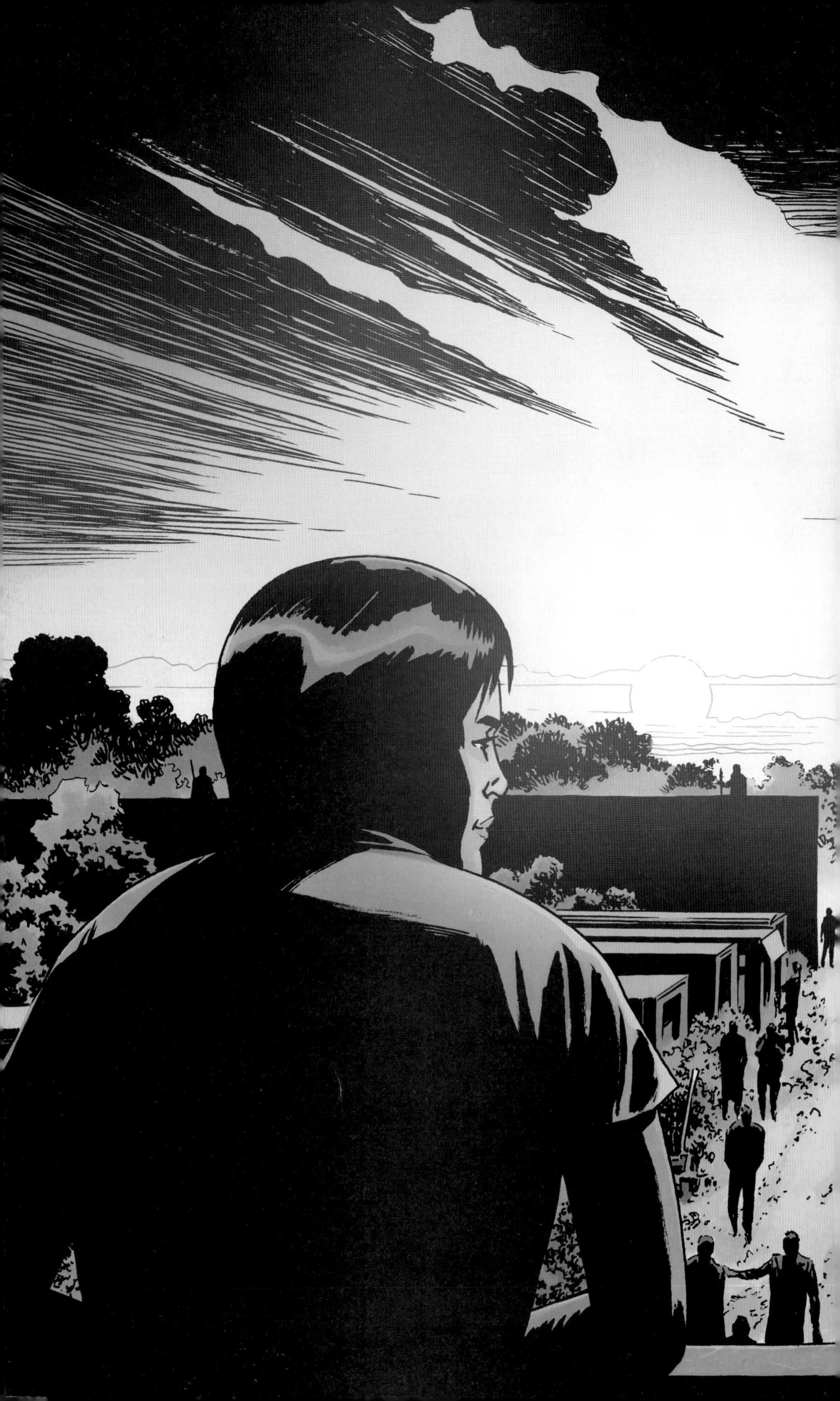

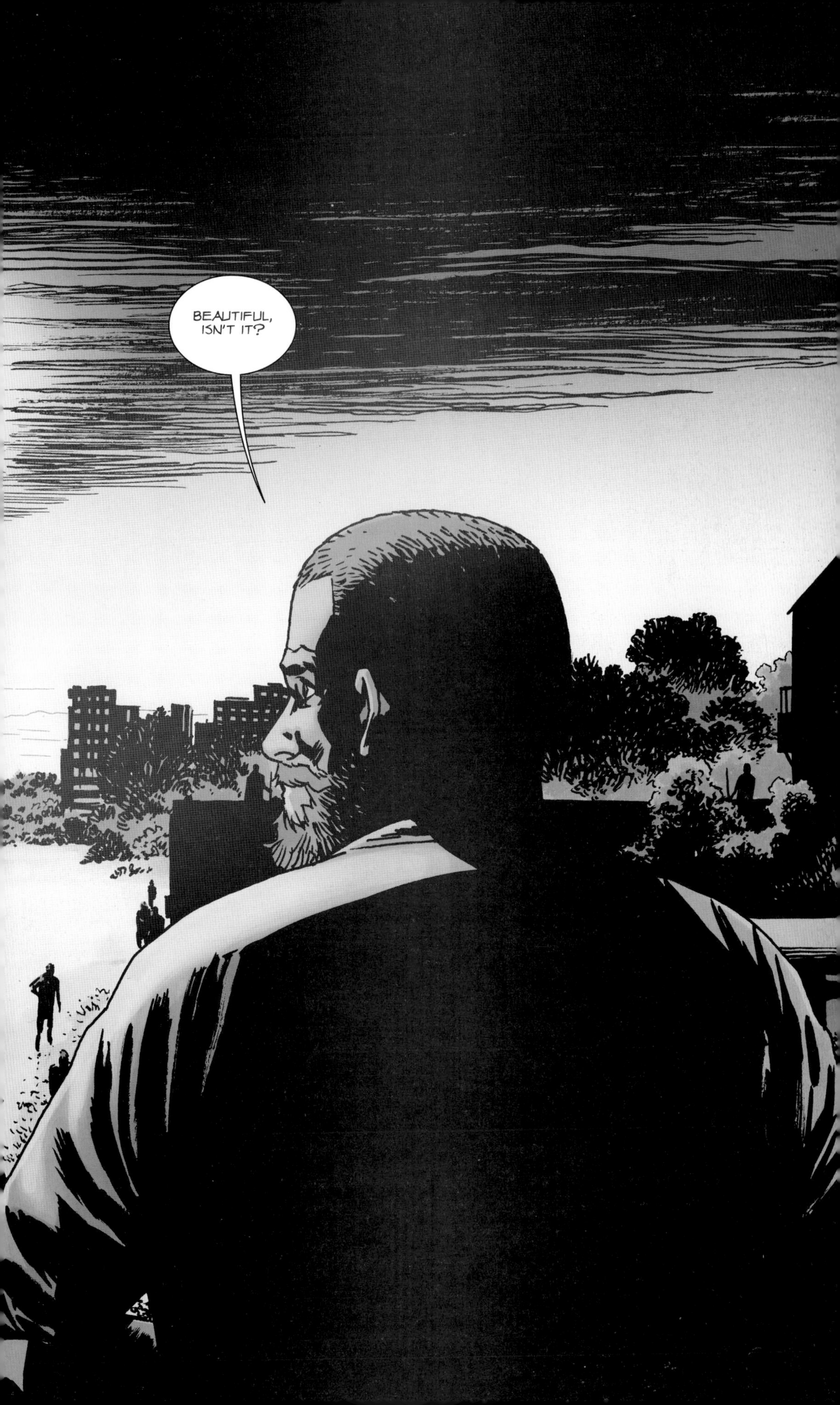
BEAUTIFUL, ISN'T IT?

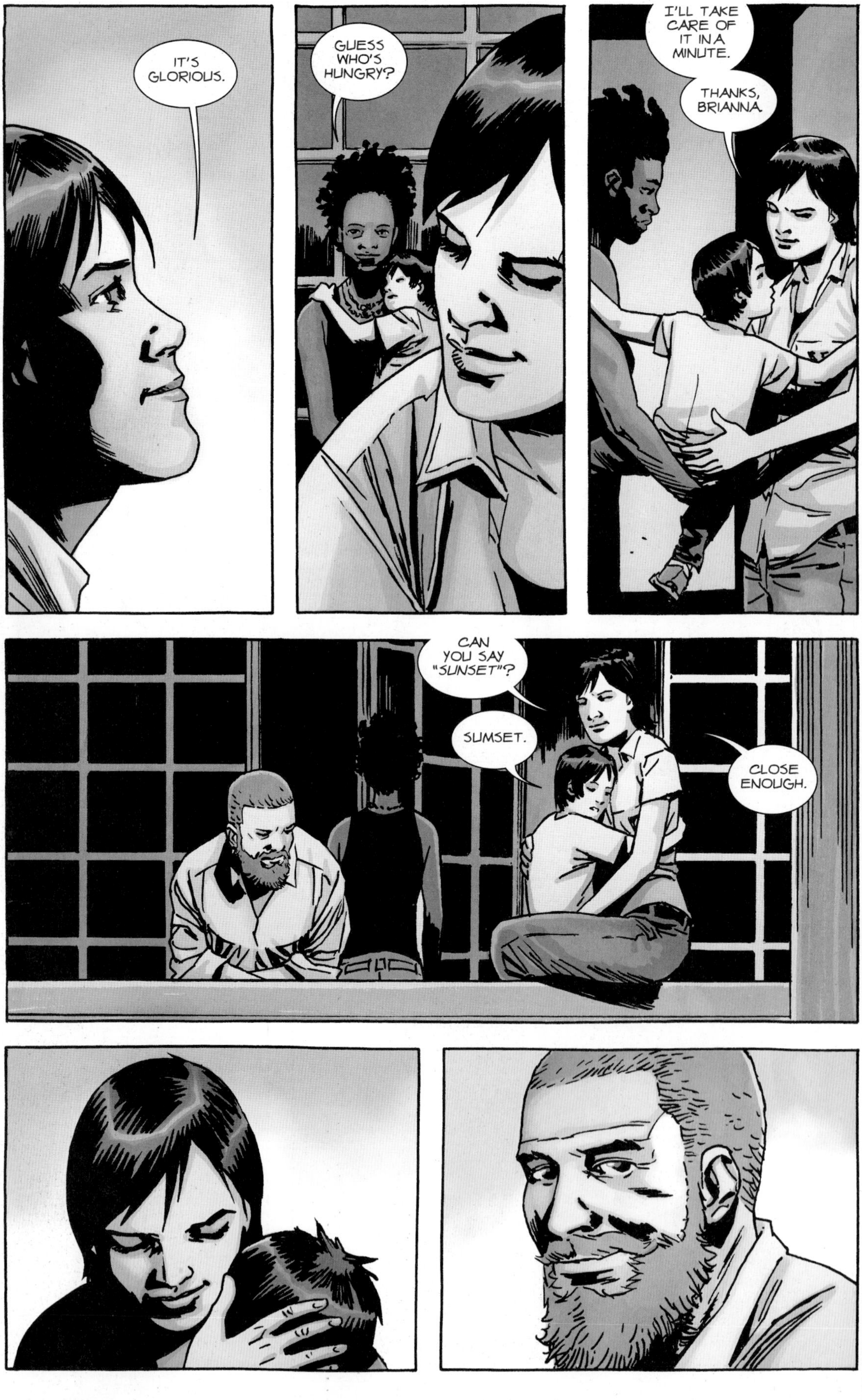
IT'S GLORIOUS.
GUESS WHO'S HUNGRY?
I'LL TAKE CARE OF IT IN A MINUTE.
THANKS, BRIANNA.
CAN YOU SAY "SUNSET"?
SUMSET.
CLOSE ENOUGH.

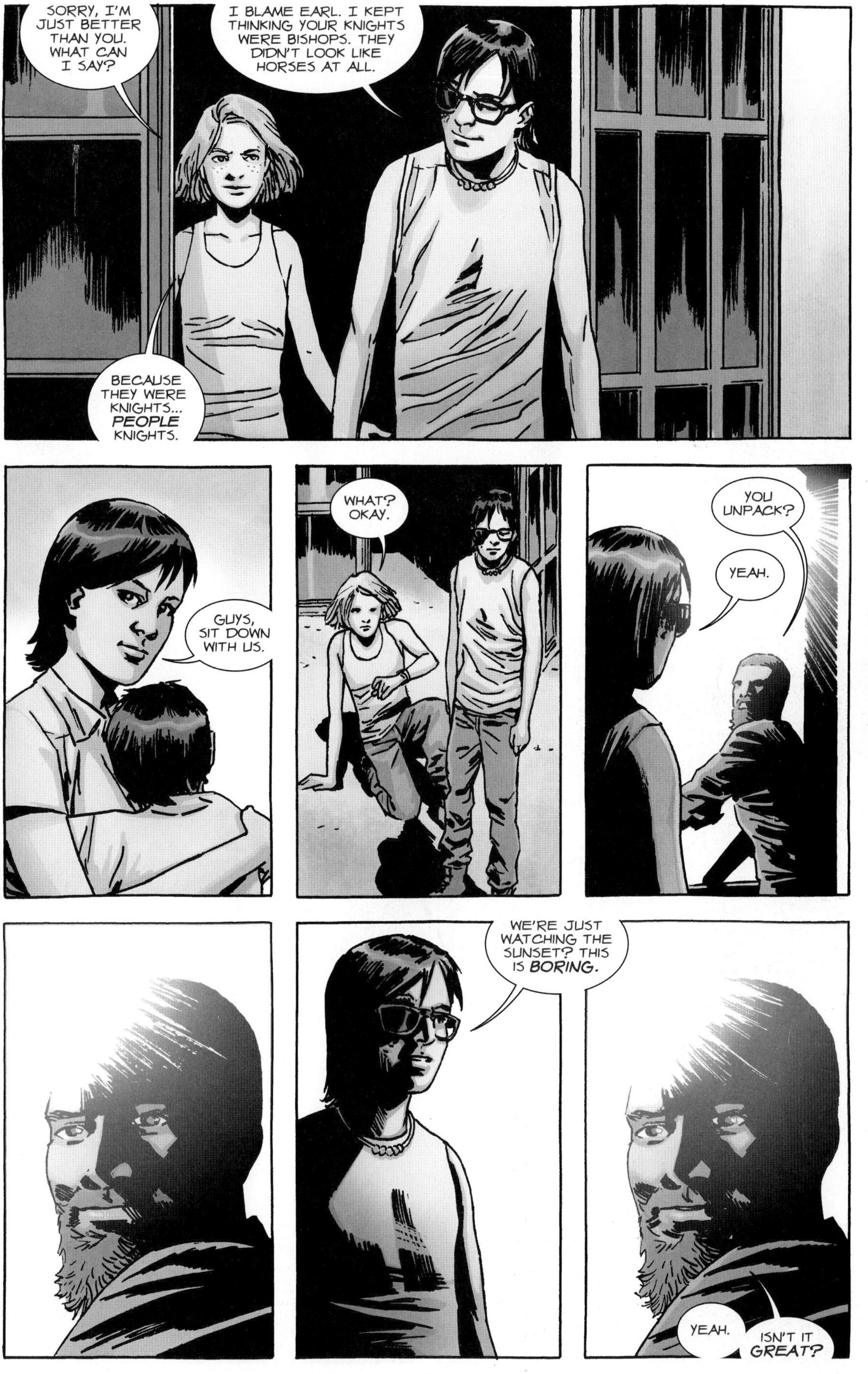
SORRY, I'M JUST BETTER THAN YOU. WHAT CAN I SAY?
I BLAME EARL. I KEPT THINKING YOUR KNIGHTS WERE BISHOPS. THEY DIDN'T LOOK LIKE HORSES AT ALL.
BECAUSE THEY WERE KNIGHTS... *PEOPLE* KNIGHTS.
GUYS, SIT DOWN WITH US.
WHAT? OKAY.
YOU UNPACK?
YEAH.
WE'RE JUST WATCHING THE SUNSET? THIS IS *BORING.*
YEAH.
ISN'T IT *GREAT?*

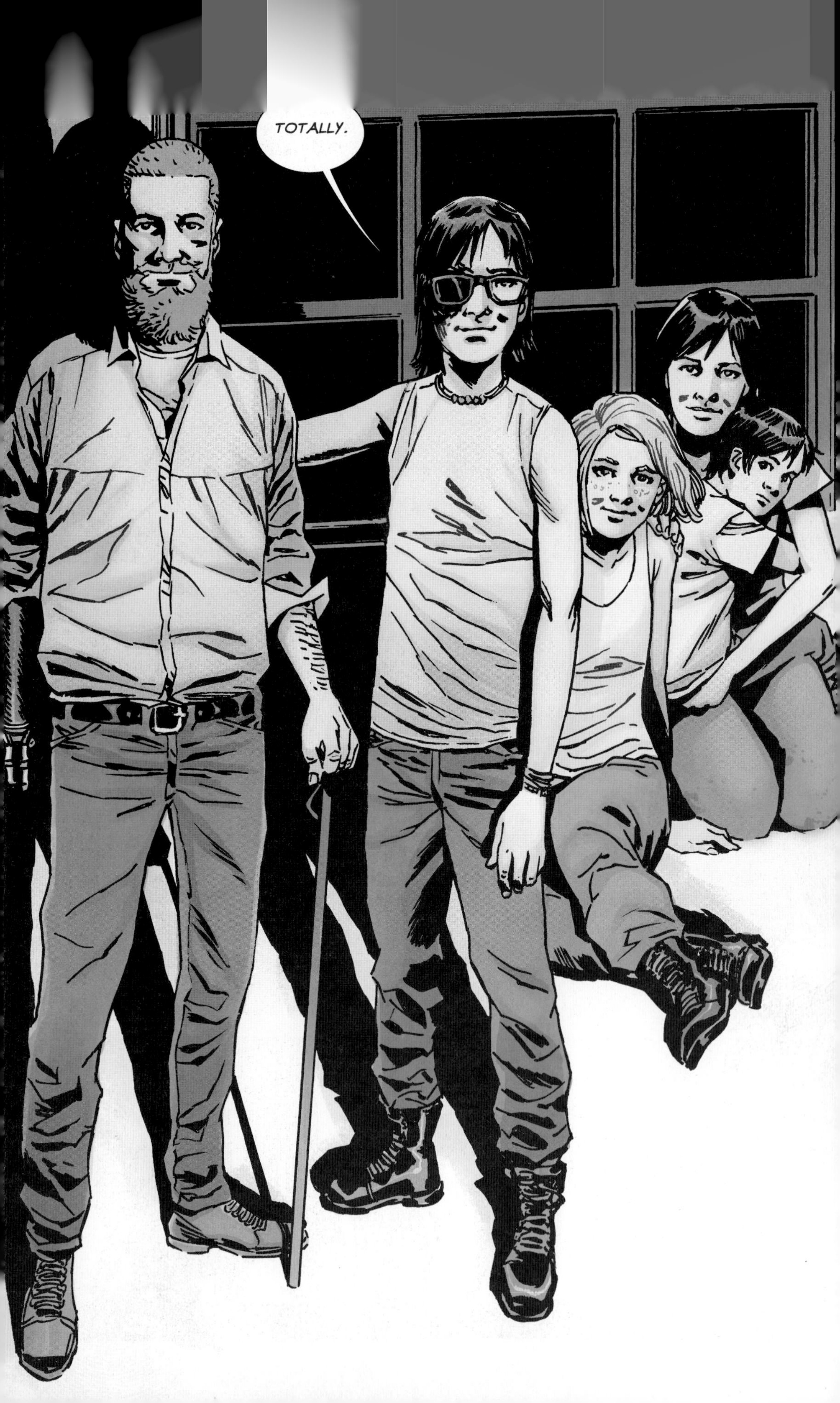
TOTALLY.

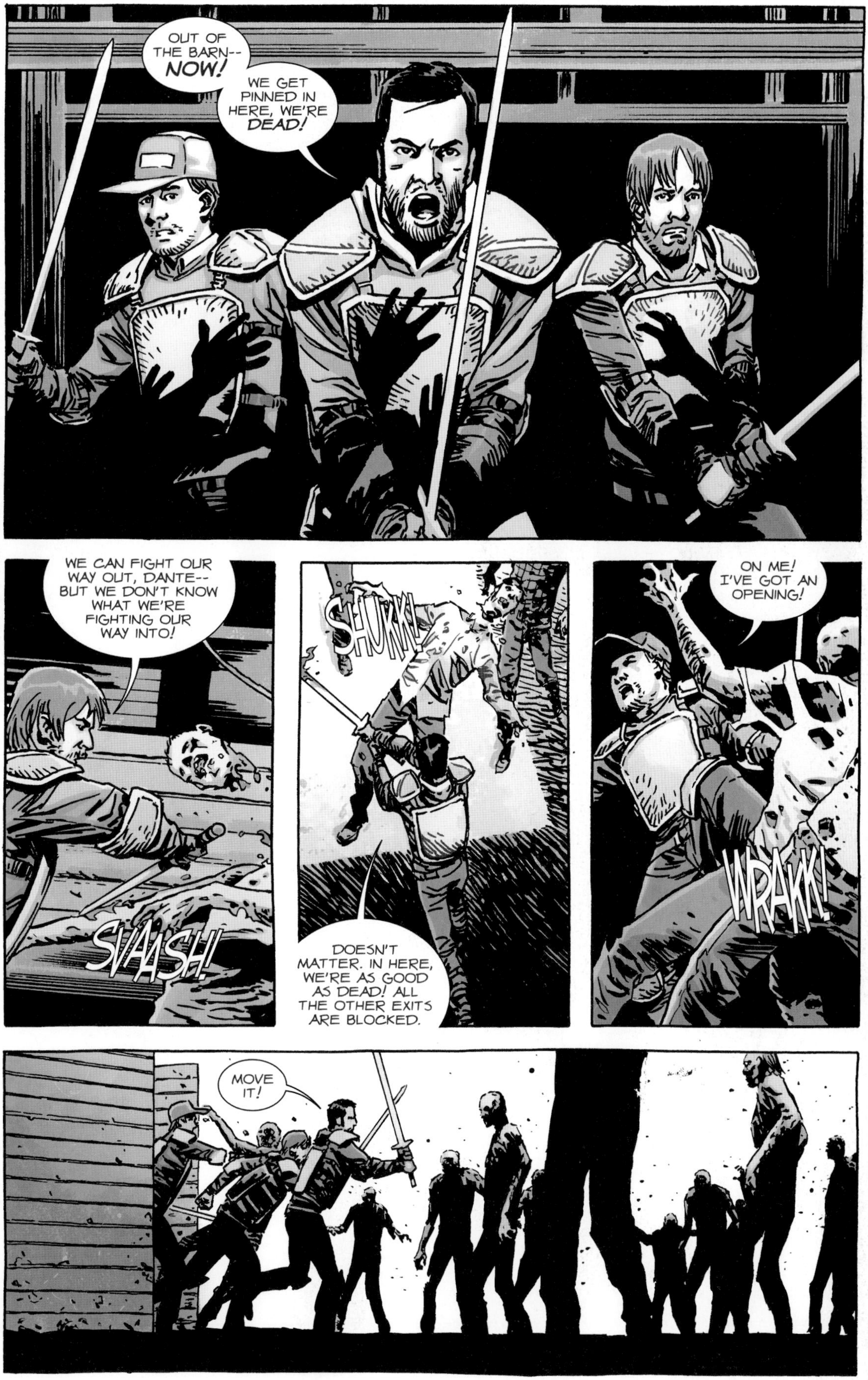
OUT OF THE BARN-- NOW!
WE GET PINNED IN HERE, WE'RE DEAD!
WE CAN FIGHT OUR WAY OUT, DANTE-- BUT WE DON'T KNOW WHAT WE'RE FIGHTING OUR WAY INTO!
SVAASH!
SHUKK!
DOESN'T MATTER. IN HERE, WE'RE AS GOOD AS DEAD! ALL THE OTHER EXITS ARE BLOCKED.
ON ME! I'VE GOT AN OPENING!
WRAKK!
MOVE IT!

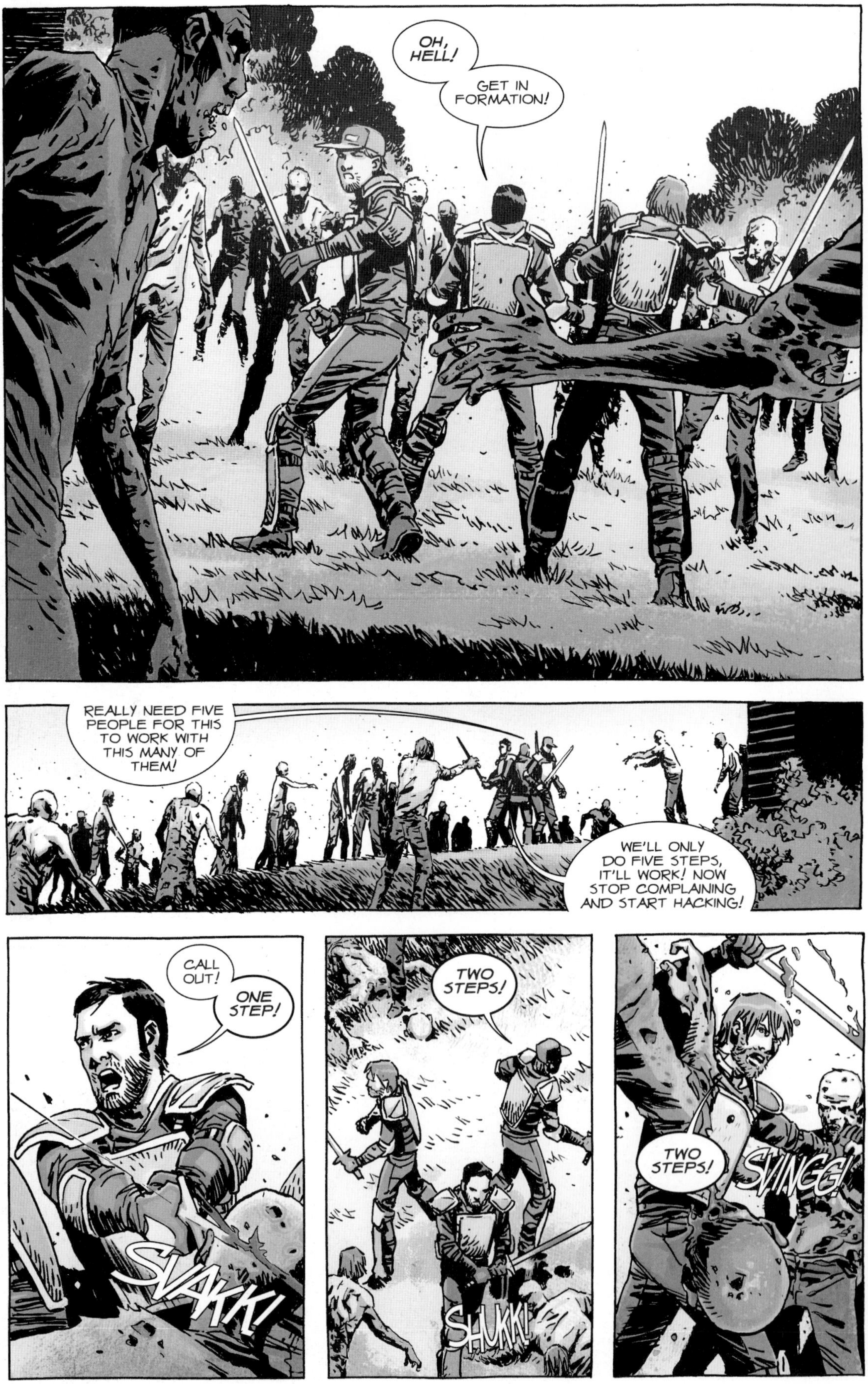
OH, HELL!
GET IN FORMATION!
REALLY NEED FIVE PEOPLE FOR THIS TO WORK WITH THIS MANY OF THEM!
WE'LL ONLY DO FIVE STEPS, IT'LL WORK! NOW STOP COMPLAINING AND START HACKING!
CALL OUT!
ONE STEP!
SNAKK!
TWO STEPS!
SHUKK!
TWO STEPS!
SVINGG!

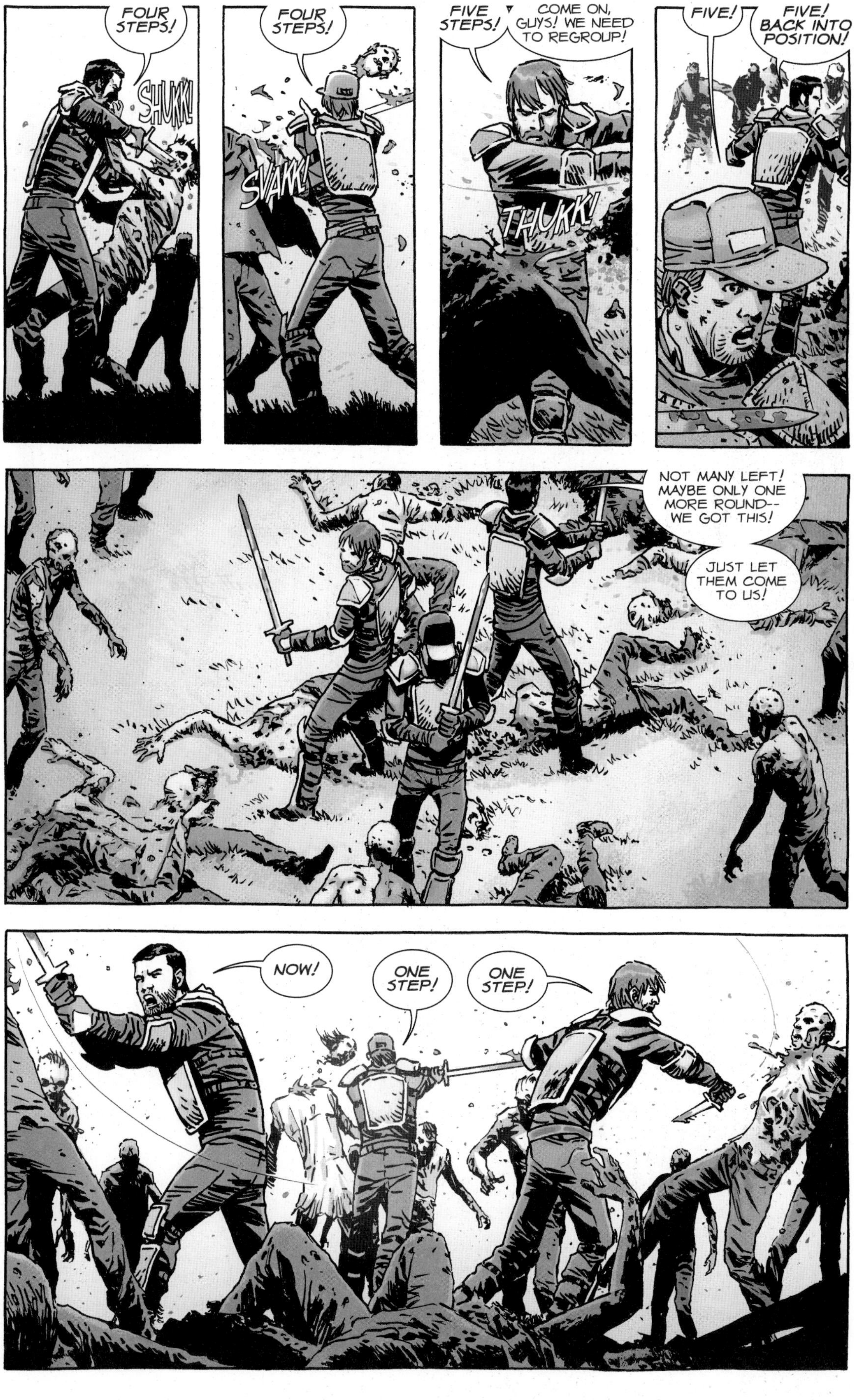
FOUR STEPS!
SHUKK!
FOUR STEPS!
SVAKK!
FIVE STEPS!
COME ON, GUYS! WE NEED TO REGROUP!
THUKK!
FIVE!
FIVE! BACK INTO POSITION!
NOT MANY LEFT! MAYBE ONLY ONE MORE ROUND-- WE GOT THIS!
JUST LET THEM COME TO US!
NOW!
ONE STEP!
ONE STEP!

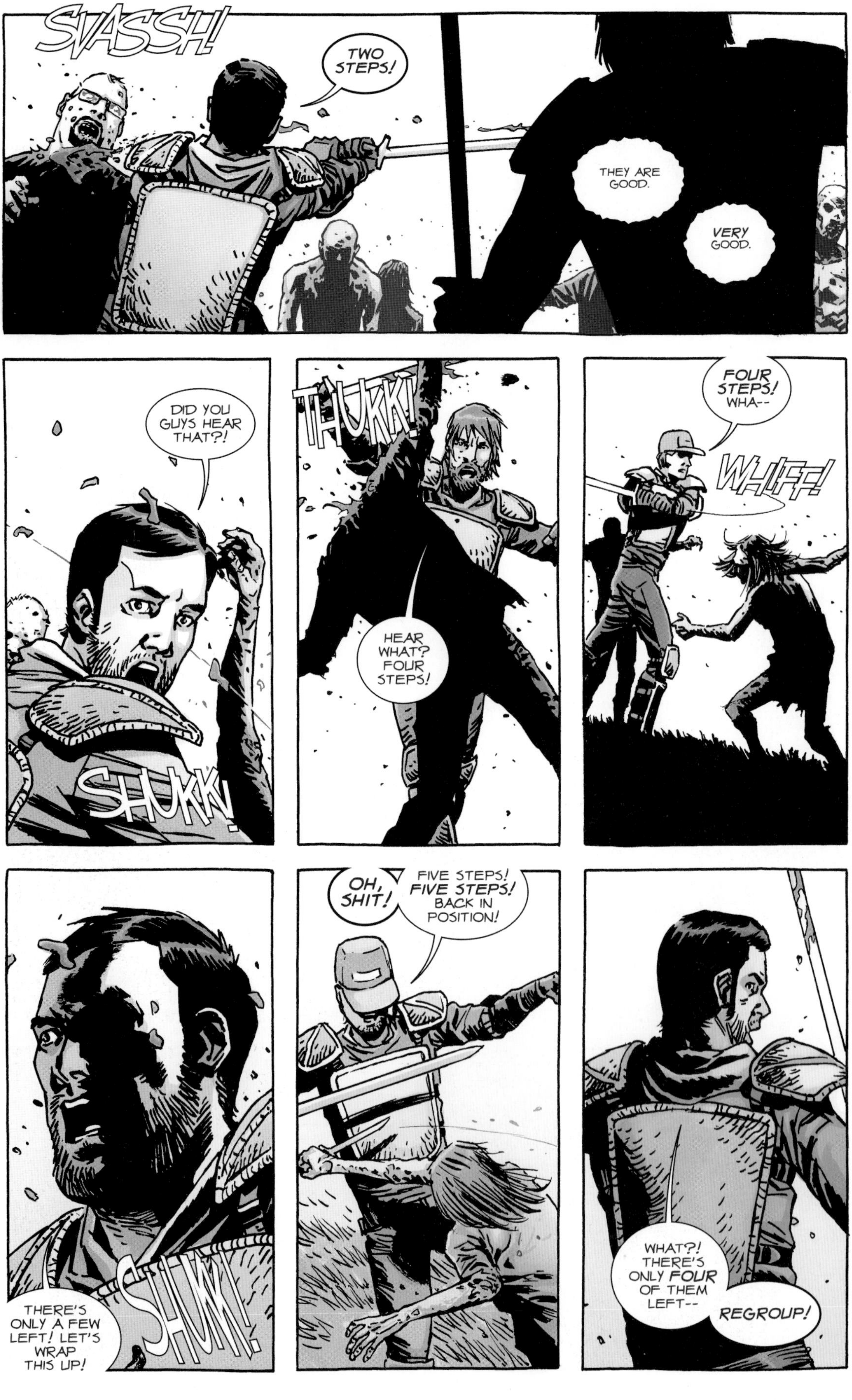

SVASSH!
TWO STEPS!
THEY ARE GOOD.
VERY GOOD.
DID YOU GUYS HEAR THAT?!
SHUKK!
THUKK!
HEAR WHAT? FOUR STEPS!
FOUR STEPS! WHA--
WHIFF!
THERE'S ONLY A FEW LEFT! LET'S WRAP THIS UP!
SHUKK!
OH, SHIT!
FIVE STEPS! FIVE STEPS! BACK IN POSITION!
WHAT?! THERE'S ONLY FOUR OF THEM LEFT--
REGROUP!

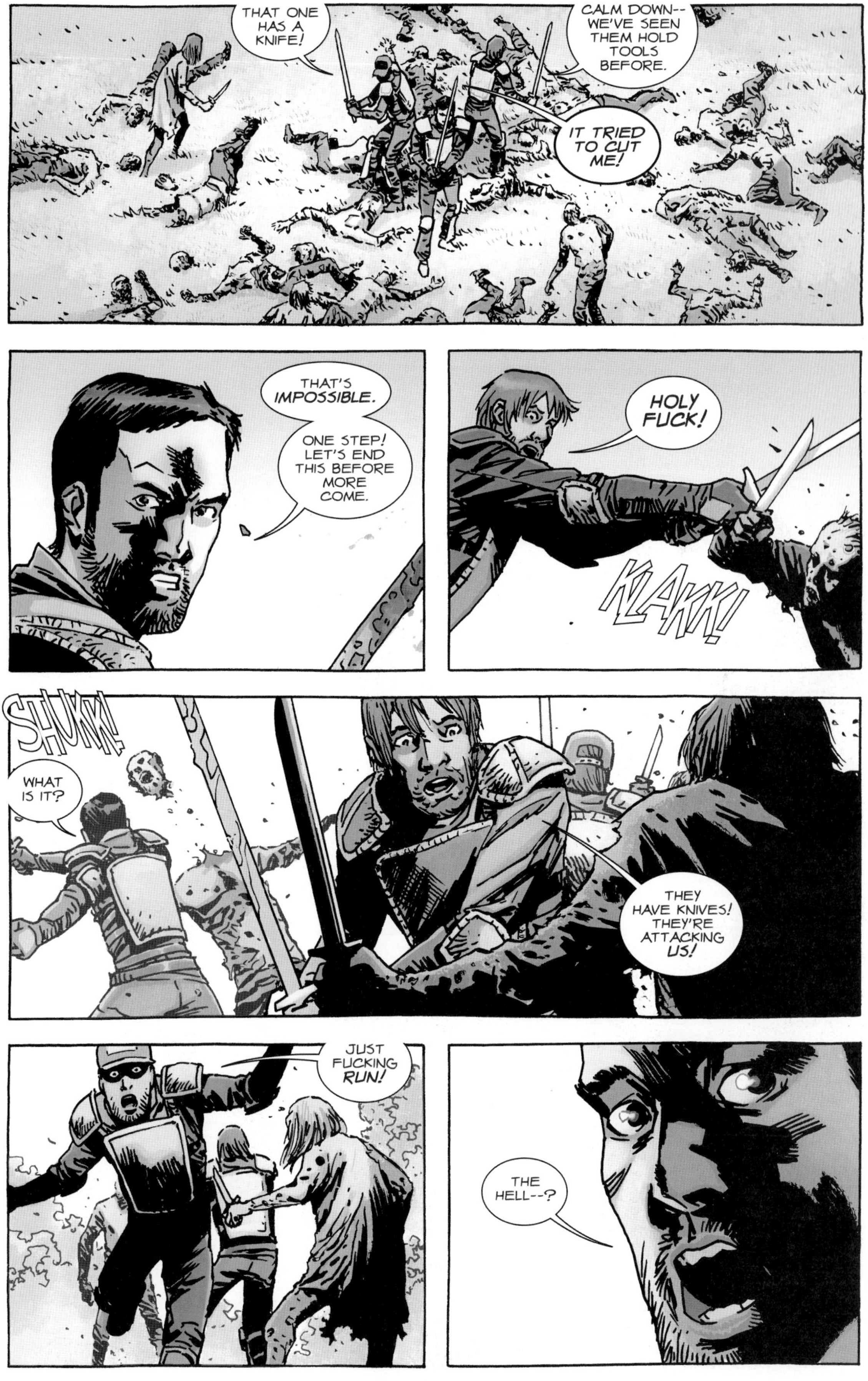

THAT ONE HAS A KNIFE!
CALM DOWN-- WE'VE SEEN THEM HOLD TOOLS BEFORE.
IT TRIED TO CUT ME!
THAT'S IMPOSSIBLE.
ONE STEP! LET'S END THIS BEFORE MORE COME.
HOLY FUCK!
KLAKK!
SHUKK!
WHAT IS IT?
THEY HAVE KNIVES! THEY'RE ATTACKING US!
JUST FUCKING RUN!
THE HELL--?

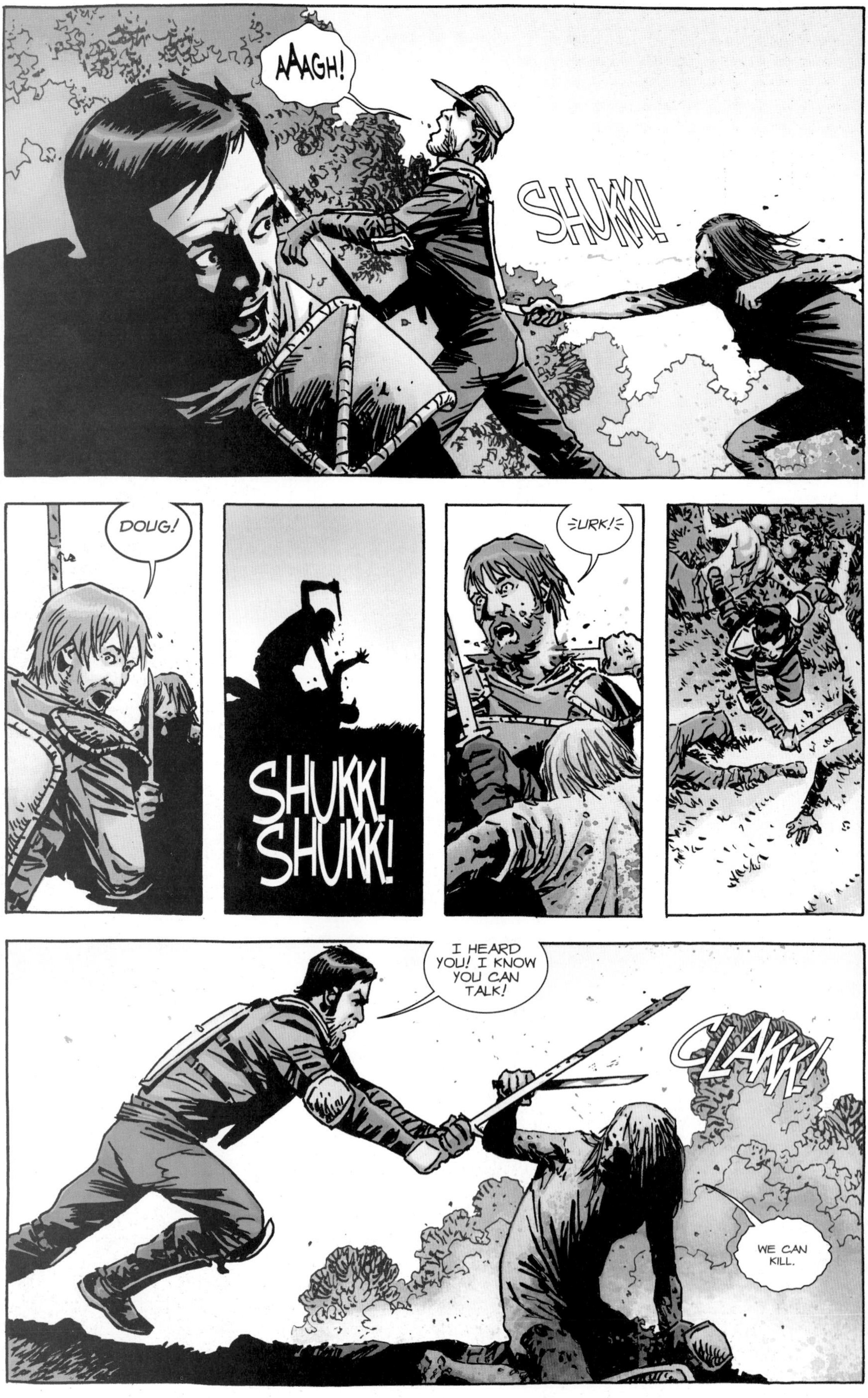
AAAGH!
SHUKK!
DOUG!
SHUKK! SHUKK!
URK!
I HEARD YOU! I KNOW YOU CAN TALK!
CLAKK!
WE CAN KILL.

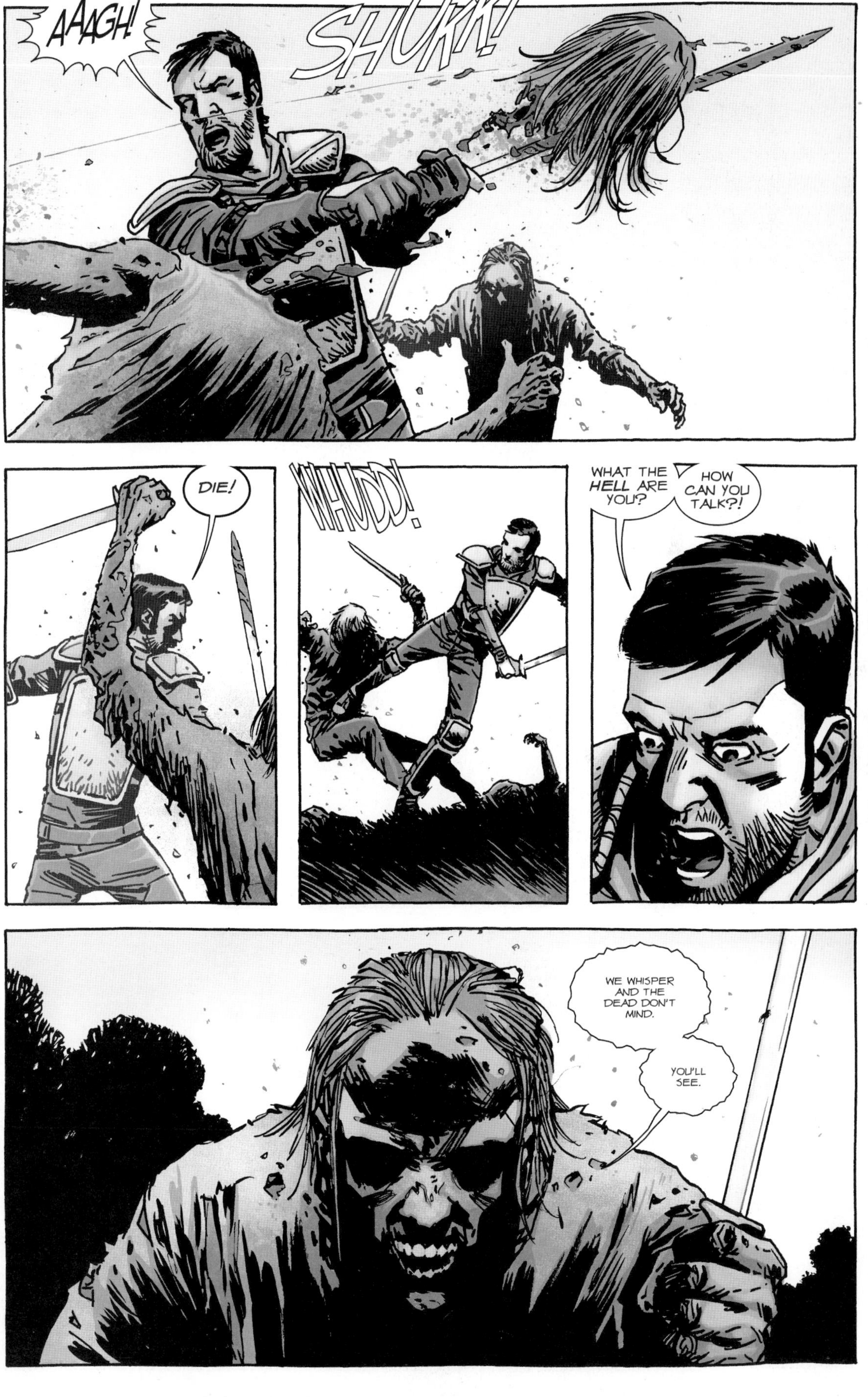
AAAGH!
SHUKK!
DIE!
WHUDD!
WHAT THE *HELL* ARE YOU?
HOW CAN YOU TALK?!
WE WHISPER AND THE DEAD DON'T MIND.
YOU'LL SEE.

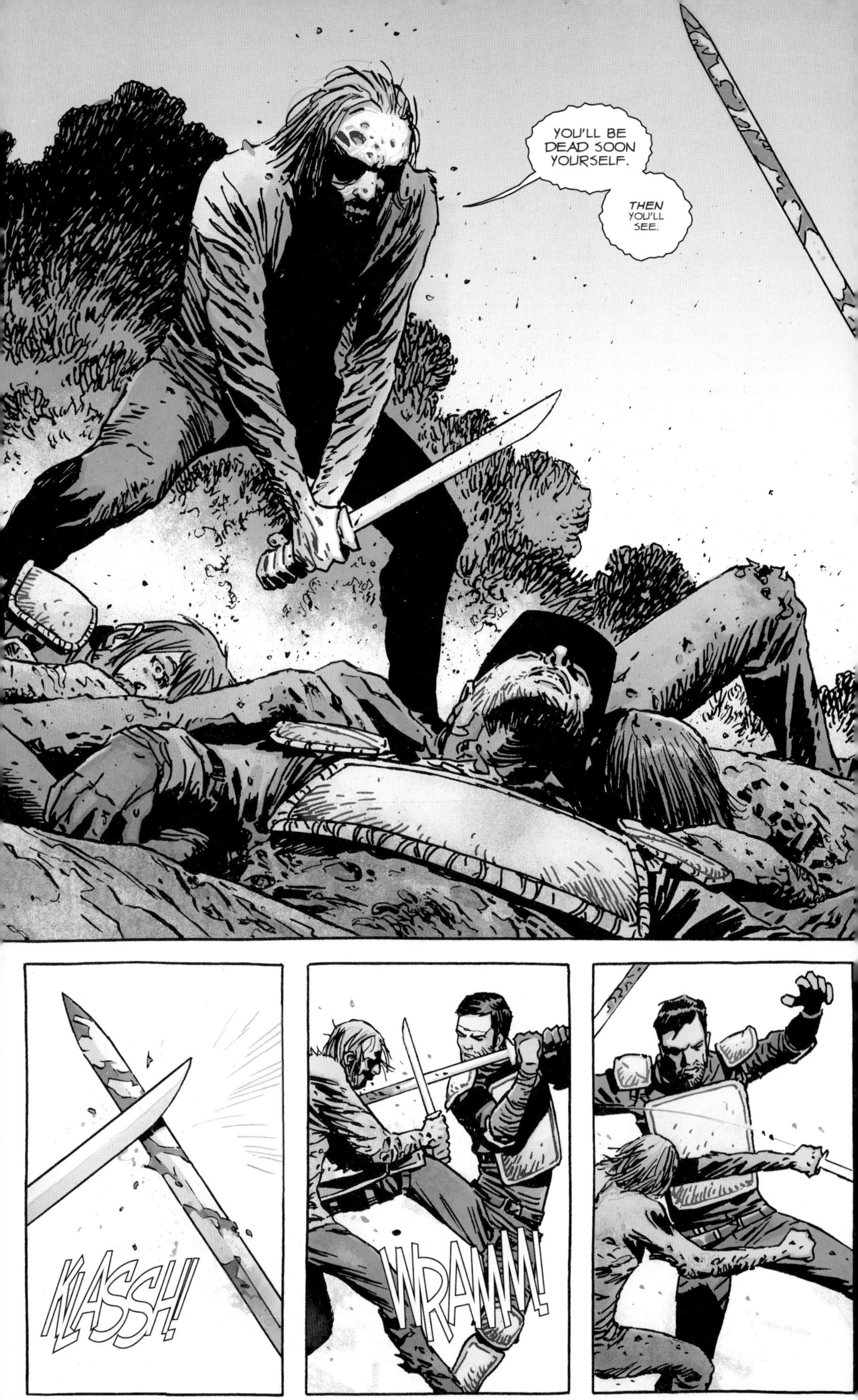
YOU'LL BE DEAD SOON YOURSELF.
THEN YOU'LL SEE.
KLASSH!
WRANNN!

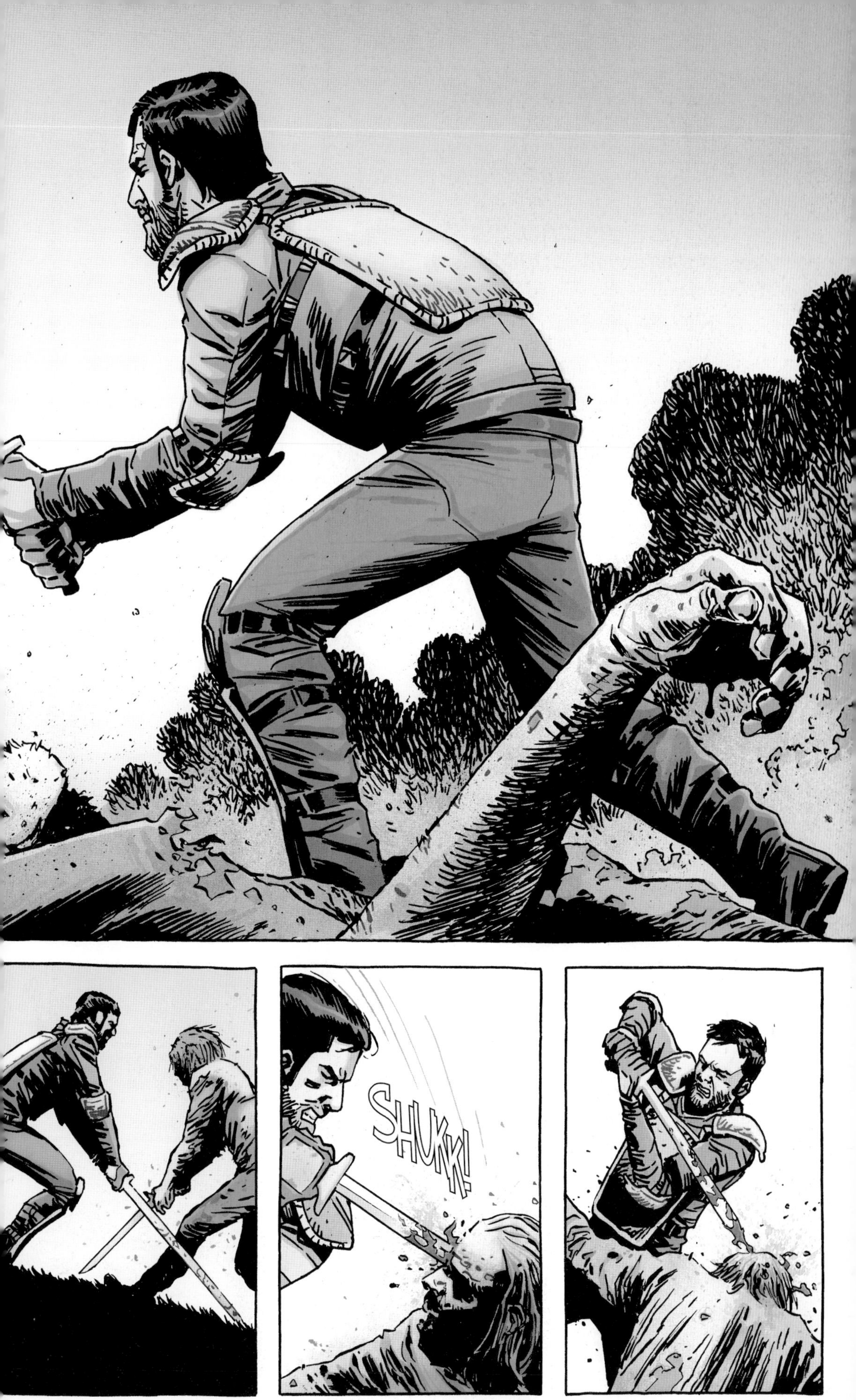
SHUKK!

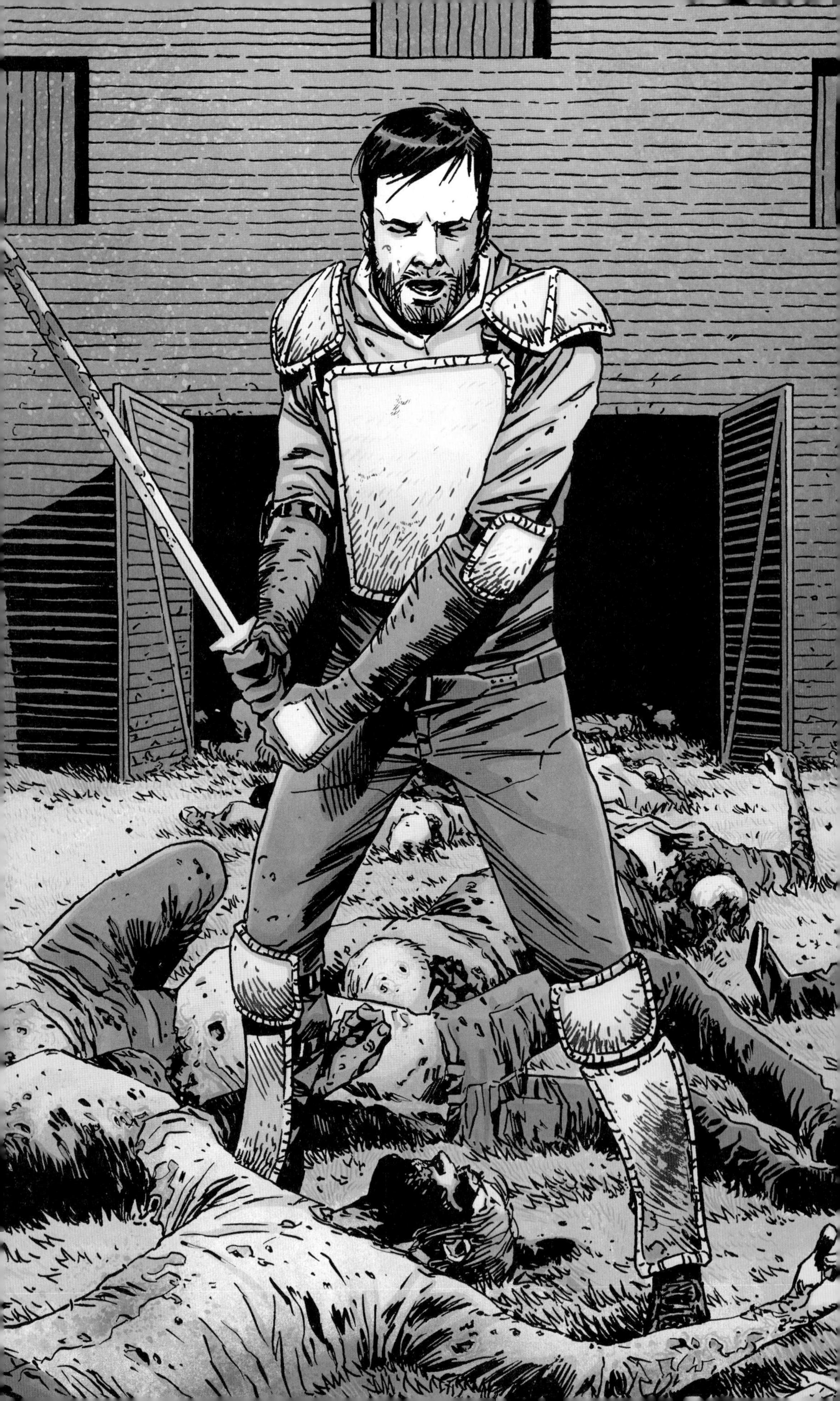

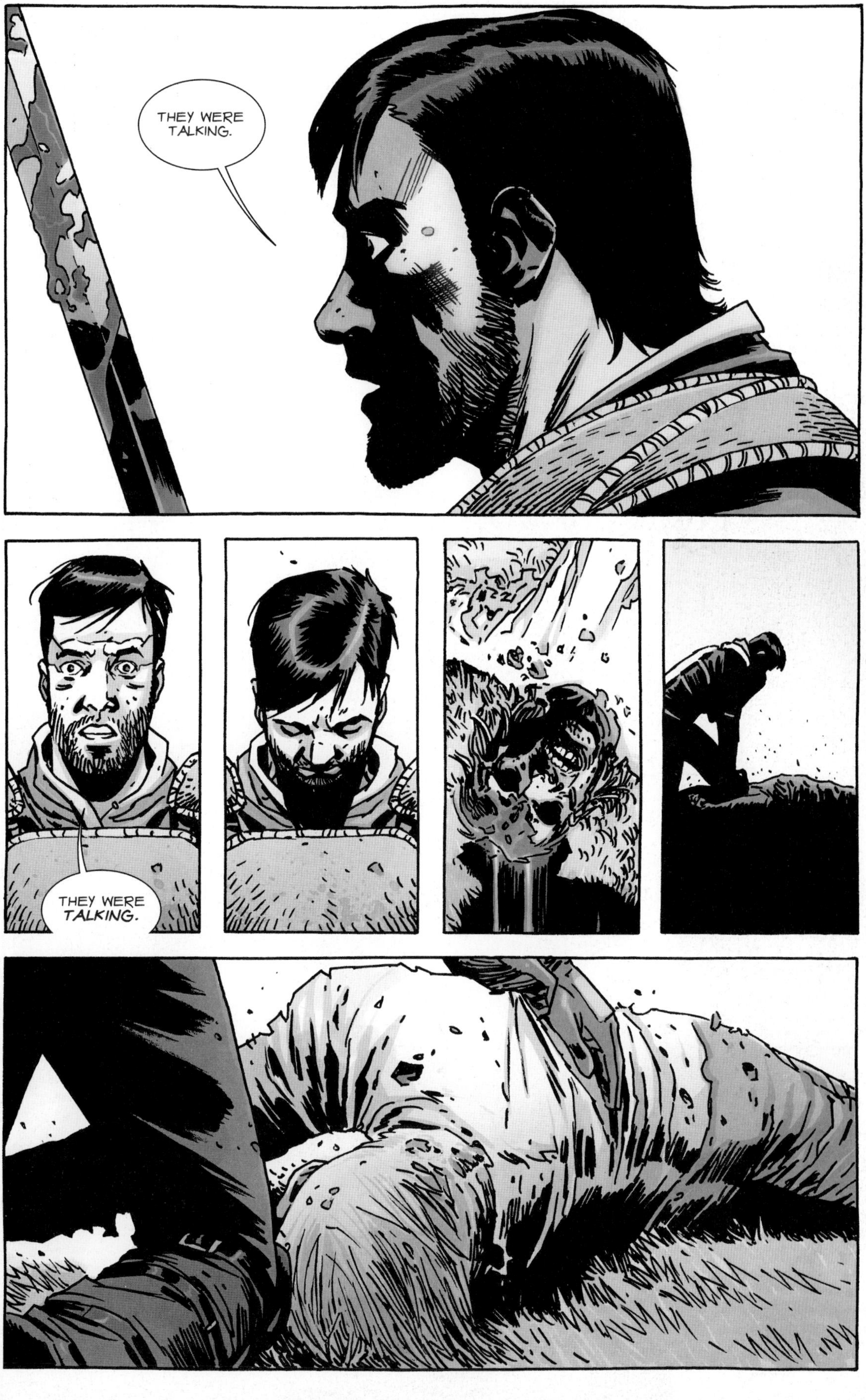
THEY WERE TALKING.
THEY WERE TALKING.

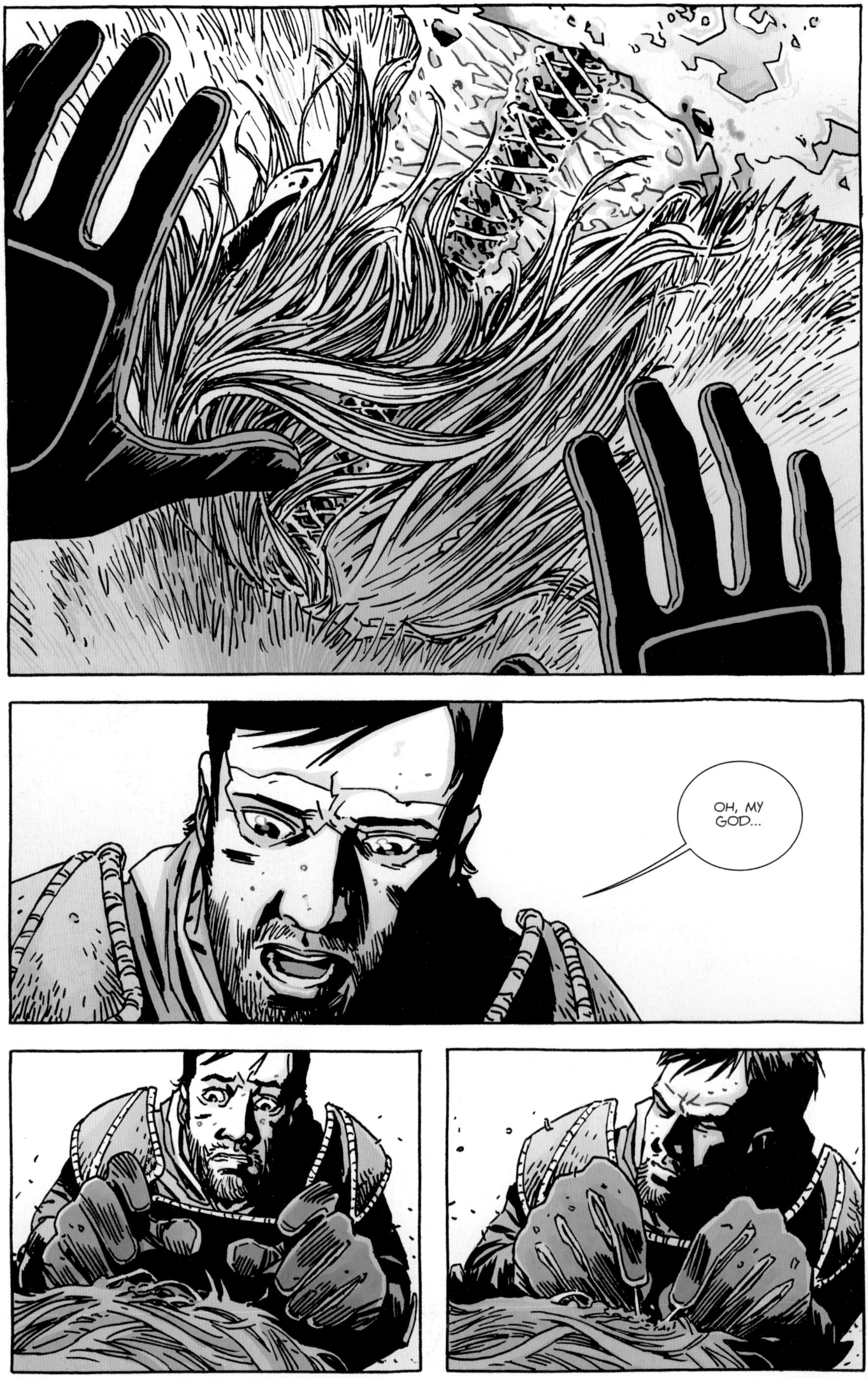
OH, MY GOD...

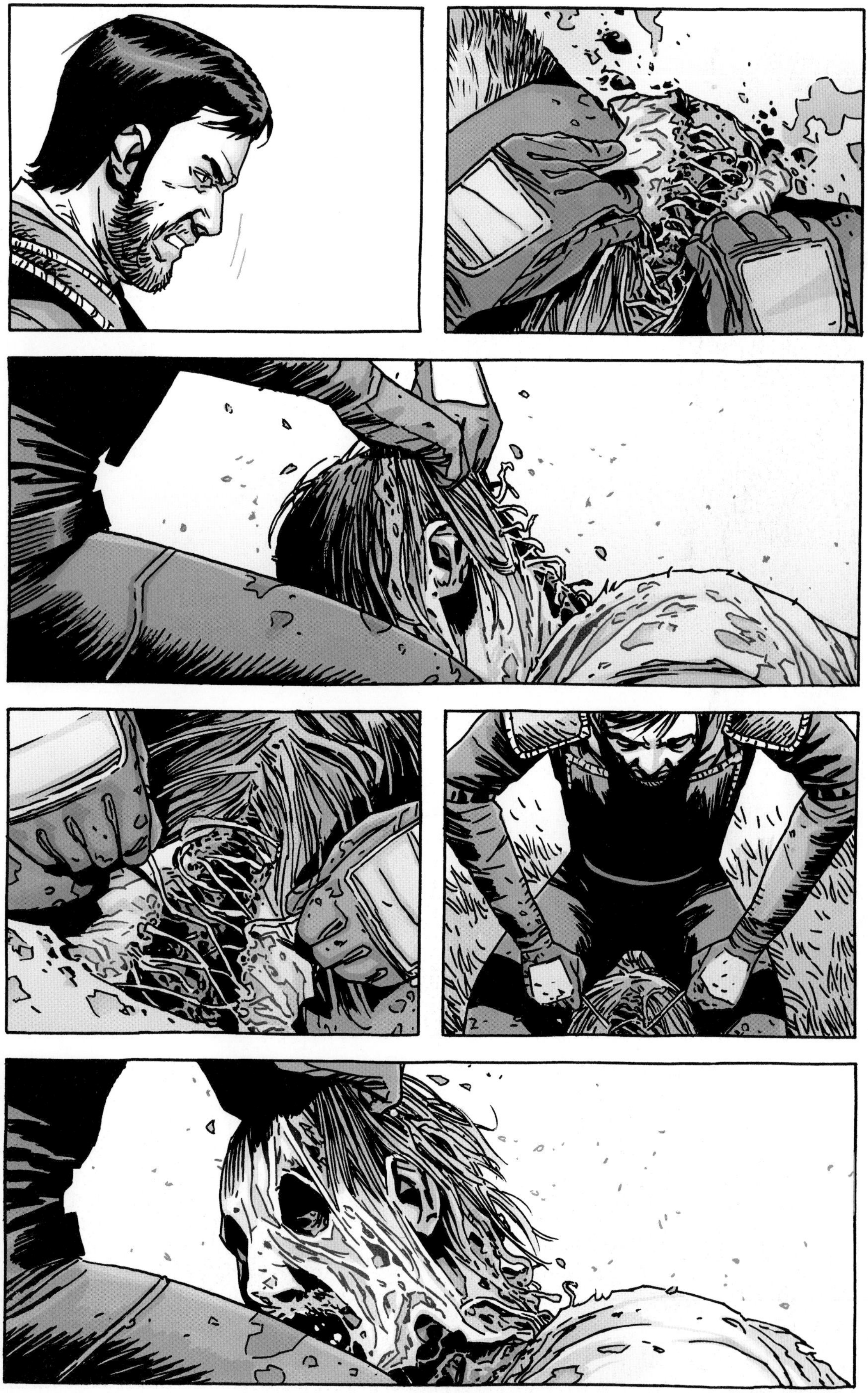

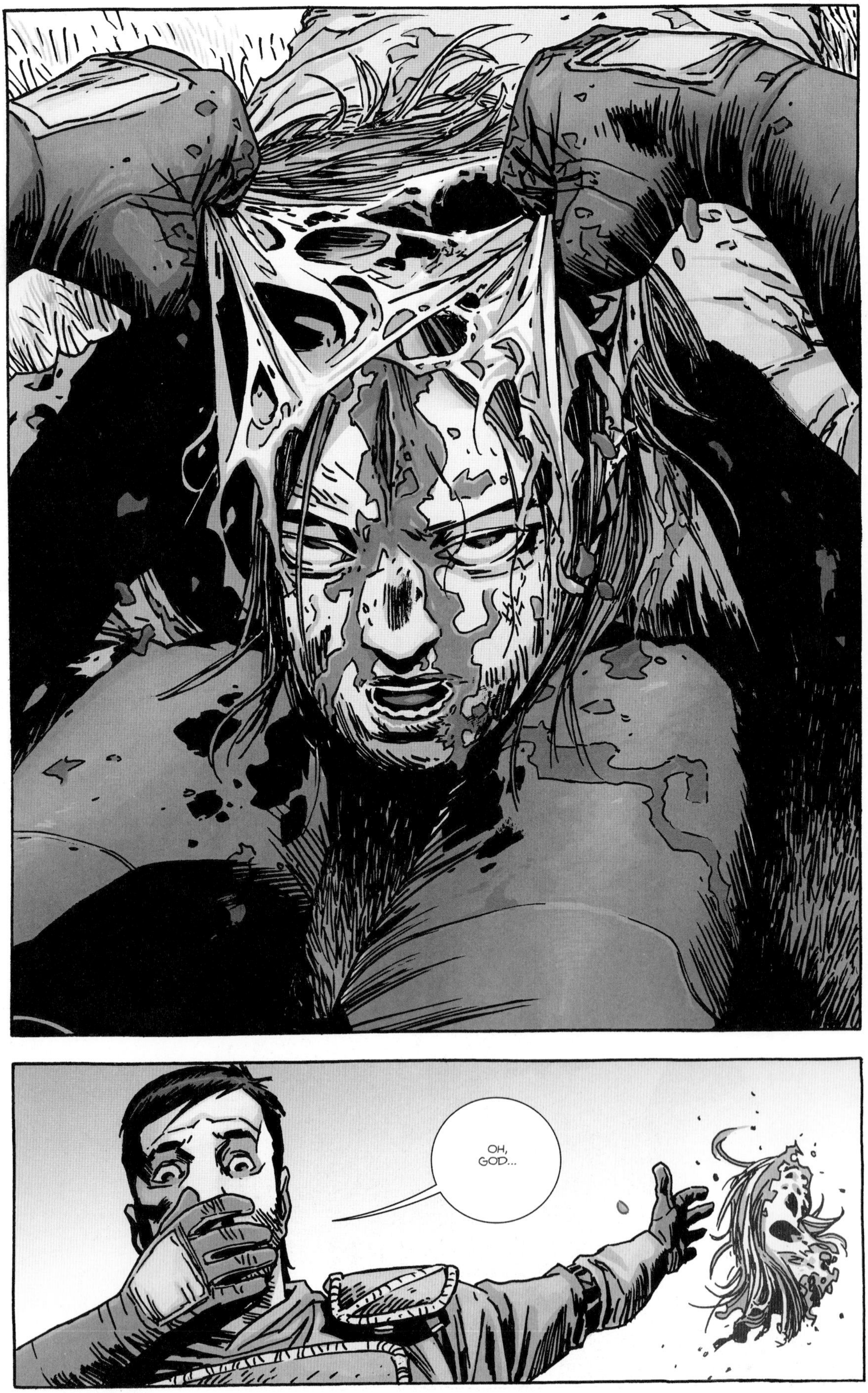
OH, GOD...

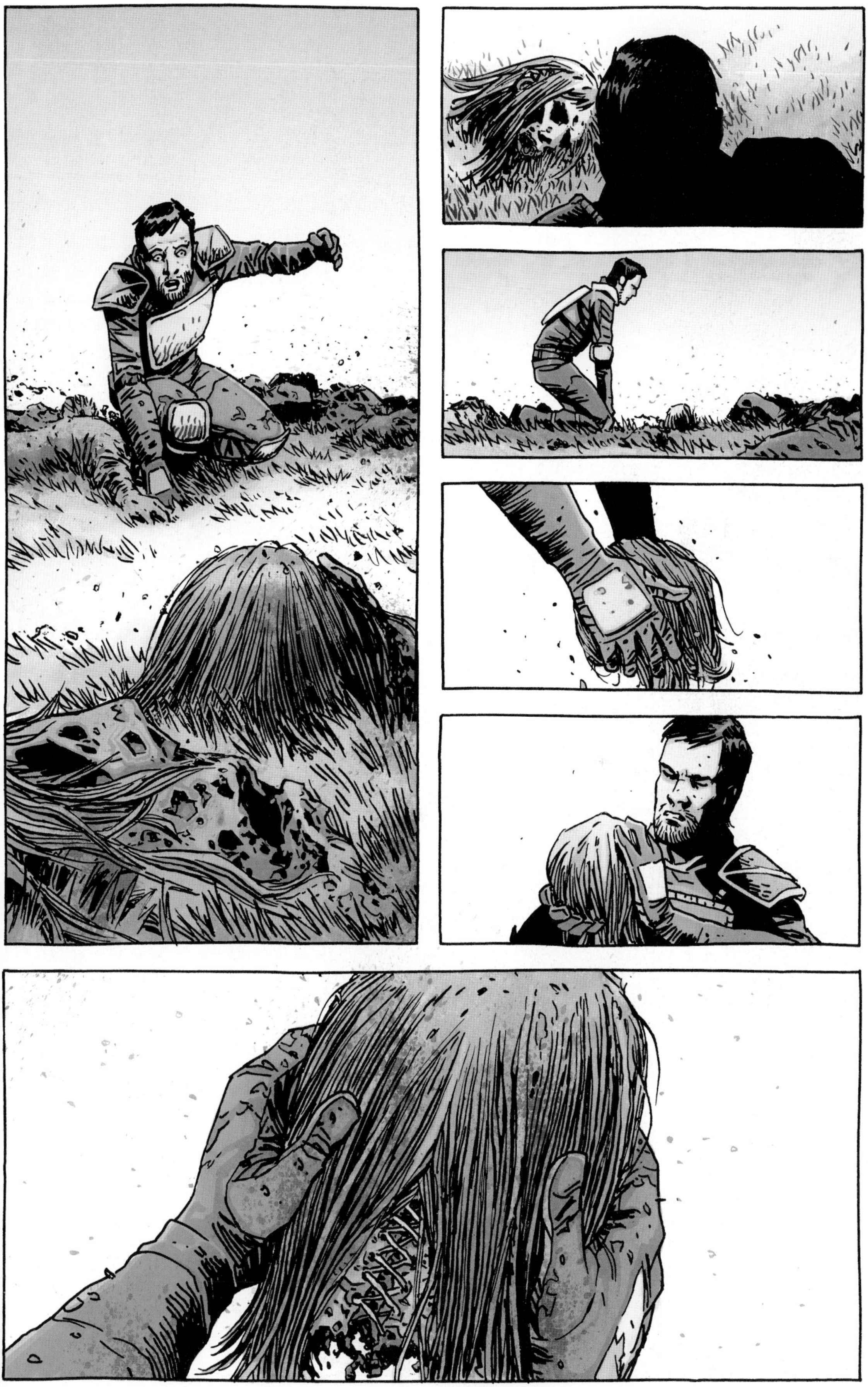

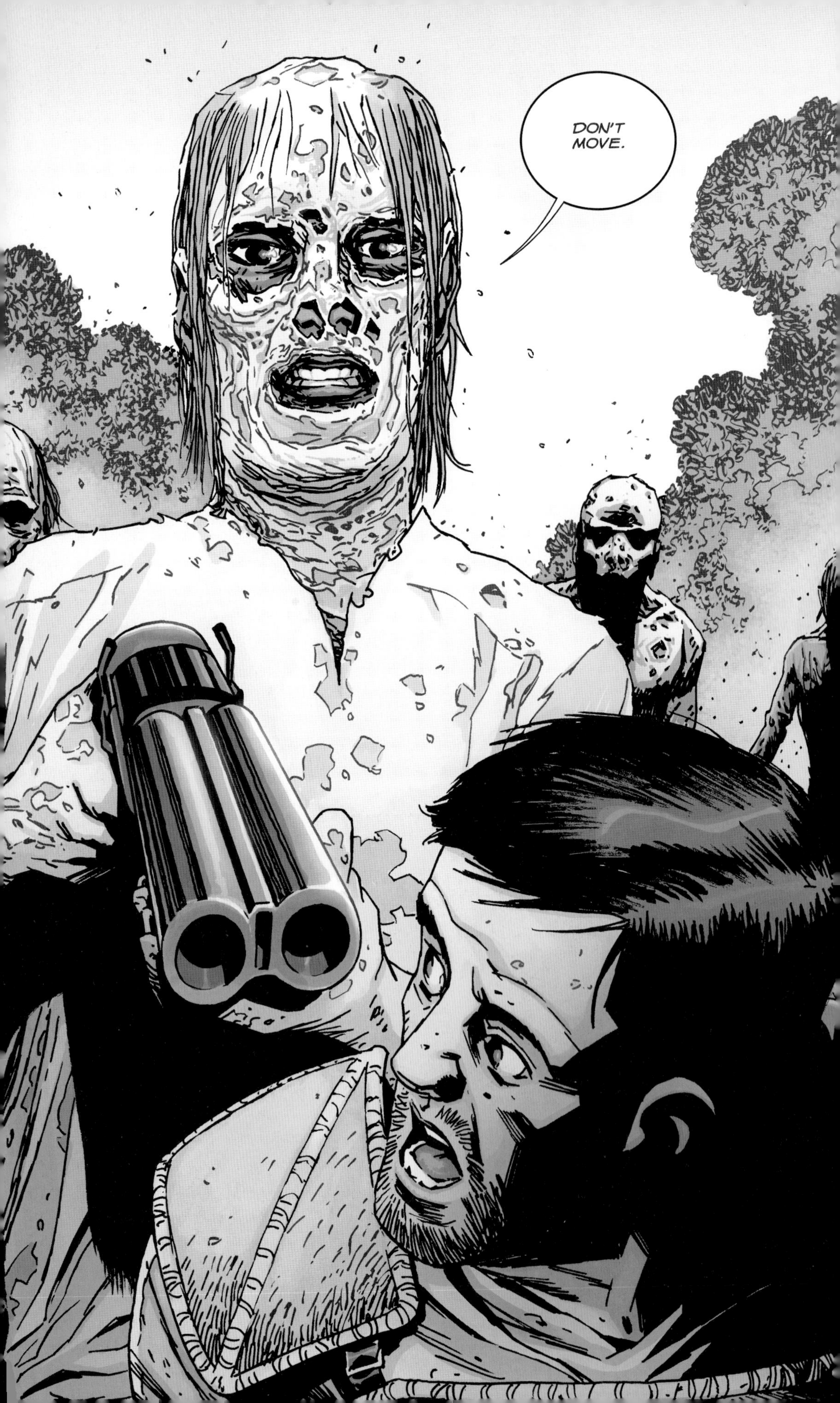
DON'T MOVE.

TO BE CONTINUED...

FOR MORE OF THE WALKING DEAD

TRADEPAPERBACKS

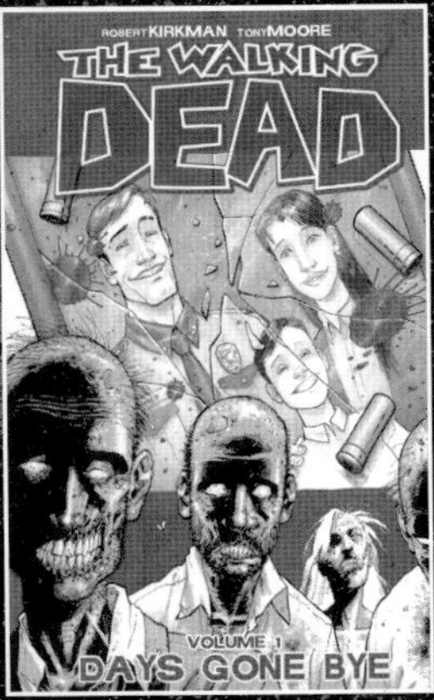
ROBERT KIRKMAN TONY MOORE
THE WALKING DEAD
VOLUME 1
DAYS GONE BYE

VOL. 1: DAYS GONE BYE TP
ISBN: 978-1-58240-672-5
$14.99
VOL. 2: MILES BEHIND US TP
ISBN: 978-1-58240-775-3
$14.99
VOL. 3: SAFETY BEHIND BARS TP
ISBN: 978-1-58240-805-7
$14.99
VOL. 4: THE HEART'S DESIRE TP
ISBN: 978-1-58240-530-8
$14.99
VOL. 5: THE BEST DEFENSE TP
ISBN: 978-1-58240-612-1
$14.99
VOL. 6: THIS SORROWFUL LIFE TP
ISBN: 978-1-58240-684-8
$14.99
VOL. 7: THE CALM BEFORE TP
ISBN: 978-1-58240-828-6
$14.99
VOL. 8: MADE TO SUFFER TP
ISBN: 978-1-58240-883-5
$14.99
VOL. 9: HERE WE REMAIN TP
ISBN: 978-1-60706-022-2
$14.99
VOL. 10: WHAT WE BECOME TP
ISBN: 978-1-60706-075-8
$14.99
VOL. 11: FEAR THE HUNTERS TP
ISBN: 978-1-60706-181-6
$14.99
VOL. 12: LIFE AMONG THEM TP
ISBN: 978-1-60706-254-7
$14.99
VOL. 13: TOO FAR GONE TP
ISBN: 978-1-60706-329-2
$14.99
VOL. 14: NO WAY OUT TP
ISBN: 978-1-60706-392-6
$14.99
VOL. 15: WE FIND OURSELVES TP
ISBN: 978-1-60706-440-4
$14.99
VOL. 16: A LARGER WORLD TP
ISBN: 978-1-60706-559-3
$14.99
VOL. 17: SOMETHING TO FEAR TP
ISBN: 978-1-60706-615-6
$14.99
VOL. 18: WHAT COMES AFTER TP
ISBN: 978-1-60706-687-3
$14.99
VOL. 19: MARCH TO WAR TP
ISBN: 978-1-60706-818-1
$14.99
VOL. 20: ALL OUT WAR PART ONE TP
ISBN: 978-1-60706-882-2
$14.99
VOL. 21: ALL OUT WAR PART TWO TP
ISBN: 978-1-63215-030-1
$14.99
VOL. 1: SPANISH EDITION TP
ISBN: 978-1-60706-797-9
$14.99
VOL. 2: SPANISH EDITION TP
ISBN: 978-1-60706-845-7
$14.99
VOL. 3: SPANISH EDITION TP
ISBN: 978-1-60706-883-9
$14.99
VOL. 4: SPANISH EDITION TP
ISBN: 978-1-63215-035-6
$14.99

HARDCOVERS

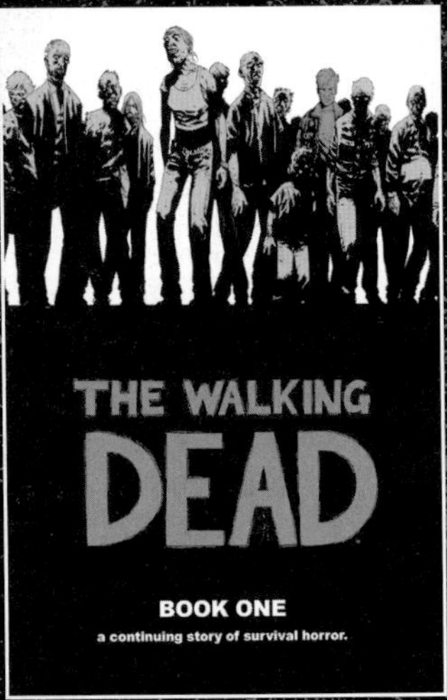
THE WALKING DEAD
BOOK ONE
a continuing story of survival horror.

BOOK ONE HC
ISBN: 978-1-58240-619-0
$34.99
BOOK TWO HC
ISBN: 978-1-58240-698-5
$34.99
BOOK THREE HC
ISBN: 978-1-58240-825-5
$34.99
BOOK FOUR HC
ISBN: 978-1-60706-000-0
$34.99
BOOK FIVE HC
ISBN: 978-1-60706-171-7
$34.99
BOOK SIX HC
ISBN: 978-1-60706-327-8
$34.99
BOOK SEVEN HC
ISBN: 978-1-60706-439-8
$34.99
BOOK EIGHT HC
ISBN: 978-1-60706-593-7
$34.99
BOOK NINE HC
ISBN: 978-1-60706-798-6
$34.99
BOOK TEN HC
ISBN: 978-1-63215-034-9
$34.99

COMPENDIUMS

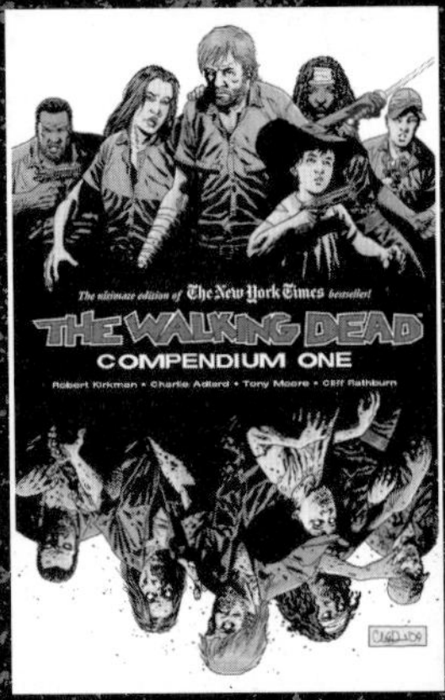
The ultimate edition of The New York Times bestseller
THE WALKING DEAD
COMPENDIUM ONE
Robert Kirkman • Charlie Adlard • Tony Moore • Cliff Rathburn

COMPENDIUM TP, VOL. 1
ISBN: 978-1-60706-076-5
$59.99
COMPENDIUM TP, VOL. 2
ISBN: 978-1-60706-596-8
$59.99

SPECIALTY BOOKS

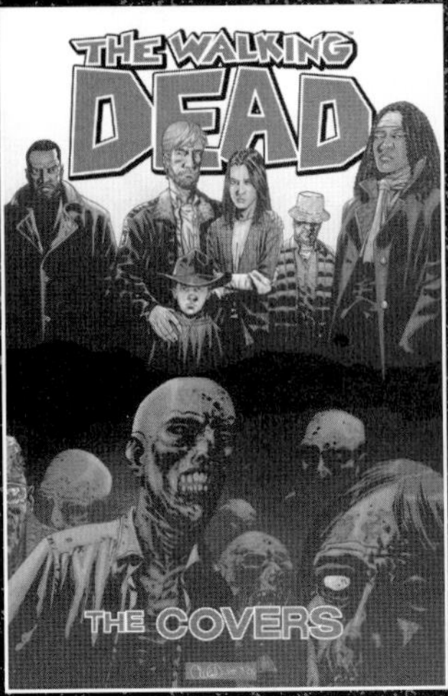
THE WALKING DEAD
THE COVERS

THE WALKING DEAD: THE COVERS, VOL. 1 HC
ISBN: 978-1-60706-002-4
$24.99
THE WALKING DEAD SURVIVORS' GUIDE
ISBN: 978-1-60706-458-9
$12.99
THE WALKING DEAD: ALL OUT WAR HC
ISBN: 978-1-60706-002-4
$24.99

OMNIBUS

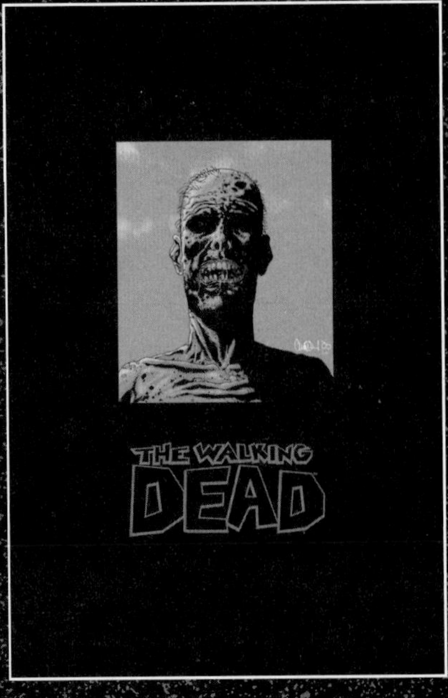
THE WALKING DEAD

OMNIBUS, VOL. 1
ISBN: 978-1-60706-503-6
$100.00
OMNIBUS, VOL. 2
ISBN: 978-1-60706-515-9
$100.00
OMNIBUS, VOL. 3
ISBN: 978-1-60706-330-8
$100.00
OMNIBUS, VOL. 4
ISBN: 978-1-60706-616-3
$100.00
OMNIBUS, VOL. 5
ISBN: 978-1-63215-042-4
$100.00

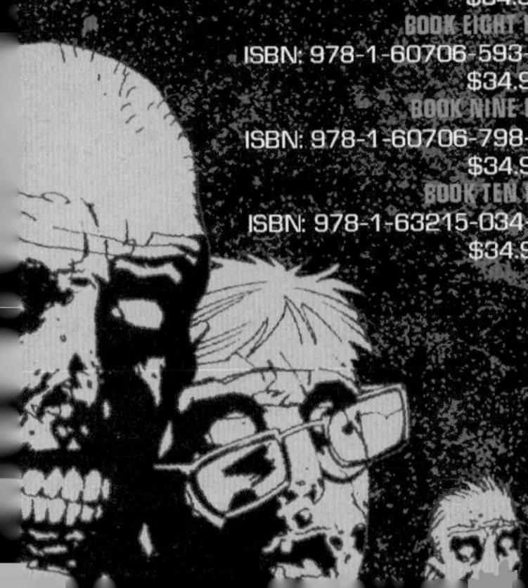

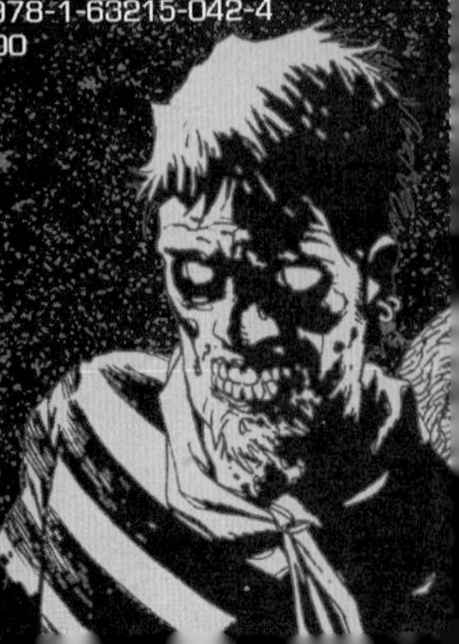

FOR MORE OF INVINCIBLE

TRADEPAPERBACKS

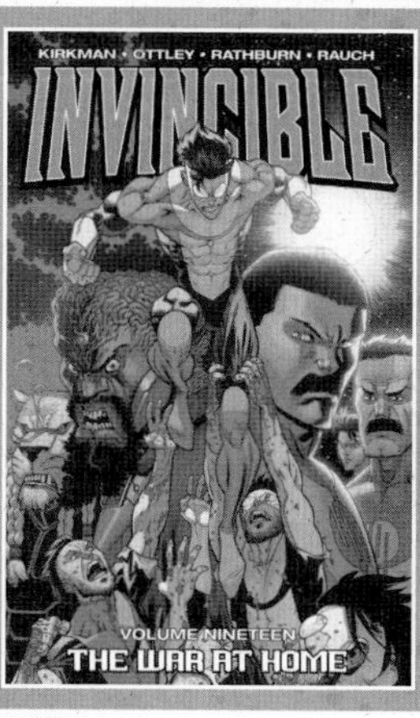
KIRKMAN • OTTLEY • RATHBURN • RAUCH
INVINCIBLE
VOLUME NINETEEN
THE WAR AT HOME

VOL. 1: FAMILY MATTERS TP
ISBN: 978-1-58240-711-1
$12.99
VOL. 2: EIGHT IS ENOUGH TP
ISBN: 978-1-58240-347-2
$12.99
VOL. 3: PERFECT STRANGERS TP
ISBN: 978-1-58240-793-7
$12.99
VOL. 4: HEAD OF THE CLASS TP
ISBN: 978-1-58240-440-2
$14.95
VOL. 5: THE FACTS OF LIFE TP
ISBN: 978-1-58240-554-4
$14.99
VOL. 6: A DIFFERENT WORLD TP
ISBN: 978-1-58240-579-7
$14.99
VOL. 7: THREE'S COMPANY TP
ISBN: 978-1-58240-656-5
$14.99
VOL. 8: MY FAVORITE MARTIAN TP
ISBN: 978-1-58240-683-1
$14.99
VOL. 9: OUT OF THIS WORLD TP
ISBN: 978-1-58240-827-9
$14.99
VOL. 10: WHO'S THE BOSS TP
ISBN: 978-1-60706-013-0
$16.99
VOL. 11: HAPPY DAYS TP
ISBN: 978-1-60706-062-8
$16.99
VOL. 12: STILL STANDING TP
ISBN: 978-1-60706-166-3
$16.99
VOL. 13: GROWING PAINS TP
ISBN: 978-1-60706-251-6
$16.99
VOL. 14: THE VILTRUMITE WAR TP
ISBN: 978-1-60706-367-4
$19.99
VOL. 15: GET SMART TP
ISBN: 978-1-60706-498-5
$16.99
VOL. 16: FAMILY TIES TP
ISBN: 978-1-60706-579-1
$16.99
VOL. 17: WHAT'S HAPPENING TP
ISBN: 978-1-60706-662-0
$16.99
VOL. 18: DEATH OF EVERYONE TP
ISBN: 978-1-60706-762-7
$16.99
VOL. 19: THE WAR AT HOME TP
ISBN: 978-1-60706-856-3
$16.99
THE OFFICIAL HANDBOOK OF
THE INVINCIBLE UNIVERSE TP
ISBN: 978-1-58240-831-6
$12.99
INVINCIBLE PRESENTS,
VOL. 1: ATOM EVE & REX SPLODE TP
ISBN: 978-1-60706-255-4
$14.99

COMPLETE LIBRARY

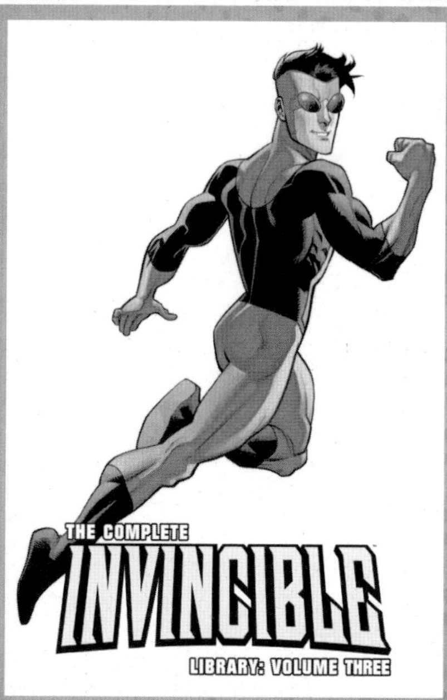
THE COMPLETE
INVINCIBLE
LIBRARY: VOLUME THREE

THE COMPLETE INVINCIBLE LIBRARY, VOL. 2 HC
ISBN: 978-1-60706-112-0
$125.00
THE COMPLETE INVINCIBLE LIBRARY, VOL. 3 HC
ISBN: 978-1-60706-421-3
$125.00

COMPENDIUMS

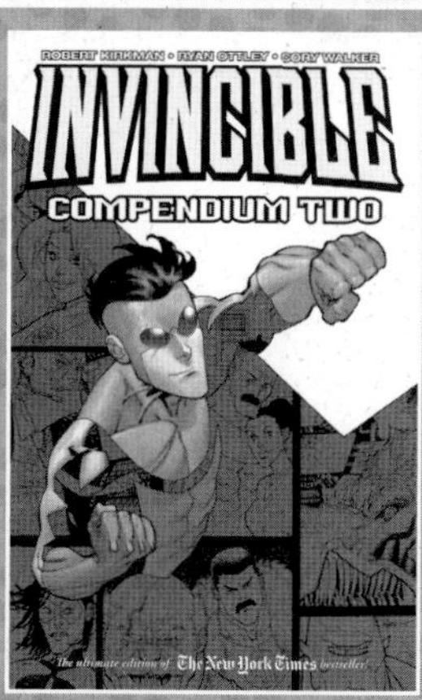
ROBERT KIRKMAN • RYAN OTTLEY • CORY WALKER
INVINCIBLE
COMPENDIUM TWO
The ultimate edition of The New York Times bestseller

COMPENDIUM VOL. 1
ISBN: 978-1-60706-411-4
$64.99
COMPENDIUM VOL. 2
ISBN: 978-1-60706-772-6
$64.99

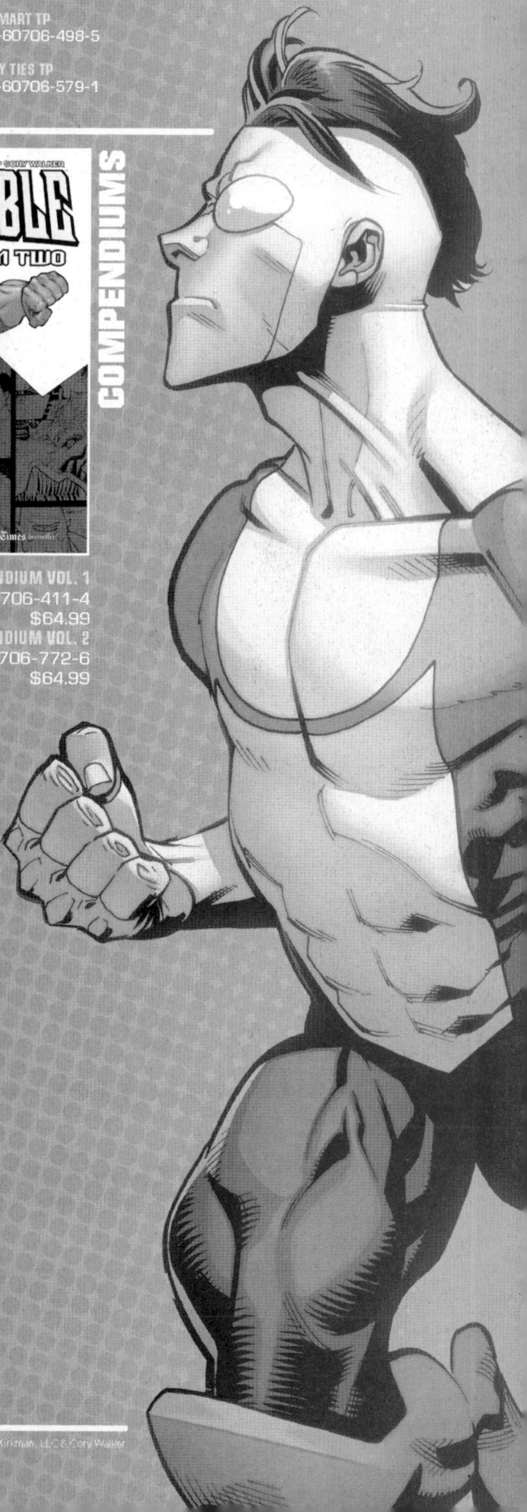

ULTIMATE COLLECTIONS

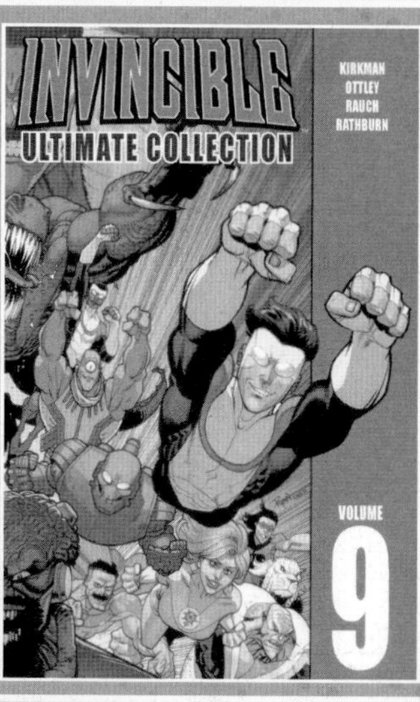
INVINCIBLE
ULTIMATE COLLECTION
KIRKMAN
OTTLEY
RAUCH
RATHBURN
VOLUME
9

ULTIMATE COLLECTION, VOL. 1 HC
ISBN 978-1-58240-500-1
$34.95
ULTIMATE COLLECTION, VOL. 2 HC
ISBN: 978-1-58240-594-0
$34.99
ULTIMATE COLLECTION, VOL. 3 HC
ISBN: 978-1-58240-763-0
$34.99
ULTIMATE COLLECTION, VOL. 4 HC
ISBN: 978-1-58240-989-4
$34.99
ULTIMATE COLLECTION, VOL. 5 HC
ISBN: 978-1-60706-116-8
$34.99
ULTIMATE COLLECTION, VOL. 6 HC
ISBN: 978-1-60706-360-5
$34.99
ULTIMATE COLLECTION, VOL. 7 HC
ISBN: 978-1-60706-509-8
$39.99
ULTIMATE COLLECTION, VOL. 8 HC
ISBN: 978-1-60706-680-4
$39.99
ULTIMATE COLLECTION, VOL. 9 HC
ISBN: 978-1-63215-032-5
$39.99